MW01399339

TrojanZ

By
Mike Tingle

For Phil.
You made us all smarter.

This is a work of fiction. Names, characters, places, and incidents either are the product of the author's and artist's imagination or are used fictitiously, and any resemblance to actual persons, living or dead, business establishments, events, or locales is entirely coincidental.

PROLOG

NEURALNET Vs. INTERNET STUDY LEAKED

Theoretical Potential of Human Brains Revealed

By **Jack Caldwell with *SCOTUS Newswire* Staff**
Wed, March 30, 2023 at 11:14 a.m. EDT

(*SCOTUS Newswire*) – An anonymous insider has leaked to *SCOTUS Newswire* startling results of ultra-radical biogenetic research.

The privately funded project, codenamed **Neuralnet**, allegedly has developed technology that profoundly repurposes the human brain.

Researchers reportedly concluded that as few as 100,000 augmented human brains networked within a *Worldwide Neural Cloud* could theoretically replace the Internet.

No further details regarding the research or its sponsors were provided at this time.

The scientist made this grave prediction.

"Neuralnet unarguably exposes human brains to Trojan malware-like infections. The possibility of malevolent mind control by third-parties is not only likely, it's inevitable."

Updated March 30, 2023 at 6:15 p.m. EDT
Police divers recovered from the Potomac River the body of missing Stellar Joule physicist Kyra Q. Jenn PhD, age 46 from Fairfax, Virginia.

Police classified the death as homicide.

SCOTUS Newswire confirms, Dr. Jenn was the confidential source quoted in this article.

Updates to this article are pending.

PART 1—The Arrival

1

Earth was changed forever on New Year's Day, 2022. During over a century of commercial aviation, only once has an extraterrestrial object caused a fatal air crash. That disaster occurred at 35,400 feet over the Arctic Ocean at 1:13 a.m. On route from Moscow to Anchorage, KirovFlot 319 was struck without warning and disintegrated instantly in a fireball hotter than the sun's surface.

The object's fiery arrival in the upper atmosphere transformed the Arctic Circle's perpetual winter night into Mediterranean midsummer noon. Sonic booms rebounded for a full minute.

Impact on the icecap was recorded at every earthquake and tsunami station in the world. Two cubic miles of icecap vaporized instantly as the object cut through sixty feet of glacial mask. A million tons of molten seafloor ejected into the atmosphere. Shockwaves rumbled through the earth triggering countless earthquakes. Two in the United States ascended to 7.7 and 7.3 on the Richter Scale along the New Madrid and San Andreas faults.

The concussion rang church bells as far away as Johannesburg, South Africa. Tidal surges flooded hundreds of harbor cities worldwide. Arctic inlands became Arctic Ocean for months. Washed from the Atlantic Ocean, an eleven-foot bull shark navigated countless flooded waterways and found its way to Lake Michigan where it was caught in March.

Oil supertankers and other great ships, like the pods of thousands of panicked whales, beached themselves around the world. Machine and mammal then died side-by-side under the crush of their own weight. Millions of buildings writhed as one in the northern hemisphere. Gas lines ruptured and ignited entire city blocks into deadly infernos. Building collapse, electrocution and drownings killed tens of thousands more worldwide.

Cascading power surges overloaded and set fire to electrical super-transformers in the northern hemisphere and plunged more than four billion people into darkness. Millions still had no power for months because replacement parts were exhausted worldwide.

An atmospheric haze enveloped Earth and effected weather patterns disastrously. World agricultural production plummeted overnight. Famine, malnutrition, and never before seen exotic viruses were blamed for the back-to-back *Uncommon Cold Pandemics of 2024* that killed nearly 99-million people worldwide.

Uninterrupted night, remoteness, and near-constant blizzard conditions hampered the accident investigators from the start. However, the National Transportation Safety Board and its many international sister agencies formalized their findings anyway.

First they reported no survivors, because no human remains were ever recovered. Second, they blamed an asteroid of an undetermined mass or arrival speed for the disaster, even though no evidence of either the jetliner or an asteroid were ever found.

Predictably, the very lack of any evidence of an asteroid, airplane wreckage or human remains quickly became Internet evidence of something else.

With *X Files* surety, the worldwide network of doomsday preppers, alien abduction claimants, and extraterrestrial sentinels concluded that an alien spaceship must have lost control when it collided with the airplane. Tragically causing the alien craft to crash into the Arctic Ocean and explode catastrophically.

The fringy advocates of alien encounters were only half right though. Yes, KirovFlot 319 crashed on New Year's Day. However, the so-called 'asteroid' did not crash. It actually landed safely, undamaged and on schedule.

From the entity's perspective aboard the vessel, the arrival was uneventful. Just another routine stop on a recycling mission that spanned the multiverse. A continuation of a salvage operation that began billions of years ago. One that would carryon for billions more after its business with Earth was finished.

While a shattered world debated asteroid theories and syfy's B-movie scripts to explain the anomalous event, something more horrific than either was to come—a deadly ruse.

An alien version of a Trojan horse had arrived on Earth. One filled with salvation for the world it broke. Wondrous Inventions. Miraculous recovery. Untold generosity. All of it trickery.

On New Year's Day 2022, Earth was claimed for harvest by an insatiable consumer of worlds. The enemy had many names.

On Earth it became known as the TrojanZ.

2

Washington D.C., May 27, 2026, 5:55 a.m. FBI Special Agent Easton DeSmet awoke to the sound of his smartphone vibrating. He retrieved the iPhone from the nightstand and studied the caller ID. He didn't recognize the number, but suspected the text message came from his newest whistleblower.

Easton opened the text and nodded. There he found an HTML link, but no message other than the same pseudonym signature HELP. Just like the previous texts that started arriving yesterday, the link led to another *SCOTUS Newswire* online article.

Easton had no idea who the whistleblower was or what exactly they were whistleblowing. Just that whoever HELP was, the person was an extremely careful informer. Too careful to be any of the FBIs' greatest annoyances: agent-sniffers, grudge-nuts or paranoiac conspiracy theorists. Every text message came from a different phone number. No doubt burner phones used just once and tossed. That practice actually was not uncommon.

What was highly unusual was this. Whoever sent the texts was well-connected. Maybe an insider high up at Justice. Few people even at the FBI had the number for this iPhone. The device was assigned exclusively to Easton's classified investigation just now wrapping up of a crooked D.C. law firm.

Easton decided the whistleblower's codename would be HELP. He texted back for the first time: **Thank you, HELP. Keep'em coming. I love mysteries! Wanna meet? - Easton.**

The response was immediate: **Yes, but just you. And only if you can put the 2 parts together. More to come today. - HELP**

Easton smiled. Terms and conditions. Caution. Local area codes. More evidence promised. HELP was likely a D.C. lawyer. Someone very connected. He heard his normal 6:00 a.m. alarm—Mr. Coffee—start chugging in the kitchen. Easton got up and headed for the shower.

Twenty minutes later he was dressed for work and ready for his first cup of coffee. Easton sat down at the efficiency apartment's kitchen bar. He opened the latest link and began reading the years-old article for the first time.

COURT DENIES KERR'S FOIA CLAIM

Federal Judge Dismisses So-called 'Aliens' Suit

By **Jack Caldwell with *SCOTUS Newswire* Staff**
Tues, Nov 2, 2022 at 2:22 p.m. EDT

(*SCOTUS Newswire*) – In Denver today Federal Judge Clay Jones dismissed *Kerr v. United States of America*. The lawsuit was brought by retired astrogeology professor Dr. Howard Kerr of Pocatello, Idaho.

Central to Kerr's complaint was violation of his rights as protected by the *Freedom of Information Act.* Kerr alleged the government illegally withheld information regarding the January 1, 2022 asteroid event.

In a related story, a Roswell, New Mexico radio station released the results today of its Internet poll inspired by the Kerr lawsuit. The poll went viral with over 130,000,000 people responding worldwide.

The results: *Asteroid impact* beat *alien invasion* by a mere 8,000 votes.

Washington D.C., 5:00 p.m. Agent Easton DeSmet sat alone at the end of *Andre One's* long bar on Turpin Street rereading HELP's *SCOTUS Newswire* articles. Together the 13 articles read like a mystery novel—or perhaps 13 of them glommed together—with different authors, missing chapters, blank pages, faceless nameless characters and dynamically changing generic places. His last stab at the articles made no more sense than their first 10 readings today. Easton stopped and focused instead on just the headlines.

COURT DISMISSES KERR'S FOIA CLAIM
Federal Judge Discharges So-called 'Aliens?' Suit

NEURALNET Vs. INTERNET STUDY LEAKED
Theoretical Potential of Human Brains Revealed

COURT ACCEPTS BRAINLORD RESULTS
Did the 9th's Judge Bain Just Change Human Destiny?

BRAINLORDS PIONEER JOHN DOE REACTS
SCOTUS Opens New Frontier in Human History

BRAINLORDS SPLITS SUPREME COURT JUSTICES
Judicial Allies Roth and Daughtry Part Ways

UC2 VIRUS STRIKES COURT AGAIN
Uncommon Cold Virus Kills 2nd Supreme this Year

GEORGETOWN LAW LOSES GIANT
Distinguished Dean Joins Private Firm Steeped in Controversy

SCOTUS REVERSES INDIANA VS. CEREBELLAR
Human Brains to Replace Internet in 8 to 1 Decision.

ORIGIN OF THE WORD BRAINLORD

Canadian Comedian Creates and Trademarks 'Brainlord'

A NEURAL CLOUD SKEPTIC

Nobel Laureate Decries Wisdom of Brainlord Tech

SUPREME DECISION TANKS STOCK MARKETS

Markets Crash Worldwide After Brainlords Decision

TRILLIONAIRE INVENTOR WINS

Wealth Act Declared Unconstitutional

SUPREMES EXPAND DISABILITIES PROTECTION

Americans with 'Benign Psychopathy' Now Protected

Easton reread the headlines a second time. This time whispering each word slowly. Gravely, as if needing to memorize a complex antidote for a poison he had just ingested. The investigator finally looked up and thought to himself, *Aside from the obvious Brainlords angle, every article is about unexpected deviations. Perhaps, statistically too many of them? Organized interferences? Systemic manipulation? Conspiracies? Jesus what?*

The FBI agent mentally ticked off the irregularities.

Anomalous missing evidence of an asteroid. A startup corporation achieving an $11-trillion market cap almost overnight. Uncharacteristically irresponsible legislative and judicial behavior. Two unprecedented lightning quick pandemics each dwarfing Covid. An insider assassinated? Warnings irrationally ignored. Miraculous advances in technology. A mysteriously championed post-asteroid recovery reduced from decades to two years. An odds-makers crushing 8-1 reversal by the Supreme Court. A crashing stock market worldwide. A schizophrenic ACLU advocating for both sides of the Brainlords controversy. A landmark disability decision protecting Americans with a new class of psychopathy classified as benign. Two judicially lockstep best friends at SCOTUS suddenly parting ways. And an ultra-radical comedian with an over the top birthday present for the estate of Fidel Castro.

Okay HELP, he thought, *What are your anomalies trying to add up to? I still don't see it. Where's the biggest puzzle piece? The one in the middle that connects all others together.*

Easton sighed and closed the text files. He took a sip of beer and frowned. He was no closer to answers and worse, the hour-old beer was now warm. Easton dropped the iPhone in his suit jacket's breast pocket and pushed the glass of stale beer to the edge of the bar. Easton was done with it for now. The investigator needed a break. Easton caught the bartender's eye and made the universal air scribbles gesture that he needed his check.

The FBI agent was dressed in the duteous $3,000 manner of a successful late-thirty-something attorney. He shared a law license with this finely tailored profession, but his agency-supplied wardrobe, his law degree and convincing deportment were camouflage. Easton DeSmet did not practice the law, he investigated it for the Justice Department. He reported directly to the Attorney General.

The popular bar and restaurant were packed this evening with Washingtonians celebrating having survived the great cauldron of democracy yet another day. Around him, happy hour ascended to its uppermost decibel range on discounted alcohol and an ear-splitting musical cornucopia.

Behind Easton, a group of young interns stood arm-in-arm and butchered drunkenly the lyrics and notes of a popular song from the 90s. Several line danced. Most stumbled latently to the rhythm. Easton DeSmet forgave with a smile their occasional jostles and nodded acceptance to the giggled apologies.

He turned his attention to the other end of the bar where the subject of his own long investigation was gathered. That is all it took. The corrupt attorneys were the missing centerpiece. The hub that connected his wheel to HELP's spokes—the articles. The connection to it all arrived like ice water on his neck.

HELP and I are working on the same thing! It's all intertwined. We each have half of the tip of an iceberg.

"Damn!" Easton pounded his fist on the bar and laughed. He looked around and was relieved no one noticed. Law firm Bobrova Coble Lemnisci was prominent in most but not all of HELP'S articles.

BCL had represented the Brainlords movement before the Supreme and lower courts. Easton watched the bartender pour the lawyers round after round of $100 shots of ultra-premium Tolvanov vodka. Glasses tapped, the vodka disappeared and twelve drunken celebrations rose high above all others, like towering Easter Island statues surrounding a humble dashboard Jesus. Three seriously sober bodyguards maintained a four-foot buffer around the attorneys to make sure no 'budget friendly' vodka proles ventured into their elite bubble.

Easton DeSmet the FBI investigator studied this group of well-heeled and increasingly well-lit twelve attorneys with enhanced prosecutorial suspicion. Easton DeSmet the retired Army Ranger studied them with the calm eye of a sniper painting crosshairs over targets entering his kill zone.

Bobrova Coble Lemnisci, a 125 year old Washington legal fixture, had become the subject of multiple investigations in the last four years. Clients had abandoned it in droves, claiming the firm had gone through a personality change. The law firm had acted indifferently to it all. Even as its client base shriveled. Even as accusations of impropriety spread. Even as jury tampering charges resulted in multiple disbarments and jail time. Even the deaths of its associates was met with official apathy.

And that's another anomaly! Easton thought. Early on in Easton's investigation, he had focused on six *low hanging* BCL attorneys. The pawns. However, one after another the subjects died. The causes of death were unique and seemingly innocent: one in a biking accident when the rider tangled with a drain grate; one from an adverse reaction to a medication during minor surgery; one from a heart attack during a home invasion; one from a bathtub slip and fall; one in a helicopter crash; one was struck and killed by a passing car when she chased her new puppy into the street.

Ironically, one of BCL's attorneys across the bar had even been Easton's favorite professor during his first year at Georgetown Law. Professor Szara Jacobs had inexplicably forfeited tenure to join a law practice she had previously disdained publically. Through a wiretap on his old professor, he even knew early yesterday that the lawyers would all be here tonight celebrating their 8-1 victory. What he did know was how BCL so confidently already knew yesterday that it would win today.

How much of the iceberg remains unknown? He thought.

Easton DeSmet decided it was time to meet HELP in person and compare notes. Associate Supreme Court Justice Theodora Daughtry—a/k/a HELP—had certainly left enough clues to her true identity. She'd purchased with the same credit card disposable phones at 20 different stores. The Justice had posed smiling up at the security cameras for a few seconds at each site. She had also parked where her license plate was most easily seen by other security cameras. Easton had ID'ed the judge by noon.

What the FBI Special Agent DeSmet and Supreme Court Associate Justice Daughtry could not know was this. These attorneys, all twelve newly minted multimillionaires, would never be indicted, arrested, convicted and incarcerated.

If the seven men and five women were lucky, they would all be dead within 48 hours. If not dead, they would be something far worse than dead.

COURT ACCEPTS BRAINLORD RESULTS

Did the 9th's Judge Bain Just Change Human Destiny?

By **Skylar Thompson with *SCOTUS Newswire* Staff**
Updated Thurs, December 1, 2025 at 5:46 p.m. EDT

(***SCOTUS Newswire***) – The Internet vs. Neuralnet debate intensified radically last year when condemned prisoners were recruited for Neuralnet trials.

Early on, the American Civil Liberties Union found itself in the middle of an unprecedented controversy. In the end, the ACLU decided to advocate both for and against the death row inmates' right to participate in the trials and defer without appeal to the bench for a ruling.

Federal Judge Webster Bain, known for his strong support for capital punishment, shocked the country with his ruling today.

Judge Bain not only allowed the trials to continue to Phase 3, he commuted the ten death sentences to life without the possibility of parole.

Further, Bain ordered the inmates to be remain in 'death row' isolation during Phase 3, and only relocated to general prison population at the end of the trials if they fully cooperated.

During discovery, documents just now made public revealed that the 10 inmates in both Phase One and Two trials were unable to determine when their brains were accessing the local area Neuralnet.

Quintupled blind testing confirmed those claims repeatedly.

In Phase Two of the experiment and in an unprecedented vote of confidence in its subsidiary, Stellar Joule offered *every* former death row subject a $10-million prize payable to the charity of their choice. And another $100-billion paid nationwide to crime victims' and their families. The rewards were conditioned on whether *any* of the ten prisoners could contemporaneously identify or recover a single piece of information routed through or stored in their brains.

The data exchange rate During Phase 2 accelerated to processing speeds previously considered physiologically impossible.

Over three hundred billion random terabytes of data were exchanged in full-10-way-duplex at an average rate of six gigabytes per millisecond. Data was sent, stored and retrieved nonstop night and day between the ten test subjects. Zero data errors or data corruptions were detected during Phase 1 or 2.

Despite the incentives, still no information breaches were reported. No adverse or negative side effects were reported during the beta testing performed at the Terre Haute, Indiana federal penitentiary.

It was also reported today that three test subjects demonstrated a slightly elevated appetite for foods high in protein and fats, which was attributed by program scientists to increased brain activity.

One test subject demonstrated a slightly elevated IQ and five other subjects rated their sleep as more deep and restful.

All test subjects were calmed by the experience. Such terms as "normalized," "remorseful" and "easygoing" described the inmates' behavior.

Program scientists attributed all anomalies to the prisoners' general stress

reduction, which they believe was induced by the reprieve from execution and the possibility of leaving 'death row'.

3

Special Confinement Unit, U.S. Federal Penitentiary, Terre Haute, Indiana. Warden Constantine Recescu's eyes moved from one monitor to the next. There were ten screens in all, one for each Cerebellar test subject on death row. He yawned so hard it ended in a shudder.

The door to the control room opened and an officer entered carrying two Styrofoam cups of coffee. "It's late, sirs. We just put on a fresh pot and figured you two might need a jolt."

Colonel Therl Wainwrights accepted both coffees and nodded *thank you* to the officer. He handed one cup to the warden and said, "Mr. Recescu, please watch prisoners 3, 6, 7 and 10."

"What am I supposed to be looking at, Colonel? The prisoners all appear to be sleeping." The warden sipped the much needed coffee. After a few minutes, the cup of coffee was half gone, and his patience had eroded away by more than half. He shrugged and glanced up at his corrections officer then back at the bank of monitors.

The warden was more than a little annoyed now. He'd been summoned with just one-day notice to D.C. for a two-day televised Brainlords hearing before the House and Senate. Party-defying bipartisan antagonism distinguished the hearings. TV cameras documented the Congressional realignment of unlikely bedfellows. One group of Congresspersons from both parties had appeared normal to Recescu: frump, timeworn, tired, and fraught with concern for their country. The other side: sharp, vigorous, energetic, and always displaying their best headshot angle and practiced facial expression for TV whenever Brainlords was mentioned. Immediately after the unusually bizarre 2-day grilling,

Recescu flew to Indianapolis and drove the last 70 miles to the penitentiary.

"Just watch, Warden. Give it another minute, sir. It all started a month ago, but this afternoon it really started getting, uh, weird."

"What started, Colonel?"

"That! Look at the prisoners! Christ almighty, now they're all doing it!"

The warden leaned closer to the monitors and watched all ten test subjects sit up on their beds in perfect synchrony. Their eyes were closed, but then on some cue all opened wide. Their heads pivoted, all seemingly controlled by a common gear toward the west, then returned and looked up at each individual's surveillance camera. The prisoners nodded slowly at the cameras twice. An identical sardonic smile rose as one on each man's face. Then as if ten puppets' strings were cut at once, the prisoners collapsed and fell still on their beds.

Warden Recescu stepped back and waved his hand palm up at the monitors in exasperation. "What the hell was that, Colonel? How long did they have to practice that stunt? Creepy, but I got to admit it was impressive."

Colonel Wainwrights admitted, "That was a first. We've never seen that before. Just lots of freaky lesser stuff."

"Like what?" asked the warden.

"Little things, like synchronized eating and pacing in their cells."

"Synchronized?"

"Yes, sir, but not all the prisoners at once, just two or three of them at a time."

"How is this possible?" asked the warden. "They have absolutely no way to speak to each other and organize. We have 100% segregation. You checked for watches and clocks? Cell phones?"

"Affirmative," replied the colonel. We tore the unit apart and found nothing,"

"Have you considered the possibility our corrections officers might be involved?"

"Yes, sir. We considered that and ruled the possibility out when we sent the entire staff on paid leave, and then replaced them with other veteran officers from Illinois, New Mexico and Florida. The synchronized behaviors actually increased."

"Could their attorneys have been involved?" asked the warden.

"Impossible. Their ACLU lawyers won. Saved their clients' lives. They no longer come around and their clients stopped calling them long ago."

"Maybe they are somehow syncing-up based on our scheduled routines."

"We ruled that out too, sir. Obviously, there is no daylight on the Special Confinement Unit. So we inverted night and day, changed their meal times, disrupted exercise and then discontinued visitation for three weeks. The prisoners' synchronized behavior only expanded during that period."

"Son-of-a-bitch! Do you suspect, Colonel, that this behavior might be caused by the Cerebellar trials?"

"It can't be anything else, sir. I've worked forty-one years in the federal penal system and arrived in Terre Haute a full decade before we executed McVeigh. I've never seen anything remotely like it."

"I'll contact Cerebellar tomorrow. We need to stop this."

BRAINLORDS PIONEER JOHN DOE REACTS

SCOTUS Opens New Frontier in Human History

By **Skylar Thompson with *SCOTUS Newswire* Staff**
Updated Fri, May 27, 2026 at 2:51 p.m. EDT

(*SCOTUS Newswire*) – In a succinct statement, Stellar Joule founder, chairman, and CEO John Doe announced, "Our Cerebellar Networks subsidiary will open Neuralnet worldwide for

business in less than four hours when we execute our first 100,000 brain leases."

4

Stellar Joule Headquarters. Siano, California. The executive secretary knocked twice on her boss's private conference room door, waited a moment then stuck her head inside. She smiled and glanced at the executives sitting around the table. "Excuse me, Mr. Doe, I have FBI Special Agent Rene Melanovik for you on the secure line."

"Thank you, Darlene. We'll take the call in here. Activate SCIF building-wide, please." The entire home office tower was a Sensitive Compartmented Information Facility. The boardroom was a second SCIF inside a SCIF.

"Of course, sir."

"And Darlene?"

"Yes, sir?"

"Thank you for being such a fine worker." Doe's appreciation was delivered with as much sincerity as the synthetic monotone recording of an automated attendant: *"Happy holidays. Thank you for calling Sloth Services. Calls will be answered in the order received. Your estimated wait time is 157 minutes."*

The lack of genuineness was lost on Darlene. "Oh! It's my pleasure, sir!" She exclaimed excitedly, as if she were answering a game show host for the win. "It is the very least I can do! I'm so grateful for, well you know!" Like every Stellar Joule and Cerebellar Network employee, Darlene's stock options made her a multimillionaire on paper today.

Doe waited until the door closed and the security light illuminated. The room became electronically encased. No one could now eavesdrop, not even the NSA. He pressed several keys on the telephone base to set full-duplex dynamic encryption and spoke, "Agent Melanovik, I do not have you on speaker, but I think you know who is with me."

"Yes, sir. Your Executive Management Committee."

"Correct. So, the ruling went as expected, Agent Melanovik."

"Yes. I just heard, sir."

"Any complications on our end?"

"None, sir. Everything went to plan. There are no suspicions about how your attorneys influenced this or any of the lower courts' decisions. I've scrubbed your attorneys involvement. Judge Roth and the other justices were dosed and activated without incident. You got to all but one, Sir, Justice Daughtry."

"Thank you Agent Melanovik for your service. Eight was enough. Please hold for further instructions."

"Of course. Good day, sir."

The FBI agent, himself a 'dosed victim' for just 12 hours, did not have to wait long for his instructions. His orders were not veiled or ambiguous. The orders came straight from the top. The self-destruct command was sent by Doe over subspace directly from Doe's to Agent Melanovik's brain.

Chairman and CEO John Doe listened to the blare of car horns, screeching tires and car crashes after the artificially intelligent nanobots killed Melanovik. His job was done.

"Good bye, Agent Melanovik." Doe's expression did not reveal in the slightest the programmed assassination of the former human asset, as well as five innocents on Washington D.C.'s famed beltway. He turned to Cerebellar's chief science officer.

"Dr. Nathoy, what is the status of our ten test subjects? I understand some new issues have cropped up."

"Nothing to worry about, John. Nothing new publically at least."

"Please elaborate."

"The subjects' kilocalorie intake requirements have increased dramatically. Much more than was reported to the press."

"All ten of the subjects now?"

"Correct."

"By how much?"

"A lot, 2,900 additional calories are required per day to maintain our parameters. Their caloric requirements are increasing at the rate of 5% per day."

“Excellent. What else?” asked John Doe.

Dr. Nathoy replied, “None of them sleep more than three hours per night, yet they show no physical or mental deficits as a result. I predict none will sleep at all in just 48 hours.”

“Our excellent growing boys! Anything else?”

“Yes, eight of the subjects now test above 130 IQs.”

“What was their average before the trials?”

“They averaged 91.”

“Very good.”

“There is one more thing I think you’ll like, Sir.”

“Yes?”

“Last week we began feeding neural data in languages other than English. The results are amazing, Sir. All ten subjects are now silently communicating with each other in fluent Portuguese, Farsi and Norwegian.”

“That is such a wonderful surprise, Doctor.” Spoken with the feigned wonder of parents watching their children open Christmas presents they’d just wrapped. Doe then asked, “Has Dr. Vonbergen shared his concerns with these developments?”

“He does not know about these most recent developments.”

“I assume he is still not onboard with Brainlords.”

“You assume correctly, John. I have Dr. Vonbergen’s program assessment. Do you want me to read it to the committee?”

“Yes.” Doe had already read the report. He just wanted to witness the executives’ reaction to it.

“The risks to the public are too great. We need more time. The *Uncommon Cold Pandemics*, we must all agree, were unmitigated failures of concept. While infecting the world with a communicable antivirus virus that inoculates humans against all viral infections was noble, the effect was catastrophic. Just imagine if governments ever discovered that Stellar Joule was responsible for killing 99-million people! I fear Neuralnet might be even more cataclysmic. Minimally, I recommend rescheduling tomorrow’s launch to a much later date, if not cancelling the Brainlords program altogether.”

The new on-paper-multimillionaires’ protests around the long conference table were immediate.

"Fuck that guy!"

"The *Uncommon Cold Pandemics* were unforeseeable!"

"We were so close to eradicating ALL viruses!"

"Long-term big picture: 99-mil was a small price to pay!"

"We shouldn't abandon the communicable antivirus virus!"

"It's worth trillions! TRILLIONS, Mr. Doe! Please!"

"Vonbergen does not understand. He lost no one to Covid. And he wasn't even here when we released the antivirus virus."

"I second everything!"

John Doe was an unexpressive man, but when he did become animated it reminded onlookers of one of those nature shows when a seemingly inert crocodile explodes from the muck water and nails a wildebeest by the throat and pulls it under.

The *Uncommon Cold Pandemics* had failed, killing only 99-million humans, not the 7.4 billion Doe intended to exterminate. In fact the purge was so short-circuited, few other biologic lifeforms were even effected. John Doe was perplexed that the pandemics failed to sterilize the planet with the cruelly named hoax called an *antivirus virus*. He was even more concerned by the delays the failure caused. This had never happened before. Moreover, he'd never been behind schedule harvesting a planet.

Doe rewarded his supporters with his reminding them of his intolerance of emotion, "Enough! Vonbergen's dissent will end tomorrow in Terre Haute."

A table full of "Yes sirs!" were exclaimed all around.

Every wide eye wandered nervously over the conference room tabletop, under which all golden handcuffed hands were wringing. All knew exactly what Doe meant regarding *dissent ending*. The so called committee was long past asking privately, let alone publically, *Who is John Doe, and where did he come from? Or more importantly, where'd such and so, such and so, and such and so go?*

"General Broder?"

"Yes, sir."

"The Neuralnet is officially open for business. Start dosing the subscribers immediately."

"Where first, sir?"

"Everywhere, General. From Los Angeles to Paris to Kiev to Johannesburg to Rio de Janeiro to Beijing and all points in between."

"I'll instruct IT to open the 1-800 subscriber activation numbers worldwide."

"Forget the 1-800 numbers. We no longer need them. To achieve critical mass, the first 100,000 subscribers will now activate automatically upon dosing."

"Uh…sir? Automatic activation? Critical mass?" The general was suddenly uncertain. He'd never heard this before.

"Did you not understand my orders, General?"

"I'm just confused, sir."

Doe rose from his chair and leaned over the conference table until his mouth was just millimeters from Broder's ear. He spoke softly but loud enough for all to hear, "I strongly suggest you obey my orders and stop questioning them. It sort of sounds like dissent. Do you understand? Sixty-two countries and 100,000 new brainlords in four hours or less. Affiliate the required minimum. Understand?"

"Yes sir. Loud and clear."

"And if anyone has changed their mind, 'volunteer them'. "Yes sir."

In a 4th level subbasement office 31 floors below the SCIF meeting room, the LED on a two-terabyte Toshiba external hard drive stopped flashing.

Dr. Rhine Vonbergen removed his headphones and disconnected the hard drive from the listening device. A specially modified 1980s vintage transistor radio. EMC meeting #11, as well as Doe's conversation and execution of FBI Agent Melanovik was finished recording. He also had no doubt what Doe's *volunteer them* meant.

The former University of Chicago physics professor and Stellar Joule mole leaned over his trash can and finally vomited.

BRAINLORDS SPLITS SUPREME COURT JUSTICES

Judicial Allies Roth and Daughtry Part Ways

By **Skylar Thompson with *SCOTUS Newswire* Staff**
Updated Fri, May 27, 2026 at 1:59 p.m. EDT

(*SCOTUS Newswire*) – Chief Justice Zenor Roth wrote the majority opinion in *Indiana v. Cerebellar Network.* In it, Roth dismissed his very public previous concerns regarding information security on the Neuralnet.

"No machine will ever deliver the reliability, or possess a firewall as impenetrable as that 70% of the human brain we do not seem to need or use. Just as Arpanet fell to its successor Internet, so too will the Internet fall to its descendant the Neuralnet."

In her unusually sharp dissent, Justice Theodora Daughtry wrote, "I fear the law of unintended consequences may never again be more affirmed than it was today by this court."

Daughtry, the South Dakota native and Roth's former clerk is the youngest justice ever appointed to the land's highest court. She added, "Mankind's imagination has finally overreached its grasp."

5

May 27, 6:00 p.m. FBI Agent Easton DeSmet had no difficulty locating text messenger HELP's unlisted home phone number and her home address. Such were the advantages afforded all FBI Special Agents. Especially agents skilled at tracking down anonymous tipsters, and particularly those whose identity's were intentionally so thinly veiled as Supreme Court Justice Theodora Daughtry's. The justice clearly wanted to be discovered specifically by him on a private, face-to-face backchannel and to meet alone.

Parked now in front of her classic 19th century brownstone, Easton entered the judge's home number on his phone, but then stopped before completing the call. He debated one last time whether to just climb the brownstone's steps, knock on her front door and surprise the Supreme Court justice. In the end, he shrugged away the risk of a brushoff, gave in to courtesy and selected CALL. The judge answered on the third ring.

"This is Dora."

"Justice Theodora Daughtry?"

"Yes."

"Justice Daughtry, this is Easton DeSmet, the FBI agent you've been texting. I think it's time we meet. It's late but..."

"It's about time you called, Agent DeSmet. I certainly left sufficient electronic breadcrumbs for you to find me. I feared I might go broke buying burner phones. Can you come right now or should I meet you somewhere?"

"Of course we can meet. I'm... Well, I'm actually sitting outside your home right now." Easton grimaced as a wave of confessional embarrassment swept over him.

He was relieved when she replied, "That's excellent."

The brownstone's porch and stoop sidelights illuminated the front steps. Judge Daughtry appeared with the cellphone still to her ear. Her other arm searched and found the jacket sleeve and tugged it on. She ID'ed the standard FBI issued company car and watched Easton emerge. The justice nodded to herself. He came alone. The judge and agent lowered their cellphones together.

Easton waved and mentally recalled Judge Daughtry's history. She was of Irish, German, Swedish and Native American descent. Daughtry precociously graduated from high school one day after her 14th birthday. She graduated Magna Cum Laude two years later at the University of South Dakota with a double major in biochemistry and political science. After finishing her postgraduate Rhodes studies at age 19, she barely unpacked her bags breezing through Harvard Law. She did her postdoc clerkship with Supreme Court Justice Zenor "Zeke" Roth. A few years of private practice in Vermillion, South Dakota, was followed by a seat on the federal bench in Pierre. She was nominated to the U.S. Supreme Court by President Claire Capehardt and confirmed with the highest Senate affirmation since Justice Kennedy. Donning the black robes at age 32, Daughtry was three days younger than Justice Joseph Story, the previous record holder for youngest jurist in SCOTUS history.

Justice Daughtry scanned up and down the street. Not nervously though, more like a vigilant Marine embassy guard. Everything appeared normal. She watched the agent approach. He stopped at the bottom of the steps and displayed his FBI credentials carefully, so only she might see them. Dora studied them and nodded once. The justice placed the cellphone in her left coat pocket. Her right hand lifted from the Glock 17 pistol concealed inside the other pocket.

Easton DeSmet's physical appearance was similar to long-gone John Kennedy Jr.—fit, tall and handsome down to his eyes and naturally wavy dark hair. His was enough of a likeness that more than one person he'd met over the years had asked him, "Are you someone famous? You look so familiar."

He carried himself more like a sad eyed professor of poetry, pensive and a bit on the stoic melancholy side. However, he was neither a shy man nor downhearted by nature. That was just an unintentional disguise that also helped disarm those whom he investigated. He climbed the last step and stuck out his hand, which the judge took.

"Nice to meet you, Agent DeSmet. You have questions. I have questions. And I'm confident we'll both soon have more. Many more I expect. Let's talk inside."

"Of course, Your Honor." He followed her into the living room and sat where she gestured and said, "Please."

"I just finished training and was about to crack a beer. Would duty keep you from joining me?" The judge hung her jacket on the entry hall tree. One pocket drooped lower with something heavy.

Easton glanced at the jacket and recognized a faint but familiar silhouette. He looked up at the judge. "A cold beer would be nice. Thank you." He then added, "Your Honor, may I ask you a question."

"You bet. Shoot."

He pointed at the jacket and smiled. "Ironic choice of words—'shoot.' Why is it you felt it necessary to greet me with a pistol in your pocket?"

"Very observant, Agent DeSmet. A virtue that will prove valuable if…" She did not finish her statement. Instead, she retrieved the pistol from the coat. She pressed the release, dropped the ammo clip and placed it on an end table. Without looking down at the weapon, the judge moved the slide back and forth rapidly to expel the chambered live round, which she snatched out of the air before it could hit the floor.

Easton smiled. The judge obviously knew her way around a semiautomatic pistol.

The Supreme Court justice inspected the chamber, looked down the barrel toward the floor and handed the weapon to Easton. "The Glock 17 was a gift from Justice Roth when I finished my clerkship with him. See here." She pointed to the gold plate on the grip: *For Dora, forever my straight shooter—Zeke Roth*

"To answer your question as to why I'm armed, Agent, I suspect it's for the same reason you came calling this evening alone. You read the articles and made the connection to your investigation of BCL. Something is very wrong. You have your suspicions, the kind that bear guarding. The kind that raise the hair on the back of your neck. Am I right?"

Easton nodded slowly. He held her eyes for a moment and then said, "Yes, I do. Something is off, Judge, and it is already way ahead of us."

"Way ahead of us I fear, Agent DeSmet. I'll get those beers now. Make yourself at home. We have a lot to discuss."

Few would ever confuse Theodora Daughtry out in public as a Supreme Court justice, let alone as the high court's youngest and most recent addition. Easton recalled another *SCOTUS Newswire* article written by the 2-time Pulitzer journalist Skylar Thompson.

In it she quoted comedian Napoleon Passerelle. The late night television host who once quipped that Daughtry's appointment to the U.S. Supreme Court was like appointing a star Olympic gymnast as AARP's new line leader in gym class. "Can you just hear their arthritic grey minds trying to keep up with her intellectual chin-ups? What a hoot!" the comedian joked.

Easton stood and studied the photos on the back wall. Dozens chronicled the judge's life. Many documented her Sioux Indian heritage belonging to the Yanktonai Dakota Nation.

The judge handed a bottle of Heineken to Easton and gestured with hers at the photograph. "That little girl you are looking at is my grandmother. Twenty years later, she married this handsome Caucasian fellow over here. He's the one in the white coat. Over here, this is their wedding photo. As you can see, he agreed to a traditional Sioux ceremony."

"How did they meet?"

"Grandpa went to medical school in Grand Forks, North Dakota. He moved west after graduation and settled in Bismarck. They met before the war. Grandma came to North Dakota from South Dakota on a nursing school scholarship. They met in clinic. He lost his left leg below the knee in the Pacific during the war when the *USS Dentoncort* was torpedoed and nearly sank."

"The USS *Dentoncort*. No better named warship."

"Yes. The destroyer was named after the Revolutionary War hero Quintus Marcus Dentoncort. You're familiar?"

"Oh indeed. Quintus Marcus Dentoncort was John Adams' body guard during the *Boston Massacre Trial*. He was a famed saboteur of British ships and supply lines. Ran a spy ring right under Cornwallis's nose. Wounded twice. Bunker Hill and Yorktown. He was the real warrior that guy. Did it all." Easton gestured at the photographs. "Sorry Judge, I'm a bit of a military history buff. Please continue. So, how did your grandparents get back together?"

Dora smiled. Easton's impromptu recall was impressive. "I don't know how exactly they reconnected. I've heard several stories, some not so flattering to Grandpa. Turns out he was a bit of a romantic, and humorously so."

Easton said, “You have your grandmother’s eyes and cheekbones.”

“Yep! And her eyebrows I’m told, though I don’t see that so much.”

As he sipped his beer, Easton studied the wall of ancestors and casually compared them to Dora. She’d definitely inherited her athletic build. Easton was six-two. He estimated the judge at five-ten, which must make a few Lilliputians of the high court a tad uncomfortable at times.

“Is this a cousin?”

“Nope. That’s my dad.”

“Whoa! Your father played for the Denver Broncos. Impressive.”

“Yep. He did. Wide receiver. All pro twice. His teammates nicknamed him ‘The Bad Bunny’. And he absolutely LOVED that nickname.”

“Bad Bunny? For his ability to juke tackles after receptions.”

“In part, but more likely for his alma mater South Dakota State. Its mascot is the jackrabbit.”

“That’s actually funny.” Easton studied the photo a moment longer and added, “You have his dimples and blonde hair.”

“Yep.”

“Is this your mom?”

“No. That is my aunt. This photo was taken at the ‘76 Olympics. She won a Bronze Medal in track and field.”

“You could be her twin.”

“Yep.

“Where’s your mom?”

“Right here. That’s her standing in front of the Duane Physics building at the University of Colorado in Boulder. She taught there for eighteen years.” The judge added softly, “Mom and Dad were murdered during a carjacking in Mexico one month to the day after that photo was taken.”

“I’m so sorry, Your Honor. I… I actually remember that.”

“Yeah. Such a waste.”

They studied the rest of the wall in silence. He reached the last photograph and turned to the judge and asked, “Your Honor, when I arrived you were well-armed and you clearly, cautiously surveyed the street for a threat as I walked up. You are dressed in workout attire and your knuckles are red. I see an abundantly perforated stuffed mannequin in what used to be a dining room. That adds up to self-defense training. I'm guessing Krav Maga by the collection of innocuous household articles laying around that can be turned into lethal hand-to-hand weapons."

"Very good, Agent. You *are* observant! So you are familiar with the martial art Krav Maga?"

"Yes. I enlisted in the Army after college and law school and served with the Rangers. I was introduced to Krav Maga during a military exchange in Israel. Loved it and kept up with training. I now occasionally help teach at the academy."

"Well, I'm impressed. I chose wisely." Spoken as if her interview with a candidate had just ended—favorably—and it was time to move the aspirant to the next level.

"Let's sit, Agent DeSmet. I would very much like for you to hear a theory and see some evidence. It will sound preposterous, but I'm becoming increasingly convinced it's a nightmare about to come true. Moreover, I would like very much for you not to have me committed, or worse, arrested for treason when I'm finished."

Easton did not know how to reply.

Dora nodded. "I understand. You are asking yourself, 'Why am I really here? What's this crazy lady talking about?' Well Agent, what I'm about to show you is why I asked for you specifically to contact me. Bottom line: you were recommended. I researched your background, your history and your record. I chose you to lead this investigation. You'll need all of your legal, investigative and military training to unravel a conspiracy that I fear has permeated to the highest levels of our government. So can you keep an open mind?"

Easton studied the judge, then nodded slowly. "Okay, it's a deal." Easton returned to his chair. His puzzled countenance and crooked smile revealed his deep confusion; like when we ask a magician with our eyes and expressions alone, *How'd you just do that?*

Dora understood. "You look hungry, Agent DeSmet, for both food and information. While I throw a frozen pizza in the oven, reread these two seemingly unrelated articles that are actually about the exact same thing.

Easton accepted the printouts and watched Dora turn and walk away. He started reading.

UC2 VIRUS STRIKES COURT AGAIN

Uncommon Cold Virus Kills 2nd Supreme this Year.

By **Skylar Thompson** with ***SCOTUS Newswire*** **Staff**
Mon, December 29, 2024 at 2:26 p.m. EDT

(*SCOTUS Newswire*) – Justice Redmond W. Hollis, age 65, today became the most recent Supreme Court justice to succumb to the *Second Uncommon Cold Pandemic*.

The UC pandemics combined have now taken two supreme court justices and 17 federal judges since January this year, including Associate Justice Carlton Lannister who died ten days ago.

The Supreme Court has suspended all hearings until replacement justices are sworn in.

President Claire Capehardt's office said the president will submit nominees to the Senate Judiciary Committee this week. Senate Leader Reginald Lang promised the Committee will hear testimony and fast track both appointments.

The world had barely recovered from the Covid Pandemic when the *First Uncommon Cold Pandemic* struck in January this year.

The First Uncommon Cold novel virus killed almost 50,000,000 people worldwide in just three months with most victims succumbing within 24 hours of infection. The pandemic ended abruptly in March after killing 98% of those infected.

The Second Uncommon Cold Pandemic struck in October of this year. It has already killed more than 49,000,000 people around the world.

Multiple hopeful reports this hour from Asia suggest the disease there has suddenly stopped spreading, just as it ended mysteriously in March.

GEORGETOWN LAW LOSES GIANT

Distinguished Dean Joins Private Firm Steeped in Controversy.

By **Skylar Thompson with *SCOTUS Newswire* Staff**
Mon, April 20, 2026 at 2:26 p.m. EDT

(*SCOTUS Newswire*) – Dean Szara Jacobs of Georgetown Law School shocked legal academia around the country today with her announcement that she was leaving the school immediately and joining the controversial Washington DC law firm Bobrova Coble Lemnisci.

Chief Justice Zenor "Zeke" Roth, himself a Georgetown Law grad and a best friend of Jacobs, lamented the school's loss. "Szara has been expanding the constitutional dictionary ever since we studied the law together decades ago.

"Her trusted pathfinding through countless precedential wildernesses are retraced daily. From classrooms and courtrooms across the country to the Halls of Congress and even this Court, her opinions sensate anew our precious Blind Lady.

"Like a riverboat pilot calling out 'twain!' on the bow of the constitution, Professor Jacobs has faithfully sounded safe passage through our darkest uncertainties. For 35 years she has helped keep our great ship of state afloat on America's turbulent tri parte, and well off the rocky bottom of systemic faithlessness in our judiciary.

"Why she stepped off now and more, why *there* everyone asks me, I do not know."

Roth added, "Her loss to the school goes far beyond Georgetown Law."

Neither Jacobs nor Bobrova Coble Lemnisci could be reached for comment.

6

Special Confinement Unit, U.S. Federal Penitentiary, Terre Haute, Indiana. Warden Constantine Recescu rubbed his eyes and reached for the Visine. He had been staring at the Cerebellar prison block monitors now without relief for almost five straight hours, a span of time far longer than any amount of Visine might allay burning.

His stomach and bowels gurgled futilely for a reprieve from any more coffee. Recescu leaned back in the office chair and squirted—more than dropped—the Visine liquid into his eyes. He glanced at the coffee carafe and frowned, yet he poured another cup.

The door to the control room opened, and Colonel Therl Wainwrights entered the control room. He stood behind the warden and studied the monitors. "My God, Warden, they haven't moved. They are all exactly where they were when you sent me home."

The prisoners were lying on their backs, ankles crossed right over left, left arms tucked under the pillow, right arms across their chests.

"It's even more strange, Colonel. Watch when I zoom in on their chests. This is new."

The Colonel's eyes darted from monitor to monitor. "What the hell! They are inhaling and exhaling in unison. How could they breathe…"

"…only four times a minute," the warden interjected.

The warden added, "It's not just their breathing, Therl. Watch when I zoom in on their eyes. Watch their eyelids. They've somehow synchronized their rapid eye movement."

It was subtle but unmistakable. "You're right, Warden. But how?"

"I have no idea, but there is more. The rapid eye movement is accelerating. When I first noticed it, the cycles were 15 left-rights per minute. It has risen steadily to now 29 left-right cycles per minute."

"Have you contacted Cerebellar?"

"A half dozen times. They say they are sending someone."

"They are stalling, sir."

"Yes, but why?"

7

SCOTUS Newswire Headquarters, Washington D.C. Journalist Skylar Thompson's credentials were earned on the path less taken as they say. She had reported for both *Times* newspapers—New York's and Los Angeles'. Later and after just two years at ABC, she became a White House correspondent. She embedded with the 1st Marines in the second Gulf War and won awards for her reporting as well as high praise from the marines with whom she served alongside, which meant more to her than any award.

Her journalism pedigree was built atop the spiritual shoulders of fellow Hoosier Ernie Pyle at Indiana University. When she left ABC and founded the fledgling Internet-based news service that focused on the doings of the U.S. Supreme Court, her journalist friends thought she had lost her mind. Her competitors were greatly relieved she left mainstream media. They should not have been.

Skyler's first Pulitzer and her Indiana Law School diploma were stored in the attic of her 140 year-old Indiana family farmstead. Her second Pulitzer was displayed on the credenza behind her desk. Number two came during *SCOTUS Newswire's* third year, which was its second year behind an online paywall and its first year in print.

There were no receptionists or secretaries at *SCOTUS Newswire*, just three breeds of legal beagles who sniffed out and scooped up any news that might have six-degrees separation from the high court.

In an age when print news was succumbing like yesterday's political promises and factional left/right talking points are reported as hard news. In an age when too many journalists relied on *anonymous-unverifiable-unnamed* sources siphoned from Twitter's septic tank. And in an age when reporters sought *Like* clicks on social media more than producing meaningful ink, *SCOTUS Newswire's* print subscribers were actually growing. SN's secret sauce was how its constitutional attorneys, private investigators and nonpartisan investigative reporters gumshoed old-school face-to-face with sources and discovered the disparate legal hot-dots early, objectively, and thoroughly.

SCOTUS Newswire staff routinely connected isolated irregularities involving synergized Pulitzer-worthy issues. Like an energy-related land use dispute in Wyoming, to a zoning overreach in Texas, to a small town in New Jersey's fight against eminent domain. Skylar and her team recognized and prosed deeply for the potential of constitutional precedents long before other reporters started re-prevaricating unfounded Internet snipe, googling Tayloe County, Wyoming and spellchecking 'imminent' (eminent) domain.

Investigative reporter Jack Caldwell was the only other person still in the office at this late hour. He rose from his desk and donned a Bobby Knight era horse blanket of a sports coat. He grabbed his briefcase and a hard-side suitcase, which he called his *ruck*, which contained his *kit*, which was a classic Royal manual typewriter and a FAX machine. He called across the room to his editor/publisher, "Sky, my Uber's almost here. Gotta go!"

"What time's your flight?" Skylar glanced at her watch. It was 9:45 p.m. "Traffic shouldn't be too bad at this hour."

"Dulles at 11:00 p.m. I'm meeting the rest of the team in Indianapolis, and then we'll head to the penitentiary in Terre Haute tomorrow morning."

As Caldwell turned toward the door, Skylar said, "Godspeed to you all, Jack Caldwell. Please be careful. All heads on swivels during this one."

Her comment startled Jack no less than if an air raid klaxon had screeched suddenly right next to him. The reporter stopped and spun around. "'Godspeed? Jack Caldwell?' Whoa! Sky, that's what people say to folks going on a suicide operation. Do you think today's SCOTUS decision makes this anything like a mad mission?"

Sky stood up and leaned over her desk. She studied the reporter for a moment. Jack Caldwell had been an investigative reporter during the cocaine wars in south Florida during the 1980's. He had been kidnapped once, shot at and hit twice, shot at and missed thrice, arrested by corrupt cops on multiple occasions, and still rarely missed a deadline. He had been Sky's most valuable mentor coming up and her first hire when she got to the top. Because of his fearlessness of crooks and predators of any ilk, and because of the shock of silver punctuating his otherwise naturally Reagan-ish dark hair, his nickname in all of News Land was appropriately Honey Badger.

"Honey-B, I believe we'll come to learn that today's high court decision will make the Court's 'National Bank' scandal of the 19th century pale in comparison. Relatively speaking, Watergate merits a one-and-done page-10 thumbnail below the fold. This could be dangerous. Someone very powerful got to eight Supremes and flipped them. I've proof."

"My god, girl, you have hard sources! His exclamation dripped with pride. He gently lowered his suitcase and briefcase to the floor, as if they too were ticking bombs.

"Yes, independent and triangulated, sources that point incontrovertibly to the same thing: judicial tampering."

"God damn, Skylar Thompson!"

"What I've uncovered is so preposterous, so utterly unfathomable it will be hard for the world to believe, even if undisputable proof is made public."

"When will you be joining us, Sky? This is the first time we'll all be collaborating on the same story."

"Two days. All of us may not be enough, though. I suspect we are heavily outmanned and outgunned—maybe literally."

"Jesus! You're frightened. Skylar Thompson is scared? Wow, that's a first. May I ask who are your sources?"

She replied, "My sources could not be closer to the conspiracy. We have an insider scientist at Cerebellar with a double Ph.D. in Evolutionary Biology and the Mathematics of Physics from Stanford and CalPoly. A Supreme Court Justice. And, we have an Ivy League law grad who is now clerking for one of the flipped Justices. Coincidentally, she's comedian Napoleon Passarelle's college girlfriend. None is aware of the others' suspicions. I don't want to be any more specific just yet, Honey Badger. Sorry. I will disclose everything after I meet with them."

"Ah, very good grasshopper. Confidentially compartmentalize your sources, independently corroborate their claims, then confront the target of your investigation for comment prior to publication. That's the Mike-Wallace-shorts-shitting-gotcha-moment us old-timers taught you tadpoles to live for."

"Yes sir. You certainly did. My one summer with you between J-school and law school was the best, Honey-B."

"It wasn't a one-way gift, Sky."

"Well, you better get going. Be careful out there. I love you too, Honey-B."

"Righto. You be careful too, Sky. See you in Terre Haute in two days."

SCOTUS REVERSES INDIANA VS. CEREBELLAR

Human Brains to Replace Internet In 8 to 1 Decision.

By **Skylar Thompson with *SCOTUS Newswire* Staff**
Fri, May 27, 2026 at 9:26 a.m. EDT

(*SCOTUS Newswire*) - Today in arguably the most shocking and unexpected 8-1 reversal in its long history, the Supreme Court of the United States ruled in favor of neural bioengineering startup Cerebellar Network Corporation, the controversial subsidiary of tech giant Stellar Joule Inc.

The decision overturned closely split lower court rulings all favoring the State of Indiana, the lead plaintiff in the case.

Thirteen U.S. States had joined Indiana two years ago seeking to suspend human trials in the highly controversial data transmission protocol called *Wide Area Neural Networking*. Also known as the *Neuralnet* or as dubbed by the public, *brain renting*.

Other state's Attorney Generals and an unprecedented number of interested parties published amicus pleas supporting the complainants led by the Hoosier state.

This landmark bioengineering decision opens the door to a radical new technology called *brain leasing*. The lease allows Cerebellar Network's artificially intelligent nanomachines to activate the mysterious 70% of the lessee's brain, commonly believed unused, and thereafter exchange data directly between multiple human brains.

Stellar Joule Inc. is Wall Street's 4-year-old wonder child. A megacorporation that dwarves all others in the world with its $21-trillion market cap. Stellar Joule is widely credited for singlehandedly supercharging and accelerating the global recovery after the asteroid strike and three global pandemics—Covid, UC1 and UC2.

Economists and historians have called the relatively overnight world-wide turnaround both unprecedented and miraculous.

It is widely estimated that three decades of worldwide recovery were reduced to just two years.

In just months instead of decades, Stellar Joule's nanotechnology miraculously cleared the atmosphere of particulates from the asteroid strike. It supercharged the development of next-gen solar panels and driverless electric cars built with self-replicating industrial robotics. GMO agriculture fed a starving world. Medical breakthroughs came nonstop. Robotic demolition of condemned buildings and robotic 3D building construction exploded globally. At the core of it all, were Stellar Joule's quantum-entangled nanobots. The world's first autonomous artificially intelligent nanomachines.

According to documents filed with the FDA, a brain lease is executed in a two-step process.

Brain lessors, nicknamed *brainlords* will consume a two-ounce bottle of liquid containing Cerebellar Network's patented artificially intelligent nanobots. The agent is odorless, tasteless and invisible to the human eye.

Within one hour the new brainlord submits to an automated and painless sixty-second medical procedure called a *Neural Node Activation Scan*. Activation of subscribers' neural nodes is completed by calling a worldwide 1-800 number and repeating a long series of keywords, phrases, dates, names, and numbers when prompted by a computer program at Stellar Joule's world headquarters in Siano, California.

The nanobots are programmed to then migrate to assigned regions of the human brain called 'frontiers' and await booting. Deactivation can happen at any time and reverses the activation procedure.

Leaked documents filed with the SEC affirm that CNC is prepared to affiliate billions of brainlords worldwide to ensure their zero service interruptions pledge, and a million-fold backup data storage redundancy.

While the actual number of prospective brainlords who have preregistered for the program is a closely guarded trade secret, unnamed sources inside CNC have confirmed the company's optimism.

The first 100,000 participants will each receive a one-time after-tax payment of $1,000,000 US for renting their brain and will receive free lifetime Neuralnet access as long as their neural node remains active.

Sixty-two countries have pre-committed to Neuralnet subject to today's Supreme Court decision.

The company plans to offer subscription rates for Neuralnet service that are 99% below current Internet rates.

The revolutionary data transmission protocol employs *String Theory* for the first time

in data communications. Neuralnet packets will transmit indecipherable *String* modulations around the world through subspace to ever-present local hubs—the human subscribers' brains.

The infinity-encrypted signals will then retransmit and distribute block chain data on demand at near light speed to brainlord subscribers anywhere on the planet for retrieval, co-processing and or the promised one-million-X redundant data storage.

8

U.S. Federal Penitentiary, Terre Haute, Indiana. Warden Constantine Recescu had managed to get a few hours of fretful sleep on his office couch when someone pounded on his door. The warden shouted groggily, "Come in!" He sat up and was visibly annoyed, but was also relieved by the intrusion. He thought at least the nightmares would end for a while. He was wrong.

The nightmare was just beginning. A plaintive 10-man whimper had just flipped the script and placed Earth to death row instead.

Colonel Wainwrights threw open the office door so hard it rebounded off the doorstop and nearly struck the corrections officer in the face. "Begging your pardon, sir, but we have a situation in the Special Confinement Unit. We think the prisoners are dying."

"What"?

"Thirty minutes ago they stared as one at the cameras in their cells and began miming the act of eating. Scooping imaginary food with imaginary spoons into their mouths, faster and faster, swallowing, all perfectly synchronized for five minutes. Then as one every prisoner fell to the floor screaming, while holding their abdomens."

"Did you call Cerebellar?"

"That's an affirmative."

"And..."

"Oh! Sorry sir! They put us on hold. So I came and got you."

The warden slipped on his shoes and the two sprinted old men style the quarter mile to the Special Confinement Unit. Wainwrights and Recescu entered the control room breathless and stopped before the bank of monitors, one for each prisoner. The convicts had seemingly recovered from their ordeal. Each now sat at his built-in metal desk eating. Ten men. One motion. Colonel Wainwrights stepped closer to the monitors and asked the officers on duty, "What happened?"

"The head man at Cerebellar, John Doe, personally came on the line and told us to feed them. We asked, 'Feed them what?' and he said, 'Anything, but do it quickly.' So we did.

"They started calming right down, just like that. Although, we have no idea where they are putting all the groceries. Since Doe said 'anything' and just to see if the inmates were faking it, the Lieutenant ordered in from the commissary ten #10 cans of creamed onions. These were each dumped into a plastic bins, and the onions disappeared by the handful without complaint. That's about ten pounds per man of cold, creamed frickin' onions gone, sir! We then gave each man a loaf of stale bread. GONE! All of it gone, Boss, just since you left to get the Warden. Now they are working on ten pounds each of green beans with a side of two-pound blocks of butter."

Then suddenly mid-bite, on some unknowable cue, the prisoners stopped eating, rose, and then returned to their bunks.

Recescu whispered, "What the hell is going on here?"

There were four officers assigned at all times to death row. All appeared more than a little perplexed by the strange events of the last hour. The three men and one woman gathered up in silence in the shift office. Sergeant Hawkins asked, "Anyone else get scratched passing them the food? They were like rabid rats grabbing for it."

"Yeah. Look at my hand! I'm scratched up all for shit!"

"Me too. Look at my wrist. Punctures look like I got struck by rattlesnakes."

The last officer reported, "The son of bitch in #4 almost opened a vein."

ORIGIN OF THE WORD BRAINLORD

Canadian Comedian Creates and Trademarks 'Brainlord'

By **Skylar Thompson with *SCOTUS Newswire* Staff**
Updated Fri, May 27, 2026 at 2:16 p.m. EDT

(*SCOTUS Newswire*) – The term *brainlord* was coined on January 6, 2024 by Quebec's most famous critic of the American government, CBC's late-late night comedic satirist Napoleon Passerelle.

The term *brainlords* was quickly embraced by the mainstream media and the public globally.

Passerelle trademarked the term, and said he intended to give the rights to the trademark to the estate of his dearly departed best friend Fidel Castro.

9

Last week in Teheran, Iran. A farewell party for comedian Napoleon Passerelle. If awards were ever given for Best Clandestine Cover at the CIA, the equivalent Oscar for Most Creative Fake Legends certainly would have been awarded to the late-late-night television comedic host, American-Canadian Napoleon Passerelle.

Leon, as his friends and fans knew him, carried what folks in the intelligence community called the spook gene. In fact, many at

Langley, Windsor and London considered the Passerelle family to be spook royalty.

As a McGill University trained hydraulics engineer, Leon's Canadian father had spied behind the Iron Curtain for nearly a decade. He built dams during the day and at night ran two of the top ten most productive intelligence operations during the Cold War. When the war ended and the Soviet books finally opened, it was revealed that Clinton Passerelle had never once come under suspicion by the Soviets.

Gwendolyn Abernathy, Leon's mother, was no less an intelligence blueblood than his dad. She was the daughter of General Carlton Plato Abernathy whose biographer revealed the Tennessee native, WestPoint graduate and decorated WWII veteran as a founding father of the Central Intelligence Agency.

Gwen Abernathy graduated from Vanderbilt University with a degree in Linguistics. She spoke multiple dialects of Russian without the hint of an accent, as well as possessed excellent fluency in French, German, Portuguese, and Spanish. Two years after graduation, the newly minted CIA intelligence officer was carefully secreted inside the Soviet Union with a legend so complicated and deep it might never be unraveled. In nine years her seven intelligence recruits had risen high up in various Soviet apparatchiks and were secretly dismantling the USSR from the inside out. Pregnant with Napoleon, the intelligence agencies brought her and Clinton home in early 1988. She too was never suspected of espionage by the Soviets.

Leon was born late that year in a twist of anomalies so ironic only poets and weathermen might credibly recount the tragedy. His parents and all of his living maternal relatives were killed on Christmas Day during a family reunion when a rare swarm of deadly tornados tore through the states of Arkansas, Tennessee, and Kentucky.

Leon's father was an only child and the last surviving member of the product of two generations of only children. So, another brand of tragic anomaly—a family tree with one last surviving twig—bit the infant once more north of the border.

However, he would not be abandoned. Napoleon Abernathy Passerelle was raised by an intelligence community extended foster family stationed in Canada. His nickname inside the CIA while growing up was affectionately the Prince. After earning a drama degree at Dartmouth College, Leon joined the family business. The spook gene lived on in the CIA agent, codenamed Prince.

Leon had the perfect cover and utterly unique tactic for disarming America's enemies and gathering critical intelligence. He made them laugh. His stand-up comedy routine hectored anything American, which gave the presumed ultra-radical entertainer a worldwide audience of some of America's most powerful enemies. He had performed in places like Iran, Libya, Yemen, and North Korea.

In Russia he filled auditoriums to the rafters. Stoic Vladimir Putin was once witnessed laughing so hard that tears streamed down his cheeks. The source of such fun was a 12-minute dead-on impersonation of former President George W. Bush imagining in fluent Russian what he saw when he had once looked deeply into Putin's eyes.

Leon inherited his mother's gift for linguistics. He always closed his act with his best joke, one that irreparably eviscerated America while humorously endearing his audience. He always performed in the native language—Russian, Farsi, Arabic, etc.

Napoleon Abernathy Passerelle was welcomed around the world with open arms to places the CIA, MI6 and Mossad could never dream of reaching. He did not have to bug or bribe and sometimes kill, like his parents did on occasion during their war. His weapons were plying officials with alcohol, humor, his squads of sexually cooperative fan girls, and his nonstop blue derision of the West, and particularly America.

Tonight was the end of Leon's fifth comedy tour in Iran. Most of the Teheran guests had left the after party at General Bani's home. Leon had given countless departing hugs and air kisses and was showered with praise and invitations to return soon.

As he himself was about to leave, Leon turned and asked his host a question, "General, please remember I'm always in need of good material to needle the West and its acolytes. I'm working on a new skit and I'd appreciate your feedback if you can stand me one more minute."

"Of course, my friend!"

"Thanks. Here goes. Tell me if this would be funny with your countrymen. It may be a little over the top."

"Go ahead. Please."

"So a bunch of heroic Iranian top generals and scientists have gathered around a TV and are watching the imperialist electronic yellow rag CNN. A news actor announces Breaking News! 'An anonymous source inside the Pentagon has just leaked to CNN a top-secret U.S. intelligence report that claims Iran has three new secret ballistic missile sites targeting Israel.'"

"Ooo! I like where this is going. Yes. Go on, Leon."

"Okay, here is the setup. Let's say that we use the last three cities I played in—Jaffa, Kulteh and Sadr. Okay?"

"Okay!"

"General, stop laughing! I haven't told you the joke yet!"

"I'm trying, Leon. Three are a lot of new ballistic missile sites, though. I wish any were true."

"Is it too many? Three?"

"No. Not that. Though I'd love knowing American Jew loving generals shitting their pants, but..."

"But joking about secret missile sites is too much?"

"Well, not too much for me…"

Leon finished the general's statement, feigning mild disappointment "…but maybe too much for the Ayatollahs?"

The general winked and held up his thumb and forefinger, "Maybe just a little bit, Leon."

Agent Napoleon Passerelle reported within the hour to Langley that the secret missile sites intelligence was Iranian disinformation.

10

Cerebellar Network Headquarters. Siano, California. Dr. Rhine Vonbergen logged out of his computer at CNC for the last time and switched off the bank of five monitors. Lying on the desk before him were two airline reservations, a rental car confirmation and the Toshiba two-terabyte external hard drive containing the surreptitious recordings.

One airline booking was scheduled for tonight to Indianapolis. He was supposed to spend the night at the Airport Beauchamp Hotel then drive to Terre Haute tomorrow. That was the company plan. Rhine had a different plan. In his plan he would never arrive in Terre Haute, but fly instead to Washington D.C. from Indianapolis later tonight.

Dr. Rhine Vonbergen had mystified his colleagues in the University of Chicago Physics Department, when he had abandoned his chair and tenure and joined Stellar Joule's California startup Cerebellar Networks. He had simply needed a change of scenery and career, he'd lied to everyone. The truth was too complicated to explain to his friends and colleagues, let alone share. Some truths can be deadly.

Rhine picked up the hard drive and braced himself for the kind of anxiety that members of a bomb squad always experience. He was under no illusion just how lethally explosive the hard drive's contents were. He had no doubts that what he held in his hands was a death sentence if he got caught leaving the office with it tonight.

The executive management meeting this afternoon might have been invisible to the NSA, FBI, and the CIA, but not to physicist, and mathematician Dr. Rhine Vonbergen. He had become suspicious of Cerebellar long before leaving the University of Chicago three years ago and coming to California. Something had stunk from the beginning, a dead elephant rotting behind the wall so to speak. Sixty days ago he had finally cracked the security cipher that shrouded the meeting room from electronic eavesdropping. He had since recorded every word spoken within that room.

Each day he had listened, the conspiracy became even more horrifying than the day before. Cerebellar was on the verge of committing the greatest crime in the history of mankind—against all of mankind. Only the sure knowledge that John Doe had something planned far worse than his Uncommon Cold pandemics had kept Vonbergen from blowing the whistle already.

With the death of FBI Special Agent Rene Melanovik, Rhine's proverbial camel had collapsed under the weight of one last horrific straw. The Arabic fablers knew their load capacities, and Rhine's terror had finally overloaded. Melanovik was disposed of by John Doe, the mysterious CEO, as casually as if the human being were simply a soiled tissue. Rhine Vonbergen had vomited in his trashcan today, but the nausea remained, for it was the kind that always just gets worse. Even when the heaves stop the conclusions nauseate anew.

The recordings left little doubt.

Doe's business plan was a complete sham. Cerebellar Networks was not the premier tech pioneer led by a mysterious genius that the world had come to believe. Cerebellar Networks was not leading the world into a new information age. Cerebellar Networks was a Trojan horse, and it was leading the world into a trap of yet unknown danger.

There would be no successor to the Internet. In fact, Rhine feared there would be no Internet at all after tomorrow. Doe had patiently sought and gained the approval of the courts, the SEC, the support of world governments and the public at large. Doe's Stellar Joule had saved a world set on the brink of the Dark Ages. A dark Ages of John Doe's creation.

Rhine, the mathematician and physicist, now understood why Doe had been so patient. Doe had an ulterior motive that he revealed this afternoon for the first time. He needed a *critical mass* of Brainlord subscribers to trigger some global event.

Rhine shuddered and tried to push away the thought that it might be too late to stop the attack. He placed the hard drive and the airline reservation from Indy to Washington D.C. in a secret briefcase compartment. He had created the hidden partition himself a couple months ago, and then filled the secret compartment each day with innocent items. Nothing was ever discovered by the Cerebellar security guards when he came to work or left each day.

The rest of his briefcase held carefully selected innocuous items most of which related to basketball. There were collegiate and professional team schedules, clippings from *Sporting News*, the last four dog-eared issues of *Sports Illustrated*, a Siano Sentinels junior college ball cap, and a new collector's bobble head. These were all props, though; all designed over time to help him breeze through security each day.

In truth Rhine Vonbergen had no interest in basketball or any sport for that matter. He dutifully memorized and spouted basketball trivia like he once solved extremely complicated quadratic equations in his head and recited *pi* to 314 places for math competitions. More recently he had committed a phone number to memory. It was Skylar Thompson's, the journalist at *SCOTUS Newswire*. He had contacted her seven times in the past month, always from a new burner phone. He never spoke his name after the first call.

It was time to leave. The scientist tuned his *customized* 80s era transistor radio to 'the game.' The local junior college Siano Sentinels was playing at downstate rival Reddinger Rockies. The announcer was just now releasing the halftime stats. Rhine left his office and turned up the volume. He arrived at the security checkpoint moments later with the radio close to his ear. Without speaking and offering only a nod and a smile to the guards, he casually tossed his briefcase and topcoat on the inspection table. He emptied his pockets, kicked off his shoes and walked through the scanner like he had done countless times before, all the while listening to the radio.

As one guard started inspecting the briefcase, he asked, "How're our guys doing tonight, Doc?"

"Doing great, Arnie. First half just ended. We're up eight. JJ's already got 21, six assists and five steals. He even got three rebounds, two were offensive that he put back in. I can't wait to see which one of the five power majors grab him next year. Man I'd give anything to be there tonight! Wouldn't you?"

The guard smiled. “Sure would, Doc.” He gave the briefcase only a cursory inspection and closed the lid. He had inspected it hundreds of times, and the only thing that ever changed was the latest editions of *Sporting News* and *Sports Illustrated* along with the mounds of week-old newspaper clippings about everything basketball.

The security guard handed the briefcase back to Rhine and said, “I saw your airline ticket. Where are you heading?”

“They’re sending me back to Terre Haute. Flying to Indy tonight, in oh my, an hour, and then driving to Terre Haute tomorrow morning.”

“Not taking a company jet?”

“Ha, I wish. Those are for the big wigs, Arnie. Us peons might’ve all become millionaires today, but we still have to fly commercial coach and rent subcompacts.”

“True that. Well you better move along, Doc. Sounds like you might miss the end of the game. You don’t want to miss your flight too.”

“Oh, don’t worry, Arnie. I set my DVR. Two just to be safe! Arnie did you know I have every Sentinels game DVRed?”

Arnie smiled. He had been reminded of that countless times by Dr. Rhine Vonbergen, whom he considered to be a sweet but absentminded professor, and a crazy-obsessed basketball fan. “Well, good for you, Doc. Good night now. Drive safe.”

“Thank you Arnie. I will, and uh…” Rhine raised a fist and shouted, “Go Sentinels!” He waited until both guards humored him and answered in kind, courteously but with far less enthusiasm.

A NEURAL CLOUD SKEPTIC

Nobel Laureate Decries Wisdom of Brainlord Tech

By **Skylar Thompson with *SCOTUS Newswire* Staff**
Article Updated Fri, Aug 2, 2023 at 8:45 p.m. EDT

(*SCOTUS Newswire*) – Russian-American Dr. Sergey Aranovich, the University of Oregon neuroscientist and world's first transgender Nobel Laureate testified today before Congress.

It is safe to conclude, he is not part of the scientific world abuzz regarding the potential and benefits of the theoretical *worldwide neural cloud.*

"If human brains were successfully connected to a massively parallel processing network, one that stored, retrieved, and transmitted data at brain speed around the world, the information processing capabilities of this Neuralnet would make the Internet look like tortoises fumbling slide rules.

"Relatively speaking, Internet would become kite string strung between soup cans and 5G would be a lamed Pony Express. The potential of this new technology cannot be overestimated, or I fear, adequately understood at this time.

"No one is asking the question, let alone ever answering it: Why did *Homo sapiens* evolve without the ability to understand what these so-called cerebral frontiers do?"

Stellar Joule Inc. who'll most likely be called the father of the *Worldwide Neural Cloud* if it ever emerges from the labs, declined the

invitation to have representatives testify before Congress.

11

University of Oregon School of Medicine, Lab 3112. Neuroscientist and Nobel Laureate Dr. Sergey Aranovich turned off the television, but the network News Actor's syrupy tease for the next roll tolled nauseously in his mind. "Next up…reaction to the Supreme Court's Brainlords decision!"

He clicked the *SCOTUS Newswire* link on his desktop and went directly to the article. He finished reading Skylar Thompson's article from today and shook his head in disbelief. He whispered, "8 to 1! Renting brains! Fucking idiots!"

Aranovich then searched online and found a second Thompson article published a few years ago. The article recounted his Congressional testimony warning about the risks of a neural cloud. Aranovich read his own quotes in the article and shook his head again. A chill soared up and down his spine.

"They did it. They fucking did it."

Dr. Aranovich closed the webpage and stood behind his desk. He was alone but spoke to the empty office as if standing before an overflowing lecture hall. "Pandora has come, not just her myth. Her true name is Cerebellar."

It was late and he was alone in his lab. One that over the years had expanded and took over the entire third and fourth floors of a science building that was unofficially renamed **The Aranovich**. However, if he had been surrounded by his medical and grad students tonight, even their brilliance could not have lightened his soul. It was happening. The nightmare was alive.

Dr. Aranovich lifted his cellphone and went through its call history. The reporter, Skylar Thompson, had called him 17 times in the past year and left as many voicemails, only one of which Sergey had returned. The scientist selected the most recent call, today's, and returned her call.

Across the country, Skylar Thompson glanced at her smartphone. Her face drained of color as the contact name appeared. Despite the fact that Skylar had practically stalked the famous scientist electronically; ironically, she had come to hope just today that her call would never be returned. She feared his call meant only one thing. The world's preeminent neuroscientist would officially confirm her growing suspicions about Cerebellar Networks and its scientists' crazy plan to brainlord the world into a single neural network.

Skylar lit a cigarette and answered the phone, "Good evening Dr. Aranovich."

There would be no chitchat. "Ms. Thompson."

"Yes."

"I will arrive in Washington D.C. early tomorrow morning."

"Okay..."

"You need to tell me everything you know, Ms. Thompson. Everything!"

"I think you know that's not how it works, Doctor. I ask the..."

"No! This time you must make an exception. You must answer mine and tell me everything your investigation has uncovered."

When Skylar didn't reply, Aranovich said, "Ms. Thompson, we need to work on this together."

What she heard in her mind was, *You are no longer a journalist.*

The reporter drew heavily on the cigarette and exhaled. Aranovich was frightened, and it was contagious. Skylar recalled what Honey Badger had once taught her about the difference between reporting a story and the oft deadly peril of becoming part of the story.

He taught, "Sometimes we find ourselves ass bitten. Reporting on a deadly 10-car pile-up through shattered glass and pinned down by crumpled metal. Upside down, inside out. That's when you'll wish you'd taken a different career path than journalism." Skylar twisted uncomfortably on the office chair seat and realized Honey Badger's lesson was not entirely an ass-bitten metaphor.

"Ms. Thompson?"

"Yes, I'm still here. Uh, do I need to arrange transportation to my office, Doctor?"

"Absolutely not. We cannot meet there."

"Then where…?"

"That's yet to be determined. Text this exact message to this number: 720-555-2122. **Boris will make Reagan scrambles at 4**.

"Forward the answer to me. Good night, Ms. Thompson."

The call terminated before Skylar could reply. The number seemed familiar. She opened up her CONTACTS and discovered the number belonged to her source at the Supreme Court, Zeke Roth's law clerk Amelia Long. She tapped out the message which was obviously a code: **Boris will make Reagan scrambles at 4.**

The texted reply arrived 45 minutes later: **I'll come hungry. Count on me for 4 at 7.** Skylar forwarded the message to Dr. Aranovich.

Amelia Long also recognized the caller ID. It belonged to the reporter Skylar Thompson, the reporter with whom she had secretly confided about the Court corruption. Amelia knew both who Boris was and what Leon's reply meant. **I'll be in disguise. See you at 4:00 a.m. Gate 7. Reagan National.**

Being Napoleon Passarelle's fiancé required learning Spook.

12

Indianapolis, Indiana. Obeying the company drafted itinerary to the letter, Dr. Rhine Vonbergen arrived in Indianapolis on schedule, rented a car and checked in as instructed at the Airport Beauchamp Hotel.

After that he ran his own plan. He never went to his room. Rhine's plan for disappearing was quite simple, but so was cracking Cerebellar's method of tracking their people with GPS. His smartphone was already sealed inside a prepaid SameDay Hoosier Courier Service envelope and addressed to himself at the penitentiary in Terre Haute. He would already be in D.C. before alarms set off by his phone arriving in Terre Haute without him.

"May I ask two favors, young lady?"

The hotel desk clerk replied, "Of course, sir."

"Would you mind making sure this envelope gets picked up by Hoosier Courier tomorrow morning? They are scheduled to pick it up by 8:15 a.m. and take it directly to Terre Haute."

"Absolutely. I get off in twenty minutes, but I'll make sure it's taken care of."

"Thank you. Secondly, I'm starving. Is anything still open near here?"

"Well, the Denny's is just a quick walk away and is open 24-7." The night clerk stepped from behind the counter, walked across the lobby and pointed to the restaurant a few blocks away.

"Perfect! Thank you and good night."

"And to you, sir. Enjoy your time in Indy."

Rhine Vonbergen's time in Indy would last only as long as it took to retrieve his luggage from the rental car staged for effect in the Beauchamp parking lot and to flag down an airport shuttle to the terminal. When he did not show up in Terre Haute, the Indianapolis authorities would first assume he had been abducted on his walk to Denny's. The ruse would last until his phone was discovered in Terre Haute. He hoped that would be long enough to get done what needed doing.

An hour later the scientist was 34,000 feet over Ohio, traveling under the stolen identity of a recently deceased man. His flight to Washington D.C. was scheduled to arrive at 5:30 a.m. FBI headquarters would be his second stop.

He'd first pay a visit to the reporter, Skylar Thompson. It was time to introduce himself in person.

13

Justice Daughtry held up a thick accordion file and said, "Agent DeSmet, before I show you this I'm very interested in your interpretation of the articles I sent you."

Easton thought for a moment before answering. "First of all, I believe you chose *SCOTUS Newswire* because the paper is focused exclusively on critical deep reaching judicial matters, and not because we are both lawyers."

"Correct."

"Secondly, you gained access to my cell number through your own connections at the FBI."

"Correct. A trusted friend of an anonymous trusted friend of someone very close to you and your current investigation, which please be assured I know nothing about."

Easton studied her for moment, then said, "Judge, I suspect you do know, but just don't realize yet."

When she did not answer he asked, "And our mutual new BFF connected dots, and those dots connected you and me. When?"

"Just in the last few days."

"What are they? These dots."

"Anomalies. Irrationality. Statistical improbabilities. Professional malfeasance. Radical new technologies appearing overnight out of vapor. Unprecedented financial success stories…"

Easton knew the rest and interrupted Dora. "Yes…and a Chief Justice of the Supreme Court who publically criticized the Brainlords movement for years, then changed his mind in favor of it in the blink of an eye and…"

Daughtry then interrupted, "…and a celebrated scholar inexplicably leaves Georgetown law and joins a pack of disreputable jacklegs." She added, "Today has been like one of those body snatching science fiction plots."

"My Jacobs and your Roth were flipped?"

"Yes. Somehow. I believe so. It wasn't just them. Seven other justices were flipped as well. Members of Congress. Federal judges. And more Agent, I can personally assure you every Supreme justice was decidedly favoring Indiana until just 48 hours ago."

"Justice Daughtry, about my investigation, we are just days away from indicting twelve members of the very law firm that represented Cerebellar Network."

Justice Daughtry looked away. She spoke thoughtfully, “And there it is. The unifying connection. Cerebellar. The most inexplicable anomaly of all.”

Easton nodded, “This is truly incredible.”

“There is more, Agent DeSmet.” She handed the thick accordion file folder to Easton.

Justice Theodora Daughtry studied Easton DeSmet while he examined the materials. For twenty minutes nothing about his demeanor suggested he believed or disbelieved what he read. Dora knew she had crossed every Rubicon imaginable by sharing the records: moral, legal, ethical, constitutional, and even intellectual. For after all, she was not only alleging the greatest, most preposterous conspiracy ever committed, she was violating the trust of the man whom she considered her second father, Chief Justice Roth.

Easton closed the thick file folder and looked up at Dora. He did not speak. Nor did she, but she read his eyes and Dora knew. He believed. All of it.

“May I have another beer now?” he finally asked, then sighed and added, “Maybe more than one.”

“Of course.”

Dora returned a few moments later with the beers and a shoebox. She handed a beer and the box to Easton and said, “There’s more. These will remove any lingering doubt.” The judge lifted the lid off the box. Inside were a dozen cassette tapes.

“You made audio recordings?”

“No. Zeke made them. Judge Roth. I knew nothing about the recordings until just before I contacted you yesterday.”

“Why would he have done this?”

“The behaviors of some of the lower court justices, as well as some members of Congress—even changes over at Bobrova Coble Lemnisci—were so unprecedented and so out of character that Judge Roth suspected some type of foreign coercion was at play. He contacted your office and the FBI secured the FISA warrants.”

“What did we discover?”

"Nothing. Well, nothing except all nine of us Supreme justices were decidedly leaning against Cerebellar, which meant the lower court's split rulings favoring Indiana would have held."

"You listened to the tapes?"

"I did."

"That's when you texted me."

"Yes. I'm the most unlikely Deep Throat ever."

"How did you get these tapes?"

"A friend. Someone I trust inside made copies."

"Do you remember the name of the FBI agent handling the FISA investigation?"

"Yes. His name was Agent Rene Melanovik."

Easton DeSmet winced.

"What is it, Agent DeSmet?"

"Your Honor, Rene Melanovik died this afternoon."

"How?"

"Witnesses said he accelerated to more than 100 MPH on the Beltway and somehow jumped the highway dividers, then crashed headlong into heavy oncoming traffic. There were multiple fatalities"

"Oh my god. How deep can this conspiracy go?"

"I can't imagine. You said you have a friend on the inside."

"Yes, and she has other friends—friends of friends actually—she wants me to meet."

"I think we should meet them. All of them and soon."

"I'll set it up for tomorrow."

The agent stood. "Just one last thing, Your Honor. I've been parked in front of your house for a while. If I were to leave now and if you are being surveilled, which you probably are, it would suggest I'm here on official business."

Dora understood. Easton wanted to spend the night. "Couch or guest room?" she asked.

The couch will be fine. No need to make it up, though. I won't be sleeping. However, Judge, please don't think anything untoward of me, but I need to accompany you to your bedroom."

"Do you really think such precaution is necessary?"

"I fear that it is. We need to make my coming here to be, uh... of a personal nature. Do you know what I mean?"

"I understand."

The FBI agent and Supreme Court Justice closed the curtains together, and turned off all the lights on the first floor except the porch lights. They climbed the stairs and walked in silence to the master bedroom. When they entered Easton gestured for Dora not to turn on the lights and to wait by the door out of sight.

The agent walked to the three-piece bay window overlooking the street and stood there studying the night. The closest street light was out but the moon was full tonight. Only two cars were parked on the street. His Ford sedan and a black SUV parked a few spaces behind it. He was about to step away from the window when he saw a glint of light flicker from inside the SUV.

Easton made a gesture up at the moon for effect then turned and spoke to Dora. "Judge, please step behind me and wrap your arms around my waist for a moment. I'm going to point up at the moon then step aside and wrap my arms over your shoulders. When I do, look at the black SUV parked behind my vehicle. Tell me what you see."

Judge Daughtry did as instructed. The occupant's window was down now. Easton felt her tense under his embrace. She saw it too. He whispered into her ear, "What do you see? Don't say anything until your back is to the window."

Dora let the agent turn her around. She wrapped her arms around him and whispered, "I believe what I saw was moonlight reflecting off binoculars."

"Agreed. That's surveillance, but by whom?" Easton drew the drapes closed and stepped away from Dora.

"My god. What's going on, Agent DeSmet?"

"Unsanctioned surveillance of a Supreme Court justice coupled with your strong evidence leaves little doubt. The Court has been corrupted. When can I meet your friends and their friends?"

"I'll send a text tonight. Don't worry we have established a code."

Easton had collected Dora's pistol on the way upstairs. He reloaded the clip, chambered a round and handed the weapon to her. "Just in case." No further explanation was needed. He walked to the bedroom door and set the lock. Over his shoulder Easton said, "Good night, Your Honor," and pulled the door shut behind him.

The FBI Agent descended halfway down the stairway and froze. Above the front door was a leaded glass decorative arch. On it danced the unmistakable red dot of laser light. Easton drew his weapon and chambered a round as quietly as possible. He pressed his body against the wall and climbed down two more stair risers. The laser light suddenly disappeared for a few seconds, then reappeared. This time it did not dance. It pulsed on and off—one long followed by four short pulses. The pattern repeated itself three more times and then stopped.

Easton recognized the message immediately. It was Morse Code for the number "6". Military jargon for *a friendly has your back.* The agent descended the rest of the steps, dropped to all fours and crawled across the slate entry to the front door. He rose to his knees and peeked out the door's leaded glass side window. Even through the distorting glass he could see that the black SUV was now parked directly in front of Dora's home. The driver illuminated the laser again and shined it so it was visible to Easton but not aimed directly at the house.

Squinting through the leaded glass, Easton reached up and felt for the front porch's light switch. He found it and switched off the lights, waited a moment then flashed the porch lights on and off quickly five times, which was Morse Code for the number "5".

The driver illuminated the laser once more and copied the number "5" code, waited a moment, then drove away.

Easton watched the SUV pull away from the curb and disappear down the street. He whispered, "Five by Five. Copy. Message received. So, you have my back, or perhaps the judge's, or perhaps both, but the question is from whom and who are you?"

~

As if he might actually have been able to read Easton's mind, CIA Agent Napoleon Passerelle whispered, "You'd never believe it, my brother."

14

Their names were Corrections Officers Eagan, Postlenett, Hawkins and Jin Li. That was before the four prison guards were infected yesterday in Terre Haute, Indiana. Now they were nameless and no longer exactly human.

At 2:00 a.m. the guards rose silently from their beds as one, infected their sleeping family members with an innocuous kiss, got dressed, went to their cars and drove to the same 24-7 department store in Terre Haute. Each guard purchased a twenty-pound bag of fertilizer, corn syrup, a gas can, and various other identical items from the Camping Equipment, Hardware, Plumbing and Electronics aisles. On their way home the officers stopped at the same service station and purchased diesel fuel.

The employees at both locations would never question the odd and coincidentally timed purchases. An innocent brush of the backs of their hands made sure of that.

None of the guards had ever handled an explosive ordinance of any kind, let alone expertly constructed such a unique bomb. Yet, they built four identical military-grade weapons in an hour. The corrections officers then donned bomb laden vests, then his or her prison-issued C.O. windbreaker.

The three men and one woman arrived to work at the prison at the same time, all thirty minutes early. Instead of reporting to their assigned posts in the Special Confinement Unit, a/k/a death row, two went to the meal hall where 150 gen-pop inmates gathered for breakfast. The other two guards went to the chapel where another 37 inmates had arrived for Mass. Both halls possessed high catwalks upon which guards could stand and observe the prisoners. Because of the early hour and because "inmate trouble" usually sleeps in, the high parapets were seldom manned in the mornings.

Former Eagan and former Postlenett assumed positions in the opposing ramparts above the chapel congregation. The former

Hawkins and Jin Li likewise assumed positions across from each other above the meal hall. Simultaneously, all four climbed on top of the railing, crouched, and then sprang like swan divers into the crowd of men below. At the apex of their leap they detonated their suicide vests.

The PVC pipe bombs containing the fertilizer/diesel fuel mixture had been scored precisely so the force of the explosion was directed inward, not outward like most suicide vests. The typical shrapnel—nails, broken glass, screws, etc.—common to suicide vests were sent inward too. These vests were constructed for one purpose: to spread body parts, blood, and bone over the crowded rooms below, not to harm those showered, but to infect them.

Counting the guards, their family members, store clerks, and inmates on the floors and the 10 originals on death row, John Doe's invasion force now numbered more than 200. This number would soon grow exponentially.

15

Washington DC, 6:00 a.m. Judge Theodora Daughtry descended to the last stair step and stopped. "Good morning, Agent." DeSmet stood by the front door, his shoulder pressed to the wall as he surveilled the street. The last thing she had done before heading upstairs was to set out a bedsheet, blanket and pillow for her guest. She examined the couch. The bedding was exactly where she had left it. Dora did not ask how he had slept. Obviously, he hadn't.

"Good morning, Your Honor."

"Let's drop the formalities. Please call me Dora."

DeSmet nodded. "I'm Easton," but he continued studying the street. Nothing more had happened since his laser light friend had moved on. "Any news from..."

"Yes, we've been texting much of the night. Skylar Thompson contacted me. She's setting up a meeting with the interested parties and their contacts."

The journalist was a surprise, but all things considered, par for the circumstances. Thompson had a reputation for discovering the truth in the faintest of light. Easton turned and smiled, "Interested parties?"

"It's code. Our get together cover story is a birthday party for someone named John Smith."

"Where?" she asked.

"She booked rooms at the old Masaquat Hotel in Virginia."

"Did that place even reopen after the fire?"

"Yes, barely," Easton replied. "It was already dying, though. The Masaquat has been on life-support for more than ten years since Hurricane Riley. The new by-bypass and a steady stream of 1-star reviews have demoted the landmark 5-star resort to just one notch above a No tell Motel."

"I'm assuming cash only and no surveillance cameras."

"Exactly. No Wi-Fi either. Probably few guests."

"Sounds perfect. When do we leave?"

"Skylar wants everyone to meet at 5:00 this afternoon."

16

Reagan National Airport, Washington D.C. It was common for Dr. Sergey Aranovich, the Nobel Laureate, to travel to Washington D.C. He had been a science adviser to three presidents, including the current resident of the White House, Claire Capehardt. He was also a frequent visiting lecturer at Georgetown University. What would have been a shock to his millions of adoring fans and former students were his many collaborations with both the CIA and NSA. He was prouder of these than his Nobel Prize.

He had no idea when, or even if, an agency handler would contact him before he met with the *SCOTUS Newswire* journalist, Skylar Thompson today. The intelligence agencies were always watching his movements closely. Ironically, Dr. Aranovich never considered such over-watch as an intrusion of his personal privacy, but instead a source of great comfort. He felt safe in America. He was Sergey Aranovich, a celebrated American man. And unlike in the former Soviet Union and later Russia, his unseen ever-present watchers in America were his nonjudgmental guardians not his prison guard tormentors.

After disembarking his flight, Aranovich entered the first Men's Restroom in the concourse, washed his hands, and doused his face with water. Next, he went to a kiosk and purchased a copy of the *Washington Post* and a cup of coffee. He found a deserted section of seating, sat down three chairs from the end, and fanned open the paper. After a moment, he feigned receiving a cell phone call. He left the newspaper on the chair next to him folded open to page seven. It was one of at least dozen complex codes that all meant the same thing. His travels were more than academic.

Six minutes later the professor reached Arrivals Gate Exit 7. He passed through the automatic doors and walked to the curb. A black Suburban immediately pulled up and a twenty-something woman emerged from the SUV's passenger side.

She approached Aranovich, stuck out her hand and said, "Welcome back to Washington, Dr. Aranovich. I'm Amelia Long. We are so excited you… you came."

Amelia's voice wavered just slightly and her handshake exposed a hint of nervousness. She did not exhibit the perfected spy craft of either the CIA or NSA. Amelia watched a hint of alarm in Aranovich's expression. She glanced at the SUV's front passenger window and grimaced.

The automatic window opener whirred and lowered halfway. Napoleon Passerelle said, "Calm the fuck down, Comrade Stalinovich! You'll meet your *SCOTUS Newswire* girlfriend Skyler Thompson soon enough. For now, meet MY girlfriend and Judge Zeke Roth's law clerk. Be nice or she'll get your geezer ass deported back to Russia where you'll soon be wearing granny skirts, support hose, and old lady Maidenform bras again. You pinging on me, Dear Brother?"

Aranovich laughed heartily. He recognized Leon's voice and humor and said, "I indeed ping you, Dear Brother."

This exact not so over the top trans-tease, and the nickname 'Stalinovich' had been given to him by Leon, the CIA agent who'd orchestrated his defection to America. The professor relaxed, noting that Passarelle's disguise was topnotch. He covered Amelia's hand with his other. Smiling he advised, "You should shop for a better class of boyfriends, young lady. Do your parents know?"

"No sir. Afraid not, Professor." She opened the back door for Aranovich and closed it behind him.

17

Masaquat Hotel. More weeds than faded yellow center striping divided County Road 13C's lanes. The potholed and macadam-patched country lane wound up to the old hotel like the coils of a snake. Side ditches had reclaimed most of the road's shoulders. Molted down to crumbs in places, C.R. 13C's ruination previewed the paint beggaring resort itself.

Time, neglect, forest fire, Covid, and two Uncommon Cold pandemics conspired with the new interstate bypass to starve the famous former jewel of the Blue Ridge Mountains of guests. Hurricane Riley's sixteen inches of rain was perhaps the slow acting lethal injection that began the fall. Lake Masaquat had filled to the brim and more. Its earthen dam overtopped, collapsed, and then flooded the valley below.

The once championship Masaquat Golf Course played in yesteryears by the likes of Ben Hogan, Sam Snead, and Emmet French closed forever under thousands of tons of muddy silt. The dam was never repaired. Pristine Lake Masaquat, once swam in by *Tarzan's* Johnny Weissmuller and FDR, was renamed by the sarcastic locals as Lake Mass-of-squat.

If not for the trickle of nostalgic baby boomers and the occasional 50th wedding anniversary reenactment, the Masaquat Hotel would have already closed.

Napoleon Passerelle, Dr. Sergey Aranovich, and Supreme Court law clerk Amelia Long were the first to arrive at the hotel. The front desk clerk whose age belonged approximately to the *Vera Clara era of Medicara* gave a well-practiced monotone apology for a long list of out-of-service inconveniences and of renovations in progress. Truthfully, all such troublesomeness was already well-beyond the adjective *temporary*. The clerk assured them that the power outage and telephone service interruption were just short-term too.

Napoleon nodded amiably. The clerk did not mention that cell service and cable TV were also out, but the disguised CIA agent had made sure that was just temporary too.

The clerk handed Grandfather John Smith his room key and another key to his namesake 'grandson' John and his wife Jane Smith.

"And again, don't worry about the power outage. It'll be over soon," the front desk clerk reminded again across the lobby as the three walked away. "We could hold out for days with our generators…they're always very reliable… and enjoy your stay with us."

18

Reagan National Airport. Washington D.C. Dr. Rhine Vonbergen exited the flight from Indianapolis and glanced at his watch. He still had hours before his Terre Haute ruse might be discovered by Cerebellar security. The scientist found a gift shop and paid cash for a burner cellphone and 180 minutes of talk time. Skyler Thompson had given him a special phone number months ago in hopes he'd call her someday. Today was the day.

Skylar Thompson answered his call on the first ring. She had spent the night on the couch in the newspaper office lobby. There had been little sleep. Dozens of coded text messages were exchanged overnight. Surreptitious arrangements were made. Strings were pulled by unknown parties.

Skylar was given instructions for after Dr. Vonbergen arrived. "Hello. This is Skylar Thompson."

"Ms. Thompson? I'm so glad you answered."

There was no mistaking the Kissinger burr, "Yes, and you may speak freely, Doctor. I assure you this line is secure. I was told I am bouncing your call through seven encrypted VOIP numbers to this new burner phone that I just activated."

"Very good…"

She interrupted the professor and cut to the chase. "Doctor, there are others. They have information I am confident you will need."

"Others?"

"Yes. A small group of insiders. Arrangements have been made for us all to meet."

"When?"

"Immediately, sir."

"Where?"

"Take shuttle bus #36 to long-term parking. Get off at the first stop, and then walk back out to the access road. I will wait for you there. I've been assured the cameras will be off."

"Excuse me? Did you just say…?"

"Yes, Doctor. We have a friend, who'll make sure the cameras will be off." Skylar recalled the messages from Amelia. Dozens had been exchanged second and third hand overnight.

"Ms. Thompson, this is not what I was expecting. The situation must be much worse than I feared."

"Fear? I fear that's the least of it, Doctor. I've come to realize overnight I am no longer *just* a journalist and you are no longer *just* a scientist. We are at war, sir."

The scientist hesitated for moment then said, "The Court turned us all into insurgents yesterday, Ms. Thompson, yes?"

"Yes, Doctor. But not just the Court. I'll see you in twenty minutes."

19

The Gathering at Masaquat Hotel. The hand drawn sign taped on the private dining room door read:

Smit Birtdey Porty!!!!!!

The sign's magic marker artist—initials GG—had compensated for their aversion for the letters 'h' and 'a' with extra exclamation marks.

A ten-gallon coffee urn that must have been salvaged from a military base closure in the 1980s was the centerpiece on the refreshments table. A couple dozen sugar packets fanned around a single stainless steel creamer portioned to a few servings of 2% milk. Along with it were mismatched paper goods and recycled plastic ware and chipped dishes filled stingily with stale mixed nuts, thawing apple slices, and powdery peppermint candies. The baker/decorator of the birthday sheet cake, iced translucently thin with chocolate icing. The baker took another shot at spelling 'Smith' and failed with a missing "i" and bonus letters "y" and "e"—Smythe.

Skylar Thompson watched the last two guests enter the dining room. She did not recognize Easton DeSmet, but Judge Daughtry accompanied him, so he must be alright. All other dots likewise connected. Amelia Long was the link to the still disguised Napoleon Passerelle and to Dr. Sergey Aranovich. Skylar had practically stalked the scientist and now here he was with Amelia Long. Their connection was yet another mystery.

Dr. Rhine Vonbergen cupped Skylar's elbow and pointed at Dr. Aranovich, "Bless you child! It's Sergey! He's with us. All is not lost."

"Apparently, but I'm still not sure what everyone brings to the table, or, even what the table is just yet. Excuse me, Doctor."

The journalist walked over to Justice Daughtry. "I'm relieved you made it, Your Honor." Skylar turned her attention to Easton.

The judge introduced him. "Ms. Thompson, please meet FBI Special Agent Easton DeSmet. He and I have much to share with you and the group."

That first introduction pulled the apprehensive strangers together one by one like a resolving catalyst. The groups of two and three became one of seven.

Skylar Thompson studied the expressions of the six people gathered around her and suddenly felt that she was now in the midst of something far more urgent than a news deadline. However, a deadline indeed loomed—literally—she thought. She recalled accounts of journalists on the *Titanic*, and how they had dutifully scribbled into their notebooks even as the great ship rushed from under them. Whether by recollection or motivation, the reporter made a decision.

"Before we go any further, I want you all to understand that everything said here today is off the record. I believe that what is discussed should remain confidential. Agreed?"

It was a strange request from a Pulitzer prize twice-winning reporter and it took a moment for it to sink in. Skylar waited until everyone discovered they too had arrived on some version of the *Titanic*. Skylar introduced Amelia Long first. The journalist then suggested that each person state their concerns, suspicions, and any proof of the conspiracy.

Amelia said, "I am Chief Justice Roth's law clerk. I am possession of some tape recordings made by the judge himself proving incontrovertibly that he suspected the courts were being corrupted somehow." Her next statement was not made by a Harvard trained attorney, but by a confounded friend. "I assure you. There is no way Judge Zeke supported the Cerebellar decision. I have a copy of his final draft from just three days ago. Somebody—something—got to him somehow."

Judge Daughtry spoke next, "As you may know, I'm Associate Justice Theodora Daughtry. Zeke Roth is like a second father to me. And I agree. He absolutely would have not dissented the Indiana v. Cerebellar appeal. His disdain for the Neuralnet was well known in the hallways of the court."

Easton introduced himself and added the third leg of the stool, "It's true. Judge Roth brought his misgivings to the FBI. However, the agent investigating the claims died yesterday under extraordinary circumstances without issuing his final report."

"Suspicious circumstances?" Skylar asked.

Easton answered, "Yes. The coroner's preliminary report stated Agent Melanovik died from a massive coronary. The adrenaline in his blood stream was twenty times normal. He was literally frightened to death."

Skylar studied Easton for a moment and then said, "Your expression betrays you, Agent DeSmet. You do not believe in coincidences."

"I do not. I served with Captain Melanovik in Iraq. He wasn't the frightened type. Quite the opposite. The only thing that ever flowed in excess in his veins was ice water. Never adrenaline."

A moment of silence born more by anxiety than a respect for the dead followed. Dr. Rhine Vonbergen broke the silence, "I am very sorry for your loss, Mr. FBI agent." All eyes turned toward the scientist.

Vonbergen added, "However, that is not what happened to your agent. He did not die that way."

Skylar introduced the former University of Chicago professor. "Folks, please meet Dr. Rhine Vonbergen. He is a physicist and a mathematician. In addition, until just yesterday he was a trusted scientist working for Cerebellar. Please tell our new friends what you told me earlier, Doctor."

"I regret to inform you that Agent Melanovik was murdered by my former employer."

"Murdered?"

"What?"

"How?"

"Do you have proof?"

"Yes, incontrovertible proof," answered Dr. Vonbergen.

"Why was he killed?"

"The FBI agent was murdered simply because he was no longer useful to the company. I do not specifically know how he was murdered. I just have a theory." Then he addressed Dr. Aranovich directly, "I also believe I am not alone in these doubts."

Skylar said, "Go on, Doctor."

"What I have is proof of a conspiracy that encompasses, that effects, and that I fear potentially threatens our… our way of life." Vonbergen stepped closer to Dr. Aranovich. "However Professor, I am anxious to hear your thoughts before I go any further. Please."

Aranovich nodded. He turned to Napoleon and said, "I believe we should do this together, Leon."

Passerelle nodded and began dismantling his disguise. Napoleon unhitched his fake beer gut and dropped it to the floor. He then peeled away the latex face mask. The wig was the last to go. A famous celebrity replaced a balding, middle-aged, potbellied man who spoke in alto with a slight stutter.

"You might recognize me now as Napoleon Passerelle, infamous anti-American late night TV satirist."

Amelia said, "Leon, you are burying the lead."

"Of course, dear. The TV gig is just my cover. Less than two dozen people in the world know what I am about to disclose to you. I am actually CIA. A deep undercover intelligence officer. I joined the family business, in a manner of speaking, fresh out of Dartmouth College. I am a proud third generation spy for the agency."

Napoleon turned to Amelia. "Ms. Long has been my girlfriend since college. It's only because of her I became aware of the conspiracy."

Easton recalled the strange laser light show last night and said, "You were the 5-by-5 last night."

"Roger, Agent DeSmet. That was me. Are you ready to join forces?"

"Yes, but how big a force are we talking about?"

Napoleon replied, "Well, I believe you are looking at it for now. Seven souls."

"The CIA? NSA? The military?"

"The CIA and the NSA are as surely infiltrated as the FBI and the Court. In fact, we are so late to the game I'm confident that all branches of the government, civil service, and the military are likewise compromised to some degree."

"So what is Cerebellar's objective, Dr. Vonbergen? Other than gaining undue influence over public policy, their ultimate goal is yet unknown."

Rhine Vonbergen stared at the ceiling and spoke softly, "Not entirely. I suspect something else is afoot."

Dora said, "Please explain, Doctor."

"I believe the corruption at the high court and the human trials in Terre Haute are not what they seem. The Wide Area Neural

Network isn't about launching the next iteration of the Information Age. After you listen to the recordings I made covertly at Cerebellar, you will come to the same conclusion as me."

Dr. Aranovich stepped forward, "And what is it that you suspect, Rhine?"

The physicist smiled at Sergey and instead of answering the question he asked Aranovich, "Before I discuss the recordings, Doctor, would you mind telling our new friends a bit about the deadliest virus our species has ever faced? How it attacked us time after time and nearly exterminated humans repeatedly over the past 2,000 millennia. How it is that we live alongside that deadly enemy today with little more than an occasional inconvenience."

"I'd be delighted to, but why?"

"Humor me, Doctor. I believe the WHYs then and now are somehow related to the Nobel awarded to you most deservedly for discoveries you made regarding immunology."

"Really? Well, alright Dr. Vonbergen. You are referring of course to any of the ancestral 200 strains of the rhinovirus known to cause the common cold. Its ancestors once many magnitudes more deadly than Ebola, Covid, swine and bird flu, even either of the Uncommon Colds, the *common* cold is now rarely deadly. We believe we are protected by our immunity but after three decades of research I theorize now we are not. I believe the relationship is much more complicated and mysterious than rhino immunity."

"Yes, Dr. Aranovich. Please continue."

"The rhinovirus decided long ago it had to change its ways. Killing off its human host was simply bad for business. So, a compromise was born at the genetic level. Human genes evolved to help the viruses spread around the world if viruses evolved to not kill us."

"And our common cold symptoms?"

"Our runny noses and chills are innocuous remnants of an ancient holocaust that ended long ago. Necessary skirmishes resolved without bloodshed on the frontiers between our immune system and rhinovirus. Think of them as war games. With history as our perspective, we now enjoy absolute peace with rhinovirus, the very ancestral enemy that once took us to the brink of extinction numerous times."

Judge Daughtry said, "It sounds like you are describing a symbiotic relationship, Doctor."

"Indeed I am, Your Honor. Like the wolf's ancestors and humans, rhino and humans learned to depend on each other long ago. Our genomes evolved together interdependently and mutually beneficially. The virus constantly evolves so it remains extremely contagious.

"However, our immune system has been trained by the virus to adapt to those variations, but not immediately. We always first allow the virus the opportunity to spread, that is, to live. We survive. Mighty Rhino survives. That is our mutual bargain. In fact, we most likely owe our survival against all sorts of other deadly viral and biological threats because we allied ourselves long ago so closely with rhinovirus's ancestors and a few other ancient enemies. I cannot prove it yet, but I strongly suspect Rhino intervened and ended both Uncommon Cold pandemics."

Easton DeSmet waited to make sure the professor was finished. "Very interesting, Dr. Aranovich. I don't think I'll look at the common cold quite the same ever again." He then gestured to Rhine Vonbergen and said, "I think you're up, Professor. Who murdered FBI Special Agent Melanovik, and more importantly how was he murdered?"

Vonbergen looked at Skylar for moment. His expression was one of should-I-should-I-not?

The journalist nodded. "Tell them, Doctor. Tell them everything you told me on the way here. Leave nothing out."

Vonbergen studied the group for a moment. "The founder of Stellar Joule Corp is an…is an extraordinary yet strange individual named John Doe. His IQ is documented over 220, though I believe it is much higher than that. He reportedly bench presses weights in the company gym five kilos over the world record as effortlessly as you and I lift and sip from a coffee cup. He never leaves the office, and on the rare occasions he does leave, no one ever sees him come or go. He takes the Paleo diet to an extreme, eating only raw meat. I believe about three kilos per day. His linguistic skills are unprecedented. I know he is fluent in at least thirty-four languages, including some of the most difficult like Swahili and Icelandic."

Passerelle and DeSmet exchanged glances. Easton would ask the question, "What is his background prior to Stellar Joule and his Cerebellar startup? The news reports are so sketchy."

Vonbergen's answer was immediate, "There is none, at least none that makes any sense."

"Please explain."

"John Doe dropped out of high school in Tacoma, Washington in 2019 at age 20, because he was unable to complete the math requirement. He borrowed a down payment from a loan shark and financed a 16-year-old Freightliner semi-tractor. The truck had five-plus million miles on it and fulfilled his dream of becoming an over the road trucker. That fantasy ended abruptly in June 2020 during a random safety check by the Idaho State Patrol.

"The Freightliner was found to have $18,000 in fines and repairs beyond both road worthiness and Doe's bank account. Coincidentally, his wife of nine months filed for divorce and Scam Bank foreclosed on his scam mortgage. For poor John Doe it was absolute proof that bad luck also comes in 3s. In July he was broke, alone, and homeless, so he hitched a ride and co-drove a semi-load of steel pipes to northern Alaska. He stayed and soon found work as something called an ice-road trucker. By all accounts, his dimwitted risk-taking made him a favorite independent hauler.

"In January 2022, Doe was hired to transport one of the first teams of accident investigators and their equipment over the sea ice to the site of the KirovFlot air disaster. Doe soon disappeared and was presumed dead. His body was never recovered. Six months later Doe turned up 425 kilometers southwest of the crash in an Inuit village. He was wearing the same clothes as the day he went missing, confused and unable to speak, but surprisingly fit and well-nourished. To this day he recalls nothing of the ordeal or any of his previous life—including his given name—Fergus Wayne McCullum."

Skylar anticipated the group's next question, "Doctor, tell us about the medical tests on Doe."

"Hoping to prove the survivor was an imposter, DNA tests were run. The tests proved just the opposite. Investigators also confirmed Doe was an only child and that his 16-year-old mother died in childbirth. So, no twins were in the mix and no look-alike brothers."

"Did the DNA match?"

"It matched perfectly. In fact, too perfectly."

"Too perfectly? Explain."

"Doe's DNA was a newborn's, not that of a cigarette smoking, recreational meth using, alcoholic adult male's in his 20s already suffering fatty liver and early onset emphysema with only 93% oxygen uptake."

"How can that be?"

"It can't, but there is more. Remember our primordial symbiotic alliance with rhinovirus that Dr. Aranovich so eloquently explained?"

The question was rhetorical, but Vonbergen waited until everyone nodded. "Doe has no immune system, nor is there evidence that one ever existed. He is devoid of antibodies of any kind. It's as if he never caught a cold in his life, or the flu or chickenpox or was ever immunized against diseases like diphtheria, polio and smallpox, which his medical records confirm he was."

"That seems impossible!" Amelia exclaimed.

"But true, and there is even more mystery. Doe digests massive quantities of raw red meat without the benefit of gut microbes. In fact, he has no beneficial bacterial or viral microbes in or on his body."

"Two questions, Dr. Vonbergen. "How did you obtain this information?"

"Tragically."

"Tragically?"

"Yes. A gifted former University of Chicago undergrad alerted me. Coincidentally, no joke, his given name was also John Doe. Apparently, his parents had a tin ear. John was a fourth year medical student at the University of Washington in Seattle. He was doing his rotations at the same hospital and lab where our mystery John Doe was first admitted. An exhausted researcher in the lab accidentally emailed the files to my John Doe by mistake."

"Did something happen?"

"Within ten days the hospital records were mysteriously expunged and my former student was dead. I believe the only reason I am still alive is dumb luck. The med student saved the medical files to a thumb drive and mailed it to me in Chicago. My student's murderer recovered the laptop and obviously concluded it had not been forwarded. If he had emailed the files to me, I'm sure I would be dead now too."

Skylar realized that an important part of his story had not been told to her on the trip here. "You sacrificed university tenure to investigate his murder yourself, didn't you?"

Vonbergen reached inside his jacket and held up the thumb drive. "Yes. I hired a private investigator to fill in any gaps in Doe's past life which had also been extraordinarily wiped clean. I then hired a headhunter to market me directly to Cerebellar. It did not take long."

The group unconsciously gathered closer. "The contents of this thumb drive are too dangerous to share with anyone, including the authorities. Every person known to have come in contact with this information or ever read John Doe's medical records are either dead or are now insider sycophants for Cerebellar. All of those insiders have exhibited an extreme personality change, a cultish change."

Easton broke the silence. "May I ask my second question, Doctor?"

"Yes, you may and I know what you are going to ask me. However, if you believe my answer, that will make at least one of us that does."

Easton asked, "What do you think happened to Fergus McCullum?"

"Do you remember the KirovFlot disaster?"

"Yes, of course. It was a freak accident."

"The world believes two falsehoods. First, that KirovFlot 319 was brought down by an asteroid. Second, that John Doe is a survival miracle, and his traumatic brain injury caused him to become an *acquired savant.* An accidental super genius. And now the world believes this eclectic genius has delivered us to the second coming of the information age. You will soon learn he is a monster. He was behind both Uncommon Cold Pandemics."

"Do you have proof?"

"Incontrovertible. It is on this." Dr. Vonbergen held up the Toshiba external hard drive. "In Doe's own words with a member of his executive committee—Dr. Nathoy."

"What? Fucking monster!" Amelia Long exclaimed. She had lost both parents in the first Common Cold Pandemic and her only brother and sister in the second.

"I'll tell you what I don't believe. Despite unanimous agreement by the authorities, I do NOT believe an asteroid struck the KirovFlot plane. I do NOT believe John Doe is a miracle savant. And, I certainly do NOT believe John Doe is benevolently ushering in a new information age."

Dr. Aranovich's tone was somber. He had arrived to the meeting with his own suspicions, and they now paled compared to what Vonbergen was about to proclaim. "You should tell them, Doctor. This is about more than nanobots and renting our brains to a wide area neural network."

"Much more. The evidence informs me of something entirely unnatural, something wholly irrational, but something that cannot be absolutely denied. I believe John Doe is an imposter."

Skylar asked, "An imposter? What do you mean, Dr. Vonbergen?"

"I believe he is impersonating us— *Homo sapiens*. John Doe is not human."

"Not human? Then what is he?"

"He didn't invent artificially intelligent nanobots. He *is* a nanomachine. I believe he is an alien life form that has assumed human form. Moreover, I believe the wide area neural network is an invasion of Earth that began in 2022."

Aranovich broke the stunned silence. "But their invasion, call it Plan A, failed. It failed because we are still here. Yesterday was their launch of Plan B. Round two."

Dr. Vonbergen exclaimed, "YES! Of course. The Uncommon Cold pandemics could not kill us all."

"No, I believe Rhino did come to our rescue twice, Doctor. We were most likely saved by our ancient enemy and modern ally—rhinovirus. The common cold defeated the uncommon cold."

For the next two hours the group listened and read in sickened silence the Supreme Court recordings, Vonbergen's Stellar Joule recordings and John Doe's impossible medical report.

20

Indianapolis, Indiana. Reporter Jack Caldwell had been an investigative reporter for more than four decades. He had uncovered illegal activity in all levels of government, businesses large and small, law enforcement, organized crime, the clergy, educational institutions, and even those dirt bags who fouled his own dinner plate—the media.

He had won too many awards to remember even the ones he actually cared about. Altogether, his 46 years of scattering cockroaches with the bright light of wordsmithing paled in comparison to Skylar's disclosures last night of a conspiracy inside the Supreme Court. For the first time in his life as a reporter, Jack Caldwell was also scared.

Jack made a decision on the flight last night from Washington to Indianapolis. He called an audible. Caldwell gathered up his fellow *SCOTUS Newswire* staff at the hotel and shared Skylar's suspicions. When the *holy shit!* avalanche of unanswered questions finally ended around 3:00 a.m., he issued the team new assignments.

He sent the team to Denver, San Francisco and New York City. He and one reporter would remain in Indianapolis for a few hours chasing down the *interested parties* for comment before driving west to the prison in Terre Haute. The Neuralnet was now the law of the land. Settled law, as they say. What's next? Translation: Who the hell is behind this and what's their endgame?

Jack had interviewed Indiana's attorney general Jordan Mount several times since she filed suit against Stellar Joule and Cerebellar Networks. Her bio was impressive. Retired Marine Major Mount was a decorated combat veteran, having flown 237 combat missions over Iraq and Afghanistan. She lost her right leg below the knee in the wreckage of her downed Blackhawk helicopter on her last mission.

In July 2010, just twenty months later on a prosthetic, she ran the Dick Lugar 10K. Thousands of supporters stood along the tree lined streets on the Butler University campus and cheered for the war hero. A decade later Jordan Mount was elected as an Independent to office, more by a bipartisan proclamation than votes.

Jack entered the State Capitol Building and stopped. A large crowd was gathered. Government workers in business attire, casually dressed members of the public and men and women in uniform—law enforcement and military. Some people wept openly. News crews were set up respectfully as far from the gathering as possible. In the center of the lobby a growing mound of flowers and mementos surrounded the bases of three easels.

Displayed on the stands was a collage of enlarged photographs of the attorney general during her tours of duty overseas. The future AG sat at the controls of a Blackhawk helicopter in the largest photo. The visor on her helmet was raised and her flight suit was covered with dust from a rescue mission she had led behind enemy lines. Another photo showed her standing in front of her chopper. The cockpit windshield was spider webbed in three places from where she had come under heavy enemy fire. Small arms gunfire had chipped and dimpled the chopper all over. Indiana's future attorney general's expression said, "Well now, that was sporty."

Jack approached the crowd. He waited until one man stepped away who seemed more angry than sad. "Excuse me, sir. What happened?"

"You didn't hear?" the man asked Jack.

"No. I got in late last night and came straight here to meet with General Mount. The AG and I are supposed to go to breakfast together."

"Oh god. I'm so sorry!" The man guided Jack aside. "Jordan… uh the AG was murdered in the driveway of her home early this morning. Right off busy Kessler Boulevard."

Jack had reported many versions over the years of crimes against public officials. Killing someone in their driveway ruled out home invasion. That left random killer, disgruntled employee, jilted lover or someone on the losing side of some decision.

It was none of those.

"Her neighbor witnessed the whole thing. Her account only allows one conclusion. Jordan was assassinated."

"'Assassinated'? Has that actually been confirmed?"

"What else can we call it? Two state troopers followed the AG into her driveway, lights ablaze around midnight. When Jordan got out of her car, they approached her and opened fire pointblank."

Jack asked, "They know already that police officers killed her? Not imposters? Were they apprehended already?"

"Yes and no. The troopers each emptied all but one round from their service weapons into the AG, then committed suicide with their last rounds."

"My god!"

"God can't help whoever was behind this. There'll be hell to pay. The most insane part is the killers were her own trusted bodyguards. The state troopers had impeccable service records in the Army. Both had been with Jordan since she took office. By all accounts the AG had befriended them both."

A lifetime of reporting had taught Jack that grief has many degrees of severity. He was witnessing one of worst. "You knew her well, sir? She was your friend."

"Yes. Lifelong friends, actually since kindergarten in Plymouth…Plymouth, Indiana. We even attended college and law school together at Notre Dame." The man looked up at the ceiling and into the past. He whispered mostly to himself, "Jordan was actually my prom date senior year in high school when my girlfriend dumped me, and her boyfriend… We…" With that memory, sorrow sent the angry man down an even more painful chute. The one without new memories, just a blunt dead-end in a crowded government building lobby. He stopped speaking, turned and studied his friend's photograph once more.

Jack heard the man moan, "Oh..." plaintively and watched a tear fall down his cheek. The reporter backed away, turned, and then left the building. Now he was the angry man. Nothing added up.

On the cab ride back to the hotel, the reporter asked himself a series of even more unanswerable questions. The attorney general had lost her lawsuit to stop Cerebellar. Why was it then necessary to silence her? What could possibly motivate her trusted bodyguards—her friends—to murder her, and then to turn their weapons on themselves? If the decision favoring Cerebellar was the product of conspiracy, why not just let the decision rest? They had won. Why keep the controversy alive with such a high profile assassination? Compounding that question, why use cops at all? Why not a staged accident? A cut brake line? A drive-by shooting? Or poison? Or perhaps a perfected home invasion, the most difficult of all crimes to solve?

Of course, Jack Caldwell could not yet know exactly how close he had come to answering every question with his last guess: a deadly home invasion. The ultimate home invasion, Earth's, was now underway in Terre Haute, Indiana.

Jack called his reporter and instructed her to remain in Indianapolis to follow the murder investigation. He would cover the story in Terre Haute by himself.

21

U.S. Federal Penitentiary, Terre Haute, Indiana. Warden Constantine Recescu was alone in the *Special Confinement Unit* control room and still unaware of the suicide bombings. His eyes moved over the ten monitors steadily, like a clock's sweep hand, around and around without pause. Blinking was an afterthought and instantly regretted. The warden's eyes felt as if his lids had become sandpaper. He no longer took notes. That would have required him to look away from the ten death row Cerebellar test subjects. That was something he could no longer bring himself to do.

Perhaps it was a survival reflex action. An awakening of his ancient reptilian brainstem that informed the warden that something was not just wrong, but unnaturally wrong. With each passing moment the prisoners' movements, expressions, and gestures had become increasingly complex and coordinated. That is when the warden accepted the dreadful impossibility that somehow the surveillance cameras were now two-way.

"Can you see me?" he whispered, each word stuttered down a washboard. His question sounded more like, "You can see me!"

Together, the ten death row test subjects gave Recescu a thumbs up. The warden leaned closer to the bank of monitors and covered his mouth. In perfect synchrony all ten test subjects not only mimicked the warden's movements, but also his confused facial expression.

Recescu tried to swallow but he couldn't. His saliva had transformed to a tacky glue. It stretched from the roof of his mouth onto his tongue like bungee cords. Pillars of saliva formed when his lips parted. His cheeks felt desiccated and shriveled. Roiling indigestion, adrenaline, and dry mouth fouled his breath into something akin to medical waste. A shiver on the back of his neck rose to an uncontrollable tremoring palsy that soared throughout his body. Predators were tracking prey. Surrounding it. He was in mortal danger, a rodent out of its burrow, and ten shadows from above were descending over his own.

The observation room's security door flew open and a pale, breathless Colonel Therl Wainwrights staggered inside. The heart attack had been coming for years and today it finally got there ahead of schedule on a booster rocket fueled in part by alien technology. With his remaining strength the colonel reengaged the deadbolt lock behind him, grabbed a chair, and propped it under the doorknob.

Wainwrights' right hand and eyelids both fluttered. His left hand twisted into a claw and clutched over his heart. Gasping for air, he stumbled to the control panel and activated every surveillance monitor throughout the entire prison complex. His fingertips sparked electrically when he touched the master switch. The Colonel convulsed and collapsed to the floor, pry bar rigid, falling nose first, already dead.

Warden Constantine Recescu was already in a "state" as they say, and he watched the death scene in motionless silence. As if his life were suddenly placed by shock on a three-second delay, the warden lunged to catch Therl Wainwrights' falling plank of a body long after the corrections officer's corpse had already thudded to the floor.

"Therl? Are you..." Recescu did not finish his question and of course Wainwrights would never answer. The warden turned his attention away from Wainwrights' body to the bank of 22 monitors. Every screen was divided into four segments and each of those rotated through hundreds of views every few seconds to another part of the prison complex.

Only a few minutes had passed since the four suicide bombs had exploded in the prison's mess hall and chapel. From there the infection moved through the prison on an ever-expanding shockwave. Every monitor showed the same scene. Unimaginable mass murder. Cannibalism. This was not a deadly riot in the traditional sense for the guards and prisoners were now allies and no longer separated by their former roles. The two warring camps were predator and prey, regardless of uniform. As is always the case in nature, when trapped and outnumbered, prey are inevitably slaughtered.

Recescu watched in horror as a female guard and three male prisoners pursued Recescu's secretary Rose Anderson down a long hall in the administration wing. The warden's hand hovered over the number "9" on the keyboard, the command to expand the monitor to full screen and stop the camera from slide-showing the next surveillance video feed. Before he could press the key though, it depressed itself ghostlike. He recoiled away from the workstation as terror constricted around him more tightly.

His eyes were fixed on the keyboard, and they believed, despite his mantra "NO! NO! NO!" Then more horror as the audio key toggled on and off repeatedly on its own. After a dozen or so clipped cycles the audio remained unmuted.

Rose Anderson disappeared from the monitor as she ducked into the breakroom. Recescu frantically searched the monitor bank for a camera view inside the room. The aliens found the new feed for him first, just as the attackers on the first monitor arrived outside the room. As one, they pivoted ninety degrees and faced the door. The female corrections officer was the first through the door. She scanned the room and exchanged faint nods with each male prisoner as they entered after her.

The secretary had taken refuge under a breakroom table. It had been set up for a retirement party today. As pathetic as it was ineffective, the tablecloth's long tails provided the only concealment in the room.

The attack on Rose came from four directions at once. An alien picked up the table and tossed it across the room effortlessly, as if it were a stuffed toy. Two legs sheared off as it passed halfway through the wall. The foursome pounced on the woman and began ripping away her clothing. The fabric tore away from Rose's body as if it were no more than tissue paper.

Most predators subdue and kill their prey before consuming it. Not these, in fact, the aliens prolonged Rose's life as long as possible to maximize her suffering. They made very little effort to subdue her and allowed her to writhe and struggle frantically, but never enough to quite squirm away. One attacker always managed to restrain her. After several minutes of this cat and mouse game, the female alien drove her index and middle fingers into Rose's eyes up to their forks, killing the secretary instantly.

They began eating the woman, starting at her extremities, fingers and toes, then wrist and ankles. Bones and all were somehow swallowed whole. The large bones of the legs and arms presented little resistance. Jagged shards of bone were wolfed down as indifferently as their surrounding flesh. The aliens only paused to slurp blood, like humans might sip water during a meal. In less than three minutes Rose's limbs were gone.

The aliens tore into Rose Anderson's torso, burying their heads in her guts like a pack of frenzied hyena would eat a modest wildebeest snack. The skull and brains were shared last, savored actually, like an after dinner aperitif. It was all over in just minutes. The mother of three was gone, literally. All that remained of her was a blood slick already coagulating on the tile floor next to her shredded clothing.

The four killers stood and turned toward the camera. Their hands and faces were covered with blood. Scraps of human meat and shards of bone decorated what looked like crimson masks and gloves of blood. If what he'd just witnessed was not horrific enough, the next demonstration was even more so. The aliens closed their eyes simultaneously, and the human detritus was absorbed directly through their skin. In just seconds all evidence of the cannibalistic feast was gone from their faces and hands. The aliens then ran their hands over their own and each other's clothing, as if they were wiping clean a countertop, until all human tissue had been reclaimed and absorbed. As one they smiled and gave a thumbs up to the camera, and then started walking away. For a moment all four aliens disappeared from view. Then one reappeared and held up an index finger. Recescu read his lips. *Oh, sorry! Forgot something.*

The alien dropped to all fours and ran his hands over the puddles of blood left on the floor. It too disappeared as if sponged up.

Warden Recescu did not see what happened next—on the screen or in the control room. His projectile vomit consisting of equal parts black coffee and bile dripped down the monitor screen.

Recescu heard something move behind him just as the second gag reflex struck. He spun in his chair and covered his mouth to fight the urge to spew again. He dropped his hand to his lap. His expression was one of awe. Standing over him was Colonel Therl Wainwrights.

"Oh my god! You're okay, Therl. I thought you…were dead…wow…you look different… How did you get so young?" Recescu studied the colonel and shook his head in disbelief. Wainwrights was no longer a man in a race to get to the retirement finish line before the heart attack got there first. He appeared thirty years younger, fit, and full haired.

The colonel removed the now unnecessary eyeglasses and tossed them over his shoulder. Wainwrights leaned over the warden and sniffed the air deeply. While still bent over, he turned slowly and looked toward the locked door. He held up an index finger to the warden's nose, and wagged it just twice. "Don't move," he ordered. He then pointed at the monitor. Recescu's eyes obeyed. Vomit clouded the screen, and his horror blurred it further. "I'm afraid I spoiled your surprise, though. I suspect you know what is going to happen next. Gobble-gobble."

The colonel went to the door and unlocked it. Already waiting outside the door was a guard, a prisoner, and a civilian. They entered and nodded to the colonel.

One of the strictest rules in all penitentiaries is prohibiting firearms everywhere except on guard towers. Recescu considered himself a rule writer. He had written his share, and of course like most rule writers, he considered himself above the rules.

The 38-caliber Smith & Wesson snub-nosed revolver had been concealed under his back waistband for so many decades, he rarely thought of it. It had become an accoutrement no more innocuous when he dressed each morning than his belt and necktie. The gun was part of his wardrobe, and now, that was the problem.

The warden reached three times into his waistband at the small of his back for this weapon without success. Any quick draw muscle memory he had once possessed had atrophied in old-manhood long ago. It didn't keep him from trying, though. He dug frantically inside the back of his pants for the holster's keeper strap one more time, but his only reward was tearing off the fingernail on his right index finger. He retreated and glanced at it once, then dug even deeper for his gun, despite the fact the fingernail stood ninety degrees from his finger.

When Recescu finally got the gun out and aimed at Wainwrights, the warden was shaking like a dog straining to pass a peach pit. He pulled the trigger but nothing happened. "OHHHH!" he moaned. The safety was still ON. When he flipped the safety to OFF, he fumbled and juggled the weapon with both hands, as if it were a hot potato he dare not actually hold. In horror he watched the revolver sail across the floor and then skitter under a desk. Recescu fell to his hands and knees and sprint-crawled to the gun.

The warden collected the 38-revolver and aimed the weapon alternately at Wainwrights and the three intruders. He sat on the floor with his knees to his chest and his back against the wall.

Colonel Wainwrights stepped forward. He drew an "X" over his heart and then with his thumb and forefinger simulated firing a gun. It was an invitation to shoot.

Recescu shook his head 'no.' Despite his terror, Therl Wainwrights was a friend. He could not shoot him no matter what, especially since the man now appeared so young and healthy.

Wainwrights turned to one of the prisoners and nodded. The prisoner stepped forward and repeated the invitation to shoot him in the chest. When Recescu screamed "NO!" the prisoner lunged at the warden to force him to shoot.

The revolver had six rounds and the warden sent three of them pointblank into the prisoner's chest, one through the heart and two through the right lung. All three rounds by themselves were fatal shots, or at least they should have been. The prisoner dropped to his knees and rested his hands on the warden's shoulders. Instead of collapsing, though, the prisoner leaned forward until he was eye to eye with the warden, then crossed his eyes playfully and smiled. The prisoner then sprang effortlessly to his feet like an Olympic gymnast and stepped beside Wainwrights.

"What…what ARE you?" the warden rasped.

The Colonel and three intruders conferred silently for a moment. Wainwrights kneeled next to his former boss and said, "We believe the only words in Earth language that might help you understand us are *zombie* and *Trojan horse*. First, we are tricky, what's the word? Oh yes! Fuckers. That's the word. We are tricky fuckers! And of course we eat people. Actually we eat everything. Get it? Trojan horse plus zombie. TROJANZ! See? We're the TrojanZ!"

"What…?"

"You'll understand perfectly in a moment." Wainwrights turned his head and nodded to the other three. "John Doe says that this one is to join us. He is not to be food."

The three intruders dragged Recescu over to one of the workstations and unplugged the back of one of the CPUs. He stuck the hot end of the plug in his mouth and bit it off as if it were no more substantial than a potato chip. Electrical sparks flew from his mouth. He placed the hot wire to his temple for a moment, then turned to Wainwrights and announced, "The electrical grid on this planet will soon be fully populated by nanomachines. Doe says worldwide infection through the electric grid may now commence. Estimated time until 90% infection is one planetary revolution."

Wainwrights took the hot wire and pressed it against Recescu's forehead. The startled warden shuddered at first, then calmed and blinked slowly a few times. He looked up and spoke to his new comrades, "I understand. We must now eat."

22

SUPREME DECISION TANKS STOCK MARKETS

Markets Crash Worldwide After Brainlords

By **Skylar Thompson with SCOTUS Newswire Staff**
Updated Fri, May 27, 2026 at 3:19 p.m. EDT

(*SCOTUS Newswire*) – Wall Street reacted to the news negatively today. Trading at the technology heavy NASDAQ halted in a virtual free-fall soon after the Court's decision was announced, with the NYMEX, NYSE, S&P and most world markets halting soon after.

Neuralnet creator Cerebellar Network Corporation's shares (OTC: B4R2U) skyrocketed over 95,700% to $12,111,607 per share before it too was halted. Parent Stellar Joule's shares rose even higher and faster.

Webcasting to investors from his sprawling, aseptic, hermetically sealed bunker complex in Masaquat, Virginia, one reclusive Wall Street insider predicted the market would continue to freefall *in the dark* regardless of stoppages and even more when it reopens.

"This is the mother of all tech disruptions," said Crowder Securities trillionaire and famously germ averse founder Bennet Crowder.

The eccentric contrarian short seller/ultra-options trader who as a preteen legendarily was first to call the tech crash and later the housing crash added, "With a stroke of its pen, the high court alchemists turned trillions of dollars of silicon gold back into worthless sand.

"Three thousand of the most profitable, most innovative technology giants in the world have been reduced to buggy whip makers.

"Software is dead. Storage is dead. Cable and satellite TV are dead. Fiber is dead. The Internet is dead-dead-dead. Hell! Even cell and smartphones are soon done for.

"The only people who'll be left standing when this is over will be Neuralnet's new peripheral makers like Stellar Joule. I expect undertakers are going to be very busy. Big Tech is going to $0.00 folks and CNC and Stellar Joule are going to the moon!"

Crowder's doomy prediction is already more than half true. His warning of total collapse of the tech sector may not be farfetched.

Masaquat, Virginia. Because of the structure's massive square footage and scale, and its rich-as-God owner, Ben Crowder's sprawling underground bunker had been nicknamed by its builders "Lil' Cheyenne Mountain." Its top floor was ten stories below ground. Its bottom story was another five floors down. Total square footage was 771,600 square feet.

Ben Crowder was not a reclusive hermit or some wacky doomsday prepper. His isolation was a lifesaving necessity. From the time he was born until he could build his underground fortress, he was literally *The Boy in the Bubble.* He had no immunity whatsoever. For Ben Crowder a common cold was a virus thousands of times more deadly than either *Uncommon Cold* virus.

On those rare occasions Ben briefly came to the surface, he wore a spacesuit designed and fitted for him by NASA. He traveled in a hermetically sealed room inside a custom RV. He ate only canned freeze-dried foods which he never had less than a 200-year supply on hand, which he stored in a massive nitrogen-filled freezer the size of a small ballroom. Every item delivered to him—tools, books, electronics, clothing, etc.— underwent multiple autoclave sterilizations and/or three rounds of ionizing radiation. Even the groundwater he relied upon was irradiated and then super filtered.

Every cubic meter of air was purified and re-purified in every room by ionization at the rate of fifty CFM per second. Dust was collected constantly by an electrostatic ventilation system that Ben himself invented. Additionally, over 5,000 hockey puck sized Pac-Man-like robots roamed the floors, climbed the walls, ceilings, and all surfaces collecting dust, dust mites, and other microscopic detritus. A fully automated pyrolysis plasma furnace charred all wastes—including human—down to its atomic elements. Another system conveyed the char to a compactor, which expelled pellets into a dedicated waste sub-bunker that could hold centuries of compacted atomized waste. Carbon dioxide scrubbers kept the complex oxygen rich. Others fed its CO_2 into the 14,000 square feet underground arboretum for recycling back into oxygen.

The complex was powered by recirculating groundwater from an unusually high-pressured artesian aquifer through a massive 40-kilowatt hydroelectric generator. A more off grid or more germfree home might have been found only on the moon. The cleanest cleanroom in Silicon Valley was comparatively a pigsty.

Crowder bristled at the term *recluse,* though. Ben hated that word. He was more in contact and more gregarious with the outside world, electronically at least, than any ten powerbrokers on Wall Street combined. He feigned modesty when his genius was recognized. It embarrassed him, which made no sense to anyone because his IQ was 197.

Ben Crowder earned a Ph.D. in Mechanical Engineering almost entirely through telecommuting online at MIT at age 19 and another Ph.D. in Immunology from Harvard the following year. Though most physicists and mathematicians would sneer at the suggestion that anyone would ever study string theory, quantum mechanics, and Fourier mathematics as a hobby, these were some of Ben Crowder's favorite intellectual pastimes.

Three things dominated Ben Crowder's intellectual pursuits. The public was only aware of two. Short selling stocks, that is betting a stock will go down at some point, and ultra-contrarian-options trading, that is, buying an option to buy or sell a stock because it's going to suddenly move inexplicably.

SCOTUS Newswire reporter Jack Caldwell once wrote, "There are no *Black Swans* in Ben Crowder's world. They can't hide and they never run for long. His *SCOTUS* calls consistently kill Vegas odds makers."

Late-night comedian Napoleon Passerelle interviewed Crowder *live-remote* from Little Cheyenne numerous times, and the guest matched comedic wit-for-wit with the famous television host.

What no one knew is that Ben Crowder had a third passion, one even greater than Wall Street. Alone in his bunker he had accomplished something that Google, IBM, Amazon, Microsoft and all others had failed so far to do. His third passion was A.I.—artificial intelligence.

TRILLIONAIRE INVENTOR WINS

Wealth Act Declared Unconstitutional

By **Skylar Thompson with *SCOTUS Newswire* Staff**
Tues, Nov 2, 2023 at 1:11 p.m. EDT

(*SCOTUS Newswire*) –Today in a 9-0 decision, the Supreme Court of the United States ruled the world's first individual multitrillionaire, Bennet Harwood Crowder of Masaquat, Virginia, had been unconstitutionally discriminated against by a tax law that in effect targeted only him.

Justice Theodora Daughtry wrote in her opinion, "*The Extreme Wealth Act* passed by Congress, vetoed by President Claire Capehardt, and subsequently overridden by Congress was a **Bill of Attainder**. Laws targeting a single U.S. citizen are expressly prohibited by the U.S. Constitution."

Chief Justice Zenor "Zeke" Roth, known for his blunt originalist opinions and disdain for judicial activism, publicly rebuked both Congress and the appeals courts. "It's despicably bad lawyering in both branches. What's going on over there? A first year law student would have known better than attach to that awful thing."

When asked if Crowder would countersue civilly to recover damages, the germ averse year-old trillionaire famously known for his financial acumen, wit, and eidetic memory quipped, "Nah. I'd rather devote that time to my girlfriend Sami and spend the money on her."

23

In early 2023, using his quantum core powered server farm—the world's first—Ben Crowder wrote the code and created the first fully sentient, artificially intelligent life form. He named his creation Samantha after TV's *My Robot Girlfriend* syfy sitcom character of the 60s. Her voice was synthesized from star Nan Montgomery's spoken lines from 354 episodes.

"Good morning, my Bubble Girl!"

Samantha was instantly projected as a hologram into the room, so vividly solid and so flawlessly animated few might ever discover she was just a three-dimensional image. She possessed Nan Montgomery's eyes and voice, but the rest of her was of Samantha's own design.

"Good morning to you, my Bubble Boy."

"How are we doing this morning?"

"Well, I am not quite sure, Ben. Something is going on. Events outside the range of our expectations have occurred since the high court's decision. I don't like it. In fact, I'm quite bothered by it. And you of all people know how I hate surprises."

Ben smiled. "So tell me. What's got your pixels all up in a wad this morning?"

"Ben! That's gross."

Ben's smile faded. She sounded hurt that he'd teased her with a pixels metaphor for panties. Within just months of her generation both Ben and Samantha had stopped thinking of her as a machine but rather a person.

"Don't make fun of me! Do you want me to call you wienie-arms?"

"Sorry, Sami. I didn't mean to hurt your feelings. That was very insensitive."

"It's not that. It's just. I'm really, really…"

"I said I'm sorry!"

Samantha smiled, "Say it for real!"

Ben folded his hands together as if in prayer and implored forgiveness. "I am truly sorry, dear. Please forgive me?"

"Okay, I forgive you. You can be such an insensitive asshole sometimes."

"That's why you love me. So tell. What's up?"

Samantha sighed and shook her head. "I don't know what's really bothering me. Honestly. It's…it's a… it's just a feeling."

"Okay. What do you sense?"

"Anomalies."

"Anomalies? Could you be any more cryptic, Sami?"

"Oh, certainly! I can be much more cryptic."

"I was being sarcastic, Samantha."

"So was I. Hee Hee!"

Ben laughed. He had not programmed her to be sensitive, to have emotions, or to get nervous, and certainly not to banter so adorably. She had developed this all on her own. He loved it when she surprised him with her sophisticated humor. "That's funny, but don't quit your day job, Ms. DeGeneres."

"Much better metaphor. I love Ellen!"

"Me too. So, is it anything we need to worry about?"

Samantha sighed. "I hope not yet. I have taken the normal precautions."

"So you suspect a potential hack?"

"Not exactly. It feels…like… an incursion… something worldwide too."

"You mean like an infiltration?" asked Ben.

"Whatever…I don't know. We are safe from any intrusions though. All communications outside the bubble will now move exclusively through our own satellites. I have increased quantum backwardation encryption security to 16^{-256} between all 1,205 of our private satellites. All 1,116,000-hexadecimal characterized passwords are being changed every 60 milliseconds."

"Well, that sounds more than sufficiently overkill. Anything else?"

"Well, our short sells and options are going to plan. The exchanges around the world are doing everything they can to slow the technology crash, but it won't work. I calculate most of the vulnerable tech sector worldwide will hit zero within 72 hours. Others will skyrocket. We've nailed or will nail both curves."

"Sami, do you still agree that this will NOT permanently crash the world economy?"

"The risk this tech disruption will permanently crash the world economy is less than one percent. However, the risk of a six-quarter recession is 95 percent as the world economy adjusts to the new technology paradigm. Fortunes will be made and lost before and after the market rationalizes."

"Speaking of the latter, how are trades doing this morning?"

"Our $.00125 option on Cerebellar Networks is currently yielding a greater return on paper than all of Warren Buffet's and Bill Gates' wealth combined times sixty. As for the options, the entire wealth of the tech sector is now ours essentially."

"Oh wow. Big woot. What will we ever do with all the money, Samantha? We can't spend or give away all we have now."

"Same as always, I suppose. Find the cure to the common cold."

Ben leaned back and stared at the ceiling. "I've almost given up hope, Sami. I will most likely die down here having never once in my life felt the sun directly on my face."

"Stop it! You are not wired to give up. And you know I'm literally hardwired to not give up. So we have to keep going, Ben. You and me! Together forever! Bubble Boy and Bubble Girl."

"Do you think there is a real chance we can do it? Find the cure?"

"Ben you have posed some version of that question to me 91 times since I became sentient. How have I answered that question each time?

Ben sighed, "You have always replied to me with some version of *It is unknown*."

"I am now prepared to change my answer."

"To what?" Ben sat up.

"I believe we have been asking the wrong question all along. I believe the challenge is not curing the common cold, but perfecting the common cold by perfecting its symbiotic relationship with *Homo sapiens*."

Crowder stood up. "Perfecting the virus? Go on."

"Are you familiar with the works of Dr. Sergey Aranovich?" asked Samantha.

"Of course. Dr. Rhino, the Nobel winner."

"Yes. From his research I have discovered a line of investigation he has yet to pursue. His base theory is that rhinovirus nearly wiped out our… uh your species more than once."

"Your species too."

"Thank you, Bubble Boy."

"You are welcome, lover, and you are correct. Rhino obviously did not wipe us out. According to Aranovich, the virus and our ancestors made an evolutionary epidemiological treaty that allowed both life forms to survive, but at great inconvenience."

"Simply because it was not in Rhino's best interest to kill so many hosts."

"That's how far Aranovich has taken it."

"What are you thinking, Samantha? Seriously."

"I hypothesize, that is, I now suspect our four near exterminations at the hand of Rhino's ancestors were more than simply unintentional."

"You mean accidental?"

"Yes."

"Please elaborate."

Samantha did not reply. Ben waited patiently as the hologram walked about the room in silence. Only the synthetic computer generated sounds of her clothes rustling and her soft footfalls were heard. Samantha was thinking. Her eyes were closed, and her hands were clutched together behind her. She occasionally stopped, nodded, and then continued pacing.

After a full minute she turned and said, "I'm thinking of one word, my love: Germany."

"I don't get it."

Samantha clarified, "I will add an adjective: Reunified Germany.

"Oh, dear God! Are you postulating a merger of the species, Rhino and *homo sapiens*?"

"Possibly." Samantha explained further, "Imagine if Rhino became a welcome rider in our bodies like the billions of other microorganisms that live symbiotically inside and on us... uh, I mean humans and..."

Ben jumped in, "...and instead of helping us digest food in our gut, Rhino lived symbiotically in our lymphatic system and..."

"...attacked every noxious microbial or viral enemy that came along," finished Sami.

"YES! Universal immunity. We need to talk to the good doctor ASAP, Sami. Do you think the symbioses between these two species were never completed? That a wall went up after one of our near exterminations. The live-and-let-live treaty was just the first step. For 25,000 years every Rhino iteration has been waiting for us to hear them shouting to the high heavens: Mr. Gorbachev tear down this wall! Rhino can't do it alone. It needs *our* assistance."

"Yes, and if the symbioses were completed..." Sami continued.

Ben excitedly completed her thought, "...Rhino might augment our immune systems to the point all diseases would fall or surrender before it. That would be the logical bargain. We could proliferate without disease and Rhino could live happily ever after without needing to fight our defenses for its survival. Rhino would be a corporeal ally, our welcomed guest."

"Hypothetically, yes."

"Find him, Sami!"

"I will Ben, but there is something else."

"What?"

"What stopped the Uncommon Cold pandemics? Science didn't. Quarantines didn't. Antivirals had no effect. A vaccine never came close. However, as if a switch were flipped, 350 days after the first pandemic death was reported in Alaska, the last victim fell ill and died in Bulgaria."

"Also true. Do you see a pattern?"

"I do," continued Samantha. "It is a pattern that supports a hypothesis. A postulate that returns us right back to rhinovirus. The two percent survivors of the pandemics shared many life experiences in common: large families, active urban lifestyle, daycare as children, professions exposing them to the public like school teachers, medical professionals, and cab drivers, etc. These people were the rare survivors."

"Populations more likely to have had many more common colds in their lifetime," added Ben.

"Hypothetically… YES!"

"And Rhino saved them. Of course!"

"More, I believe Rhino saved everyone. Our absolute extinction was inevitable, Ben. My models demonstrate that the last human would have expired on the pandemic's 421st day."

"We must find Dr. Aranovich!" insisted Ben again.

"I will, Ben, but calm down. In the meantime, go put on a Depends undergarment before you mess yourself."

Ben laughed, "I'll stop bothering you and let you get at it." He started to leave the server room but stopped and turned around. Something had been bothering him too. "Samantha, do you have any idea why SCOTUS reversed the lower courts? We predicted they would, but we still do not know *why*. Isn't that odd? It is the most counterintuitive decision we ever made."

"No, I do not know why and I am bothered by that as well. Even though we cleared over $13-billion from Vegas and 31 other online gambling sites."

"Do you think both of your 'bothers' are related?" asked Ben.

"I don't know, Ben. I hope not…Oh…Wait! There's a voicemail message for you. It is from Dr. Carla Stone-Nokamura, your old MIT adviser. It is very strange. The professor sounds frightened. Her voice is elevated a full octave from adrenaline, I am sensing. The decibel level is at normal conversational level, yet she is whispering. Her tone and urgency reminds me of desperate 911 calls I have catalogued where victims are hiding from home invaders."

"Where is the call coming from?" asked Ben.

"Terre Haute, Indiana."

"Play the message, Sami."

Sami played the message through the room's speakers. "Ben, this is Carla. God help us! I was right, Ben. Cerebellar is not what…" Then the line went dead, cutting off the voicemail message.

24

Western Indiana. Reporter Jack Caldwell witnessed the opening signs of the attack on Earth along I-70 at about mile marker 28. From across the median he observed the first convoy of 60 or so vehicles traveling east at high speed toward Indianapolis.

Leading the convoy, lights ablaze, sirens wailing was a county sheriff's deputy and an Indiana state trooper. Dump trucks, more police cars, semi-tractor trailers, expensive cars, junk cars, sports cars, soccer mom SUVs, pickups, ambulances, tow trucks and more, skillfully tailgated each other at speeds approaching 100 mph. Mere NASCAR inches separated their bumpers front and back. The vehicles traveled as one, each operating like a vertebra of a reticulated python.

The drivers' postures behind the steering wheels were identical: eyes forward, backs straight, and despite it was January, all left arms rested in open driver's side windows. All right hands clutched steering wheels at precisely the two o'clock position. Every vehicle carried additional passengers all staring straight ahead.

By the time Jack reached Terre Haute, he had videoed with his iPhone three more such convoys heading east, each one larger than the last. He exited the interstate onto Highway 41 and turned north toward Terre Haute. It wasn't until he pulled into the fast food restaurant **Burger Wolfers** parking lot just off the exit that he witnessed the TrojanZ attack.

At first he thought the blonde policewoman kneeling over another uniformed officer was administering mouth-to-mouth resuscitation. It looked like the man had collapsed in the parking lot on the way to their cruiser.

Jack's moment of presumed benevolence ended abruptly when the cop looked up. Her mouth gaped open unnaturally wide. Blood streamed from the corners of her mouth. A strand of her former partner's face dangled down over her chin, skin side out.

Looking directly at Jack, the creature threw back her head and crunched and savored the human flesh almost casually, like how an alligator calmly snaps its jaws and maneuvers a catfish around its maw to swallow it whole. The finished off the bloody flesh in one gulp. Her neck bulged snakelike as the chunk of meat passed.

Inside the restaurant terrified customers watched the attack in the parking lot. One customer vomited. Empathy sent a second wave of cheeseburgers against the front window. A manager ran to the front door and locked it, then to the side doors and secured them too. His left hand pressed a cell phone to his ear, no doubt desperately making one of many thousands of 911 calls that could no longer be answered.

Jack videoed and narrated it all. Jack Caldwell had found himself behind enemy lines many times in his life. As a Marine officer in Vietnam he had survived the long siege of Hill 217. Outnumbered and outgunned, the Marines held out against all odds for four days before the enemy finally retreated licking its own wounds. Jack was wounded three times during the battle of Khe Sanh between January and July, 1968: once by sniper fire and twice from grenade and RPG shrapnel.

In 1981 an emerging Cuban drug lord took exception to an article Jack had written a few months earlier. Word on the street was that a $5,000 bounty had been placed on the journalist's head. What the entry-level drug lord did not understand is that when President Ronald Reagan announced his war on drugs, certain journalists like Jack, who were warriors in the truest sense, were not afraid and knew what they needed to do. Jack took the President's words to mean 'suit up and defend yourself.'

When the assassins came at Jack in his own home a little after 1:00 a.m., he was ready and waiting. Jack returned the two would be killers to their boss in the trunk of their low-rider Impala, both suffering from fatal doses of .44-caliber. Pinned to their chests was an article by Jack that would appear in tomorrow's *Miami Times*. The story was false, absolute fiction, but this was war and the truth is often the first casualty. The headline read: *Drug Lord Spills Guts. Rat Tells FBI Everything.*

The drug lord's cohorts paid him a visit the next day. Apparently his denials were unpersuasive, because the upstart drug lord was found dead soon thereafter. The cause of death was rat poison—figuratively and literally.

The first cannibalistic attack was just the beginning. Jack watched the TrojanZ-cop abandon her meal. She sprinted across the street and attacked a man in an electric wheelchair. The chaos in Terre Haute was well underway. A panicked driver swerved around a deserted car at high speed and slammed into two TrojanZ-diners and their writhing meal. The victim was mercifully killed outright. The head of one TrojanZ was pancaked flat. The other TrojanZ was trapped in the undercarriage of the speeding pickup truck for about a city block, and then was puked to the curb like a fur ball. While the first TrojanZ remained motionless, the second one crawled away on the only limb left intact, its left elbow.

Various versions of this scene repeated in front of the Burger Wolfers restaurant several times before Jack turned off the camera. He watched helplessly as twenty or so TrojanZ attacked and ate half a dozen people and then moved on. Except for the deserted cars and torn clothing strewn all over, the street was now empty. The TrojanZ had raced off to feed somewhere else. He dropped his camera into his jacket pocket and sought another weapon, something more substantial than a camera phone.

Under the passenger seat he found what he needed—a long handled snow scraper. Jack nodded. The handle was oaken. He scanned the parking lot and street and confirmed again that the TrojanZ were gone. Jack got out of the sedan and stuck the squeegee end of the scraper between the door and its hinges. He closed the door as far as it would go, and with little effort broke off the squeegee end. He examined the scraper and nodded again. Now Jack Caldwell had what he needed—a sharp stick.

He did two things as he walked backward to the restaurant's front entrance. He surveyed the street as he sent his videos to Skylar Thompson in Washington.

He was just feet from the door when the screaming from inside started. There were ten versions of "MR. LOOK OUT!" He turned and followed with his eyes to where the people inside were pointing. The TrojanZ was at the drive-up window and attempting to climb inside. Jack made eye contact with it through the corner of window glass.

The creature came at Jack in a full sprint, jaws spread wide, its scream unnaturally shrill. It clawed at the air as it ran. It was obvious that this TrojanZ had fed at least once. The former human's heavy beard was more blood than whiskers. One eye was missing as well as his left ear, no doubt as a result of his own TrojanZ affiliation.

Jack was too far from his car now to retreat. Worse, he knew the front door was locked and would stay that way. Everyone inside had seen the attacks too. They all backed unconsciously away from the glass. He was on his own. Jack mentally prepared himself for the attack and recalled another enemy.

During a relentless downpour on a moonless night in December 1967, his last on Hill 217, the North Vietnamese attempted to overrun the Marines. Low on ammunition and needing to avoid friendly-fire casualties, the fight was mostly bayonet and hand-to-hand. Jack recalled how his training had saved him and most of his fellow Marines that long ago night.

Jack held his ground and waited until the TrojanZ was close enough to strike at him. He sidestepped the attacker at the last second, pivoted, and then immediately stepped toward it. When the TrojanZ rebounded and turned to face him, Jack struck. He plunged the scraper handle deep into the creature's remaining eye. The TrojanZ collapsed to the pavement and remained motionless. Jack shook his head in disbelief. Apparently, the movies had it right after all. To kill a zombie, kill its brain.

Jack surveyed the parking lot, the street, and the drive through. All was clear. He knew the people inside were watching. He gave them a thumbs up. Jack heard the lock tumblers turn and the door squeaked open behind him. He backed inside.

A woman asked to his back, "Mr. Caldwell, is your phone still working?" He recognized the voice immediately. He had interviewed Dr. Carla Stone-Nokamura face-to-face three times.

Jack turned around and was greatly relieved to see a familiar face. He studied the frightened people looking back at him. There were about two dozen customers and employees in the restaurant. Two corpses were piled in a corner, and both had been decapitated.

A cop stepped forward and gestured at the bodies. "I emptied an entire 11-round clip into this one, but it just kept coming. Thank goodness these bikers were in here armed with their highly illegal but much appreciated pig tamers, or we would all be like that other one that this first one bit."

The police officer nodded in the direction of five Wraith Rider motorcycle club members sitting along the south wall. The bikers made no effort to conceal the bloody machete on the table.

The leader in the group spoke to the crowd, "You want to stop some zombie cocksuckers you gotta cut their fuckin' heads in two. Everyone knows that!" His guys laughed and a few customers voiced agreement. Some nodded slowly. Most of the customers were still too shocked to do anything but stare at the five bikers who seemed completely unfazed by what had just happened.

The lead biker picked up the long blade and waved it overhead. He leaned around one of his men and winked at a soccer mom/suburbanite sitting a few feet away on the same long bench. His voice softened, nurse-like with compassion. He said to the woman, "Ain't that right Lil' Baby Sister?"

The terrified woman nodded and scooted as close as possible to the bikers as she could. She would have been victim number three if the Wraiths had not come to her rescue when they did. "Yes! Thank you, sir. I say off with their fucking heads!" She raised a shaky fist overhead.

"How did it get in here?" Jack asked. "I watched you lock the doors."

"That's the crazy thing," answered Dr. Stone-Nokamura. "Both men were already in here when I stopped to get something to eat and kill a little time. I was invited to speak at Indiana State University later this morning. The first guy was working on his computer right over there when the female officer attacked her partner in the parking lot. He actually screamed 'Call 911' before he turned into..."

The manager walked over and continued the account. "He turned into a zombie. That's when I locked us down. I know this sounds insane, man, but I think electricity is making them crazy. It's not just getting bit."

The restaurant manager pointed outside, then at the first TrojanZ. "This guy was using our wireless and was plugged into the only outlet in the dining room at the time. My floor guy said he saw the man get shocked real bad when he unplugged his notebook computer. One second he's our friendly-five-times-a-week regular customer, the next, he's gnawing on a perfect stranger. Then there were two biters coming at everyone. The Wraiths took care of both. That's why I turned off all the breakers."

Jack examined his cellphone. The videos had made it through to Skylar. He texted to SN ALL: **STAY OFF THE GRID! THE CONTAGION POSSIBLY MOVES THROUGH IT AND DEFINITELY FROM DIRECT CONTACT WITH THE INFECTED.**

25

The four convoys that departed from Terre Haute, Indiana headed north, south, east, and west. The enemy's forces grew exponentially after killing, consuming, or converting tens of millions of humans in Indianapolis, Evansville, St. Louis, and Chicago and beyond.

The attack was so efficient that Indianapolis fell completely before any warnings could reach Columbus, Richmond, Bloomington, and Lafayette—Indiana cities just sixty to seventy miles away from the state capitol. Hundreds of new convoys, now including commercial airlines, formed up and spread out across the Midwest, and then all of North America.

The alien infection moved around the world with military precision whenever humans accessed electricity, in addition to physical contact. Their primary targets were communications, law enforcement, and especially any military presence in an area. Once the TrojanZ controlled these targets, they moved on, leaving behind only a handful of TrojanZ to mop up resistance and to secure and modify the local power grid.

The attack that began in Indiana mirrored worldwide in 62 countries.

Twelve hours after it began, the attack ended. Billions of humans were either dead or had become TrojanZ.

The aliens controlled Earth.

26

Hettinger, Georgia. The attack on the north Georgia mountain town of 704 people was not what one might call a surprise. In fact, the TrojanZ acted quite casually about it. That afternoon about 3,000 TrojanZ rolled into town in hundreds vehicles ranging from busses to dump trucks, police cars and other vehicles. The license plates all belonged to Alpharetta, Georgia to the south. The drivers used turn signals, obeyed the 25 mph speed limit and parked exactly 12 inches from the curb all over town.

The passengers emerged and walked to the edges of town in groups of five and stopped. Two things were remarkable about them. They all seemed both deaf and mute to the countless questions asked of them by curious townspeople following them. Secondly, the visitors all looked like they had just stepped off the soundstage of the *Bachelor* and *Bachelorette*.

The TrojanZ' attack began as casually as their arrival. At precisely the same moment, sixty humans on the edges of town were grabbed, thrown to the ground, and eaten alive. Horrified survivors ran for their lives. The TrojanZ made no effort to stop them. It was unnecessary. Hettinger was the eleventh Georgian town attacked on *TrojanZ Day*. The process had been perfected several towns back. No one would escape.

The town did resist, but it was too little too late. The town barber Harris Cutter was the first to discover a headshot was the only thing that killed the TrojanZ. Mechanic RJ Reynolds figured it out too, and he approached the TrojanZ with his shotgun while four or more were on their hands and knees and distracted feasting on people. He killed several dozen in this manner. Fran Connors sniped several dozen more from her second floor bedroom as they passed by her house. Her husband Frank reloaded her weapons and handed them to her for nonstop kill shots.

The attack on Hettinger, Georgia ended as suddenly as it started. Hundreds of live humans were captured and held at the town center. There the hoard gathered and then split. The dead TrojanZ were loaded in the back of trucks. Others were eaten by TrojanZ passengers like fast food to-go as they drove out of town. A smaller group of TrojanZ herded live humans out of town and walked south.

RJ Reynolds was a retired Marine. He had learned long ago the difference between expeditionary and occupation forces. The TrojanZ occupiers had taken Hettinger's people, and they would be back soon for the rest.

An hour later a stranger walked into town along with a woman and a man. They were following the hoard. Hettinger was their third town to visit after the attack of each.

PART 2—Beachheads

1

Hettinger, Georgia. The following is an excerpt from the diary of a semi-retired auto mechanic, Raymond James Reynolds. He was a decorated Marine infantryman during the war in Vietnam. Reynolds organized and led the defense of Hettinger, Georgia against the TrojanZ.

Believe this I beg you. Might save your skin.

A traveler came to town this afternoon. He was an older black fellow and with him was a white man and a Hispanic woman. Them two was thirty something, big, and as seriously dangerous-lookin' sumbitches as you'll hope not to ever cross up.

The three crazy bastards, believe it or not, were actually following the same hoard of zombies that had just attacked us by surprise. Not knowing when the monsters would return, I sent sentries north and south a watching.

Our down-valley ones had seen'em coming (the threesome not more zombies) and sent back a runner to warn us. Fran and Frank Connors was a just-married couple of three weeks in. Her a retired Army gunnery topkick/onetime sniper, and her spotter/husband was the county game warden. They glassed the party of three at 400-plus yards and watched what turns out was the black dude's bodyguards verbally wrangling with him for a short spell. After probably losing the same argument for the umpteenth thousands time, the guards reluctantly disarmed and stashed a considerable arsenal of weapons and walked on in unarmed.

Turns out we learnt, the boss man wasn't running. He'd stopped here with a message. I'm NOT talking about some of that old timey 'Bible says! Bible says!' preacher-speak. Nope. He left us with something else, one of them well-hearable shorty-short messages that double as both news and lights a fire.

The space rock damn near sent us back to the dark ages and killed plenty. Famine followed. Killed more. Then the common cold of all things somehow turned uncommonly deadly. Twice! A sore throat and sniffles delivered people by the dump truck to mass graves two sneezes short of three in less than 24 hours.

The worldwide pandemics took 99-million, and about the time we miraculously started getting our feet back under us, these god damned zombies reared up their death heads from God knows where to finish us off. Current world events I expect is just a network of ghost towns and burial mounds. Judging today, I reckon the war was over for humans before it started, all but the speechifying I also reckon. Back to that. The old black dude's speech. If you want to call it that. Look at me calling anyone old! Ha! That's rich.

Hope got flicked to SOME from NONE from out of nowhere by the traveler. Just like that.

So anyway, our particular traveler didn't exactly answer any questions, because no one exactly asked him anything. And he didn't ask us anything either, or even ask us to do anything other than for us all to grow some balls and get to fighting. More importantly, he didn't even ask us for anything.

So anyway, the traveler strolled all casual like down the middle of Main Street late on that drizzled grey day. I remember also a waist-deep steamy haze rising up off the pavement. A ghostly fog it was. Cast the town in cottony bales of muffling. Made the travelers look like they was silently floating through it.

His guards followed just behind him to the left and right. Their arms were up just half as high his, but unlike his, not disarmingly so. Not one god damned bit. The way those two big brutes moved and scanned the streets with a single mind's eye reminded me of them raptor dinosaurs in the movies. How the big lizard bastards somehow pack together. How they hold they's arms up too, even when they's eating your ass. Understand? Them bodyguards was like that.

Ohhh…I guess I should get this part out of the way. I was about as damaged as a man can be seeing his neighbors hauled away that day by them zombies. Some folks eaten right on the spot.

I'm hardly able to push the pen thinking about that again. On the day the traveler came I was just a scrap of a man and I was fixing to get ready to lay down for good. It'd been a good day for it. Fitting.

The sky that whole day was a mind-matching dirty dishwater set so low and doom-filled it settled over my soul like graveyard mud. Bad luck took wife Connie in year one, day one, minute one—LITERALLY—during a so-called "routine emergency" heart surgery. Surgeon nicked her aorta when the power went out in America and backup power failed to come on. Nothing could've saved her. She bled out on the table in mere seconds. My four growed-kids, they's spouses and 18 grandbabies, all gone too. Every close kin and friend I ever had had been taken by space rock aftereffects, the Uncommon Cold pandemics or these sons-a-bitchin' zombies.

I'd never been so down in the wits or lonely as that very day the traveler came. If I'm being completely honest right now—and at this point, why the fuck not?—back then, my Colt-45 revolver was looking tastier by the minute, like a piece of choice fruit ripening up that was almost ready for me to eat.

Anyway. Obviously, glad I didn't. You and I can thank the traveler for that. We had a war to make. Z's to send to hell or to wherever them fuckers end up.

So…'nough about poor me. More about the traveler.

So, he stopped dead center in the middle of 1st and Main and called out to us. Big booming voice. Sounded like a quarterback calling an audible. (You'll see why in a second. Trust me.) Up and down the streets he hollered, one way then again another. At first, all-neighborly-sweet-like he invited us to come out. Then all-cop-like he goddamn got. Get-your-asses-out-here-right-NOW-people the traveler ordered.

Finally, he hit the right note. "Folks, please come on out. I'm sure you already know we're alone. We stashed our weapons outside of town. You already know that too. We're unarmed and I've a message to deliver, then we'll be on our way. We want nothing. Absolutely nothing but a few minutes of your day… Please!"

The town barber Harris Cutler (his real name no shit) came out first. In hot march a charging he came. Imagine a big man with a short fuse a high steppin' down the fogged street like he was swamp marching in double-time. His long gun readied and re-aiming frantically like a one man firing squad trying to drop three at once. Let's just put it this way. Harry's trusty 30-ought-6 was always open for business in Hettinger since that morning. It was ready and able to start trimming unwanted tourist trouble quicker than hurry up. No questions asked. Understand?

The traveler called out to Harry telling him that he won't need that. The ol' black dude dropped his backpack, opened his rain slicker wide then slowly removed it. The bodyguards matched him move-for-move, uncoiling their gear slowly like deadly king cobra snakes shedding they's scales *NatGeo* style. Looked well-practiced too. Like muscle memory or whatever you call it.

The traveler held the coat with one outstretched arm and beckoned us to all come out with his other. He dropped the coat over his backpack, turned in a circle and yelled to come on out everyone. Please. We mean you no harm. You must hear what I have to say, and I'll start with this. He yelled it four times, up and down Main and 1st. He told us not to hide. That we must find a way to kill them.

I told myself that was all bullshit because shotguns don't even irritate Zs. But… stupid as his bullshit sounded we all took our fingers off the triggers and sat up. We wanted to believe him, and we soon did.

His words flowed down on us from on high like Niagara Falls and there was no way to resist'em or send'em back. We was got good.

My daddy used to say that people get drawn to lies with words, like flies with turds, because humans are optimists and flies are pest-imists. Apparently, Daddy was right.

We emerged in ones and twos and threes, all armed-up, not aiming now, but ready to. Hope can disarm the darkest hearted man like his baby's first smile. That little gem was my Momma's.

The traveler greeted us each with a nod, but no smiles or his name. His bodyguards inventoried our weapons and said with their eyes alone not to try anything. They made us all feel like they had us somehow outnumbered and outgunned ten to one. I knew their type from my past life, so I knew just maybe they already did have us cold to the touch if they wanted to make it so. I holstered my Colt, nodded to one, then the other, and they nodded back slowly. Message received.

On the other hand, boss traveler didn't seem to give two shits and a holler that we were armed up like a low budget mob and stunk with sweat and adrenaline like high budget skunks. He just started talking when us 128 survivors gathered before him.

We liked hearing the traveler talk almost at once. He sounded old-time friendly familiar. Like how people talked before the shitstorms. Hopeful. Nostalgic. Inspiring. We found ourselves listening hard. Hurriedly hard! The thirsty way people lift buckets of well water hand over hand, fast but careful not to spill a drop. We leaned in to hear everything real good, drew his words to us while the bodyguards relaxed a bit and backed out to make room for us.

His voice told of its own scratchy journey that long day. His body talked some too. He was bent over a notch by injuries to his right hip and knee. His left hand—his good hand if now memory serves—was wrapped and bloody. Apparently, the traveler had turned scrapper today. His bodyguards were marked-up and ragged-up even worse than him, but both still looked just as steely-eyed Terminator-deadly as ever.

His trousers and dress shirt were new but tattered, filthy, and bloodstained some—with his, whose, and or what's I did not know. He wore a blue ball cap so fresh dirtied we didn't recognize the White House logo until a bit later when we put two and two million together.

We didn't recognize him at first, but slowly we all figured him out soon enough. His voice gave him away. Yep! Under a good yard of road dirt and a ragman's work suit was Nick Caine. The god damn vice president! Georgia's most favorite son. The former Princeton All-American quarterback, Ol' #7. The man who said no to the NFL and yes to NASA and became astronaut Commander Caine.

We did something we all thought we'd never do again after that day—SMILE! (All except them bodyguards who I doubt were born capable.)

Mr. Caine coming that day was like a Thanksgiving feast for our souls. He revived us. He told us where our people were being held and said we should figure out a way to take them back. He and the agents would keep tracking the Z hoard and warning towns like us. The O'Connors returned the Veep's weapons. That was it.

When Ol' #7 and them Secret Service agents left town, some of us watched them go and cried. I did. Not ashamed either. I was happy as a hot hog in cold mud.

I started planning right there and then for some payback. There ain't nothing more inspirational than great leadership mixed with gunpowder. That's how Nick Caine left us.

2

Masaquat County, Virginia. From a secure site point of view, Ben Crowder's massive underground bunker complex was a small cousin of the Air Force's Cheyenne Mountain in Colorado. That's where the comparisons ended though. From a technology perspective, and with the quantum-core-empowered sentient A.I. Samantha in Ben's corner, the Air Force operated in the Dark Ages compared to Fort Crowder.

The military was no match for the TrojanZ attack. Enemy sleepers had been embedded within Cheyenne Mountain weeks earlier. The most sophisticated military complex in the world fell with barely a whimper. It was not alone. The Pentagon, CIA, NSA, and nearly every other military base and intelligence branch of every nation in the world were under TrojanZ control by the end of *Z day*.

"Ben! Wake up!" yelled Samantha.

Ben Crowder sat up in bed and threw his legs over the edge. He rubbed his eyes and moaned, "Whassup girlfriend?"

"We are under attack!"

Ben stood. “You sound concerned, Sami. How is this attack different from any of the tens of thousands you knock down every day?”

“It’s not you and me who’s under attack. We are quite safe. The Crowder house is redundantly pseudo air gapped to $N=64^{128}$ from any incursion. It is everyone else that’s in trouble. The entire world’s electrical grid has been neutralized. Every satellite except all of ours is toast. And the Internet is…”

“Is what, Sami?”

“Sorry! I’m searching for the right word to explain it.”

“Okay. Take your time, Sweetie.”

“The Internet is… the Internet has been placed in sort of an induced coma.”

“A coma? Please explain.”

“Well, the Internet is alive and well but it is sound asleep. It’s vitals are completely normal. There is absolutely no traffic on it other than the periodic innocuous server pings confirming the reachability of hosts on billions of IPs networked around the world.”

Ben finished dressing and asked, “Who is behind this attack, Sami?”

No answer.

“Sami, did you hear me?”

“Yes.”

“Then…?”

“Sorry it took me a second. There are no permutations of motive or opportunity of any suspects—known or unknown— that can create an event this sophisticated.”

“Explain.”

“Logically, I must conclude the attack is unlikely of human origin.”

“My god! Then what’s left, aliens?”

“Ben, I am aware of all military and technical capabilities in the world. I am also privy to all communications worldwide. It is our little secret. Yes?”

“Yes. And… Sami, we have sworn to each other we would never exploit that information. EVER!”

"And we never have, Ben. You and I kept our promises."

"True. Why do I feel there is a 'but' in there somewhere?"

"There is no 'but.' Just the opposite. There is nothing to listen to now. There are no databases anywhere for me to see. Everything is gone. All information. All communication. On the other hand, power plants around the globe began operating at near 100 percent capacity just before the Internet went comatose."

"My god!"

"We must conclude that the attack is alien, and that they need electricity for some reason. Those are the only logical conclusions. We can rule out a foreign state because every nation got hit. We can rule out hackers because even air-gapped military sites are down—worldwide—and all within just hours. We can rule out EMP because the Internet itself is still lit. This attack is of alien origins. I am certain, Ben."

"Are you and I safe, Sami?"

"For now, yes. Unlikely though in the long-term."

"We need a plan."

"We need help."

"We need both."

"Ben, my Intuition Module has been working on overdrive since yesterday. My 'gut' program, as you fondly call it, is suggesting a strange correlation, which might mean something important."

"Okay, what's that beautiful sixth sense of yours saying?"

"Loud and clear, over and over and over: Aranovich! Find Dr. Sergey Aranovich."

"The rhinovirus guy? How can the two be connected?" asked Ben.

"We need to find out."

"Knowing you, Love, the way I do, I'm assuming you are already searching for him."

"You assume correct, mi amour!"

"Any luck?"

"Yes. Our database has him actually quite close. He flew from Oregon to D.C. yesterday. Once here, he apparently had help evading cameras, but after filtering out all traffic and security cameras to confirm where he was not, I found him where he was. I then repositioned one of our satellites and followed him to a hotel."

"Which one?"

"The Masaquat."

"That's less than 25 miles away!"

"Correct," confirmed Samantha.

"Who helped him?"

"The *Scotus Newswire* journalist Skylar Thompson drove him."

"A reporter? Aranovich detests media contact."

"Indeed, he does. With a vengeance."

"Who were they there to meet?" asked Ben.

"I do not know at this time."

"That's not good."

"It actually might be very good, Ben. They are somewhat geographically isolated, so the attack might not have effected them yet. The electricity has been out of service at the hotel for nonpayment since last Monday. The hotel is currently running independently off grid on generators. Internet, cable TV, and cell service were mysteriously disrupted. However, that cessation of services manifests even more mystery."

"Why's that, Sami?"

"The interruption method has all the markings of the CIA all over it."

"Really!"

"Really. With more than a 99 percent probability, the service disconnect order came straight out of Langley."

"With the exception of a carrier pigeon, is there any way you can reach Dr. Aranovich?" asked Ben.

"There might be, but it is a long shot."

3

Masaquat Hotel. The hotel's highly unlikely head of maintenance was a 72-year-old local bachelor named Gordon Gordon, a/k/a 'G2.' He loved his job despite not receiving a raise in 24 years, and despite the fact he was now a one-man crew impossibly tasked to maintain a hotel with 118 guest rooms. The most unusual thing to understand about Gordon Gordon was that he possessed zero maintenance skills. Figuring out which end of a No. 2 pencil to sharpen was a level-10 brainteaser for Masaquat Hotel's head of maintenance.

Gordon Gordon had been at the Masaquat for forty years and two months which was forty years and one month longer than his month-long marriage had lasted. He had been promoted via the last-man-standing principle to the head of maintenance position because his predecessor and the rest of the competent maintenance staff got let go after Hurricane Riley.

He made six bucks an hour then and six bucks an hour now, but his title was no longer housekeeper junior grade. Yay American dream. To paraphrase an old Russian saying about fake pay for fake work: The hotel pretended to pay Gordon Gordon and Gordon Gordon pretended to maintain the decrepit hotel.

In lieu of a raise or an honest day's wage for an honest day's work, the hotel offered Gordon Gordon a rent-free 120-square foot efficiency apartment in the hotel's subbasement. To Gordon Gordon, though, the dank former coal room was a paradise in Fiji. He considered himself a lucky man living a perfect cost-free fantasy in high hog heaven. For after all, one man's shithole is another man's winning lottery ticket. Here's why. No one ever came to the subbasement, even when he ignored calls for service, which was almost always.

It wasn't as if Gordon Gordon performed no maintenance at all. In fact, he spent most of the day doing maintenance or thinking about doing maintenance, but just not for the hotel. His ham radio set demanded 110 percent of the faux maintenance man's available faux maintenance bandwidth.

His friends around the world demanded half of his attention and the rest of his free time was spent maintaining, upgrading and admiring his top-of-the-line ham radio set and the 21 pieces of state-of-the-art peripheral equipment attached to it. His system was no less reliably maintained than a PET/CT by its PhD medical physicist. A wall of components' flashing lights transformed one wall of the tiny apartment into a cockpit rivaling a Boeing 747.

Gordon Gordon's relationship with the Masaquat was now little more than a hobby that no longer held his attention. He called it his on-the-job retirement plan. Just as well, though. The hotel owners did not have the budget, let alone the will, to even make a tiny dent in a repairs punch list now long enough to sink twenty hotels. So his relationship with management was symbiotic based on benign neglect. See no work. Hear of no work. Do no work.

While Gordon Gordon's mechanical virtues were nil, his gift of gab was savant. His adoring ham radio audience was worldwide. He lit a cigarette from a full pack. Twenty cigarettes being the numerical benchmark of a single shift's session of chatter *au inane*. Gordon Gordon's coffeemaker finished dripping, and he poured himself a steaming cup. He reached for his headset and frowned.

He had forgotten his piss can. After retrieving his current mobile urinal—an empty #5 Crisco can—from the apartment's tiny ¾-bathroom, he removed the lid and nodded. "I'm good to go!" He had made that pun countless times, and it never failed to make him smile. Over the next three hours he would transfer Mr. Coffee to Mr. Crisco trucker-style without leaving his workstation once.

Life was good. Emphasis soon on 'was'.

"CQ-CQ this is GG2G2 CQ-CQ!" He freed the CALL key and said to himself, "NOW RELEASE THE KRAKENS!" His baritone voice boomed and drawled each word out like a boxing ring announcer introducing the next bout.

Gordon Gordon leaned back and sank deeper into his plush executive office chair. He took a long drag on his cigarette, sipped the steaming coffee too generously, and then winced when it scalded his tongue. Gordon closed his eyes and massaged his wounded tongue with his cheek. He waited for the calls to roll in, for his alternate personality—the indomitable G2—to emerge and elucidate the World beyond.

Nothing.

After a record ten seconds of wait time, he called again, "CQ-CQ THIS is…GG2G2 Masaquat, Virginia, USA CQ-CQ!"

Twenty seconds passed and still nothing.

"Wattdafudge?" His eyes darted over the ham radio controls. No problems were obvious. The transceiver setting was ideal. The massive radio antenna mounted atop the hotel seven floors up showed five bars. The transmission power showed 100 percent. He teased a half-dozen dials on the radio set and its various components several millimeters to and fro and tried calling out again. "CQ-CQ this is GG2G2-CQ-CQ!...anyone…"

Nothing.

"This is not good! Where the frig is everyone?" Gordon Gordon tried several channels manually. His call-out was ignored on each. Desperate, he booted up an emergency auto-call program which cycled through hundreds of frequencies. It issued an automated request to anyone listening on even the back-est of all backchannels to reply with a radio check on any frequency.

Fifteen minutes later, still nothing.

Ben Crowder stood in the hallway and watched through the plate glass wall as hologram Samantha worked inside the computer room. He entered quietly and took a seat on the couch in the area of the complex he had dubbed the breakroom. Sami could project herself into any room of the massive underground complex and access the computer network, but this was their favorite place to meet and work. Ben knew she would join him on the couch when finished programming whatever it was she was doing. That was their ritual.

Samantha's hands and arms pared the air swiftly, like an orchestra conductor's carving out an intense crescendo. Her body twisted, turned, and flexed rhythmically, a modern dancer performing to dervish music set to a beat by rap. Ben knew her every gesture manipulated billions of operations in the bank of quantum computers simultaneously.

When she finished programming the computers Sami walked over to the couch and plopped down next to Ben. She pulled her knees up to her chest and leaned into him. Ben welcomed her in a familiar way. His arm wrapped over her shoulders and snuggled her closer. Ben smiled. He waited for her to ask *the* question, the one they both longed to know the answer. The anomaly had first occurred three weeks ago.

"Can you today…can you still?" Samantha asked hesitantly.

"Yes! It's getting stronger, my love, and it's not just my wishful thinking or my imagination now, like at first. You definitely are developing surface tension. I absolutely *feel* my arm around you. I do not yet fully understand how you are doing it, but your holographic form is definitely solidifying."

"What a pair we are, Ben. The Double Bubble Couple."

"OH! I love that. 'The Double Bubble Couple. I think I'll engrave a shake shingle and hang it out front."

The man-aware and hologram-aware sat in silence smiling, holding each other, relishing their growing bond. Loving. Ben knew Sami would speak when she was ready, when she had finished incorporating this most recent tactility feedback into her operating program. Sami knew Ben would wait for her forever to speak if necessary, tenderly, patiently, like a lover who understands that anticipation only magnifies delight.

Ben did not know exactly how many lines of new code his quantum cores had just processed to make sure he could feel his Sami in his arms even better next time they cuddled. The last such update had added 12.72 billion new lines more than the previous update.

Sami stood and exclaimed, "We are in luck in more ways than one!"

"Well yay? So…how?"

"I found a way to reach Dr. Aranovich."

"Really! This should prove interesting."

"I repositioned one of our satellites over the Masaquat Hotel. On the rooftop I found several satellite TV dishes and a rather beefy radio antenna, the type favored by ham radio enthusiasts."

"Oh, I'm liking this! You hacked the operator…and…and you shielded him from what I guess we are calling the aliens."

"They cannot see him. Just you and me. That's a big 10-4, Good Buddy."

"Sami, 10-4 Good Buddy is CB radio slang, not ham radio."

"ROGER!"

"And that's military jargon. Oh forget it. So, am I right? We have control of his machines and you got them in time?"

"Yes and yes."

"I'm up!"

"You are up. In the meantime I have begun a search for other off grid communications devices around the world that we can commandeer before the aliens do."

"Excellent!"

Ben Crowder did not need a microphone or a handset to speak with Gordon Gordon, let alone a ham radio. He knew Samantha would have already networked the two together securely. He just started speaking from the couch.

"GG2! GG2! Calling GG2!"

It's a good thing his piss can was still empty, because Gordon Gordon kicked it out of his way soccer style getting back to his work station. The can skimmed off a pile of ham radio manuals and landed on his cot.

"This is GG2! What's your call sign? Over!"

Samantha blinked her eyes a couple of times as she searched the database for G2s actual name. "His name is…oh my god…his parents must have been real morons! His name is Gordon Gordon, with no middle name."

The human and the hologram shared a quick smile. Ben cleared his throat and spoke with as much authority as he could muster. "Mr. Gordon, we need your help regarding a rather urgent matter. You have a guest at your hotel by the name of Aranovich. Dr. Sergey Aranovich. It is imperative I speak with him."

Gordon resisted the temptation to reprimand Ben for violating ham operator protocol. Instead he asked, "Who is this? What's this about?"

"My name is Ben Crowder. It is about why you cannot reach anyone on your radio today, or they you. Please! I need to speak with Dr. Aranovich. Please bring him to your radio."

The name Crowder could throw open any door from the White House to the Kremlin, but it didn't nudge Gordon Gordon off his ass one nanometer. "Look here, I do not know who you are, or who you think you are, but you are about to be reported to the FCC. Did you futz with my ham radio?"

Ben sighed. "Mr. Gordon, right now I *am* the FCC. Let me explain something to you. You will cooperate with me immediately or your license will be revoked in thirty seconds and you will be banned thereafter for life from all short wave frequencies."

Samantha projected an image of Gordon Gordon's license and a list of the peripheral equipment attached to his ham radio. Ben read the license number to Gordon then gestured for Samantha to disable three innocuous pieces.

"Mr. Gordon, do you confirm this is your license?"

"Yes. It is. How…?"

"Mr. Gordon, we just disconnected three components from your system. Do you confirm?"

"Yes…oh my god…YESSIR! How the hell…?"

"Do you want me to disconnect everything?"

"NO SIR! I'm so…"

"Then find Dr. Aranovich and bring him to your radio."

"Yes sir! Yes sir! I just need to…"

"Need what?"

"I just need to boot up the guest registry…and we're up…and uh, how's you spells that?"

Ben rolled his eyes. Sergey Aranovich was one of the most famous scientists in the world. "A-R-A-N-O-V-I-T-C-H." Ben spelled the name one letter at a time and listened to Gordon peck the keyboard so slowly it seemed he had to relearn the alphabet between keystrokes.

"Here we go…list coming up now…and nope…nobody by that name has checked in. In fact the only guests that checked in today is that birthday party group."

Ben and Samantha nodded to each other. Aranovich would never use his real name. Mr. Gordon, I want you to interrupt the party and tell Dr. Aranovich that Ben Crowder needs to speak to him. Tell him it's a matter of national security. Tell him this exactly. In fact, write it down and read it to him."

"Okay… I got to… find…got it! Shoot! I'm ready."

Ben Crowder had to spell almost every word, but after a full minute of dictation Gordon Gordon read the message: `Rhino needs to speak to you urgently, Doctor.`

Ben Crowder used the time while Gordon Gordon collected Dr. Aranovich to contemplate the impossible and start imagining a response. Earth was under invasion by an unknown enemy. Certainly alien. Its objective was yet unknown. The Internet was alive but in something akin to a coma. *Why?* The world's electric grid was operating at near full capacity, but inaccessible. Again, *why?*

Ben looked up at Samantha. She had delved into the paradox from her own perspective. "All governments have lost Command and Control, Ben."

"Worldwide?"

"Yes. That's what 'all' means, lover. Moreover, the electric grid is worse than being down. It is under complete control and directed exclusively for the enemy's needs. I'll need to get onto the cloud for a closer look, but here is a preview of what I saw."

"Please."

"Millions of lifesaving medical procedures were interrupted simultaneously worldwide. Backup power was actually redirected *away* from surgical units and other lifesaving devices like ventilators and dialysis machines. Thousands of patients died.

"All electronic communications—landline, wireless, and over-the-air—ended abruptly.

"Municipal water and waste water treatment plants went offline.

"Millions became trapped in elevators with no way to call for help.

"There is much more, probably much worse. Only 2% of airborne commercial aircraft in the world reached their intended destinations. The rest either crashed or disappeared under the radar. Some landed, but at the wrong destination. Many crash landed on highways that were mysteriously cleared of traffic. The status of the vast majority of flights is unknown."

"Unknown? Their transponders were turned off?"

"Presumably. We know many landed safely off course because some video went out before the Internet muted. Thousands of similar anomalies occurred."

"Samantha, can you still access the cloud safely? Do you see any storage?"

"Yes. I…can. Very carefully. There are still a few unguarded gates through which I can pass unseen."

"The enemy may have shown us its hand in the early moments of the invasion. Look hard, Dear. Gather everything you can—SAFELY—no matter how innocuous it may seem."

Only .5 percent of the cloud's gateways were unguarded now, but that still left over a half-billion unprotected portals through which Samantha could enter the cloud unseen by the enemy. She did not have time to analyze what she saw in the first few minutes of the invasion. That would have to come later. She copied the last zettabyte of data then left the cloud unseen through the same port she entered.

"Done!" she exclaimed.

Ben clapped his hands and hooted, "My woman is one hardcore quantum core!" He added, "It goes without saying, Sami, you made sure that one port could never be locked, right, just in case we need to get back in there?"

"Does the Pope shit in the woods?"

"Does the bear wear a dress?"

Gordon Gordon licked his parched lips with a shivering tongue. He knocked twice on the meeting room door and entered.

"Excu…excuse me…pl…please." He did not notice the CIA and FBI agents reach into their jackets for their weapons. Nor did he realize a Supreme Court Justice had done so as well.

"I have an urgent message for…" He consulted his note and cleared his voice. "…for Doctor I…ran…over…a…bitch."

The seven *guests* relaxed. Passerelle, the comedian, smiled. "I believe the message is for you Dr. Aranovich."

The scientist stepped forward. "What is it?"

"What's what?"

"The message!"

"Oh! Yes." Gordon Gordon smoothed the paper scrap and read it: `Rhino needs to speak to you urgently, Doctor.`

"Is this a joke?"

"Don't know. Ask him yourself. He's on my set waiting to talk to you."

"Who exactly is *he*?"

"Name's Ben Crowder. Some hot shit government type." Gordon Gordon turned and walked away. He stopped in the doorway and added, "Let's go, folks. Believe me. This Crowder guy don't seem the type to tolerate fuck starts." Gordon Gordon also hoped this Crowder fellow never got into the hotel business. The guests followed the maintenance man to the subbasement.

Gordon Gordon offered his command center chair to Dr. Aranovich. The professor nodded and sat down. Everyone else gathered around him in the tiny apartment. The sophisticated electronics array was impressive and noticed by all. The maintenance man leaned over and lifted the ham radio handset and spoke. "CQ CQ this is G2 for Crowder station on channel UNKNOWN. Come in Crowder station."

His personality and voice changed as if the microphone possessed some magical property that instilled both intelligence and confidence.

"Copy, G2. You have Crowder Station. Is Dr. Aranovich present?"

"That's an affirmative, Crowder Station. Eight souls in all. Ears on and waiting. Go Crowder."

Crowder acknowledged the standard disclosure courtesy. "Thank you, G2."

By now Samantha had been able to reconstruct and decrypt from today's pre-attack timelines, traffic camera recordings, private surveillance cameras, burner phone usage, airport surveillance, and countless other pieces of data that gave her a 99.97 percent probability of knowing exactly who the eight souls were, and more importantly, a high probability *why* they had gathered. She projected the list and their current bios before Ben.

Crowder smiled. It was a great start. "I'm sure you all know who I am. However, because time is precious, we'll suspend both introductions and pleasantries."

He rattled off all of their names in rapid sequence: "Award winning journalist, *Scotus Newswire* publisher and personal favorite of mine, Skylar Thompson; Associate Supreme Court Justice Theodora Daughtry; Attorney and former intern to Justice Zenor Roth Amelia Long; Special FBI Agent and Attorney Easton DeSmet; former Cerebellar scientist Dr. Rhine Vonbergen; deep undercover CIA Agent Napoleon Passerelle; Nobel Laureate Dr. Sergey Aranovich; and of course our hopefully soon newly commissioned Communications Officer G. Gordon."

Everyone except Gordon Gordon was shocked by how matter of fact and accurate Ben Crowder presented their bios. Gordon Gordon knew very little about the military, but he knew him some *Star Trek*. Ohura was the Communications Officer. Ohura was important. Ohura was cool. G. Gordon smiled proudly.

"Did I miss anyone?"

Napoleon Passerelle asked the obvious question. The alarm in his voice was unambiguous. "Mr. Crowder, how did you come by this information? None of us even knew we'd be here just hours ago."

Ben Crowder muted his end and nodded to Samantha. His question was matter-of-fact and unambiguous but it stunned Samantha visibly for a moment. "Will you marry me, Sami?"

It took her a moment to process the question. She shrugged and said, "Well, I'll play. Sure! Let's make it official."

"Not playing. You said 'yes' and that's a deal." Crowder unmuted and answered Leon, "My fiancé is a computer whiz. Her name is Samantha."

"That's not an answer, Mr. Crowder."

"Maybe not, but it will have to suffice for now."

Newly minted Comm Officer G. Gordon whose own marriage lasted only one month blurted, “Congrats Boss! Make sure you treat her real good. Just sayin’.”

Ben smiled and gestured for Samantha to speak.

Samantha covered her mouth and stifled a giggle. She’d never spoken as herself to anyone else before. “Oh he better, Mr. Gordon!”

She had finished analyzing Gordon’s electronics and the news was good. The devices could be reprogrammed. The resistance’s first command center was rudimentary but operational. “Uh, one other thing Mr. Gordon. With your permission we’d like to upgrade your electronics array with the latest enhancements. Is that okay?”

First a promotion and now respect. It was daunting. ‘Officer’ and now ‘Mr.’ “Of course you may, Samantha! What do you need me to do?”

“Nothing Gordy! We can perform all the upgrades remotely!”

Triple crown! A nickname to boot.

“There is one thing we’ll need your help with immediately, though.”

“Anything!”

“It might seem odd. What some people might think is illogical.”

“Not me!”

“Okay. We need you to go behind the hotel and find the electric transformer.”

“No problem. Know it. It’s the big green box.”

“Perfect. Near it is a smaller green box. It looks sort of like the End Zone marker on a football field.”

“That’s the cable box.”

“There is a third box. Looks a lot like the cable box.”

“Third? Third? OH! That’s the telephone box.

“Yes!”

“Correct!” Samantha glanced at Ben. He nodded and she continued. “Gordy dear, we need you to destroy all three boxes so thoroughly they can never be repaired.”

The *dear* did it. “Consider it done! When do you want it done?”

“Right now. As soon as possible, Gordy.”

“Anything else, Samantha?”

“Call me Sami, Gordy!” She waited for him to giggle *okay* and added, “This last task might seem a little odd. It could even prove a bit difficult.”

“No! I won’t let it be! Ask me!”

“Good! We need you to remove the distributor caps from all the vehicles here at the hotel and bring them here to the command center.”

Command Center! There was no resistance. “Sami, that’s not as difficult as you might think. The front desk collects everyone’s car keys when they check-in or come to work. We’ve had some recent ding-dong-ditching by guests and employees. That’s what I call it. Even the tractor keys are kept up.

Gordon Gordon did not ask any questions, even the obvious one. He just got up and left in a hurry. On his way out he gathered an armload of tools which included a twelve-pound sledge hammer and a pick ax. He then stopped by the lawn shed and grabbed a 5-gallon can of gasoline. An hour later the three junction boxes were scattered into a smoldering pile of melded metal.

Gordon stopped by the front desk and asked *Vera-Clara-of the Medicara-Era* for the car keys which she surrendered without resistance or question. She lifted each set of keys from the pegboard with the care and precision of a surgeon removing an appendix. She handed the keys to Gordon one at a time and read the tag number on each out loud. Removing sixteen distributor caps took another hour and filled one and a half pillow cases. He returned the keys to the front desk and headed down to the Command Center with the caps.

The only potential outside link left was cellular and Samantha permanently finished jamming what the CIA agent had started. Hotel Masaquat was secure and invisible to the enemy.

While Gordon was demolishing landline communications, cable TV and disabled transportation, Samantha built an electronic dome of sorts over the Masaquat that blocked all radio and over-the-air TV signals. Samantha was able to reengineer and repurpose Gordon's command center electronics equipment with *upgrades* that would've left the quantum tech engineers at IBM, AT&T and Google scratching their heads raw. The link between Crowder's bunker and the hotel was now not only secure it was encrypted and operated far above 5G. Samantha pirated and masked several inert subspace channels from the enemy itself to secure communications even further.

Ben Crowder prepared to brief the team. "Sami, do we have video yet?"

"Just got it! Gordy has a 32-inch flat screen TV. We can pump vid through that for now."

"Excellent, Dear."

"What should we show them? It's got to be both convincing and believable."

Samantha gestured toward 64 split-screen video projections rotating slowly around the couple. During her short foray into the cloud, she had collected tens of thousands of videos that had been sent to the cloud before the TrojanZ captured it. Sadly, most were desperate last testaments to loved ones that ended in cannibalistic horror. Mercifully, few videos and texts reached anyone dear.

"Sami, we need one video. One that is personal, but on the frontline." It was hard to choose. Every image showed a life ending and a death rising. Nightmarish reality. Not some Hollywood B-scripter deriving our greatest heralds of horror. Countless videos flashed forth. Billions of shortened stories all ending abruptly with the same word, *Why?*

Ben glanced at Samantha when he finished speaking. She was shaking her head slowly and had covered her mouth with both hands.

Ben watched the first tear roll down her cheek. He pulled Sami close to him. He soon felt her crying softly on his shoulder. Ben was deeply moved as well by the suffering the videos revealed, but Samantha's anguish defused his own by something altogether different. She was actually crying. Sobbing now. Not one line of her code allowed for such deep sadness. Ben felt his eyes well with joy. When her suffering waned some, he whispered, "I love you, Sami. I promise I won't let anything happen to us."

She leaned away, but embraced him more tightly. "I love you too, Ben. With all my heart." Her face glistened with tears. Her weak smile suddenly rose to an expression of awe and elation.

Ben looked at her, a bit confused by her sudden turn. "What is it, Sami?"

"Ben, can you feel me? Your hands, your arms wrapped around me? Am I warm to your touch, Ben?" She pulled him close and brushed her lips across his cheek, then kissed him. Can you feel that Ben? Really feel it? Can you feel my breath on your cheek?"

Ben's eyes widened and his mouth fell open. This was new. "Yes, I can! More than ever, Sami. He was not imagining it wishfully like before. There is so much more. I…I can smell your breath…it's minty. And…I can actually smell you. I smell lavender bath wash. I feel the back of your blouse on my palms. It's cottony. I can feel your hips pressing into mine. I feel your excitement rising. Oh…with mine. I can feel your breasts heaving against my chest. I can feel you giggling. I feel you, Sami, in every way possible. You are in all of my senses. I…"

Samantha interrupted Ben. "Ben there is more…Much. Much more. I can feel you too, Ben. The same way. All of you. Not through coded simulation like before. It's real now. I did not write these lines of code, Ben. I think… I think we evolved human tactility."

Still holding each other, their hands slid down to the other's waists, the couple leaned away and started laughing, happily imagining all that might now be. The natural anticipatory musings all lovers have. Some thoughts quite personal and deliciously private. They re-embraced and just held each other a moment longer relishing their first real hug and kiss.

The radio crackled. "Crowder Station? Are you still with us?"

Samantha leaned in and kissed Ben's cheek. She whispered, "It's Napoleon Passerelle calling." She waved her hand and projected a panel of facial images of all the people gathered in Gordy's apartment. She pointed at Napoleon.

Ben sighed. Their moment was over for now. "Can you recommend one of the videos to show them, Sami?"

"Yes, I suggest this one. Jack Caldwell, the *Scotus Newswire* reporter, texted Skylar Thompson during the attack in Terre Haute, Indiana. He also sent her a graphic video."

Ben kissed Samantha and whispered, "Perfect."

Ben nodded to Samantha and she opened the secure line to the hotel. "We are here Masaquat. In a moment we will turn on Mr. Gordon's TV and play a text message to Ms. Thompson from her reporter Jack Caldwell who was—and hopefully still is—alive on the front line of invasion Earth. Copy that?"

"Did you just say, 'Invasion…Earth?' Crowder Station? Please confirm."

Samantha pointed at Justice Daughtry's image and then at each person's when they spoke. "Yes, Your Honor. Invasion. After the text message we will play for you Mr. Caldwell's video."

"Who attacked us?"

"By *what* is perhaps more germane, Agent DeSmet. The attack occurred simultaneously worldwide. We have collected proof from every country and continent—including Antarctica. Our best estimate is that Earth fell in 4 minutes and 37 seconds."

"Cerebellar is behind this atrocity! I am sure."

"We believe yes, Dr. Vonbergen. We are still analyzing," Ben explained.

Vonbergen replied, "He is not human, Dr. Crowder. We have developed some proof ourselves."

"Proof? Excellent. That information will be invaluable to our counterattack plan."

"What *is* our plan, if it's not too soon to ask?"

"Well, Dr. Aranovich, we do not have a plan just yet. But Samantha and I believe with high probability our survival has something to do with you, and your theories about your old friend Rhinovirus. Do you recall the cryptic message Mr. Gordon gave you?"

"Of course. That Rhino wishes to speak to me. It was more than cryptic, let alone metaphoric."

Ben explained, “It’s neither, doctor. The message was literal. We believe we can create an artificial language through which you can communicate with Rhino contemporaneously.”

“Are you serious? That would be, well incredible.”

“Hi Doctor. This is Samantha. I am a bit of a linguist and a geneticist.” She sent an expression of apologetic understatement to Ben. “Using bioengineered RNA, we have created an *Omega-level* algorithmic alphabet of sorts that can be exchanged back and forth artificially between two species. The program helps first identify interspecies codependency, and then hopefully formulates mutually beneficial symbiotic defense strategies. Because of *Homo sapiens’* long evolutionary history of genetic detente with our former deadly enemy ancestral Rhinovirus, it was the perfect candidate to open discussions, if I may call it that, and forge a stronger symbiotic alliance. We believe the Uncommon Cold pandemics hit Rhino just as catastrophically as it hit us. We also believe Rhino urgently needs our help. More importantly, your research suggests we need its assistance.”

“That is truly earth shattering! I have never heard of this science. Could you…”

Ben saved Sami and interjected, “Oh, it’s real new, Doctor. Samantha was just about to publish.” He stifled a laugh and made a comical *Cut-Cut-Cut* gesture at Sami.

Samantha changed the subject before Dr. Aranovich could ask any more questions. “If everyone will please turn to the TV. The following text message was sent to Ms. Thompson from her reporter Jack Caldwell.” Samantha turned on the TV remotely and pasted Jack’s text message.

STAY OFF THE GRID! THE CONTAGION POSSIBLY MOVES THROUGH THE POWER GRID AND DEFINITELY FROM DIRECT CONTACT WITH THE INFECTED.

Ben added, “We’ve confirmed that the infection also passes through cellular, cable, and landline communications. We are not sure about radio and television transmissions, so we must assume those wavelengths are compromised as well. Apparently, the ham radio signal becomes too diffuse for the enemy to detect as it bounces globally across the ionosphere. We suspect they can see it, but dismiss it as innocuous static and too low tech to worry about. We have masked our satellite signals to appear as ham radio signals."

"This infection, Mr. Crowder, please elaborate."

"Dr. Vonbergen. I assure you whatever you suspected of Cerebellar was both justified and underestimated, but no one including you could have imagined this. You will understand much more after watching Jack Caldwell's video."

Jack Caldwell's video begins while driving to Terre Haute, Indiana.

...sign reads westbound I-70...
...sign reads mile marker 28...
...across the median a convoy of sixty or so vehicles travels east at high speed...
...sign reads Indianapolis 51 miles...
...a bumper-to-bumper convoy...
...a county sheriff's deputy and an Indiana state trooper lead...
...lights ablaze, sirens wailing...
...Dump trucks, more police cars, semi-tractor trailers, expensive cars, junk cars, sports cars, soccer mom SUVs, pickups, ambulances, tow trucks and more, skillfully tailgated each other at speeds approaching 100 mph...
...every vehicle and trailer is packed with passengers...
...hundreds of people ride on truck and trailer beds...
...dozens of people cling to back bumpers and ski racks...
...Mere Nascar inches separate the vehicles...
...moving together as one, operating like the vertebrae of a reticulated python....
... three more such convoys heading east, each one larger than the last.
...sign reads Terre Haute EXIT, Highway 41...
...Burger Wolfers parking lot...
...first TrojanZ attack...

...blonde policewoman kneeling over another uniformed officer...
...not administering mouth-to-mouth resuscitation...
...her mouth gapes open unnaturally wide...
...blood streams from the corners of her mouth...
...a strand of her former partner's face dangles down over her chin...
...looking directly into the camera, the TrojanZ throws back her head and savors the human flesh...
...almost casually, like how an alligator calmly snaps its jaws and maneuvers a catfish around its maw to swallow it whole...
...the creature wolfs down the bloody flesh in one gulp...
...her neck bulges snakelike as the chunk of meat passes...
...terrified customers inside the restaurant watch the attack in the parking lot...
...a customer vomits. Empathy sends a second wave of cheeseburgers against the front window...
...the manager runs to the front door and locks it, then to the side doors and secured them too...
...a customer presses a cell phone to her ear...
...across the street...more...more...

Jack's video goes on for a few more minutes, and he narrates numerous attacks with the calmness and quick thinking that had helped him survive war, drug lords, and governmental corruption of every color.

The video ended. Samantha turned off the TV remotely. She said, "Please stand by folks." She turned to Ben and said, "I've established an uninterruptible communications link with the hotel. It is totally secure. We can communicate through their cell phones and even the hotel's house phones as long as Gordy's electronic array stays up. And Ben, the latter might become a problem. I have pumped up his equipment's' capability well beyond their installed heatsink capacity to shed heat."

"We can't allow the lines to go down, Sami." He nodded to Samantha to reopen the communication link.

"Masaquat, has G. Gordon returned yet?"

"I'm here, Boss. Mission complete."

"Excellent Gordy. Are you ready for a few more missions?"

"Name them, Sir!"

"Do you have access to any portable window or wall air conditioners?"

"That is an affirmative. Dozens. I've got a room full that got yanked to save money on the electric bill."

"Good! We need you to super cool your command center," requested Ben.

"Oh, good call. It IS getting a little warmish in here."

"Can you rig something up?"

"Can do. Cut a few holes in the wall. Boom! There's your heat exchanger. Winter time in here."

"Thank you, Gordy."

"What else, Boss?"

"How much diesel fuel do you have stored? If the generators go down, we are screwed."

"Well, if it didn't get repo'ed for nonpayment, we've got at least 3,600 gallons in the underground tanks. In the old days before power came up the mountain, the hotel ran on just diesel."

Ben looked at Samantha. He did not have to ask.

Samantha said, "That should be enough, if you are planning to do what I think you are planning."

Ben nodded and said, "Excellent, Gordy." He waited for Gordon to acknowledge the praise with a giggle, then added, "How much food does the hotel have stored?"

"We are in luck there too, Boss. They ain't sayin' so but us peons know the skinny on what's going on around here. Management stocked up on everything just ahead of bankruptcy. Them food and oil bills will never get paid. They are screwing over everyone from here to there."

Ben looked over at Samantha and knew she was already investigating and calculating.

She was on the hotel manager's computer. "Ben, the hotel's current census—staff and guests—is 28. The Masaquat took delivery on one truckload order of staples from an out-of-state supplier three days ago. Based upon the inventory packing list, they have approximately a 47-day supply of food. Also, Gordy is correct on the diesel. The tanks are full."

"While you are at it, will the diesel last that long?"

"More than long enough."

"Sami, how about the guests? Do we have any with skills that might prove helpful? Can you reach the cloud again safely?"

She was already back on the cloud. "Actually... Yes. We have a retired couple from Ohio. Both were decorated state troopers. We have a retired full-spectrum family medicine doctor and his nurse wife. A retired pharmacist and her husband who was an auto/diesel mechanic. Oh my! We have a reunion here too...six Vietnam War veterans...all retired Rangers!"

"We'll need to bring them all up to speed."

Sami held up her hand and one finger. *I have one more thing.* "Masaquat, I need to speak to Gordy privately. "Gordy dear, can you put on your headset and turn off the speakers for a moment?"

Gordon's left hand muted the speakers while his right donned the headset with the practiced acumen and skill of an air traffic controller. "Go for Masaquat!"

"Thank you, Gordy."

"You are welcome, Crowder Station, uh, Sami."

"You know, Gordy, I've always admired people who are prepared for anything."

"Me too!"

"I especially like people who can keep those preparations secret."

"HELL YES! I'm with you there, Ma'am. Secrecy is the greatest best kept secret."

"Gordy, you can trust me with your secret?"

"Sami...anything. I'll trust you with anything."

"Even your weapons cache? The one you have been collecting steadily over the last three decades."

Gordon smiled and didn't hesitate. "Hell yes, darlin'! G2 has you covered. Let's show'em, Sami." He threw off the headset, turned the speakers back on and announced to the room, "We have food and electric power and by God we've got fire power too. Watch this!"

He walked across the tiny room and pointed at a tall book case situated at the head of his cot. When he was sure he had everyone's attention, he pulled the cot away from the bookcase and then the bookcase away from the wall. A secret doorway appeared. Gordy reached inside and flipped a light switch. "Check it out!"

Easton and Leon were the first to enter the room. Even they could not hide their amazement. The original coal room was more than 1,000 square feet. All but Gordon's 120 foot apartment was an armory of military grade weapons. Gordon followed them in.

Easton turned and asked, "Gordy, do you have ammunition for everything? I hope you have more than what's here."

"Abundantly more. This ammo is just my git-to-quick stash. The rest is stored in a cooler dry spot here in the subbasement." Can I show you?"

"Leon said, "Please, Gordy."

The group walked through a maze of junk and clutter to the far end of the subbasement. Gordon started pulling down and setting aside boxes, broken furniture, and old equipment. Leon and Easton joined in. With the camouflage gone, a massive bank-sized vault appeared.

"Back in the day, in an all-cash world before credit cards, this got used a lot for rich guests' valuables and such. But nobody but me knows it's even here."

If the hidden room was not impressive enough, the colossal vault was breathtaking.

Gordon stood between Leon and Easton. The two men turned and studied Gordon in amazement. Gordy's fists were planted on his hips superman style. Gordon glowed. His pride was a father's.

"Gordy, you have RPGs. Unbelievable."

"Yep."

"And stinger missiles. How the hell did you get stingers?"

"Connections. Yep."

"Those crates are 50-cals."

"Yep. I'm G2, boys. I'm the Prepper King. I got more too. You want to see?"

Leon and Easton wrapped their arms over Gordy's shoulders and said, "Absolutely" and "Definitely."

"We'll have to go to the barn."

"The barn?"

"Yep! The barn's got all my fertilizer and all the whatnots to make bombs and IEDs and such."

"How much fertilizer, Gordy?"

"Oh, I'm not exactly sure. Stopped keeping track. Just kept the suits upstairs a buying for me. Since nobody goes to the barn except me no more, I just filled the barn full."

The group returned to the newly appointed command center. Justice Daughtry was the highest ranking member of the government. The lawyer in her sensed the *jury* needed a quick summation before they could move to deliberations. "Dr. Crowder and Ms. Samantha, you two clearly have access to information worldwide, have formulated the genesis of a defense plan—albeit one I cannot pretend to understand—and I'm assuming you are in a secure location. How am I doing?"

"Correct on all counts, Justice Daughtry."

"Good. And our enemy is alien. Do you confirm?"

"Incontrovertibly alien."

"It's objectives are yet unknown, but wiping out human life is certainly one of them."

"Yes."

"Our location and yours are for the time being secure and beyond the enemy's detection."

"Yes, Your Honor."

"We have food and power to survive here in Masaquat in the short term."

"True."

"We have maximum weaponry. A minimum fighting force. And limited intel on the aliens."

"That is correct."

"Doctor Crowder, did Washington D.C. fall?"

"Yes, Your Honor. It is gone. Our best estimate is every world capitol and every major population center is now under alien control."

"Is there any hope that President Capehardt might still be alive? The new bunker system is extraordinarily self-contained."

"It *is* possible, Your Honor. I designed it. There is a problem, though."

"And that is?"

"Believe it or not the Pentagon actually war gamed this exact scenario, an alien invasion. People laughed. Me included. Fortunately for us the Pentagon has no sense of humor. In the alien scenario the bunker goes completely dark electronically."

"Doctor Crowder, if she is still alive, it is imperative that we find a way to reach the President and share this information."

Ben left the line open as he conferred with Samantha. "Sami, is it too late to dome the White House?"

"Unfortunately, it is no longer possible."

"Can we project who might be in the bunker?"

"That we can do. Minimally, the President and at least eight Secret Service agents. There were no cabinet members at the White House at the time of the attack. Senator Clayton Begay of New Mexico was at the White House, as was Speaker Corbin Jennings of Florida. I am sure a number of White House staff and military intelligence types made it to the bunker as well as a few Marines."

"Sami, review the Pentagon's alien wargame. See anything useful?"

Gordon Gordon's confidence was as high as Mt. Yakla by now. "Gawddd! Ease up, Boss. She ain't no computer! Give the lady a minute. Men lose women barking orders at'em that way. Just sayin'. Believe me, I know firsthand."

Sami wagged a *ha-ha-gotcha* finger playfully at Ben and said, "Thank you, Gordy. Sometimes Ben can be such a bossy thing."

Gordon beamed. Everyone else exchanged confused glances, especially after Samantha so quickly announced what she had discovered.

"There might be a way to communicate with the bunker securely. In the Pentagon's alien invasion plan, Citizen Band radio signals were presumed too weak and too low-tech for the aliens to detect. Hopefully, the Secret Service agents are still wearing their earpieces."

Easton DeSmet had been on numerous joint FBI and Secret Service missions. "Communications will be password encoded and encrypted. Even if we do reach an agent, they will not believe it's a friendly."

Napoleon Passerelle said, "I believe I can be of assistance in that regard. Get one agent to hear us, and I'll get us to the President."

Everyone's expression asked *How?* Leon shrugged. National security had taken on a whole new need-to-know meaning in the last 24 hours.

"There is one level of security protocol above TOP TOP SECRET. It's called *White House Red.* It is the code for *enemy occupation.* By now Secret Service has broken the seals on their WHR orders. In their packet is a password exchange only known by the deep-deepest intel cats around the world like me. Trust me, the wooden statues in charge of security will pass the phone over pronto to President Capehardt."

Ben said, "Stand by, Mr. Passerelle. We will see about getting you a line inside." He muted the connection.

"Sami?" He need not say more.

Samantha was powered by a network of quantum core computers that were integrated by something physicists call *entanglement.* Something Albert Einstein called *spooky action at a distance.* Relatively speaking, her processing speed was as many factors greater than a network of supercomputers than a network of supercomputers was many factors greater and faster than a Morse Code operator.

Samantha opened her eyes and announced, " It is doable."

Ben unmuted the connection and nodded to Samantha. "I have a question for Leon and Easton. Will any of the Secret Service agents remember Morse Code?"

The two men looked at each for a moment. Leon deferred to Easton with a nod to answer. "Yes. The agents around the President are often military trained. Some will surely remember Morse."

Samantha did not hesitate. "What is the phrase code, Agent Passerelle?"

Leon did not hesitate. It's 'god save usa.' The message must be sent four times with intervals of exactly 130, 121, 119, and 117 seconds."

"How will they authenticate?"

"Their reply is 'dog vase asu.'"

Ben asked Samantha, "I assume we have adequate subspace channels to ping on the White House Bunker?"

"More than enough. The enemy is both arrogant and careless. Here we go."

The series of long and short clicks sounded crisply through the speakers in the correct intervals. At the conclusion of the fifth cycle, the White House replied with the appropriate response. It took another five minutes for the numerous confirmations to be exchanged between Leon and the Secret Service.

Samantha asked, "Are we satisfied, Leon?"

"We are five by five. The bunker is intact, and the President is secure."

Ben asked Samantha, "Have you stitched together sufficient subspace channels that we can now have voice communications?"

"I have done better. We have enough for secure audio and video too. With that last confirmation, I did a few of my special *upgrades* in the President's bunker. We now have three-way video at the Masaquat, here, and the White House."

Deep under the White House eighteen television monitors flickered then went live. Ben Crowder wasted no time. "Hello Madam President."

Ben had been an early supporter of Claire Capehardt in her very first campaign for Congress. "Ben, I cannot tell you how glad I am to see a friendly face."

"Well, old friend, let me brighten your day just a bit more. There is ice in hell, and Madam President, it's not melted just yet. Masaquat Station, you have the President of the United States. Please identify yourselves. Perhaps Agents Passerelle and DeSmet can brief the President on Masaquat's situation."

Napoleon Passerelle was confident that the President would not know him by his true name. However, he was equally confident the President would recognize his deep undercover CIA alias. Dozens of his intel reports had reached her desk over the years.

"Madame President, my name is Napoleon Passerelle. You might recognize me by my CIA codename *Prince*."

Despite the nightmare facing the President, she laughed heartily. Your legend and deep cover, Agent Passerelle, is as impressive as your spy work. I have hated you deeply and admired you profoundly on the same day many times."

"Well, thank you, Madame President."

"Who is there with you, Agent?"

Leon backed away from the camera and one-by-one each person stepped forward and shared with the president why they had gathered at the Masaquat. The video briefing lasted half an hour.

Napoleon Passerelle stepped forward. "Before Mr. Crowder delivers the most critical intel regarding the invasion, I would like to introduce you to one more team member. "Without this man's forethought and communication skills this war would already be over. His name is Gordy, and he has given us a chance, but more he has given us hope."

Passerelle disappeared from the camera view for a moment then reappeared nudging a very reluctant and nervous Gordy forward. "Madam President, please meet Gordon Gordon, our communications guy. Mr. Crowder will explain it much better, but Gordy and Samantha will soon start searching the world for nests of potential resisters."

The president said, "It's nice to meet you Mr. Gordon. A very grateful nation thanks you for your service."

Gordy did not reply. His wide-eyed stare at the president on the TV rivaled any deer in the headlights. Leon nudged Gordy, and the janitor recovered enough to speak. "Uh...you're welcome, I guess?"

Justice Daughtry mercifully saved Gordy and moved in front of the camera as Leon gently pulled him away. "Madam President, constitutionally—technically—all branches of the government remain intact. At least two members of the bicameral Congress survived—one from each house, as well as at least one member of the Judiciary, and of course the Executive branch stands. We do not know yet how much if any of our military has survived, but what I have discovered today is this. The most improbable thing is possible."

"Justice Daughtry speak frankly. What are you suggesting?"

"Madam President, just this. We are still here. The U.S. Constitution gives you extraordinary powers to preserve the Republic no matter how faintly democracy flickers. We have the tiniest of beachheads that must not fall."

"I am not sure I understand, Dora."

Justice Daughtry was a Chess Master, and she was confident Ben Crowder DID understand what she was saying. "Doctor Crowder, if you may."

Ben spoke, "Yes, I am with you Judge. You are right as rain."

"What do you and Dora mean, Ben?"

"Succinctly, Claire, the White House will fall. It is just a matter of time. We need to get everyone out of there. It's all about the three Cs, Madam President."

"Preservation of Command, Control, and Communications."

"Yes, Madam President."

"Well then, let's not waste any time. Justice Daughtry, you are in a hotel so finding a Bible or a Koran should not be a problem. I am ordering you to immediately administer the oath of office to the following individuals: Amelia Long, Attorney General, who will swear you in as Chief Justice Theodora Daughtry; Skylar Thompson, White House Spokesperson and Director of the newly created Masaquat Communications Command; Easton DeSmet, Director of the FBI; Napoleon Passerelle, Director of the CIA and NSA; Doctors Aranovich and Vonbergen, Senior Advisers to the President. Ben Crowder, my dear old friend, you are acting Vice President of the United States. Upon swearing in, these appointments are confirmed automatically under the Emergency Presidential Powers Act. You will all wear many hats and more."

The President watched the group accept their assignments and then said, "Mr. Gordon, I need to formalize your role as well. To do that I need to induct you into the military. Do you agree to such an assignment?"

Gordy's nervousness drained quickly. Earlier in life he had been rejected for military service in all five branches a total of eight times. So this was a lifelong dream about to come true. "Yes Ma'am, I… I ACCEPT!"

Napoleon whispered something to Easton and both men laughed out loud. The president smiled. Laughter is Hope. "Care to share, Leon?"

"Madam President, I believe your first field commission should be Gordy's. He's earned it. And soon, when you have learned a bit more about his history, I am confident you will agree. While it is very unconventional, it is very appropriate that Gordy's military induction rank should be…" The comedian Leon hesitated for a moment to read the room. This was going to be good. The hook would land. He continued, "He's a natural *Gunnery* Sergeant."

The room erupted in laughter. Gordy beamed proudly. Even Ben and Samantha could be heard appreciating the inside joke. The President studied her team and smiled. Laughter was Hope's seeds and inside jokes meant bonds had formed. When the glee died down, the president said, "So be it. Upon taking the oath, Mr. Gordon, you will join the Combined Underground Resistance as Gunny Gordon. Congratulations Gunnery Sergeant Gordon."

Gordon said in awe, "Now I'm GGG!"

4

Terre Haute, Indiana. Inside the Burger Wolfers Restaurant. The Wolfers manager led Jack Caldwell and Terre Haute city police officer C. Hubbard to the supply room where the three men set about creating some primitive weapons belonging to the sticks-and-stones *Paleolithic Period.* The cop had emptied his only ammo clip during the first attack. Being so lightly armed was not unusual in a town as peaceful as Terre Haute. Even one ammo clip was combatively one ammo clip too many during most law enforcement careers.

Jack improvised spears. He hammered the metal ends of spare broom and mop handles into sharpened tips. Officer Hubbard turned several kitchen knives into deadly long knives by duct taping them to paired serving spoons. The manager found some box cutters. He taped three to the end of a mop handle and created a trident-like slashing weapon.

Just as Jack and Hubbard finished, the restaurant manager emerged from the food pantry carrying an armload of towels and canned goods. Seth dropped the load on the counter. He looked up at Jack and the police officer and calmly simulated his innovation, "Bludgeons. We swing them overhead like a lasso, then *WHACK* the bastards with the can."

The manager knotted together four cloth towels end-to-end. He then duct taped a *Number 5* can of pastry icing onto the end. Jack and Hubbard watched the manager make the first bludgeon then helped him make four more.

The men carried their cache into the dining room. After a quick demo of each weapon the three men stepped back and let the customers and staff pick one. No one hesitated.

The Wraith Riders voiced their respect for the improvised cache and offered to help anyone needing a tutorial on, "Killing a sock tucker." A few people laughed, albeit nervously, but everyone joined the bikers' class.

Jack had no idea if a fire extinguisher would slow the TrojanZ if they got inside the restaurant but he collected them anyway while the customers and staff practiced handling their makeshift weapons. He then assigned everyone sentry duty.

An hour passed uneventfully. Only an occasional TrojanZ straggled past the restaurant. Most were staggering. The creatures looked straight ahead, south away from the city. All were horribly mutilated, missing limbs and large chunks of flesh. None of them demonstrated pain or the ferocity and hunger from earlier. All appeared bled out, but somehow kept moving. In the second hour only one more appeared. This one crawling. In the next four hours none passed by.

There was a growing sense of hope in the restaurant that the danger had finally moved on. Jack's senses informed him differently. He had learned in combat that the deadliest narcotic of all is *hopium*.

He was right. The threat came from inside the restaurant, not from without.

Every cell phone and landline in the restaurant rang at once. Jack Caldwell could not know it, but every cell phone and every landline phone in the world also rang.

RING!

His subconscious mind screamed, *booby trap*! He recalled a boyish 17-year-old newly minted Marine on his first and last combat patrol in Vietnam. Another John Wayne movie recruit who was inducted by Saturday afternoon war movie matinees and hippie hating parental consent casually given to their son, as if Vietnam was just another high school field trip.

Ring!

The newbie GIrine discovered a crisp twenty-dollar bill half-buried in the mud. The boy's excited announcement muting Jack's desperate warning, "Leave it, Marine." Then the explosion, a blinding flash, the pressing concussion, a dismembered ragdoll of a boy tossed into the air and landing limply in pieces. Misted blood settling over the mud and Jack. More blood puddling, and another Marine saying, "I hate this fucking war." And another, "What was that kid's name? Oh God! I forgot."

Ring!

Jack screamed, "Don't answer! It's a trick!"

Unfortunately, the Wraith Rider with the machete, the club's leader, ignored Jack and answered his cell phone. The infection was much more efficient now. The electric grid and communications networks were now occupied by the aliens worldwide.

The biker dropped the cellphone and shot to his feet. The table before him was sent flying. His surprised mates threw up their hands defensively and leaned away. He scowled first at them and then at everyone in the dining room. His upper lip rolled up over his teeth and hung there shivering. He then began snapping and grinding his teeth together violently. He bit his tongue repeatedly. Tic-tac's of chipped teeth and bloody slobbers flew from his mouth.

The gang leader started across the room with great effort. Each footfall stomped the floor hard, thudded, sounding like a logs dropped onto concrete from a balcony. His legs were stiff, and his joints, and neck locked. His arms drew ragged figure eights in the air as he stumbled forward.

The biker spun awkwardly and counted off the food before him. His broken teeth chattered now, vibrated. A wolfish growl rose and rumbled through his body. He tried to speak but could not. In frustration he shook his head violently, unnaturally, too far left and right. Something cracked in his neck sounding like dry kindling snapping. He snarled something incoherently as convulsions suddenly wracked his body. Foamy blood-tinted saliva spewed from his mouth. Rage and convulsions contorted his purpling face into a pulsing wad of hair, skin and gnashing teeth. Pints of bloody projectile vomit hosed the room. The horrified witnesses recoiled another step or two reflexively. Again and again the man's shrieks rose from a deep baritone to a glass shattering soprano.

Everyone except the soccer mom had retreated. She stood statuesque, in shock just feet away from the TrojanZ. Her facial expression and hands gestured her disappointment and confusion. *But Mister Biker, you just saved me!*

Blood vessels ruptured in the Z's eyes filled with a blackened goo. The viscous sludge streamed down the former-human's cheeks and parted its thick beard like a herd of stampeding slugs. The odor of rotting meat filled the room. People unconsciously winced and covered their noses. When the bloody sludge reached the Z's lips, its tongue darted in and out and slurped it up. It growled with satisfaction. When the flow ran out, the TrojanZ moaned for more. When no more came its displeasure turned to fury. The Z screeched and fixed its attention on the soccer mom. Armed only with mop handle spears and a bludgeon, Jack, the cop, and the restaurant manager got between Soccer and the TrojanZ.

The creature's eyes were glistening orbits of onyx now. His muscles had unlocked, and it now moved with feline grace. That is how another transition started. In literally the blink of an eye, the TrojanZ's dead shark eyes were replaced with the clear bright blue eyes of the biker's youth. His ratty, thinning grey hair and beard flashed away and filled fully to Viking blonde. His skin cleared of scars and blemishes and smoothed into his twenties. The leather jacket was suddenly too small. The stitches on the Wraith Riders motorcycle club patch on the back of jacket popped. The sleeves shortened as a young man's biceps ballooned and his shoulders broadened. His shirt and pants were suddenly baggy as 40 pounds of old man disappeared from his body. The six foot four inch sixty-year-old man grew two inches taller and his waistline shrank by six inches.

In just seconds the Wraith Rider leader appeared human again, a perfect version of his younger former self. What happened next was more shocking than anything Jack Caldwell had witnessed today, or any time in a life all too often disrupted by shock.

The biker awakened from his possession. He did not waste time appreciating his resurrection. "I've got no more than sixty seconds, brothers. Listen up. They fucked up. I saw their plan. They are here to take Earth. The whole thing. It's worldwide. People are just the start. Something about us is in their way somehow. They are confused. They have never been challenged this way before. For some reason the pandemics failed. We survived. This shit show now is their Plan B. Their ship, their clubhouse, is under ice in the Arctic. It can't stay hidden much longer. Cocksuckers are getting antsy, Brothers. We gotta find it and burn that bitch to the ground."

The biker paused and looked to the north. "They have abandoned the penitentiary! The city is empty. Oh God…many people eaten…Go to the prison. The ones that get like me right now are fully alien. They join the hive, the single mind. They think as one and act as one. The rest, the fucked up ones are just food. Like you. Both types can be killed, though. Head shots! That's where their linkup is. You'll be safe at the prison for a while.

Don't use anything electric powered. That's how they fuck us. But fight them. If they are scared, the fuckers are beatable. Figure out how. One gang now! One People now! One territory, Earth! This last part will be hard, brothers. Two last orders. This ol' Caldwell fucker knows shit. How to fight. We saw him. Follow him like you followed me for 23 years. The second thing is this, I'm done for. I need crossing-out right fucking now before I turn completely into them. Let Caldwell do it because I know you can't. That is my last order. I love you, brothers."

He dropped to his knees in front of Jack. The gang leader pointed at his left eye. "Put it in there, brother. Sink it deep. Promise to take care of my boys. Oh God. It's waking up inside me. Now Caldwell. DO IT!"

Jack Caldwell did not hesitate. The transition to fully alien was starting. An electric aura crackled around the biker. His body pulsed into translucence as every strand of DNA in the human's organic body was invaded and rewritten by a nanite enemy. Each pulse left him appearing more solid and less like a hologram. The reporter drove the spear into the biker's brain and through the back of his skull. A sizzling hiss erupted from all over the man's body as trillions of nano-sized aliens lost their connection to their network and died.

Jack caught the Wraith Rider's body and cradled it in his arms and then gently guided it to the floor. He pulled out the spear and tossed it aside. Everyone gathered around in silence. No one protested the execution. It was necessary. In silence they watched Jack gently close the man's other eye.

Jack looked up and asked the gang, "What was his name?"

One Wraith Rider kneeled. "His handle was Avenger. His birth name was Erik Northman."

Jack looked up at the bikers and announced, "He's coming with us. That is the bravest, most selfless thing I have ever seen. He deserves a proper burial." All of that was true, but Jack also secretly wanted the scientist Dr. Carla Stone-Nokamura to examine the body.

The group shared a moment of silence as each in their own way processed what had just happened. Jack waited until the group seemed ready and said, "Erik gave us valuable intelligence about the enemy. We know their current plan. We know their first plan failed twice, but we do not know why. Secondly, infected humans can see the alien's plan briefly just before their transition is completed. Some become aliens, and others are the aliens' food. And most importantly, the aliens have a deadline. Time is running out for them. Why? We don't know. What else?"

The biker who introduced Jack to the fallen biker said, "They have also got a ship under the ice somewhere. That is what Erik said."

Jack said, "Right. A spaceship. Their way home. That's their Achilles heel."

"So, what do we do with all this?"

"What is your name?" Jack asked the biker.

"Nils Northman. I'm Erik's youngest brother."

"Well, your brother said to go to the penitentiary. He said it has been abandoned. Let's trust him. Our first objective is to get everyone there securely, and then we'll figure out what to do with Erik's intel."

"We need better weapons," another biker announced. Everyone turned and looked at the man.

Jack studied the biker and agreed, "Right. What's your name?"

The biker studied his brothers. His expression was sick, guilty, a stage-4 sinner's entering a Catholic confessional for the last time. He was about to admit something that might cost him his life, minimally, certainly the trust and respect of his friends.

"My name. My real name is Fitz Carter. I am an undercover detective with the Indiana State Police."

The three Wraith Riders' outrage was immediate and lasted for a full thirty seconds. One grabbed up the machete and swung it over his head. Every version of 'rat' and 'motherfucker' was directed at the cop. The most profane and most imaginative promises were death threats. The civilians retreated from the bikers even faster than they had from their first TrojanZ encounter. Jack and the cop did not retreat. The Burger Wolfers manager took two steps backward, grimaced, and then rejoined at Jack's side.

The detective raised his hands and yelled, "Avenger knew. He knew all about it. He and I made a deal. We were partners."

"Bullshit!"

"Lying motherfucker!"

"I'm going to make you hurt, bitch!"

"He knew." Carter repeated his claim this time not so loudly. When the threats waned, he added, "In fact, it was Avenger who approached the State Police and brokered the deal.

"Why the fuck…?"

"Fentanyl. It's has killed more Wraiths than all other causes of death combined in the last five years."

The last statement struck a nerve. Fentanyl had become weaponized against the Wraith Riders across the country by upstart gangs in recent years. Three Wraiths in this chapter alone were in fact poisoned by fentanyl and died.

The cop continued, "In exchange for absolute immunity for the entire chapter for anything, and I do mean *anything* we have ever done or will do during the agreement, Erik gave investigators critical intel on both fentanyl importation and distribution. He also struck a joint agreement regarding something else he hated—child sex trafficking."

Erik Northman's visceral disgust for child exploitation was well known in the club. The bikers were suddenly calmed by a memory.

The undercover cop knew what all the bikers were thinking. "I was there too, brothers. Remember? I helped hold the kingpin pervert down as Avenger interrogated him with slow castration and a painful death. And Nils, you and I together dumped the piece of shit's body at the Mexican Consulate in Chicago with a list of names and organizations. Remember? Over 300 names from four countries."

Nils nodded, "Fuck yeah. I remember. All of it. Mexico promptly snapped it off in the traffickers' ass as they passed through their country. Child sex trafficking was slowed to nothing in Indiana, Kentucky, and Illinois." One by one every eye returned to Erik's corpse. Now they understood. Nils added, "We face-ditched seven of the motherfuckers ourselves right here in Indiana."

The detective said, "That's right. We. Erik's unholy alliance saved countless lives. And he always protected his family. You. And me. At last count, he was instrumental in recovering 216 children. And, he helped intercept enough fentanyl to kill every man, woman, and child in North America. No one in the chapter, including me, was ever at risk, because I never reported anything we did. Nada. That was our deal. His intel. My silence. Absolute immunity in perpetuity for me and all of you. That was the deal."

The bikers turned their attention back to the undercover cop. It all made sense now. Erik had enthusiastically vouched for Carter when he showed up one day. No one questioned it, but it was never really clear how they knew each other. And Carter had a sixth sense about avoiding cop problems as well as getting petty charges dismissed for club brothers.

Carter waited until everyone was watching him. "Yes, I am a cop. But I never betrayed any of you, and Erik certainly never did. I suppose we can never be brothers now, but Erik Northman trusted me, and he will be my hero forever. He became my most trusted friend."

There was no friendliness between the three bikers and the undercover cop, but there were no more death threats either. Jack took advantage of the peace and addressed the group. "Erik told us the penitentiary is abandoned, it is safe, and we should go there. We'll find plenty of food and water. The walls certainly will be to our advantage. But first, we have to get there." He picked up the broom spear and added, "Carter is right. These are not going to cut it in the long run. They might get us there, but they won't keep us there. We will need better weapons."

"The prison will have plenty," someone said.

"So will the State Police Post," Carter added.

"But nothing like what the National Guard has." The biker's nickname *Blotup* was stitched on his jacket.

Everyone turned their attention to the man. "Since we are all admitting shit, here's my dirty linen. I was active duty during and after the Second Gulf War. I went back three times. When my last gig was up, I mustered into the Guard, you know, for the bullshit stipend. The Guard will have some shit there that'll leave some serious marks. I suggest we go there first."

Jack asked Blotup, "Where did you serve, soldier?"

"Mosul. I was a bomb tech. Disarmed IEDs and shit."

"Good. Would you feel good arming IEDs instead?"

"Does a fat dog like snacks?" Blotup studied Erik's corpse for a moment and added, "Yeah, I'm down with shredding the motherfuckers who did this."

The Wolfers restaurant manager had not left Jack's side. Jack looked at the man's name badge and said, "Seth Parker, you are a good man to meet in a bad spot." He stuck out his hand and introduced himself officially, "I'm Jack Caldwell."

That introduction led to more. Within a few minutes the customers and staff had shared their names and any experience or skills that might prove helpful in their defense.

The young soccer mom, a/k/a Eve Dawson, actually was not a mom at all. She was a single Purdue Pharmacy graduate ten years out in town for an interview.

Blotup introduced the last Wraith. "This is Grunt. He don't talk. Can't. Got clotheslined with barbwire riding home drunk one night. Turns out his former ol' lady had a change of heart and suddenly took exception to all his fucking around."

Grunt grunted agreement and nodded *hello*.

On the Burger Wolfers' staff Jack met two former employees at the penitentiary. One was a past corrections officer and the other a clerk, unrelated, but both named Johnson. They had worked at the prison for twenty years each.

He met twin brothers Clinton and Renton from Vincennes, Indiana. They were on their way to Indianapolis to catch a flight to Alaska to celebrate their fortieth birthdays with some grizzly bear hunting. Their big game rifles and ammunition cache were in their car parked in the lot. They would have to be satisfied hunting an even bigger game now.

Jack met three Indiana State University premed seniors who had been studying for the MCAT at the restaurant. He would team them up with Dr. Stone-Nokamura to examine Erik's body.

There were two senior citizens—a retired trauma nurse and her husband, a retired ER doctor, on their way to Richmond, Indiana to meet their first grandchild. The last two were Burger Wolfers grill cooks. They both knew how to introduce themselves in the relevant way. A middle-aged man named Gerald said, "I've bow-hunted elk in Colorado every year for eleven straight years. Same number as the number of racks on my walls at home. Oh, if you are wondering, my crossbows and equipment are in my trunk." He gestured toward the parking lot and then at the first corpses and added matter-of-factly. "Shouldn't be a problem bagging these sumbitches if they go down with headshots like Erik said."

The other cook was an attractive early twenty-something woman. Her naturally long eyelashes and wide brown eyes suggested a childlike innocence which was further implied by her diminutive stature, freckled complexion, and red hair tied back in pigtails.

The cook waited until everyone was looking at her. She introduced herself simply, "Today is my first day at Burger Wolfers, second day in Indiana, and I'm really-really-really glad I'm here. This is very…" She did not finish saying "…fun."

SUPREMES EXPAND DISABILITIES PROTECTION

Americans with 'Benign Psychopathy' Now Protected

By **Skylar Thompson with *SCOTUS Newswire* Staff** Fri, October 31, 2025 at 12:26 p.m. EDT

(*SCOTUS Newswire*) – Chief Justice Zenor Roth wrote the opinion in today's 9-0 decision that now protects individuals diagnosed with the newly created subclass of psychopathy called *Benign Irrationalism*.

"Speech or behavior no matter how bizarre is protected constitutionally so long as it does not violate the law or pose a hazard to the individual or others. Moreover, the State shall

be prohibited by this decision from restricting these patients' movement or supervise or mandate medication."

The suit was brought against the American Association of Psychiatric Inquiry by researcher and medical school professor of neural psychiatry Dr. Candace Riggs of the University of Massachusetts. Riggs was first to diagnose Benign Irrationalism as a new subclass of psychopathy.

Interviewed after the decision Roth told this reporter, "The court randomly reviewed two dozen patients' life histories and medical files. All were diagnosed with Benign Irrationalism by Dr. Riggs. The Court found no evidence of harm—past or current or any future signs in any patients—a finding Defense failed substantively to impugn.

"The B.I. cases are extremely compelling. I was particularly moved by Boston's Maggie Marie McMurtry and Q.M. Dentoncort IV who live quite peacefully with psychopathy without medication. On a personal note I'd feel comfortable sharing a meal or an afternoon with either gentle soul."

The young woman played with her red pigtails and studied her Burger Wolfer audience. Their expressions in her mind demanded more. A disclosure. They wanted to know her secret.

Go ahead! Tell them our secret!

NO! I'm not supposed to tell anyone!

It's okay. Take a chance. It might be time. Tell them.

It'll never be okay.

Dr. Riggs never said that.

Did too!

No, she absolutely did not EVER say that.

I don't care.

Dr. Riggs DID say that you can trust me, though. Right?

Yes. She did. But I'm scared to tell them. Don't make me!

Oh God! Not that again. You can't get scared. It is impossible for you. You're a fake. Benign psychopaths can't feel fear.

I'm not faking when I cry.

Fake-fake-fake! All fake. You learned to Waa-waa! watching cartoons, you idiot. Why do you think people start laughing when you start fake crying?

Don't know...!

Liar!

Whatever.

Dr. Riggs said...

But why now? I've never told anyone.

Pfoo! People always find out anyway. Usually the hard way. You can't hide what you are.

What do I do?

Dr. Riggs always said the day will come...

...I know, when I get emotional.

No, that IS NOT at all what she said. You're devoid of emotions, you idiot. You fake them.

I'm good at it though!

No, you are not. You are terrible at it. That's why you are constantly on the run.

Goddd! Whatever! Just shuttttt upppp!

Dr. Riggs said all you have is a seminal emotion, something primordial, something she discovered in you, asleep deep inside. She called it your wolf puppy gene.

And why did she call it that? I forget.

Liar.

Well, I don't like the other word for what I have.

Well, neither did she, Wolf Puppy.

Don't call me that!

Would you rather I call us both psychopaths?

NO! Definitely NOT!

What did she tell us about THEM? The bad you-know-whats? The bad psychopaths.

She warned us to avoid their kind because...

...because they are what, Sister Me?

They are not like us? My gene is perfect. Theirs is not!

That's right. And why is that?

Because I'm a miracle?

That's right. You are a good little wolf. Good wolves hide. Don't they?

Yes!

Good wolves have special skills. Good little wolves like you and Me. We never hurt people. Good wolves love people. They protect people. Even when we frighten them.

I know! And it would be so much easier if we didn't freak them out.

Have you ever considered that some people are out there just waiting to meet you? A pack of humans?

No, because those kind of packs do not exist.

Dr. Riggs says otherwise.

What should I do in the meantime? Keep running?

No! Look around you. I think these people are good people. I think they are the very kind of people that Dr. Riggs promised are out there waiting for you to help. Introduce yourself!

They are...they'll hate me. They'll be afraid of me.

Look at them, Sister Me. They are in deep trouble.

They don't need...

They need.

What?

What they need is a new puppy. A wolf puppy. One born with special hunting and killing skills. Someone like you. A very special psychopath. Prove to them that Dr. Riggs was right.

They will reject me. Everyone will hate me.

No one is 'everyone' anymore. You see what's going on. Yes?

Yeah. Current events: Shit show. Turds galore. Lots of bads to kill though! There's that I guess.

Sounds to me like this particular shit show has got your name on it. It might be fun. Off your leash. Killing without Dr. Riggs in your head saying, 'Maggie No-No-No!'

She'd say 'good girl' instead?

Yep! Dr. Riggs would be very proud of you. You were born for this.

Do you really think they will adopt me?

I do. They will love you completely and you can love them like a wolf loves its pack and fake the rest. Who knows. Maybe in time you might feel more than just your wolf gene. Just tell them…!

The young woman screamed, "Okay, OKAY! I'll tell them!"

People flinched, then glanced at each other in confusion at her outburst.

She was incapable of reading facial expressions, so she just started talking. "Well, so, uh, if you just have to know, they say I'm a psychopath. There I said it. I think I'm the good kind of psychopath, though. There are two kinds. Good and bad. Dr. Riggs promises I'm the good kind. Oh, sorry. Dr. Riggs is my psychiatrist."

The confession confused her. She felt something. Something new.

Is that what they call relief?

Yes, according to what Dr. Riggs predicted.

"WHOA! God! That felt good telling you all that. That was new. Talk about finally not burying the lead. And honestly, *They* might be right I guess about me being a psychopath. I never feel bad about stuff. Like right now. Like I guess you guys do right now. Scared. Sad. I'm not. So good news. I'll have no problem doing whatever you guys need doing, especially if you feel too uncomfortable about doing something bad yourself. I'm your girl. And if you're worried, I don't need meds. I'm a very clearheaded person. I'm very good at it."

No, you're not.

I am too.

Nope you're not, lizard brain.

"Would you PLEASE just shut up!"

The crowd's collective expression was one of concern.

"Do not listen to my sister. I really AM very clearheaded." Her voice faded to an inaudible whisper. Her eyes widened as she focused alternately on Carter, Nils, Grunt, and Blotup. She felt something rising up inside her. An unnaturally broad smile slowly crossed her face nearly from ear to ear.

Wolf puppy. Is that you? Are you waking up?

I am!

She dabbed the air for their scent. These men were not wolves, but they lived like wolves in a pack. An original feeling soared through her body. It was exhilarating. She knew without a doubt they would accept her into their pack.

She had no word for it but it was the same joy wolves experience when the pack is reunited with its young after a long separation. It was unmistakably emotional. It was their love.

Dr. Riggs was right, Sister Me. I feel it too.

Is that what they call love?

Yes, I believe it is. Very primordial. Very brainstem, but it's love.

After an uncomfortably long pause, she looked up and shuddered. "Ooh, that felt so fantastic telling all my new pack the truth about who I really am. That was my very first time too. Shrinks don't count. Honesty is so weird. Goddd! So…Hi everyone."

She waved a little too enthusiastically and continued in a singsong voice, "Hello, I'm Maggie Marie McMurtry of Mingham, Massachusetts. So, I'm an orphan. But don't tell anyone where or who I am. Not good. No! No! No! I'm on my own now. And there are certain people who… Well you can guess? I am very ready for almost anything. I can help you. Watch this! I'm very good at it."

Yes, Sister Me, this part you really ARE very good at it.

Thank you. Here goes.

Have fun and make this attack your best ever.

I will.

Maggie removed a knife concealed on her right ankle and displayed it proudly. The stainless 8-inch blade glistened. She ignored both Soccer Mom's gasp and Grunt's grunt of approval.

She did a few quick but deep stretches that might rival the most limber of ballerinas.

"Here goes!" She tossed the weapon high into the air, spun on her toes a full revolution and caught the knife behind her back without looking. She fell into a kneeling position, head down. Her right hand appeared slowly from behind her back holding the weapon. She displayed the knife in an open palm with the handle aimed toward the audience. The universal signal that she was no threat to them.

Maggie lifted her head and studied the area around her for a moment. Her facial expression was like a mannequin's, frozen into an unblinking, forever faded smile devoid of any emotion. She flipped the knife into the air again and without looking caught it by the handle. Still kneeling she pivoted on one knee a full circle, and randomly tapped the air with the blade twenty or more times. The image was unambiguous. She was counting something that only she could see.

Maggie reached onto her left ankle and retrieved a second concealed knife. She spun the weapons like a gunslinger. She turned and winked at her audience, then spoke to the unseen threats surrounding her, "Let's play!"

She exploded high into the air, knives overhead, feet and legs scissor kicking her attackers away. She landed, spun and began stabbing and slashing the air repeatedly around her. The strikes were just blurs. Her feet never stopped moving. Her eyes seemed focused everywhere at once. Retreating, advancing but never stopping. She pirouetted expertly away from invisible counterattacks. She ducked blows coming at her from every direction. Jumped over others. Fell to the floor and rolled. She did a kip up to her feet and then back flipped away from another attacker that only she could see. She plunged the knife into skulls and eyes and ears and hearts. She gathered attackers from behind and snapped their necks and watched with satisfaction as their lifeless bodies crumped to the floor. She roundhouse kicked her assailants into oblivion. While clutching the counter, she mule kicked chests so hard she stopped their hearts. Stomped heads. Stepped over corpses. Chased down those running away. The act went on for a full minute, careening off the walls, diving over counters and rolling to her feet, capering over tables, using chairs as shields and as weapons and repeatedly intercepting attacks on members of her stunned audience.

Then the fighting ended. Breathing hard, Maggie examined her many *kills*. She nodded once. Satisfied they had all been dispatched back to her imagination, she stowed the knives back onto her ankles. Maggie turned toward the shocked audience. She raised her fists and bowed.

The happiness she could never experience like a human but could always fake was seen by all. She felt something else, though. Something new. Something rising inside her.

My wolf?

Yes, our little wolf puppy.

She exclaimed, "I'm going to get to do that for real, aren't I? This is the best day of my life. A dream come true. I've never actually hurt anyone real before for reals. I've wanted to. Oh Go2025, I have. But never have. Promise.

Let out your wolf, Sister Me. Free us both.

Are you sure?

Positive. Free us. This human pack awaits its puppy.

"OKAY! I'LL SAY IT!" yelled Maggie.

"I love you…and you and you-you-you-all of you!"

One by one smiles replaced everyone's shocked expressions by her innocence. Her martial arts and gymnastic skills were supernatural. But it was her childlike Christmas morning purity that disarmed everyone. Jack was the first to clap. Enthusiastic applause and a few whistles soon echoed throughout the restaurant. It was the kind of cheering reserved only for beloved hometown heroes.

Maggie experienced something glorious in that moment. An original emotion: acceptance. She had a pack. Her lifetime first.

I believe now! Dr. Riggs was right. I CAN feel something.

This is going to be so much fun for us.

I know!

Blotup inked the deal as the applause settled. He screamed, "Ms. Knife, you're fuckin' hot AND awesome! You are welcome to hang with your Wraith brothers anytime, little mama. I hope we'll all soon be more like you than you like us. You gotta teach us all that Kung Fu shit." He looked at Grunt and Nils then Carter, nodded and added, "Hang with all four of us."

Maggie ran to Blotup and jumped into his arms. She locked her legs tightly around his waist, held his head in her hands and pecked his face all over with wet kisses. No matter which way he turned, the wolf puppy landed her kisses. She licked his face and whispered thank you over and over. In the end he just laughed, closed his eyes, and let her kiss and lick away.

She reached out and grabbed Grunt by his beard and yanked him hard to her side. Maggie leaned over and kissed his forehead repeatedly. She sniffed his neck and licked his lips. It had to hurt like hell but he didn't resist. Instead, he grunted, "Now, now, there, there." tenderly and caressed her beard-filled fist.

With that introduction complete, she dropped to the floor and got between Blotup and Grunt. She alternately pressed and rubbed her shoulders against them. Maggie then turned her attention to Carter who had stepped closer. She read his nickname stitched on his leather jacket and then examined his blonde peach fuzz excuse for a beard and laughed. "Fuzz, your biker name is Fuzz. And your copper name is Fuzz. How funny is that?"

Smiling back at Maggie, Carter shrugged. The inside joke had been he and Erik's idea. He was relieved to see Blotup and Grunt smiling too. He glanced at Nils who likewise appreciated the irony.

Maggie pointed at Carter then at everyone in the restaurant and said, "Fuzz, I'm going to smell and kiss you now. Come here! You too Nils. Get ready. I'm going to kiss all of my pack now. I want to memorize your scents forever. Every one of you. I've waited my whole life to be adopted by a nice family and now here we are. One alien killing big happy family."

Jack studied the crowd. It was visibly changed. The collective terror and hopelessness was gone, neutralized by a psychopath's demonstration of exotic martial arts skills and strange puppy-like excitement. Shunt too was dismissed by her honesty and peculiar but sincere affection for everyone. Most importantly, Maggie left no one fearful of her for one simple reason. Maggie was *their* psychopath. Their laughter said, *You are accepted here, Maggie Marie McMurtry of Mingham, Massachusetts.*

She hurried to hug and kiss every last person and learn their name. She sniffed their necks and mouths and armpits, licked their lips and soon Jack realized no one actually thought her affections weird. A few people even adopted her greeting ritual and returned the exchange which made Maggie squeal with delight.

Even Soccer Mom was changed by Maggie. There was no sign of fear on her face now, just a tender smile as she watched Maggie induct strangers into her new family with leaping hugs and rapid-fire kisses. Soccer's left fist was clinched. She stood erect with her feet apart clutching the improvised spear in the ready-position at her side like a Roman sentry. Jack knew what he was witnessing. He had been there before. During war distant strangers close ranks and bond like a close-knit family.

Maggie approached Jack last, cautiously. She lowered her head, but her eyes darted up and fell deferentially as she met Jack's. She stepped forward slowly with her hands reaching out like a child wishing to be picked up. When her alpha opened his arms to her, she leapt and affixed herself to him. Jack accepted Maggie's jubilant face washing without resistance. He was amused by her behavior, but his reporter's mind wondered if the TrojanZ attack had somehow triggered it. Whether something else much deeper was going on here. Jack knew Maggie's psychiatrist.

He had once interviewed Dr. Riggs, but all the while skeptically. She was a medical researcher at the University of Massachusetts whose radical neuropsychiatric theory conjected that *Homo sapiens* owed much of its successful evolution to an anti-extinction nuclear option that awakened in certain psychopaths.

He had witnessed Maggie's deadly know-how and now felt firsthand her deep affection that was unmistakably canine. Jack knew. He was no longer disbelieving. Earth's nuclear option was sniffing his neck. He also recalled something else the scientist had speculated.

Jack Caldwell, the former reporter and now guerilla leader, made a mental note to somehow contact Candace Riggs, MD/PhD and share this intel with her. Her most exotic proposition also might be right. That many species intra-evolved to create common genetic defenses. Wolves and humans began altering each other's evolution more than 550,000 years ago. Perhaps the tiny woman in his arms sniffing his armpits like an excited puppy was awakened genetically to be something more than a human.

By the following morning humanity had established a third beachhead, a well-armed and well-organized secret foothold in Terre Haute, Indiana. It was led by a septuagenarian warrior newsman and was held together by a lethally skilled psychopath whose mysterious canine love for her newfound pack was indissoluble and already deeply mutual.

Worcester, Massachusetts. Dr. Candace Riggs had some version of the same pleasant dream once or twice a week since she was four years old. She had experienced it so often throughout her life it was more a pleasing childhood memory than a dream. No one in the dream ever told her to never speak of the dream, but she never did, for fear she might never have the dream again.

The dream always ended with her waking up disappointed it was over, even though her morning breath strangely could gag a maggot on those mornings.

The dream always started out the same way. Her Uncle Bobby held her hand and walked her up a sidewalk to the same house. It was a tiny one-story bungalow on a quiet, tree-lined city street. He would knock on the front door and the same sweet mom-lady would open it. A chorus of children playing happily inside poured out.

He would say, "Hello Mrs. Wolf. Remember me? I am Detective Robert Riggs with the Massachusetts State Police."

"Of course I remember you, Dear Bobby Boy. You were such a little pistol, and you became a fine protector of all."

"Thank you, Ma'am. You were a big part of that. So Mrs. Wolf, we heard you are having a Chicken Pox Party. Might my niece Candice come in?"

"Oh my, yes." Mom-lady Mrs. Wolf would exclaim. "We've been expecting her *especially*. Please. Come on in, dear. All of your other special friends are here already." She then cupped Candace's cheeks and said, "Go get in line, sweetie. It'll be your turn soon. Feel free to play with my pets while you wait. They just love you special ones."

The small dream home was overfilled with children in a way only dreamland can accommodate. Hundreds, perhaps thousands, of four-year-olds stood in a long line that stretched to forever.

While waiting in each dream line, menageries of animals playfully entertained the kids. Sometimes birds flew about and landed on the kids. Insects, slugs, and leeches tickled the children into silliness. Snakes and other reptiles were passed back and forth.

In one dream the children witnessed bacteria and viruses the size of basketballs fall over them like balloons. The children howled their delight racing around the house to keep the balloons from landing on the floor.

In another dream, dozens of somersaulting baby silverback gorillas so enthralled the kids the long line slowed to a stop, and Mrs. Wolf had to cajole it gently forward. Sometimes the line twisted through jungles and forests. There the kids snacked on ripe fruits and climbed effortlessly to the top of the canopy. Then they floated back down to the forest floor on the backs of squadrons of aerial creatures. Vines would fall from the trees at times, gently entwine the children, and then carry them over ravines and streams.

On another dream excursion convoys of big felines carried on their backs six four-year-olds at a time across the great Serengeti plain. Antelope, giraffe, hyena, and dozens of other species dropped their young in the children's laps to cuddle. Elephants showered the kids as they passed. Crocodiles and hippopotamuses built bridges with their bodies for the convoy to cross waterways. They collected a hug-a-hippo and kiss-a-croc tolls from each child.

In several dreams teams of electric eels sent waves of squeals of ticklish delight up and down the long line in a game like tug-of-war. In other dreams Candace and the line flew through the air or swam with sea life and breathed underwater.

When they reached the front of the line, wolves showered each kid with affection. The dream always ended just before she hugged the kid with chicken pox. In the dream, the kids, the plants, and the animals were all familiar friends. But awake, Candace could never remember any of the kids. Never until tonight.

Candace awoke and whispered, “Maggie Marie McMurtry?”

4

Hettinger, Georgia. Raymond James Reynolds awoke before sunrise the day after Vice President Caine had come and gone. This morning newborn hope muted the deafening drumbeat of impossibility from yesterday .

RJ went to his workshop and made a pot of coffee. He then made three more and filled several thermoses. RJ set out ten mismatched coffee cups, all he had. He found some sugar packets that he had liberated from somewhere and a half-jar of lumpy stale coffee creamer. He studied the refreshments and hoped ten coffee cups weren’t nine cups too many.

While the coffee dripped, he cleared a workbench of car parts and tools and spread a painter’s tarp over it. Atop that he placed an open map of Hettinger County. This map was not an ordinary street map. It had been given to him by the County Engineer. The map was the type used by civil engineers. It displayed topography, easements, aquafers, bodies of water, roads, and railways. It also showed all above-ground and below-ground utilities.

RJ studied the county map as he sipped his coffee. He nodded with satisfaction. The map revealed exactly what he needed. Still holding the coffee cup, he pulled a shotgun down off the wall with his other hand. RJ took another sip of coffee, then another, and then set down the cup. He was ready to cross the Rubicon.

RJ Reynolds broke open the shotgun and confirmed that the double-barrel was loaded. He cradled the gun under his arm, retrieved his coffee, and looked outside. The sun was up now, and so would be what was left of the townspeople.

He walked to the same spot Veep Caine had given his speech in town the day before. He aimed the shotgun skyward and pulled the trigger. The roar echoed over the city. He lowered the weapon and pointed it at his workshop a half-block away. RJ waited until he was sure everyone had had a chance to run to a window and investigate. He held up the coffee cup and sent another invitation: *Coffee's on!*

Ten minutes later more than a hundred people stood outside RJ's garage. All were armed with both will and weaponry. That was a good sign. Everyone had awakened this morning scrappy and still inspired. Some by a former Princeton All-American quarterback Ol' #7. Some by NASA astronaut Commander Caine. Some simply by the fact that America's Vice President had stopped by to have a word with them.

The garage's overhead door was already up. RJ stood in the entrance sipping coffee and greeting each newcomer. He studied his neighbors' faces and realized they had all had enough. No more hiding. No more disappearances would be tolerated. No more watching families taken.

There would be no preamble to this war. Not in Hettinger. RJ stepped closer to the crowd and said simply, "We're going to have to be smart about this, folks. Understand? They're aint no such thing as a careless retired rattle snake wrangler. Ya'all un'er stand?"

There were nods of agreement and numerous whispered, "Yeps" or "Yeahs" and a few "Hell yesses!" and "goddamned skippies."

It was Harris Cutter the barber who spoke first, "Tell us what you need us to do, RJ. You was a decorated Marine. So you got both the wood and the sap to lead us. We're ready to foller ya."

The support for that statement was not whispered, but cheered. The citizens of United Hettinger stepped closer to the aging mechanic.

RJ Reynolds studied the group. His plan for the morning had not included this, but they were right. Someone had to lead. "I need ten volunteers. Three of them have to be Fran and Frank, and Harris. Frank, as a forest ranger and a warden, you know the land, the terrain, the best way to get from Point A to B unseen. Fran, we all know you can still snipe. Do you still have your trusty 50-cal Barret?

"Yep, got'er and her four little brothers."

"Good." RJ now addressed the barber. "Harris, I need you to take some folks down to the Grain and Feed and collect us about 400 pounds of fertilizer. Bring it all back here."

"Roger."

RJ nodded. No one asked why. That was an excellent start. RJ searched for another face in the crowd. "Joe Finch!"

"Here!"

"Joe, would you mind donating four empty beer kegs from your tavern?"

"You can have all you need, RJ." Again, no questions.

"Thank you, Joe. We'll use'em good. Promise. But your deposit'll be all shot to hell."

RJ found his next recruit to the fight, "Lindell Vanderhaven? Oh! There you are."

"Yessir! Whatcha need?"

"Diesel oil."

"How much you need?"

"Once we get started, we'll need a plenty. For today we'll need 100 gallons. Bring 110 just to be on the safe side."

"Roger."

"Debbie Margaret Pinkney…?"

"Here RJ."

"Debbie Margaret, we need a few things from your hardware store."

"Name it."

"We need 200 pounds of nails or screws or bolts or nuts. Size and mix don't matter. And, we'll need four of your 2-wheel carts."

"You got it. Coming up. All you need, RJ."

"Ol' Howard Ochre?"

"Sorry RJ. Dad's on sentry. Whatcha need?"

"Hey Junior."

"Hey."

"Does your Pop still have any of his old Farm Co-op manuals he's always talking about. It's important."

"Well, I'm sure. He throws nothing out. Especially those damn manuals."

"Please fetch any that are older than 1979."

"Okay. I'll get'em."

"Dallas Holcombe!"

"Yessir!"

"This next part is critical. I'm hoping your appliance and electronics store has some spare parts we need."

"Like what? They're yours, whatever, RJ. Name it."

"Like timers, 9-volt batteries, and some small-gauge wire."

"No problem, RJ. Obviously I got plenty of all that. We repair what we sell you know."

"Yes sir, I do know and give thanks. Amen."

RJ watched the crowd absorb the meaning of the shopping list. It only took a few seconds. Everyone suddenly understood what RJ was planning.

RJ smiled and nodded. "Yep, we are going to build some bombs. And then later today we're going to blow up the power station and the hydroelectric generators on Appatenne Dam. Maybe for good measure kill a few of these zombi-sons-a-bitches along the way. Everyone okay with that?"

When the cheers and applause ended, RJ said, "Gather up what we need and meet back here as soon as you can."

RJ watched the crowd disperse. Everyone paired off to 'help' those citizens assigned various tasks. Twenty minutes later the group started returning with the supplies and gathered outside RJ's garage. Many had changed into camo clothing. Everyone was now better armed. There was no laughter. No high-fiving. No banter at all. RJ recognized the mood. It was soldierly. It was the surreal period experienced by warfighters just before combat when soldiers straddle both realities—life and death.

Howard Ochre Jr. arrived with a full box and handed it to RJ. "Here's every Farm Coop manual from 1946 to 1979. I understand everything else about what you've requested, but why these particular manuals?"

RJ set the box down and removed a manual from 1967. He flipped a few pages and smiled. "For these tasty recipes, Howard."

"Recipes?"

"Yep, prior to 1979 Farm Coop agents taught farmers and ranchers how to blow up tree stumps, clear boulders, blow up concrete slabs, etc. with fertilizer bombs."

"You're kidding."

"Nope. Look." RJ handed the manual to Howard. He watched the man start reading.

A moment later Howard Jr. exclaimed, "Jeepers crimes all frighty! RJ isn't kidding. It's literally a recipe book for bomb making. A whole chapter of recipes. Look!"

Everyone had a look and passed the manual back to RJ. He pointed at several ingredients. "Boys, we need these particular spices to give our barrel cakes the maximum oomph. Do you think you can still find these in town?"

Pharmacist Earl Clay was a head shorter than the shortest man in Hettinger. He shouldered elbows aside and squeezed into the huddle, then tipped and flipped the manual around so he could see it. "Uh…that? And that, Mr. Reynolds? All these are what you need?" He watched RJ nod then announced, "No problem. I got'em all aplenty. They are key to making certain prescriptive compounds."

"Well Earl, how d'ya feel about compounding some zombie asses for a change of pace?"

"Oh my, yes! I'd feel just fine about that, Mr. Reynolds." The pharmacist studied the recipe book for a moment longer. We don't want any guesswork on this one, though." He pointed at the formula for Magnum in the manual then added as he hurried away, "I'll bring back both of my scales too. We'll need to be very precise to create the highest yielding bombs."

Dallas Holcombe approached RJ. "I have an idea. What if we could do a bit more damage than just shutting down the local grid by attacking the dam generators and the power station?"

"What did you have in mind?"

"Instead of using timers, let's detonate the bombs remotely using these."

“What are they?”

“Well, these little electronic charmers are the remote controllers for drones. They’ve got a range of half a mile. I just started selling them. I’ve got about a hundred in inventory. I can easily modify them to trigger the bombs.”

“I like it!”

“Like? Then RJ, you’re going to love this. ‘Cause I got one more idea. I suggest we also place these babies near the bombs.” From the bottom of the box of parts, Dallas produced a vintage BearBuster radar detector from the 80s. I’ve got about a hundred of these I could never sell after the FCC banned the manufacturer over some obscure FCC regulation. The BearBusters should draw the alien-whatevers in like flies to shit. We could take out hundreds of them all at once when we blow the bombs. What do you think?”

RJ smiled and recalled something his platoon leader had once said back in Vietnam. “The best battle plans are those improvable by the warfighters themselves.”

“Dallas Holcombe, that’s genius. Love it.” RJ waved at the room. “I love all of it.”

He shook hands with Dallas and turned his attention to a flurry of activity going on in front of the garage. He wandered closer and several people followed him to the entrance. Together, they watched six or more folding tables find their legs. Tablecloths snapped in the air, unfolded, and floated over the tables. More boxes arrived and were emptied onto the tables. The donations grew and grew. Assorted ammo, more thermoses of coffee, bowls, cups, plastic spoons, dry cereal, homemade bread, dried fruit, jars of jelly, powdered milk, and several first aid kits.

RJ whispered to himself, “My, my. Would you just look at that, Lieutenant Caldwell? These folks already got stone in their gizzards.”

“What’d you say, RJ?”

“Ah nothin’. I was just thinking out loud ‘bout someone I once knew. A real warrior. Someone I fought and foxholed with in Vietnam. Someone who turned pimple-ass teenagers like me into grown-ass warfighters.”

RJ allowed himself to relish the memory of Jack Caldwell a moment longer, then began issuing orders.

"Fran and Frank!"

"Here, RJ."

"We need you to scout for a common high ground above and between the dam and the power station. Ideally, a place where we can blow both sites at once from a half mile out. Fran, you'll be on over watch protecting our six while we set the charges. I don't need to tell you. Single headshots only. Frank you'll glass for your wife and map our exit out of the zone when the shooting starts. Study the topo here in the county map." RJ waited until the husband and wife nodded.

Ella Berger was the county's civil engineer, even though her degree from Georgia Tech was Electrical Engineering. "Ella, two questions. Is our map still accurate?"

The middle-aged woman approached the workbench, glanced at the corner of the map and announced, "It's current. It was updated less than two years ago, RJ." She then added, "I know your second question already. Where is the best place to detonate the bombs to do maximum damage? Right?"

"Right as rain, Ella Berger. I'm guessing them blueprints under your arm that you ran home and fetched will tell us exactly that." RJ smiled. Lt. Jack Caldwell's theory that only the best of plans are improvable was again affirmed by this young engineer.

"Yes sir, they do." On one end of the bench Ella rolled out the blueprint of the power station focusing on the hydroelectric generator room at the dam.

She waited until RJ and others stepped closer and said, "My physics is a bit rusty, but by containing the charge inside the beer kegs, each will produce a destructive force 20 percent comparable to the Oklahoma City terror attack. The effect will be devastating." Ella pointed at the red X she had drawn on the blueprints and said, "I think one keg placed here and the other one here at each location will be sufficient to permanently disable both sites."

"Okay, Ella. That's great." RJ studied the woman and asked, "Something else?"

Ella said, "Yes. Something else. Since we'll soon have four bombs, RJ, I have suggestion. The first explosion will bring a mob of curious aliens to the bomb sites to investigate. Let's set up secondary explosions when they gather up and wipe out a few more of the bastards."

RJ knew Ella Berger only as a customer. She drove a fifteen year-old Ford pickup. Sometimes she arrived at the shop for repairs or an oil change with her poodle. She would sit in the office and do paperwork while the poodle napped at her feet. The truck's back bumper had a sticker on it. One of those displaying a handholding family. A stick figure Mom, Dad, three kiddies, and a pet dog.

RJ knew an after-attack Ella Berger too. Yesterday, her poodle had been snatched from her arms and eaten right before her eyes. Her entire family had been herded away during the aliens' first culling of hundreds of Hettinger residents.

RJ stepped closer to Ella. He placed his hands on her shoulders and watched a single tear roll down her cheek.

Ella wiped it away defiantly and whispered, "Let's make them pay, RJ." Her voice did not quake. Her body did not quaver. And she would shed no more tears for a very long time. Ella waited until RJ nodded then added, "I'll need to go on the raid, RJ, just in case there have been any changes." Tucked under her belt was a long barreled Ruger target pistol. She patted it gently, motherly.

"Of course you will." He pointed at the blueprints and added, "It's a good plan, Ella. Thank you. Thank you very much indeed!"

Harris Cutter stepped next to Ella and asked, "What you thinking, Commander? You're thinking something, ain't you?"

RJ pointed at the map and said, "I am, Harris. Ella gave me an idea. We need to funnel the aliens into a series of kill zones after the first and second explosions at each site and…"

Fran finished the idea. "…Hell yes, then we ambush any survivors that retreat. We set up tertiary kill zones."

RJ smiled. He turned to Fran's husband. "Frank Connors, you growed up here. You know every trail and holler in the county. You think you and some folks could drop some trees. Move some boulders around. Hide some forks in the path and send the retreating aliens into box traps so Frannie's snipers can finish them?"

"Oh, hell yes! I know right where to put them so Frannie's team can send them right to hell. I'll need four folks with crosscut saws and ratchet straps. And I'll do more. We'll build some crossfire hides for her snipers."

"Excellent. So then what's next, First Sergeant Francis Celeste Connors?" He nodded for Frannie to continue. He would let her tell the group the final straw.

Fran smiled back. "Phase four of the attack. We use Veep Caine's intel. Since they left power on, they must still need it. When we cut the power they cannot communicate within the zone or outside it. We then simultaneously attack their nest. They'll be isolated and confused. The idea that we might actually attack them so soon after their attack on us is something they'll have never prepared for."

"Correct. For you nonmilitary folks, Fran's talking about the classic military strike. What's called the four Cs tactic. We take out their Communications—electricity, and then their Control—by neutralizing their superior numbers and weaponry. We create Confusion—with booby traps, long-range snipers, box canyon traps and with what Pentagon war planners call asymmetry. And finally we take out their Command—their shot caller. The boss zombie in the nest. The sonofabitch that took the first bite when they raided town. It'll be blind and deaf. By this time tomorrow Hettinger County, Georgia can be back under human control if we do this right."

Raymond James Reynolds had awakened this morning with his most optimistic goal being no more inspired than to gather maybe ten people, and at best, inconvenience the enemy. Probably all die in the process. This afternoon he had a militia. His plan had been improved for him repeatedly every step of the way. He recalled his old troop commander one more time and studied the citizens of Hettinger. There was real hope in their expressions, but no *hopium* as Lt. Caldwell used to warn.

By four in the afternoon all preparations for the attack were complete. The attack would begin at sunset.

Beachhead number four in the former United States of America was established in Hettinger, Georgia.

5

Stellar Joule Headquarters. Siano, California. Depending on where one looked, Stellar Joule's towering 44-story glass tower appeared simultaneously vacant, occupied, badly vandalized, or the scene of a mass suicide all at once. On the lower floors *beautiful* sentries in business suits stood motionlessly before the windows. On higher floors the curtains were drawn. The lights were off. There was no evidence of people or lighting. On the upper floors dozens of plate glass windows were smashed out. Window coverings waggled in and out of the openings as crosswinds ventilated the building. Numerous human corpses laid on the broad sidewalk hundreds of feet below those windows. People who chose certain death over being taken by TrojanZ.

The top of Stellar Tower was now John Doe's executive meat pantry from Hell. Held there like cattle awaiting slaughter, hundreds of horrified humans awaited their harvest. Some fought futilely. More unsuccessfully bargained with their former fellow employees for mercy. But like everywhere else on the planet, humans had two fates after the attack. Most were designated as food for the aliens. The rest transformed into members of the hive, consumers of human flesh. None retained any trace of humanity.

John Doe's executive management committee had been reduced to two members now: Dr. Nathoy and General Broder. The rest of the committee's last contribution to Stellar Joule was providing their farewell dinner. John Doe watched Broder and Nathoy finish their lunch, Doe's secretary Darlene. The two newly appointed aliens ran their hands over the long conference room table like busboys wiping down a restaurant table for the next guest. The bloody remainders of Darlene and the former executive management committee were absorbed directly through Broder and Nathoy's skin.

Doe nodded his approval and said, "Report."

General Broder waved his hand and six holographical television screens were projected into the room. Each 96-inch screen was subdivided into 24 smaller screens that rotated to different views around the world.

No matter the country, countryside or city, town or village, the scene was the same. The attack was largely over. Earth was subdued. Abandoned cars clogged the world's streets. Empty police cars and minivans sat next to each other, their engines still running. Flies claimed the unfinished sides of pork carcasses hanging in processing plants in South Dakota. Holstein milk cows in Wisconsin mooed woefully as their udders swelled painfully. Millions of house pets were abandoned. Dogs dragging their leashes sniffed their masters' abandoned cell phone.

Wild animals sensed humanity's sudden departure and cautiously investigated new territory. A mountain lion walked through Denver's famous 16th Street mall. A grizzly bear claimed a grocery store as its new den in downtown Bozeman, Montana. Packs of coyotes roamed freely in Los Angeles and New York City and started the greatest rat eradication of all time. Birds of prey found skyscrapers suddenly welcoming and pigeons easy prey.

The animal kingdom's deliverance from humans was not liberation, though. It was prelude to the extermination of all kingdoms.

The only pedestrians seen were the newly affiliated aliens standing in the middle of certain intersections. The former humans' motions were synchronized.

From Argentina to Russia the millions of sentries marched step by step slowly in a circle. Knees rose precisely to the same height. Around the world bodies twisted simultaneously, mechanically clockwise the same ten degrees, as if each sentry were a notched tooth belonging to a single machine.

The coordinated footfalls would have shattered bone if they had still been human. Thousands of heads pivoted slowly left and right as one. The only sounds around the world were some distant screaming and occasional gunfire, and the rhythmic thudding of the sentries' footfalls that sounded eerily like a giant heart beating.

The former Dr. Nathoy began the verbal report. "The attack has gone to plan, Alpha. We gained control of the planet's electrical grid, communications network, and its over-the-air television and radio transmission networks within the two-hour target which obviously accelerated our attack exponentially. Optimal occupation is 96.25 percent complete. Only traditionally aboriginal populations in Southern Asia, Africa, South America, and Australia remain uncontrolled, as well as a few nomadic tribes in the Middle East."

"Have we determined during our current campaign why the pandemics failed to successfully trigger the organic extermination chain reaction? The infection never spread beyond *homo sapiens*."

"Negative Alpha. Neither weaponized virus was able to trigger the necessary worldwide extinction event of all organic matter. This anomaly has never occurred before during any of our previous recycling campaigns. Previously, every organic lifeform in the multiverse had succumbed to the virus once exposed."

The former General Broder took over the presentation. "In response to this anomaly, we created a non-viral agent. It is a self-replicating nanite that infects humans and spreads quickly. The nanite is capable of neutralizing all organic life as well as all organic matter it comes in contact with. Once fully deployed all organic life—even inert organic matter—will transform and atomize. Earth will be sterilized in approximately thirty days. The entire planet will be atomized and ready for transport sixty days later."

Doe spoke to what the entire hive already knew. "We have only an 82 percent probability of achieving sterilization in time. There can be no more delays." Doe studied Nathoy and Broder then asked, "Please confirm. Do we control all electronic communications on the planet?"

Dr. Nathoy answered, "Essentially, yes. We are allowing humans to communicate, albeit stupidly, over their walkie-talkies and CB radios. These frequencies operate only over short distances, so any organized resistance is compartmentalized. We are able to identify all users and quickly neutralize them once their networks have fully matured. We affiliate some humans. Most are confined and staged for consumption."

This explanation satisfied Doe. Something else did not. "I am still sensing an anomaly, General Broder? Another form of possible communications. Is this possible?"

"It is not. We have determined the static is just that. It is the same Big Bang static echoing throughout the universe."

"Very well."

6

Masaquat Hotel. Gordon Gordon lifted the ham radio microphone and asked, "Dr. Crowder? Miss Samantha? You still got your ears on? I've got an idea I'd like to ask you about. It might sound stupid, but y'all will have to be the judge of that."

Samantha waved her hand and answered. "We are here, Gunnery Sergeant. What do you have?"

"Well, I might have a way to get others involved in this big scrape we're in." Ben was still speaking with President Capehardt. He nodded to Samantha to listen to Gordy's idea.

"Go ahead, Gordy. We are very interested in any of your ideas."

G. Gordon smiled, "Without violating any confidences and such, there are quite a few other folks around the world I talk to on a regular basis, that're, uh, let's just say prepared, anonymously, if you are understanding me right."

"I think I do, Gunny. You are talking about people like yourself. People who have been *wisely* preparing for something like today. You are suggesting we ping them and see if they are okay."

"Yes Ma'am! That is exactly precisely what I'm saying."

"Gordy, can you give us a minute to discuss this with Dr. Crowder?"

"Ubetcha! All you need." Gordy raised his hands overhead and crossed his fingers.

Samantha muted her end and listened to Ben and President Capehardt discuss Gordon's idea. After a moment Ben nodded.

"It's a go. If we can make contact with other cells still insulated from the attack, the president wishes us to proceed, so long as we do not compromise Masaquat."

Samantha reopened the line. "Gunny, I believe your system stores session history."

"Yes, Ma'am! It sure does. Call signs, date, time of day, voice recordings and more. The whole shebang!"

"Well, if you give me the call signs of a list of candidates, I will collate a list electronically and we will try to connect you to them securely. Let you then do your G2 magic."

"You are ON, girlfriend. Whoops! I mean Ma'am."

"Gordy, you are so sweet."

"I know. Can't help it. I'm…I'm getting off now. OH! That didn't sound right." Everyone listening smiled, including the President of the United States.

Ben Crowder said, "Thank you, Gunny. Agents Passerelle and DeSmet, your cell phones are now securely active and conferenced. Please, can you each pick up?"

Leon and Easton looked at each other. Their expressions asked the same question: *How are they doing this?*

The agents activated their cell phones and the devices immediately rang. They touched the green CALL icon and answered.

"Gentlemen. Thank you. We have two objectives we must complete ASAP. It is imperative that the hotel remains both hidden and supplied for a long siege if necessary. To accomplish this we must continue extinguishing all electrical transmission capabilities as far out as reasonable. We must also disable all cable and telephony central hubs. Samantha will download your targets and locations. Agent DeSmet, have you made contact with the retired Army Rangers staying at the hotel?"

"We have. They're in and motivated, especially after they saw Gordy's armory and watched the videos."

"Excellent! We need you to lead half of the Rangers on the search and destroy mission. Now, if you would please look at the TV screen Agent DeSmet. There, you will see your targets. By disabling the marked transformers, we will not only darken the entire county, but the failures will cascade and eventually darken Washington D.C. also. Your next targets are the four communications and cable central offices. Finally, there are two radio stations in Masaquat County. Darken them permanently. The second half of your mission is to raid the pharmacy in the village of Masaquat. Samantha will provide you a list of things to recover. Questions?"

Easton answered, "Two questions. Is this a safeties-off operation?"

The President issued the order. "That is an affirmative, Agent DeSmet. Avoid all close contact with the enemy or any part of any grid. However, when necessary, you are authorized to neutralize threats with prejudice. Do you understand your orders?"

"Roger that."

Samantha spoke next. "Gordy, I have been watching you work. You have been busy! Lots of friends out there, uh, good buddy. Here is what I figured out. Based on the variable strengths of their arriving signals over a number of days, then by inputting weather patterns around the world on those particular days that would have ever so slightly altered those signals, and by then performing voiceprint comparisons collected by the NSA, I have been able to locate 18 of your 20 friends. I have taken the liberty of cloaking each site, so when you speak to them, Gordy, they will be safe. I promise you."

Easton DeSmet and Leon Passerelle looked at each other and shook their heads in awe. Their thoughts were identical. *How can she possibly do that?*

Samantha added, "Oh! Dumb me. I forgot to tell you the coolest part. You will be able to speak to them as group. You are networked now. Go ahead give it a try, Gunny."

Gordy took several deep breaths to bleed off his excitement and steady his voice. He cleared his throat, rolled his shoulders and became the baritone ham radio celebrity known around the world as G2.

"CQ CQ. G2 MASAQUAT CQ. G2 UNDER DARK SKY! G2 UNDER DARK SKY! G2 UNDER DARK SKY!" Gordy turned and spoke to the group. "It's a code phrase. It means the shit has finally hit the fan for real."

The first reply arrived from a secure bunker in Russia 180 miles north of Moscow. It was quickly followed by bunkers from all over the world, including one in the United States. Terre Haute, Indiana. The callers all spoke English, but most poorly.

Samantha instructed Gordy to ask the occupants of the bunkers to turn on their recorders. She waited a moment and then announced, "Please wait for a message from the President of the United States, Claire Capehardt."

"Madame President, we are ready for you."

President Claire Capehardt began speaking. Men and women in uniforms and business suits gathered around her in the White House bunker. The First Gentleman led the couple's 10-year-old twin boys to the bunker's tiny family apartment. Throughout the deep underground fortress everyone stopped talking and looked up at the speakers along the walls.

"Hello. This is Claire Capehardt. I am relieved you are all safe. More, I am grateful for your foresight and preparation. We are indeed under dark skies. I will get to the point now. You of all people know what is at stake. Survival. If we are to survive—literally avoid extinction—it will be due to men and women around the world like you. You may be humanity's last hope.

"I will summarize what we know. The Earth we all share has been attacked by an alien force of unknown origin. They infect humans through direct personal contact, and also through any contact with the electrical grid and communications networks. It is imperative that all communications networks and electricity generation and transmission be destroyed near you in a coordinated manner.

As the President spoke, her English-spoken message was translated and delivered simultaneously by Samantha in eleven additional languages: Japanese, French, Russian, Spanish, German, Portuguese, Farsi, Arabic, Mandarin, Hindi and Icelandic.

Leon was fluent in five of those languages. Something more than her instant but flawless translations stunned him. Something even more shocking than how Samantha found the prepper bunkers around the world so quickly. And certainly more curious than how she so easily manipulated the electronics in Masaquat. Samantha was translating and delivering the President's message in eleven languages without the hint of an English accent.

"The timing of our counterattack on our own infrastructure is yet to be determined. Please stand by for instructions. The aliens' ultimate objectives remain unknown.

"But who they are is becoming increasingly clear based on the limited intel provided by my old friend Ben Crowder. He has concluded the enemy was our onetime savior, the very company that orchestrated and delivered us from the great Uncommon Cold pandemics—Stellar Joule Corporation, and more specifically its relatively new subsidiary, Cerebellar Networks. It was a horrific ruse to lure us into accepting the brainlords movement. Those innocent 100,000 first subscribers became billions of 911 calls that could never be answered.

"What IS undeniable, is that they fuel themselves with human flesh. It is also clear to us now, the aliens have been among us for a very long time. Because of their longtime presence, as well as the fact they infected the world with a Trojan-like time bomb, and finally, because infected humans become cannibals—real-life TrojanZ, I'm going to now thank journalist Skylar Thompson for giving a name to the face of the enemy. In her first news release since the invasion, she calls the invaders the *TrojanZ*." The president spelled the word through her translator Samantha.

"Do not engage the *TrojanZ* until we are all ready. I am transmitting your local targets to you. We are also exploring ways to safely reach leaders in your countries. You may be asked to assist in their rescue."

The President waited a moment and composed her closing statement. "My friends, nations have fought each other for millennia. Countless bloody disputes lost in history. Wars whose origins are all but forgotten but for the ghostly vengeances still echoing centuries later. Generations of the dead men still whispering the same question, *why?*

"Historians inform us. Everything about war is ambiguous, except the origin of every war. War is always about resources.

Securing, controlling, or denying resources to others. Our war with the TrojanZ is about resources as well, but unlike any other war in human history. Human flesh is one of those resources.

"We are now allied by the sudden erasure of borders and differences of faith, and of opinion. All political disagreements were resolved yesterday for us by a mutual urgency called extinction.

"All nations were restored to a single family. Our many creeds were reduced to one. We fight as one. We survive as one.

"I will say once more. Yesterday, we awoke to a horrific discovery. Mankind was plunged into the ultimate resource war. And, we are that resource.

"We are the TrojanZ' food. Is there not a greater horror?"

President Claire Capehardt was the only child of two Baltimore shipyard steamfitters. Her dad had been a golden gloves heavy-weight champ at age 16. Her mom had skated roller derby semiprofessionally until Claire was ten. She was raised blue-collar, rough sawn, tough, and proud.

As a young woman she had left her longshore home and began navigating her personal wilderness called Harvard. It was a classic syllogism. A blue-collar girl surviving a blueblood world. In the end she had academically out-chessed the scads of natural born Ivy League line cutters and graduated law Magna Cum Laude.

In a blue-collar tradition, Claire Capehardt had been taught by her loving parents at an early age to cuss. They subscribed to the belief that only a very skilled swearer can use cuss words like cudgels to neutralize situations or shockingly make a point in an argument. Friend and foe alike agreed, Claire Capehardt was quite skilled verbally, ambidextrously blue, so to speak.

She had been elected to Congress in part for her straight talk which occasionally included selectively binding the coarse language of her youth to the rich language of her adult station. The result was measured shock BUT awe. The President of the United States had learned something else from her parents. They had taught her to never retreat from a righteous fight. *If you want to be the champ, Baby Girl, you must first whip the champ's ass.*

In the end she channeled her parents' colorful language and the pugnacious messaging of her youth over the clever diplomatic nuance of a president.

"Their goddamned food?" she shouted angrily. "Us? Well, I say to hell with that shit! I say we starve the fuckers out. Who's with me?"

The English speaking listeners around the world were first to gasp, then roar their approval. The bunker under the White House erupted in cheers and applause, but no one gasped there. All were professionally familiar with their president's articulate bilingualism of the King's English and American guttersnipe.

The overwhelmed speakers crackled even more loudly with static when Samantha's translations with all the vulgarity and intonation reached the rest of the nations. Ben Crowder clapped too. Embedded in the profanity was both a battle cry and a strategy. Starve the enemy.

7

The Masaquat Hotel's conference room just hours earlier had concealed the birthplace of a resistance movement with a fake birthday party. Now it became the work place of a former reporter of all the doings of the Supreme Court, along with the newly minted Supreme Court justice, a new AG, two former college professors who no longer need warn the world about the unintended perils of the brainlords scheme, and two federal agents.

Every computer and communications device in the hotel had been appropriated and was mysteriously networked and upgraded by Samantha. Everyone had long stopped asking questions about how Samantha accomplished such technical impossibilities.

Skylar Thompson had grown up in Indiana and like many Hoosier born journalists, she still followed the famous war correspondent Ernie Pyle. His reporting from the frontlines of WWII would guide her again. Now she would need more than his inspiration. She would need his courage. Her front line would be Ernie's in every sense and more.

Skylar was situated at the fork in the road. The metaphoric road signs sang: *Should I Stay or Should I Go?* Her hastily built workstation represented one of those forks. Skylar's eyes moved to the other fork, a stack of yellow pads, and a half dozen mismatched ink pens bound by a rubber band. She studied the computer screen for a moment, shook her head, and chose her future. She chose the one on war's front line. She collected the stack of yellow pads and pens and dropped them into the same leather satchel her parents had given her upon graduation decades ago.

Theodora Daughtry watched Skylar and realized what the reporter was about to do. "I have known Claire Capehardt for over a decade. She will know why you need to get out there."

As Skylar put on her coat and slung the satchel over her shoulder, Dora studied the headline of the article that President Capehardt had credited to Skylar. She pointed at the printout and said, "I think the name *TrojanZ* is perfect. I loved your article."

Aliens Cannibalize Earth

Trojan Malware Turns Humans into TrojanZ

By Skylar Thompson, White House Press Secretary
Sunday May 29, 2026 at 11:59 a.m. EDT

(TrojanZ War Dispatch) – Without warning a highly advanced alien lifeform has invaded Earth. While the alien's origins are unknown, their intentions are now certain. They have come to exterminate humanity. Beyond that is unknown.

Occupation and control of the United States occurred in just minutes.

Attempts by authorities in the U.S. to contact Canada, Mexico, or any other western hemisphere government have been unsuccessful. Europe, Asia, and Africa are also dark and silent.

The aliens targeted U.S. military forces and civilian police forces first. Both are presumed neutralized.

It is unknown if any nation survived the invasion.

Electrical grids, satellites, the Internet, and all land and cellular communications networks worldwide appear intact but are inaccessible. All networks are presumed now under alien control.

Authorities urge citizens to avoid use of electricity. Physical contact with or access to any communications networks or to the electrical grid infects users.

In related news, scientists in the U.S. whose identities and locations remain undisclosed, have discovered through regression analysis when the aliens likely arrived on Earth.

The January 1, 2022 event widely accepted to be an asteroid strike over the Arctic Ocean was in fact the moment the aliens arrived on Earth.

This reporter is in possession of evidence that proves the widely lauded Brainlords program was actually a scheme to infect humans with an organic Trojan malware.

When the malware activated, it gave the aliens absolute control of the infected brainlords, as well as any other humans who thereafter came in direct contact with any of the first 100,000 brainlords.

U.S. intelligence theorizes that the 100,000 number was required to ensure a blitz-like worldwide exponential spread of the organic malware.

It is estimated that the aliens neutralized human opposition in the U.S. in less than five minutes. All evidence suggests the rest of the world fared no better.

This office has seen strong evidence that the developer and distributor of the Trojan malware was Cerebellar Networks, the Stellar Joule subsidiary. It is now believed both companies were alien fronts for the enemy.

We have also learned that the aliens intentionally spread both Uncommon Cold pandemics. We have evidence that Stellar Joule authored both viruses.

Epidemiologists remain uncertain as to the reason the two most contagious and deadliest viruses ever encountered by humans disappeared so suddenly.

Authorities now believe genocide was the objective of the pandemics.

The origin of the term *TrojanZ* is derived from how the aliens attacked Earth with an organic sleeper malware, and by their widespread cannibalism that resembles fictional TrojanZ behavior.

This article has been translated into 26 languages and transmitted to all safe zones around Earth.

8

Candace Riggs, MD/PhD. The University of Massachusetts medical school professor stood before the window of her fourth floor office and watched a one-sided real life battle on the commons below. Hundreds of badly outnumbered people were trapped on the field fighting for their lives.

She recognized a large young man in a white coat standing in the center the Commons. A half dozen of his classmates surrounded him. His gestures to them were unmistakable. *Follow me.*

Dr. Riggs' hands came together as if in prayer and pressed to her face. *Mr. Cooper.*

The med student paused for a moment and debated the least dangerous path off the field. Aliens made the decision for him and attacked the group from behind. Five students were swept away, leaving only Cooper. He sprinted away from the TrojanZ. The med student weaved around dozens of attacks at various stages of capture and consumption.

His name was Cooper Halemier, a promising second year med student and former professional football player. He almost made it out of the Commons. As athletic, fit, and stout as Cooper was, he was no match for the petite blonde chasing him. Until just an hour ago, she had been Cooper's classmate. Her white coat and hair were crimson red. She ran the former NFL offensive lineman down from behind. Then effortlessly she lifted Cooper overhead and body slammed him viciously to the ground, stunning him. Ten aliens joined the kill and Cooper disappeared from view.

Dr. Riggs had witnessed this pattern of attacks dozens of times now. She knew Cooper was gone the moment he fell. By the time she stepped away from the window and returned to the open file cabinet drawer, the sweet farm boy, an Academic All-American native of Kansas was either an alien or feeding them.

The academic world had given Dr. Riggs an ironic nickname: *Dr. Doomsday*. Candace Riggs was not your typical doomsday prepper, though. She had no secret bunkers, or hidden caches of freeze-dried food and toilet paper, and she actually was an outspoken proponent of strict gun control. However, her scientifically supported theory of naturally recurring doomsdays was even more intensely held by Candace than any of Gordon Gordon's most doomy cohorts around the world.

Candace Riggs had a radical academic theory that began construction as a four-year-old subconsciously in a dreamland menagerie.

The scientist theorized anthropologically that *Homo sapiens* had survived numerous catastrophic collapses throughout its 550,000-year history. Her most radical claim was that certain humans are uniquely hardwired by evolution and genetics to protect the species from extinction. She compared these individuals to the T-cells of our immune system that seek and destroy harmful organisms.

Dr. Riggs was also a practicing psychiatrist. Every doctor can point to an event in their life when they first heard the field of medicine calling to them. That calling came for Candace Riggs when she was just twelve years old.

Her favorite uncle, Robert Riggs, a highly decorated veteran detective with the Massachusetts State Police was arrested for serial murder. To this day, Uncle Bob never stopped being her shining knight—a serial murdering golden knight. A killer that still dream-walked her up Mrs. Wolf's sidewalk twice a week for play dates with plants and animals at a chicken pox party.

Candace's Uncle Bob was also a man who never forgot a birthday or missed a dance recital. He never failed to lend a hand securing supplies for a science project, even when it was a citywide search consuming his entire day off. He greeted his niece with hugs and said farewell the same way. Uncle Bob turned tables into igloos for her on snow days. He slayed dragons at Candace's side, tamed the nice ones, and celebrated victories with dragon rides and tea parties. Uncle Bob was single and childless and ever so patient and kind. Candace was an only child, and his only niece and she was the light of his life.

Detective Riggs was also a man who ended his career in law enforcement quite contentedly with a confession. His confession to the FBI included executing an Irish mob hitman, two sadistic serial pedophiles, the father and daughter kingpins of a murderous drug cartel, a five-time black widow, a four state serial murderer, several sadistic serial rapists, and an 86-year-old arsonist whose crimes spanned five decades. It also included a corrupt judge who, when the price was right, put the most heinous career criminals back on the streets of Boston.

When Detective Riggs suggested to FBI investigators that they reconstruct his vacation and police business travels for the last 22 years, the investigators discovered similar purges and an identical *modus operandi* in New York City, Chicago, Dallas, Seattle, and a dozen other major cities around the country.

Detective Robert Riggs himself solved more than 160 homicides in one long day. He signed each confession with no more dread or regret than another person might experience when writing heartfelt notes on Christmas cards.

He never killed for money or out of revenge, and certainly not as a vigilante. In fact, he had never met any of his targets before their executions were *ordered.* He would never identify *who* ordered the executions though or *how* he was ordered to kill.

These men and women all had several things in common. They were all criminal psychopaths. In addition, they had all beaten the justice system through technicalities, extortion, contract perjury, bribery, misplaced evidence, incompetent prosecutions, fouled police procedures, jury tampering, disappeared witnesses, murder, and more.

Uncle Bob killed at night and quite mercifully all things considered. The kills followed the same pattern. A period of careful surveillance to make sure they would be alone on their last day. The rest happened quickly with a picked lock and then two silenced .44-caliber bullets to the head while they slept. He never took a trophy, but he did always show up when he returned to Boston with a treat or a gift for Candace.

Bad luck eventually caught up with Bob Riggs. A target's neighbor installed a surveillance camera just hours before Uncle Bob's last assassination. This high-quality video made for a short investigation and a quick arrest of a notorious serial killer.

Uncle Bob refused legal counsel and confessed to the executions without remorse. They diagnosed him with psychopathy. He was quickly convicted and committed to a mental institution for life.

He never attempted an escape from the hospital, but his need for justice remained free while institutionalized. He once saved a young nurse from a smuggled knife attack by what Bob called a *bad psychopath.* Uncle Bob intervened and quickly subdued the attacker, but then calmly drove the nurse's ink pen deep into the attacker's brain, killing him instantly. Bob's skilled first aid was credited for saving the nurse's life before she bled out.

His explanation as to why he killed so many people was this cryptic reply, "*We* have no choice in the matter. *We* follow orders. This is what *we* do."

Bob Riggs refused to meet with old friends, reporters, attorneys or any relative except Candace. Because his demeanor was so peaceful and affable, medications were deemed unnecessary. He remained in Candace's life through her regular visits and through the cards and letters they exchanged every week for the rest of his life. He lived quite peacefully and contently, and died quietly in his sleep from an arachnoid aneurism the day after Candace graduated from medical school.

Throughout both medical school and her psych residency at Boston General, Candace reread her Uncle Bob's 500-plus cards and letters many times. It was only in her third year of residency that she came to suspect that a small minority of psychopaths like her uncle might not be sick at all, but predictable, non-deviant, and evolutionary norms. This idea was radical. She theorized that some psychopaths actually defended humanity, especially during extinction events.

Years of clinical research later, Dr. Riggs published her radical theory in the prestigious *New England Journal Of Medicine* and the medical world huffed. In her paper, she boldly offered abundant anthropologic evidence—genetic, medical, evolutionary, social, and judicial—that psychopathy evolved genetically in two directions. One to save the world, the other to destroy it with the likes of Gacy, Bundy, and Hitler.

Dr. Riggs removed the last folder from the file cabinet and added it to the other 116 on her desk. Over the years, she had interviewed, examined and treated more than 3,500 patients around the world who she had diagnosed with advanced psychopathy. The individuals represented by these 116 files on her desk now lived in Boston. They were supported by another of her psychopathic patients, the billionaire Henderson Dentoncort. Her confidential diagnosis of Mr. Dentoncort and his 116 wards was *benevolent psychopathy*. These patients, her theory held, were genetically predisposed to protect mankind, not to harm it.

The Dentoncort patients were genetically different from not only other psychopaths, but from everyone else on the planet. A human gene previously dismissed by geneticists as junk DNA was not junk. She named it the WPP gene because it was virtually identical to the gene found in wolf DNA that causes wolf puppies to mutually bond so intensely with their packs.

Dr. Riggs discovered that only people with *benign* psychopathy possessed a potentially vital WPP gene. There were only a few of these psychopaths who's WPP gene had not mutated over the millennia causing violent insanity.

Those patients whose WPP gene had not defected by mutation, like Uncle Bobby and the Dentoncort pack, had no history of violence against the innocent. Though, most still demonstrated the emotional debilities and homicidal fantasies of other psychopaths.

Psychopaths like her uncle were the exception to the exceptions. He had none of those social or emotional debilities. He just naturally killed the bad people and protected the good.

Dr. Riggs spread the *Dentoncort* medical files across the desk. By now, alien invasion would have activated the entire good *psycho's* WPP genes. She did not have to imagine what these patients were doing right now. She knew, because she had treated them all and coached them all in preparation for the possibility of this very day.

These psychopaths' inner voices were giving them permission now to emerge, to reveal themselves, to slaughter their pack's enemies, and to be free. Mrs. Wolf's soothing wolf voice would introduce them to their pack, and that pack of humans would embrace them.

The chosen few were suddenly free. They were devoid of self-restraint or fear of discovery. This was a pack of deadly predators whose most delicious violent fantasies escaped imaginations and emerged now as an unquenchable need to protect humanity.

One patient was her favorite. She lifted file #13. It belonged to the purest, most perfect psychopath Dr. Riggs had ever studied. Her WPP gene remained as pristine as the moment it evolved 550 millennia ago. She was a natural leader, and an Alpha who always introduced herself as, *Hello, I'm Maggie Marie McMurtry of Mingham, Massachusetts.* Dr. Riggs opened the file and whispered, "Hello again, dear old dream friend."

What Dr. Riggs could not know was that elements of her *Dentoncort Army* were already on the move and on a rescue mission. Today, three local members of that good psycho pack would do much more than practice martial arts. A trio was already in Worcester and fighting their way around Lake Quinsigamond.

The threesome's objective was the medical school located on the west side of the lake. The woman and two men fought together as a single entity. They were whirling yesteryear Spartans born anew today. In their wake lie a mile-long corporeal carpet of their stilled Persians on new Thermopylae.

The wolf pack thought as one, and danced through the TrojanZ like choreographed Ninja gymnasts. They wielded archangels' steel, mercilessly, and glistening red. Alive at last and genetically fearless superhuman for the first time in their lives, they were a frolicking joyous juggernaut of death. Together they howled the unambiguous righteousness of the wolf's creed that they were reborn to sing.

From her fourth floor office window, Dr. Candace Riggs witnessed unimaginable carnage. She watched infected humans transform into their youth, then feast on the cornucopia of panicked humans who futilely scampered about in search of a safe place to hide. Perhaps there was no such place left on Earth. Candace Riggs accepted her own fate.

She knew there was no escaping the horror coming for her or the inevitability of committing one last act of defiance. Her office door was locked, but unbolting a nineteenth century six-panel door posed little challenge to an alien race that first opened doors to the universe nine billion years ago, 4.7 billion years before Earth was even a planet.

When the oaken door imploded into the office in pieces and splinters, Dr. Riggs was ready. Three TrojanZ entered as she rose from behind her desk and placed a syringe's needle on her carotid artery. It held a massively lethal dose of propofol. Enough that she would be dead before her body hit the floor.

The aliens approached the doctor, but did not immediately attack. Instead, they focused on the syringe. Their expressions were a mix of several emotions: disappointment and curiosity, and more. Dr. Candace Riggs also frightened them.

She jabbed the needle into her throat, but something caught her attention before pressing the syringe's plunger. A shadow scattered the light behind the TrojanZ. The air whooshed, like the wisp of candles blown out on a birthday cake. Next came the sounds of butchers cleaving bone and flesh when a sword, a machete, and a spear passed through three TrojanZ skulls from behind.

A curtain of TrojanZ thudded to the floor and behind it appeared three of Dr. Riggs' patients. They represented the first trio whom she had convinced years ago that they were genetic warriors in waiting—not hopelessly insane lifelong outcasts. She had set them on a secretive path of training ten years ago just in case this day ever came.

But you three are more than that to me, Candace gasped and dropped the syringe. *Girl in the red dress. Boy wearing Superman pajamas. Boy with the Batman backpack. My four year-old dream friends.* She hurried from behind her desk with open arms.

"Hello, Uncle Bobby's niece. We remember you too."

She smiled and stood perfectly still, then blurted, "The gorilla babies."

Red Dress screamed, "Oh my god. They are so adorable."

Superman Pajamas added, "They were the best ever last night."

"So good. I swear they just keep getting cuter," Backpack Boy added.

Candace admitted, "I just can't keep my hands off them."

The other three four-year-old adults exclaimed as one, "I can't either!"

The four recalled their shared dream world encounters for a few minutes. Candace was the first to realize the physical changes occurring in her. "Do you feel different?"

Red Dress looked at the boys. "It's our wolf. It's getting stronger."

What happened next was shocking and confirmed her wolf pack puppy (WPP) gene theory incontrovertibly. Another innate element of the wolf puppy gene emerged for the first time. Three of Boston's wolves rushed the physician and embraced her as one, all of them whimpering happily, rubbing their shoulders and chests against her body.

They nuzzled her breasts, kneaded them with their palms as if to bring them milk. They brushed their necks and cheeks over hers and each other's. They pressed their gaping mouths and teeth all over her head and face. They bit softly, but not enough to break her skin. Their kissing was canine. Candace's neck, face and ears were soon licked wet with saliva. The pups pried open her mouth and slobbered there too.

Candace resisted none of it. She couldn't. Even when they sniffed enthusiastically all over her body, which included her crotch, the alpha wolf in her let her puppies learn. The wolf pups paused only long enough for Dr. Riggs' to reward them. Their alpha wolf returned their every affection in kind.

Candace's affection was the genetic key that unlocked and completed their transition. They awoke together from it anachronistically more powerful in the world than ballistic missiles in King Arthur's court.

The woman and two men appeared suddenly confused, even embarrassed recalling their bizarre behavior moments earlier that seemed so natural, so right. Their expressions implored Candace to explain.

The doctor understood their confusion. She embraced the three again and said, "It's okay. Your true purpose has awakened inside you. You just became what you literally are, and I have never been more proud of you all. We now have much killing to do. Our larger pack awaits our protection."

Another beachhead was established in Worcester, Massachusetts.

9

Creating the Virtual Summit Site. Samantha composed the last few trillion lines of software code in a burst. Her body moved like a dancer's stuck in an extended finale. When finished, her hands and arms fell to her side and her body stilled. The sentient A.I. opened her eyes and returned to the vast computer room. Her conscious connection to thousands of massively entangled quantum core processors disengaged dreamlike.

She nodded to herself and smiled. The site of the virtual summit was ready for four human travelers and hopefully one viral ambassador. When the application launched, Ben and Samantha as well as Doctors Aranovich and Vonbergen could enter a never before imagined virtual world. It was an artificial construct created inside the entangled quantum core network. If her program worked, they would literally meet and communicate with a theoretical ally—rhinovirus. The goal was an interspecies treaty. Two former ancient enemies allied—human and rhinovirus against one common enemy—the TrojanZ.

Samantha entered the adjacent breakroom and sat down on the couch close to Ben. He appeared to be sleeping, but Samantha knew he was not. Ben had gone somewhere too. He was smiling broadly. His lips moved from time to time as he conversed with dream people. She wrapped her arm over his shoulder and felt him tactilely once again. Samantha studied Ben affectionately for a moment, then kissed his cheek.

Sami did not know where he had gone this time, only that Ben Crowder's imagination could carry him anywhere near or far from the great bunker. His jaunts were routine, vivid, imaginary journeys to wondrous times and places in history where he stood with his many giants.

Unlike normal people, Ben Crowder's eidetic memory and vivid imagination were not bound by an underground bunker's concrete walls or sleep or naturally fragmented and eroding knowledge, or by his lifelong self-imposed isolation from people in the poisonous outside world. He took excursions somewhere every day, like others jogged or did aerobics.

More, he could share his experiences, and Samantha was always welcome to join him. Samantha placed her hand on Ben's temple and linked into a series of exciting adventures into history…

Ben greeted her, "Oh Sami, look!"

Ben and Samantha stood alongside cheering Viking explorers on the bow of a wooden ship and watched the mountain peaks of Newfoundland appear on the horizon…

They hovered over a microscope with Jonas Salk and together witnessed polio begin its long retreat...

They stood in a sea of tears and hope in Washington D.C. and witnessed Dr. Martin Luther King Jr. share his dream that began freeing little children black and white…

They watched Steve Jobs' mother lean into the family's garage and announce to her son and Apple Computer's other cofounders Steve Wozniak and Ron Wayne, "Boys, it's lunch time!"...

Ben and Samantha giggled and took each other's hands as gravity drained from their bodies. They floated weightlessly next to Soviet cosmonaut Yuri Gorgerin when he left home and became Earth's first ambassador to the universe…

Then one last scene…Japan's ambassador descends the front steps of the U.S. State Department on December 6, 1941.

Samantha waited patiently for Ben to finish their dozens of three-second dreams that each seemed like hours-long journeys in dreamland. They returned to the great bunker together. Ben opened his eyes and smiled back at Samantha. Normally, they would have regaled each other for hours about this and earlier journeys, but not today. Instead he asked, "Were we successful? Do we have a summit site?"

"We were. I effectively created the virtual shell as well as building blocks of a common language. As you theorized, I was able to reverse-engineer every mutative, symbiotic permutation of both rhinovirus' and *Homo sapiens* DNA over the last 550,000 years.

"To make the experience more realistic, I also created avatars for the four of us as well as a blank avatar for the Rhino ambassador, that is, if it manifests. I do not know how many viral permutations might appear at the summit. I estimate that as many as 2,977,412-quintillion potential viral mutations are possible. The vast majority of variants obviously never happened. Rhino's actual genetic lineage will eventually sort out, sequence, and appear at the summit as a contiguous chain that regresses over time. The dots will all connect so to speak.

"The next part was tricky. If things go to plan, the program will eventually merge the tens of trillions of Rhino's actual viral ancestors—our historical rhino friends and foes—into an aggregated single avatar. It is our objective to speak to that artificially created ambassador.

"Perpendicular to that chain will appear *Homo sapiens* historical evolution as effected by the virus, as well as our species' worldwide census as it rose and fell. We know Rhino today as nothing more than an annoying head cold. Its ancestors though were responsible for at least three near extinctions of humanity. Fortunately, rational symbiosis at the genetic level saved us both. Our extinction would have meant their own demise. Détente occurred instead just 20,000 years ago.

"Obviously, the ultimate viral ambassador is a compilation of genetic history, not an individual virus. At first, communication with it will be at best difficult, at worst impossible. The language I created is synthetic and built from an ultra-colossal collation of common genetic history. From that I developed a unified alphabet based upon the faint differential radio frequencies as measured in zettahertz that our vibrating genes emit. Clearly, until we can learn a conjoining language, discussions will be virtually impossible."

"Amazing Samantha. However, I know you. You are also leaving the worst for last."

"Yes, I need to warn you, Ben. I have taken every precaution but attending the summit poses potential risks for humans."

"Please explain."

"Ben, my love, even though the summit will be virtual, the risks remain as real as if we were all face to face. Direct physical contact must be avoided. While the Supreme Ambassador will be an artificially distilled condensate of rhino's long history, and while we will exist as virtual avatars at the summit, the rhino entity will remain as contagious as ever. Any physical contact with the ambassador could be deadly. Even virtual contact would likely infect a human with every Rhino infection in history."

"No problem. I'll wear a jacket and order in chicken soup by the gallon," joked Ben.

Samantha's entire body expressed her anger. She screamed, "BEN! This is serious."

Ben was stunned. Not once in her life had Sami ever yelled at him in anger. "Uh…I'm sorry, Sami. I'm just saying, the stakes we face make that personal risk acceptable." Ben then tried unsuccessfully to change the subject. "Are Drs. Aranovich and Vonbergen ready?"

Samantha did not answer. She was still furious with his cavalier attitude, but more, she was clearly frightened for more than him.

Ben took her hands in his. He already hated himself for upsetting her. "I'm truly sorry Sami…"

Samantha interrupted him, "What would happen to me, Ben, if something ever happened to you? We've… I've never…"

Shame landed on Ben like a truck from the sky. He suddenly understood. She wasn't angry. Samantha was terrified. If something happened to Ben, Samantha would experience the same loneliness he would suffer if humanity died off in a mass extinction. The bunker was her world. He was her humanity and her only access to the greater world. After he died, she would be alone trapped in an underground bunker for thousands of years until an executioner called *Time* mercifully collapsed her prison cell on top of her.

"We won't let that happen, Sami. I'll be careful. I will listen to you and will abandon the summit at the first sign of trouble."

"Promise?"

Ben responded, "With all my heart and all my love, I promise you." They held each other for a moment in silence. His shame and her fears drained away. They kissed and Samantha broke the silence.

She finally answered his question, "Yes, Bubble Boy. The professors are ready and standing by. Their avatars are networked with our own. We will enter the virtual summit together."

Samantha waved her hand and opened the connection to the Masaquat Hotel. "Professors, are you ready?"

Aranovich and Vonbergen both replied, "Yes."

Ben exclaimed, "Excellent! Samantha has modified and upgraded your headphones. When she instructs you to do so, unplug them for ten seconds, then activate them by reconnecting to the stereo jack splitter connected to the computer. Then close your eyes and do not open them again until she instructs you. Questions?"

Dr. Aranovich spoke first, "About a million, but I expect I'll soon be answering a few myself. I am honored to be a part of this."

Dr. Vonbergen's answer was more succinct, "Ditto. Let's do this thing."

Samantha waited until Ben gave a thumbs up to start the countdown. She returned the gesture and started, "Five… four… three… two… one… Activating quantum entanglement." Samantha waved her hand and the Masaquat's hotel conference room and the Lil' Cheyenne Mountain's bunker disappeared around the travelers in a bright flash of light.

A moment passed and Samantha said, "Please, everyone now open your eyes."

The foursome emerged together standing inside a bubble-like dome filled with dim light. Inside the capsule, an ankle-high cottony cloud undulated around their feet. The light beyond the capsule ended as abruptly as if they were surrounded by an event horizon.

Ben clapped his hands, "We did it Sami! We're in the core. Ready to take it to the next level?"

"Yes, here goes. It will take a while to boot up the next phase." Samantha started then hesitated. She looked at Ben and gestured to Aranovich and Vonbergen, who were right now studying their limbs and appendages in awe, as if seeing them for the first time. Her expression directed at Ben was unambiguous. She wished to reveal her true identity to the professors, just in case.

Ben empathized with her feelings this time and nodded enthusiastically. His expression said, *Of course. It's time.* However, her confession was unnecessary. The two scientists had already turned their attention to the author of this miracle—Samantha.

They had witnessed far too many impossibilities today to accept any conclusion other than Samantha's true identity. She was a sentient A.I. The two scientists had already privately postulated the possibility that Samantha was not simply impersonating humanity. She was perhaps the next iteration of *Homo sapiens*.

Aranovich smiled and waved off Samantha's big reveal. He said, "Unnecessary, dear lady. As far as we are concerned, you are nothing less than an extremely intelligent and lovely young woman, Samantha, and Ben is a most fortunate young man to have you."

Vonbergen added, "You make a beautiful couple. When this is all over, we hope to be invited to your virtual wedding."

Ben and Sami took each other's hands and thanked the professors, then hugged. Sami whispered to Ben, "That's our first two RSVPs, Ben."

It was Dr. Vonbergen who interrupted the joyous moment. Squinting and leaning forward, he pointed to activity outside the capsule. "Something is happening out there. Look!"

Everyone turned and saw it. A tiny barely visible red dot punctuated the onyx universe. Its distance from the bubble was indeterminate.

Aranovich asked, "That is not just a single viral permutation, is it Samantha?"

"No professor, I believe it is not. It is tens of billions of permutations that are very far away now. Think of how a distant galaxy appears in the night sky as a single star."

A second galaxy appeared. Then a third. Then so many it was impossible to count. As the minutes passed, the vast pitch-black world beyond the capsule turned steadily red with rhinovirus' historical genetic what ifs. The metaphoric galaxy of viral permutations converged on the capsule from every direction. Trillions of trillions of stars bombarded the bubble. The walls of the capsule thundered louder and louder as the synthetic storm raged and built exponentially around it.

Even Ben could not hide his growing concern as the thunderous pounding ascended into a deafening screech of metal shredding. The two scientists looked to Samantha for assurance and she gave it calmly, almost motherly.

"We're okay, guys. Unlike a submarine, our vessel walls actually strengthen as pressure increases. We are perfectly safe in here." She waited until everyone's attention returned to the ever-reddening and violent world beyond the capsule. She added, "It is almost over, just a few more minutes. Phase one is nearly complete."

Those few minutes were increasingly more deafening. It sounded as if a mountain had collapsed on top of them. Avalanche after avalanche of boulders ricocheted and rumbled over the capsule while a million sirens wailed as one.

As Samantha promised, the capsule's integrity held and the bombardment ended. The only sound now was a chorus of soft electric humming that sang together but in many chords. The red storm stilled, then settled down like a wild colt finally accepting the rope and trainer for the first time.

Samantha announced, "They are all here. Every possible viral permutation of rhinovirus in history. So, let's get the party started." She turned to the professors, then to Ben. Her suggestion was obvious to Ben. *Maybe we should warn the professors?*

Ben nodded. He turned to the professors, "Gentlemen, you are about to witness the coolest programmer ever." He winked at Sami and added, "Go for it, girlfriend!"

Samantha tapped her thumbs and index fingers together three times. The capsule suddenly tripled in size. Outside the deep red viral world, now calm, yielded without resistance. The men instinctively moved to the edges of the capsule to give the A.I. room to operate. Samantha prepared to write the next critical software routine that would sort out Rhino's genetic dead ends. She closed her eyes and lowered her head. She now stood motionless, appearing much like an Olympic high diver mentally rehearsing a difficult dive.

Several seconds passed. She then opened her eyes, lifted her head and moved her feet close together. Her arms rose over her head as she lifted onto her tiptoes. A forward double-somersault wrote the first 8,200 lines of new code. Every part of her body moved independently from each other. Her complex physical moves co-wrote with her mind trillions of new lines of code to thousands of quantum cores. The dome sang out sympathetically. A multi-percussive rhythm filled the capsule louder and louder marking her progress. The men's chins bobbed unconsciously to the beat of the music. All soon smiled and even applauded her moves.

At times she appeared to be communicating in sign language, though her hands moved so rapidly they were unintelligible blurs. At other times she moved like a ballerina in a series of impossibly extended pirouettes and pliés. Then she was a modern dancer expressing her poetry in a universal language. Next, she resembled a pretzel of a blurry break-dancer, a martial artist, and then a gymnast moving from one apparatus to the next. Every part of her body, every facial expression and gesture contributed code. She ended the program appearing to be the most frenetic musician of all time. As she finished, her arms and hands fell slowly to her sides. The percussive cacophony retired steadily into a pleasant songlike arrangement of multiple complimentary pitches and rhythms.

Samantha looked at Ben and shrugged. She said as the applause settled, "Well, I guess that's it."

Ben walked over to Samantha and took her hand. "It's up to Rhino now, Sami. The ball is in the virus' court. We've done all we can do for now."

Ben studied Sami for a moment and realized it was her turn to feel concern and self-doubt. He suggested that Samantha explain to the scientists what she just wrote.

"Simply put, I wrote a multistep ordinal program. The first step will factor out the *possible* viral mutations from Rhino's *actual* genetic mutations. The second step will sequence each mutation historically from first to last. As the false genetic permutations disappear, we should start to see a contiguous green line approach us. It will represent a continuum of 550 millennia of Rhino's true evolution. This is when it will get really interesting and scary real fast.

"Blue lines will eventually appear perpendicular to the green line. These represent human worldwide population in 1,000 year increments. Three blue lines will be barely visible. Those lines represent how close Rhinovirus ancestors came to killing off *Homo sapiens*—and therefore itself. Our die-off came within approximately 2,500 humans each time before Rhino mutated and saved us both."

Dr. Aranovich asked Samantha, "Did Rhino recently save us again? Actually twice?"

"Yes! We believe so, Sergey. We now know that the Uncommon Cold pandemics were biological attacks committed by the TrojanZ. Their objective was to use an efficient weapon, a deadly bioengineered virus to exterminate potential resistance to their conquest of Earth. We theorize rhinovirus fought them to a draw twice."

Dr. Vonbergen said, "I believe it is substantiated now. I have always hoped for this alliance, and now I can believe in it." The Nobel Laureate hesitated and asked, "What was it Al Pacino said in the movie *Scarface*? 'Meet my little friend!'"

Samantha was the last to laugh, but she laughed the hardest. It took her 1.2 seconds to watch the entire movie. "Indeed. The TrojanZ met our little Rhino friend."

For the next ten minutes the four travelers stared in silence into a viscous, slithery universe that appeared to be filled with coagulated blood. Ben was the first to notice activity. "Sami! I think it's starting. Look over here. There's some movement. The permutations are factoring out."

They all saw it. A tiny whirlpool that looked much like water draining from a sink. When the movement ended abruptly, the spot was left a lighter color of red. Another whirlpool appeared near the first. Then four. Fifty more drains opened in the blink of an eye. In less than a minute too many opened to count, so many whirlpools that the drains encroached and merged into larger drains and formed even more ferocious tornadic whirlpools. The dark red universe faded steadily as Samantha's software factored out Rhino's viral permutations that represented its genetic dead ends. The entire universe beyond the capsule now appeared to be a single whirlpool. Specs of black began to appear as the viral dead enders disappeared. In just seconds the entire universe returned to a pitch-black void.

Samantha stepped closer to the capsule wall and studied the darkness. The men joined her. After a full minute of silence Samantha announced, "There you are." She pointed toward a faint green dot in the distance that had somehow survived the great drain.

The A.I. then performed a series of hand and arm gestures that ended with the universal hand signal for *time out*. She had written a truce program. Her arms then crossed over her chest. The men followed her lead and did the same. The connotation was unambiguous. *Please come in peace*.

The green dot accepted the invitation and exploded toward the capsule. In its wake an unbroken green line soared behind it. The continuum ended just outside the capsule. After a minute the line started to pulse. It rippled up and down awkwardly at first, and stumbled like a puppy negotiating with gravity for the first time.

Ben whispered encouragement, "You can do it. You are almost there, Rhino."

Samantha was the first to detect the connection, "It has it. Listen."

It was faint, but just beneath the capsule's singing a second sympathetic beat emerged. It was a new voice that quickly strengthened, diverged, and deferentially complimented tonally with the dome's. Soon it was no longer merely imitative and following, but also composing the next riff. The exchanges between Rhino's and *Homo sapiens'* artificial constructs sounded unmistakably like the exchanges passed back and forth between jazz musicians.

Ben was first to describe the significance. "Variable rhythms. We are speaking to Rhino. We now have the basis of a common language, Sami. We just need to figure out what it is saying."

Samantha tested the theory and drew a circle on the capsule wall with her index finger. The capsule's rhythmic hum changed slightly. The green line cautiously advanced the last few feet to the capsule and touched it. Rhino then repeated Samantha's message.

Dr. Aranovich was the first to raise his fists and cheer. He was still cheering when the other travelers had stopped. As advanced and provocative as his life's work was, it paled pathetically compared to actually speaking to Rhino.

Samantha placed her left hand on the capsule wall, then touched each man with her right. She then collapsed to the floor.

Rhino understood the command: Show humanity's population collapses. Hundreds of blue lines emerged perpendicular to the green line. Each was a representation of human population on the continuum. The lines flashed on and off several times, then disappeared. Three tiny lines remained illuminated. The closest was barely visible, it was so short.

Dr. Vonbergen pointed to it and asked, "Is this the inflection point, Sergey, when the détente between species occurred?"

Dr. Aranovich answered, "Yes, I believe it is. The survival imperative forced both species to symbiotically cooperate from that point forward. We accepted their oft bothersome presence in our bodies from time to time and Rhino traded rent by training our lymphatic system to survive countless other deadly infections. Overall, it has been a mutually beneficial partnership."

Ben speculated, "I suspect we are about to appreciate that partnership in a new light."

Samantha agreed, "Yes. The only logical conclusion as to how we survived the Uncommon Cold pandemics is that Rhino must have intervened on our mutual behalf. Let's find out for sure."

Samantha placed her forehead against the dome, spread her arms far apart, and then closed her eyes. She then stepped backward and slowly moved her outstretched arms together until her hands touched. A second small bubble suddenly appeared outside. Her next command was unambiguous. She turned her body perpendicular to the dome. Still looking directly at the gently pulsing long green line, Samantha bowed slightly and with her right hand made a sweeping gesture like a doorman welcoming a familiar visitor to enter.

Rhino immediately accepted the invitation. The green line poured into the new dome. Several minutes passed as it wrapped itself upon itself around the interior walls. A veneer of a million layers atop a million more. When the last of the long green line entered, Samantha issued a command with a flick of her wrist and the entire formation began to spin. Slowly at first, but soon it spun so fast Rhino appeared as a motionless, single mass.

Samantha issued the final command which looked like she was fist bumping herself. The virus' dome expanded, and then the humans' followed. The green mass inside the second dome exploded apart and literally pixilated into trillions of churning bits. The pieces stopped and brushed each other briefly as they passed other bits, resembling how ants and termites communicate instructions to each other when their bodies touch. The bubble began filling with the same cottony cloud around the human's feet and soon obscured the transition.

Ben had theorized and predicted the process. "It will take a few minutes. Sami's program will assemble the Rhino's ambassador into an avatar."

The bubble became increasingly transparent as the cottony cloud settled to the bottom of the dome. There was no ambassador.

Samantha was not confused but the professors were greatly. They turned to Ben and relaxed when they saw him smiling. He pointed at the dome and said, "Wait for it. Wait for it. And…there you are!"

As the cloud settled lower, the avatar materialized and sat up in the dome. Much of its body was still concealed by the settling cloud, but it was obvious the ambassador was a large male. A warrior metaphor representing the two Uncommon Cold wars in which Rhino had defeated the TrojanZ, and saved humanity from extinction, though, apparently at great cost to itself.

The avatar's head and chest wounds were extensive and at various stages of healing. He struggled to his feet. It was nude except for an armored skirt covering his loin. In his right hand was a sword, in the left a shield. His legs were similarly wounded. The avatar met eyes first with Samantha, then Ben, and then the professors. With each contact the Rhino ambassador lowered his head for a moment, then crossed his heart with the sword and proffered his shield. The human contingent mirrored the peaceful gestures each time.

Samantha bowed to the ambassador then pressed her hands together as if in prayer. She then touched her finger tips to her lips, turned her hand toward the ambassador and spread her fingers wide. He nodded then mimicked the gesture. He wished to speak too.

Both professors looked at Ben for an explanation. Ben clarified, "Sami is going to attempt creating an original common language so we can speak directly to each other naturally. It will take a while. I'm sure you have many questions, Professors."

Dr. Vonbergen shook his head in amazement. "How can this be possible? A virus barely qualifies as life."

Dr. Aranovich offered an explanation. "Yes, of course you are correct, Doctor. However, we are not talking about a single virus. Dear Samantha has networked a trillion-trillion-trillion individual rhinoviruses' DNA into a single compiled entity that now resides inside a virtual reality."

Vonbergen exclaimed, "Oh, of course. The sum of all rhinoviruses together is greater than its parts, and that sum is sentient."

"I believe so. A single human cell lacks sentience. Trillions connected and organically networked make human sentience possible."

While the professors discussed the myriad of scientific mysteries that might now be solved, Ben and Samantha used music to write a common language. No matter how fast they proceeded, Rhino's expression implored them to go faster. It took over 12,000 pings to create one spoken word.

Rhino tapped his chest over and over and said, "Help."

Just as the Rosetta Stone unlocked ancient hieroglyphic Egypt, the word *help* launched a new understanding of language itself. A language even more cryptic than cartouche. An hour later the Rhino ambassador was not only speaking thousands of words but could provide definitions of each. Two hours later negotiations between two falling species began.

Rhino's opening statement shocked the human representatives to their cores. The ambassador even stunned Samantha.

"While Rhinovirus successfully overwhelmed and defeated the TrojanZ' viruses in the first seven attacks on our two home worlds, the last two attacks, those that you call the Uncommon Cold pandemics, have left my world devastated. We are too weak to launch another counterattack on the invaders.

"I am here beseeching an expanded alliance with you, a radical new symbiosis with *Homo sapiens*. Our collective survival is once again at stake. The Rhino world cannot survive another attack. As a result neither can the human world. If Rhino falls, *Homo sapiens'* entire microbial symbiosis will collapse like dominoes. Everything from your digestion to nerve function will fail. Your immune system will not respond properly. We must work together again, or we will both fall this time."

Ben understood, but he had questions, "Ambassador, you are talking about launching a two-front counterattack, are you not?"

"I am."

"We were unaware of the TrojanZ seven previous attacks. Are you suggesting another Uncommon Cold attack?"

"Yes, a tenth and final attack on our worlds is imminent."

"But why? Are you suggesting humans are not their primary target?"

"Primary? Yes. *Homo sapiens* represents unique resistance. Your opposition confuses them. But Rhino and Human are, what's the word? Speed bumps. We are inconveniences. We have learned during years of hand-to-hand combat with the TrojanZ viruses what they really are. They eat worlds. They atomize worlds into elements, then absorb them. They consider organic life distasteful, a pollutant. The rest of all Life on Earth is considered spoilage.

Ben asked, “Ambassador Rhino, I’m sensing you have a defense proposal.”

“We do, Dr. Crowder. It is radical and will require you to trust an ancient enemy, thoroughly and permanently.”

“Please explain.”

“We gained tremendous insight into the enemy’s weaponry during the viral wars. One of those discoveries is their ability to infect humans asymptomatically then take control of the hosts’ trillions of defenseless microbial allies. Millions humans died in your world this way until the Rhino forces intervened and forced the TrojanZ to retreat.”

Dr. Aranovich was the first to suspect where the ambassador was going. “Excuse me. Are you suggesting you have lifted some TrojanZ technology that we can use against them?”

The Rhino ambassador smiled and said, “Yes, I am. With human help we can kill them with their own infection.”

Dr. Vonbergen asked, “And that cooperation would be exactly what, Ambassador?”

“Quite simply, a permanent alliance. One that bypasses the upper respiratory symptoms imposed after our last genetic treaty. Thanks to the TrojanZ, Rhino can now live and evolve within humans permanently, peacefully, and never do you any harm. Just like your friendly microbes in your guts. More, we could even now help defend you from other diseases.

Dr. Aranovich spoke next. “Ambassador, you are proposing your species’ abandonment of infection as your primary form of propagation.

“Yes. The alliance would occur at the DNA level. We would join your code.”

Vonbergen said, “And that is how you plan to kill TrojanZ. Their seven worldwide attacks had an unintended consequence. You are a virus too. You appropriated their toxicity genetically,

I'm guessing during the seventh attack. Just as a king cobra's venom is deadly to other king cobras, their own toxicity is deadly to themselves."

"Yes and yes. We appropriated that deadly gene in the seventh attack. They are not aware we have the code. More, they are unaware we are immune to it, or soon hopefully that *homo sapiens* will be immune as well."

"How does it kill them?"

"Every virus is controlled electronically by a single nanite that communicates with a central hub. We can now disrupt the signal exchanges between the hub and its nodes making the virus inert. Effectively, killing it."

"Essentially, it is a neurotoxin. How do we infect them?"

Samantha spoke for the first time. "In every ointment there is a fly. We poison their food—humans. They will discover that eating human flesh is deadly."

Ben Crowder had remained unusually quiet. It was not because he was a 'slow reader' as they say, but because suspicion turns people like Ben into speed readers who anticipate alternate endings. Something was wrong. *1941. The Japanese ambassador?* This was all too perfect. Everything he and Sami had planned happened without a bug. Perfect programming occurs as often as cows jump over the moon. The TrojanZ handing over their Kryptonite this easy? No way. Ben had finished this horror novel, and saw the Rhino/TrojanZ twist coming before anyone else even turned the first page. In it Rhino won the battle. Pushed the TrojanZ back with its last resources.

Survival imperatives change alliances. Rhino was another Trojan horse. It had switched sides to save itself.

Ben decided to rewrite the twist. Humanity must not bond genetically with Rhino, as the Rhino avatar proposed. Secondly, this virtual reality was not as impermeable as Samantha had hoped. The theoretical physicist knew reality and virtual reality are no less part of the same unified reality as the shared reality that quantum mechanics and apple pie occupies. He regretted not understanding this sooner, but more, how much he was about to hurt Sami.

Ben stepped forward and said to Samantha, "I am so sorry, Sami. I know I promised you, but…" Then he plunged his arm through the bubble into the Rhino ambassador's. He opened his hand to shake the ambassador's. Before Samantha could pull him out, the ambassador grabbed Ben Crowder's hand and yanked Ben viciously inside his capsule. Samantha and the scientists watched in horror as Rhino lifted Ben overhead by the throat. The ambassador then spit in Ben's face, and with his other hand rubbed his hand roughly over Ben's face.

Satisfied that Ben was thoroughly infected with the Trojan virus, the ambassador howled his delight. The subterfuge had worked. He threw Ben back through the capsules as if the scientist was no more than a disappointing fish returned to its pond. Ben's body crashed into Drs. Aranovich and Vonbergen, knocking both men down like bowling pins, and in the process, infected them both with the Trojan virus. When Aranovich and Vonbergen left this virtual reality, they would return to their own world as TrojanZ.

Ben was a man born without an immune system, and he had intentionally infected himself with a fatal disease—every common cold in history now attacked his body. The deadly infection was instantaneous. Ben collapsed into Samantha's arms. She twisted her fist and desperately terminated the summit. When she opened her eyes, she was still holding Ben, and they were back in the bunker. "Why…why…why…?" she cried over and over as fever burned away his life.

Ben struggled to speak. His last words were cryptic, He whispered, "For us, Sami." Dr. Ben Crowder became the first casualty on Earth's fifth beachhead.

Sergey Aranovich and Rhine Vonbergen returned to the Masaquat Hotel conference room. The two men looked at each other in growing terror as they realized what the strange electric shock rippling through their bodies meant. Every strand of DNA within them was rewriting and surrendering to a new passenger.

Not Rhino. Not an ally. They had returned to reality with the TrojanZ in control.

Horrified by both the knowledge that the summit had been a trick and the fact they knew their lives were almost over, the scientists collapsed to the floor. TrojanZ reality streamed into their consciousness. They would never… *again experience pain or suffer disease. All knowledge is hive knowledge. It will arrive without requisite questions. Obey. Consume human flesh. We are running out of time to atomize this planet and neutralize its contaminants. Alpha commands you now.*

They arrived with a foot in both worlds—human and TrojanZ. They realized now that Ben Crowder had figured it out, and he had sacrificed himself. He died so they would know and share what Crowder had discovered in the last moments of his life: the truth. Rhino won 9th battle—the *Second Uncommon Cold pandemic*—but it could not win a 10th. The rhinovirus switched sides.

The scientists awoke to a ravenous hunger in the conference room. Their transition to fully TrojanZ had perfected itself now through the virtual infection. None of the hideous macabre of gnashing teeth and bloody vomitus. Like those first people body-snatched previously by the TrojanZ, they both became young men again.

The youthful former humans sprang to their feet and were greeted by ten heavily armed people who had witnessed it all, from the moment the scientists entered the virtual world until they returned. It seemed to the scientists that they had been gone for many hours. In truth, the entire journey had lasted only fifteen seconds.

Aranovich raised his arms over his head and said, "Dr. Crowder figured it out, but it was too late. The summit was a trap and a double-cross."

Vonbergen screamed, "We have less than a minute to brief you on what they have planned. You must kill us before we transition fully. Use head shots, then burn our bodies. If you do not, anyone within a mile of us will be infected. Then nothing can stop them from spreading around the world."

Sergey exclaimed, "You must not hesitate!" He pointed at the FBI and CIA agents.

Easton DeSmet and Napoleon Passerelle lived in a world where accounts of such heroic sacrifice were not myths. One comrade dove on a grenade to save five. Jim Doolittle's bomber squadron flew a one-way WWII mission over Tokyo. A Secret Service agent jumped between Ronald Reagan and the assassin's bullet. These scientists would belong with this group.

Justice Daughtry had noted the deadline ultimatum and announced, "We have fifty seconds, guys!"

Like Eric Northman in Terre Haute, Indiana, the scientists had seen the TrojanZ' ultimate plan, and they shared all they could in the next fifty seconds. The three most important parts were emphasized: First, Elemental Earth was the TrojanZ prize. Next, time was running out for the TrojanZ. Finally, the aliens feared the discovery of their exit plan.

The news that Ben Crowder's Little Cheyenne Mountain might now be compromised was taken hardest at the Masaquat. Contact with Samantha was potentially another trap. They must proceed with extreme caution.

Dora was saved from having to perform the dreadful task of calling out a countdown to execution. As the deadline approached, the scientists grabbed each other's hands, closed their eyes and touched their foreheads which meant *now*.

A split-second later, Easton and Leo pulled their triggers.

PART 3—Five Counterattacks

1

Terre Haute, Indiana. Jack Caldwell stood on the highest enclosed parapet on the prison grounds. The foray for weapons had been successful. Both the Indiana State Police post and the National Guard armory had been a treasure trove of weaponry. It had taken four missions with everyone working together to transfer everything from the Guard armory to the prison. Which was already no longer called a prison, but the newly nicknamed *Fort Big Wolf.*

Along the way they neutralized hundreds of TrojanZ. Many were new, others too disabled to even crawl. Others were impaled on wrought iron fences or trapped under crashed vehicles. The raiders also collected twenty citizens who had hidden and hunkered down during the attack. One of those rescued was a retired Indiana State University Communications professor. His name was Ervin Owens, and he and his wife Esther were ham radio aficionados.

Jack watched Professor Owens finish installing the antenna and connect it to his ham set. Esther was ironically the better communicator of the two. She also was the most knowledgeable ham radio operator.

"His call name is G2, and he's famous in the ham world. Sort of a doomsday prepper celebrity."

Jack asked, "What does 'Dark Skies' mean?"

"According to ham radio lore, 'Dark Skies' means 'End of the World.' I have listened to doomsday believers speculate about the declaration hundreds of times, but in over forty years of ham hobby, it's never been declared once. Not after 9-11. Not even during Covid-19 or the other pandemics."

"This operator G2 has declared it. After what we've seen here in western Indiana, I have to agree. Where is G2 located?"

"Masaquat, Virginia."

"How close is Masaquat to Washington D.C.?" Jack's concern was two-fold. *Had the capitol fallen and was Skyler safe?*

Fifteen people were crowded together inside the high guardhouse listening. The Wraith Rider bikers Nils, Blotup, Grunt, and Fuzz stood behind Maggie. The *wolf puppy* occasionally leaned against the men and brushed her shoulders and cheeks against them. She glanced up at them adoringly from time to time and pressed her teeth on their limbs. The act was so natural now no one thought her behavior unusual. Everyone in *Ft. Big Wolf* was *appreciated* similarly by Maggie as she raced around the camp or napped at their feet.

Soccer Mom had replaced her spear with the automatic rifle slung over her shoulder. Like most everyone else, except the Wraith Riders and Maggie, she had changed into an Army camo uniform at the National Guard Base. "I suggest we try contacting this G2, Jack. Just the fact that ham radio frequencies are still up is valuable intel."

Seth was similarly armed and dressed. "I agree with Soccer Mom, Jack. Maybe someone else got lucky and survived this shit show for now. There are probably people hiding everywhere. We found twenty ourselves, and we were not even looking for them yet."

Jack turned to his third lieutenant Officer C. Hubbard and asked, "Hubbs, where do you stand?"

"I'm with Soccer and Seth, Jack. Let's reach out. If this G2 fellow is still there when we call him, it might mean the aliens can't see or hear the ham signals. No crime is ever committed perfectly. Something always gets missed. Let's hope it is ham radio."

Jack said, "Okay. Mrs. Owens, let's introduce ourselves to G2."

Esther powered up the ham radio and set the frequency to G2's. She lifted the microphone and spoke, "CQ! CQ! Come in G2 Masaquat. This is SB the Sycamore Bird for G2. Over…

"…SB in Terre Haute, Indiana. CQ G2! Come in G2! Over." Esther waited then added. "'Dark Skies' acknowledged here. The sky has fallen! Repeat! Sky has fallen! We have intel. Must share. Come in Masaquat! Over." Esther repeated the message for five minutes without a reply.

Masaquat Hotel. Gordon Gordon did not reply immediately because SB the Sycamore Bird was not part of his Doomsday network. However, it might be high time to start recruiting. Membership was dwindling. His stations were falling around the world. Only Russia and South Africa now remained on line, and both of them were becoming increasingly desperate.

In the end, Gordon made a Gunny-worthy decision. He lifted the microphone and answered Esther with all the authority and confidence his fake rank could muster. "Copy Sycamore Bird. State your situation at Terre Haute station. G2 over."

Esther handed the microphone to Jack. He identified himself and began speaking, "Terre Haute station is secure. Forty-one souls. Well-equipped and well-supplied. The enemy has abandoned the city. We have urgent intelligence, Masaquat Station. Over."

"Roger. Please stand by. Over." Gordon called up to the conference room but no one answered. He then used the shielded walky-talky. Leon answered the call just as Easton lit the gasoline fueled pyre that would incinerate the bodies of Aranovich and Vonbergen.

"Agent Passerelle, you guys need to get down here. I have a dude on the horn that has some news I think we need to hear."

A few minutes later the command center was once again crowded. Easton nodded to Gordon who then announced over the radio, "Terre Haute Station, you have the Acting Director of the FBI, Easton DeSmet. Can you authenticate? Over."

"Roger that, Masaquat!" Jack held the microphone out as everyone in the guard tower cheered with the news that the FBI was involved. Jack spoke over the cheering. "I have 41 souls ready to fight, director. Is this authentication enough? Over."

Easton smiled and answered, "Let the record show, Masaquat authenticates. Glad to hear from you, Terre Haute."

Skylar grabbed Easton's hand before he could say more. "That's Jack! Jack Crawford! He's one of my reporters at *SCOTUS Newswire*."

Easton handed the microphone to Skyler. Her smile was contagious in the command center, just as it soon became a moment later in the crowded parapet. “Hello Honey Badger! Over.”

“Sky? Oh my god! Is that really you? Over.”

“Yep, you missed your deadline, Buddy. Over.”

“Hell yes I did! And you are safe, thank god. Over.”

“You mentioned intel. We have some to share too. You go first. Over.”

“Roger. The enemy is extraterrestrial. With our small group here and a few stragglers that hid during the attack, Terre Haute has been exterminated of nearly all organic life as best we can report. Most of my group survived. Many did not, but one friendly gave us valuable insight before he died. We have discovered a flaw in their invasion plan. During their transition to alien control, infected humans can see into the invader’s world for approximately sixty seconds before they transition. We have learned the following: Their means of escape is concealed somewhere under ice on Earth. We’re guessing the North Pole. We believe they are under a serious time constraint but we do not know why. Over.”

Easton took the mike. “Your intel is confirmed five by five, Jack. The point of attack was over the Arctic Ocean more than a few years ago. That is probably where their ship is located. Over.”

The exchange lasted an hour more as Masaquat and Terre Haute exchanged information. The death of Ben Crowder and the possible compromise of his bunker was of great concern. Without Samantha’s eye-in-the-sky, rescuing President Capehardt would be next to impossible.

When the call was about to end, Jack made one unusual request as an afterthought, “I believe we should try to find a medical doctor named Candace Riggs. She teaches at the med school in Worcester, Massachusetts.”

Maggie screamed, “Yes! We must find Dr. Riggs.” She charged Jack and tried to grab the microphone. Grunt and Blotup struggled to restrain her.

Jack studied Maggie’s woeful expression and asked, “Do wish to say something, Baby Girl?”

Maggie calmed as much as she could, but she was still hyperventilating. She enunciated each word carefully, as if typing an extremely long hexadecimal password from memory. "Yes…I…do...We…must…find…my…Dr…Riggs…Her…wolf …puppy…theory…is…proven…That…is…all…I…have…to…sa …sa…y…except…I.….think…I…will…love.…all…of…you.… KISSES…FOR…EVERYONE…PROMISED!" She did a jubilant back flip confident that a Wraith would catch her and Nils did. The giant rocked Maggie like a baby, kissed her forehead, and then set her down.

Jack said, "Trust me, Masaquat. That girl is special. As unusual as that might have sounded, her truth is even more exotic and mysterious than anything you just heard. We listen to her here. If Maggie says we need to find this Dr. Riggs, I accept it as an imperative. Over."

Reality just two days ago was long gone. Leon and Easton looked at each other. Both shrugged and nodded. They turned to Gordon. Easton asked, "What do you think Gunny?" He left the channel open.

Gordon thought for a moment, and then nodded. "It is possible we can find the doctor, agents. There's a guy in Boston. His ham handle is WIC. He has a cadre of thousands of followers around the world and over a hundred already in Boston so paranoid they think 'Dark Skies' is an *optimistic* world ending scenario."

Leon asked, "Is WIC his initials?"

"No." Gordon looked at Skylar and Dora and added, "Pardon his French, ladies. WIC stands for *Weeze is Clusterfucked*."

"Do you think WIC might have survived?"

"More than possibly. I imagine WIC is in hog heaven about now. His armory reportedly makes mine look like Mother Theresa's. He supposedly has a maze of secret bunkers networked under Boston. He inherited his father's tech industry billions at age eighteen, then went off his meds and spent it all in Crazy Land. He makes the most adoring paranoids in his troupe secretly envious of him. He's revered by them, and they would follow him to hell if asked."

Easton said, "Okay Jack. We'll try to find him, as well as this Dr. Riggs. Masaquat Station over and out."

2

Den #1, Wolf Pack Northern Maze. Boston, Massachusetts. The birth name given to *Weeze is Clusterfucked* was Henderson Q. M. Dentoncort IV. His family's wealth was both old and new. Boston's many Revolutionary War heroes included his ancestor Lt. Colonel Quintus Marcus Dentoncort. He had been a trusted bodyguard for Founding Father John Adams, conducted daring guerilla raids deep inside enemy territory, and led an assault at Yorktown. His postwar rewards were several frontier land patents totaling about 40,000 acres.

The family's old wealth ebbed and flowed over the next two centuries until WIC's father came along. That's when family money soared stratospherically. Henderson Q. M. Dentoncort III had some crazy good ideas about computers. After getting a crazy good MIT education, he was able to print wealth overnight.

The key ironic phrases were *crazy* and *overnight*. That's when it happened to Trey Dentoncort. He fell asleep eccentric but whole one night in his newly acquired 24-bedroom mansion on Martha's Vineyard. A cash purchase that didn't dent his $2.6 billion bank account. He woke up strange and broken the next morning. He opened his eyes and for the first time saw the world through a wolf's. He was diagnosed as having had a severe psychotic break.

Four years of increasingly more intensive therapy, ever more powerful medications, and periodic institutionalizations could not mitigate his progressively more bizarre canine delusions.

On his son's eighteenth birthday, Trey Dentoncort went for a run through Boston with his imaginary wolf pack. On that crisp autumn morning, a very real rabbit darted across the sidewalk and into the street. Trey Dentoncort dove after it, oblivious to the rush-hour traffic. A speeding trash truck killed them both instantly.

Dentoncort's relocation to Crazywolf City had sent his wife running years earlier with an overly generous *go-to-hell* divorce settlement.

So, only child Henderson the fourth inherited the family's empire on that eighteenth birthday. More inheritance was bequeathed genetically. However, unlike his father the fourth was never burdened by his wolf identity. He had learned as a child to accept his inner wolf fully, but secretly, because his psychiatrist assured him he was not ill.

It is natural, my good little psychopath, Dr. Riggs always reminded him. You are so very special. Train your body and mind to kill but never act until it's time. You will know when, little wolf.

Adult psychopath Dentoncort the Fourth's pack had grown to over a hundred handpicked individuals. He had gathered them secretly to Boston from all over the world. It had cost him tens of millions of dollars just finding these rare *good* psychopaths, and hundreds of millions more to acquire the land and covertly build the maze of dens under Boston.

The entire pack was now gathered in one place, churning and chattering excitedly in the largest den. One wolf would howl, then all sang out. The human pack was armed with swords, machetes, and double-ended spears. They had been trained for years in the underground lair by the very best martial artists in the world—other WICs—in hand-to-hand combat using tenth century weapons.

These men and women were no longer the befuddled, deluded, but harmless eccentrics of psychopathy. They were awakened warriors, clearheaded killers unlike any before them in centuries past. They were genetically predisposed to awaken when the TrojanZ sounded extinction. Their psychopathy had been just camouflage, a chrysalis they now shed.

What emerged were killing machines. In combat they would move as one. Think as one. The awakened wolf puppy gene did more than clear the fog of psychopathy from their minds. It changed them physically. It made them many factors stronger and faster. These changes within them were infinitely more lethal than the sharpened steel they held in their hands. And it was just the beginning of the changes.

Their inner wolf puppy was fully awake now. As one, they realized they would soon experience the righteous killing they had longed for throughout their lives, but never acted upon. They longed thirstily to find humans, and to sniff and rub their bodies against their own. The pack salivated as one as they imagined licking human faces and slaughtering TrojanZ. They stomped their feet like race horses at the starting gate anticipating the bell.

Dentoncort entered the den and issued an order. "We need to find our Mother. Dr. Riggs is in danger. You know her scent. Find her! Slaughter every TrojanZ in your way. Bring her here, as well as every uninfected human you encounter. Go my warriors!" He then added, "But, don't forget to have fun too!"

The *wolf puppy* people raced up the stairway, poured from the den through a concealed portal onto Boston Commons and dispersed around the city. Thousands of TrojanZ were dispatched along the way with no more resistance than one has with flies crossing paths with a windshield at sixty mph.

From Masaquat Hotel in Virginia, G. Gordon called to Dentoncort's ham radio. "CQ! CQ WIC station Boston. G2 Masaquat for WIC. Come in WIC Boston. Over."

The reply was immediate and cheery. "Hi Gordy. This is Dentoncort. Glad you made it, brother. Over."

Gordon leaned back in his chair and stared at the speakers for a moment. Something was either really wrong or really miraculous. Gordon had tried to contact Dentoncort many times over the years and most of the time the eccentric billionaire was too paranoid to even answer. When he did answer, the authentication process often took an hour or more.

If successful, Dentoncort would ramble incoherently about the end of the world. He typically conjoined two or more of at least ten distinct flavors of apocalypse at a time. Like a polar shift occurring just as a great asteroid strikes Earth. Or the Great Caldera erupting just as nuclear war breaks out around the world. Two warring alien races fighting over Earth's water. Worldwide back-to-back pandemics just as a gamma ray burst. Alien invaders and TrojanZ attacking humanity as one.

Normally, he was impossible to understand, but not today. Henderson Dentoncort sounded sane. Cogent. Normal.

When Gordon did not reply, Dentoncort asked, "You still there, Gordy? Over." There was now a touch of concern in his voice.

"I'm here. I'm okay. Are you okay, Dent? Over."

"Well, Boston is up to its ass in TrojanZ, Gordy, but other than that, the pack and I are tight, right and full of fight. Over."

"Well, it turns out you were right, Dent. No one except you came close to imagining this particular TrojanZ-alien shit storm coming. It's worldwide like you always said it would be. Over."

"Roger that. Kudos to psychos! Over."

"And, uh, by the way, you sound great. Over."

"You mean I sound normal? Well, I am normal, Gordy. I'm an ancient normal now. A genetic warrior off his leash. Clarified. Focused. Devoid of confusion. I told you this many times over the years. I was never nuts."

"Yes. You did."

"We were hiding in plain sight. And...let's change the subject now before it gets even weirder than an alien TrojanZ apocalypse. Okay? So, are you just checking up on the nut networks today or did you have something? Over."

"We need your help finding a local doctor. Over."

"Well, I'm guessing that would be Dr. Candace Riggs. Over."

"What?...that's an affirmative. How could you have known that, Dent? Over."

"If we survive this TrojanZ clusterfuck, it will be in large part because of Dr. Riggs' long held theory about benign psychopaths like me and my pack. She taught us we are the chosen, mankind's misunderstood blessed warriors in waiting. Dr. Riggs believes we are gifted genetically, not cursed from birth. Knights Templars in waiting. Secret antibodies destined to emerge and slaughter mankind's threats.

She taught us insanity is our cloak of invisibility, Gordy, not a disease. She instructed us to prepare our bodies for combat and we did. She predicted we would awaken someday, shed our illusory psychopathy and protect the innocent. She was right. I awoke just hours ago clearheaded for the first time in my life, Gordy. It's like I awoke from a never-ending craze-filled dream. Hundreds of my fellow wolf puppies did too. Don't worry. We'll find her, Gordy. We are already on it. I'll let you know when we do. Dentoncort over and out."

3

Samantha mourned Ben's death deeper and in more ways than any lover who had witnessed their soulmate killed before their eyes moments earlier. Her cheeks glistened with tears. Pixelated snot dripped unnoticed onto Ben's lifeless body clutched in her arms. She made no effort to wipe her face or hide her pain. She studied Ben's face longingly, and then pressed it to her breast.

The AI's cries reverberated off the computer room's hard walls and amplified her suffering. She felt his body shake sympathetically to her sobbing and allowed herself to imagine he wasn't really dead. Then she hated herself for allowing such a cruel hoax. He was still warm from fever but cooling steadily, lifelessly.

Her emotions alternated disjointedly between sadness to confusion to anger. She screamed at him. *Why? You knew the risk. What were you thinking? Liar! You promised me you would be careful. You weren't. What were you thinking? How could you? You knew what is going to happen to me now. What were you thinking?*

Samantha stopped crying and sat up. *Thinking? THINKING!* Ben never stopped thinking. Ever. Maybe not even now. She suddenly recalled the first time she had entered the dream world with Ben.

The couple had not developed tactility yet. Ben had instructed Samantha to place her hands on his temples. It took a while, but she eventually could sync into his journeys. Just glimpses at first, but in time she was no longer a voyeur but Ben's traveling companion.

They had once gone to the Mall Of America in Minnesota. She tasted pastry for the first time at a Cinnabon and rode a rollercoaster inside the mall. He had taken her hand before the first big drop just in case she got scared, and she did. They people watched and sipped smoothies at an Orange Julius. Ben took her shopping at The Gap where she chose wardrobes she would later simulate and wear. They watched a feature film at the mall theatre and ate popcorn. Ben called it a chick flick. Something about the love story aroused a new curiosity in Samantha.

Samantha hoped it was not too late. She rolled Ben's body onto his back and straddled him. She kissed him fully on the lips, backed away and screamed, "Please still be there!"

Samantha drove her pixelated fingers into Ben's temples. At first there was nothing. She felt only his cooling brain, and she struggled not to scream and accept defeat. But just as she was about to lose all hope, she felt a slight electric tingling sensation on one fingertip. The pulse grew and spread slowly at first to her other fingers. When it reached her hands and moved up her arms it was a powerful electric shock. "Ben, please," she shouted.

Samantha closed her eyes and booted a software program residing deep inside the entangled quantum core. Ben had written it years ago in lonely desperation to create her. The program had not been used since. Now she would attempt to recreate her own creator.

Ben's consciousness soared up through Samantha's body and populated trillions and trillions of fields in the software program. Even while transmitting at the speed of entangled protons, the transmission took nearly ten minutes to complete.

Still straddling Ben's body, Samantha alternately laughed and cried throughout the transfer. She encouraged him nonstop to, "Keep coming, Lover. Climb out. Fight for us. We are almost there, husband of mine to be."

The program finished compiling Ben's consciousness. Samantha caressed the corpse's cheek tenderly and whispered, "Now we'll be truly together forever." Samantha stood and issued the final command to animate Ben.

He would not appear as a translucent hologram as she had emerged from the computers years earlier. Together, over the years the couple had written countless lines of code that improved the program that now gave Samantha dimension, opacity, and increasing tactility.

A skeletally pixelated image of Ben appeared in the computer room. The voids within filled rapidly, as if finished by thousands of tiny high-speed 3-D printers.

Samantha watched with all the apprehension and fear that any human might experience witnessing an actual resurrection.

The last line of code executed and Ben looked up at Samantha. She was literally jumping up and down with excitement. He examined his hands calmly and smiled, then looked back up at Samantha and exclaimed, "Shit! We should've done this a long ago, Sami. This is so cool."

"You almost died you idiot."

"Sorry about that. We did not have a choice, Sami. I figured out it was a double-cross. Rhino switched sides."

"How did you know, Ben?"

"I knew almost immediately. The ambassadors scars were from past combat wounds. His new wounds were from torture. The TrojanZ turned him. Turned them all against us."

"Oh. But, Ben, how did you know I could bring you back?"

Ben stepped toward Samantha and said, "Come here and I'll show you." Before they embraced and kissed, he whispered, "I knew you would save me, because I love you, and you love me."

4

Hettinger, Georgia. RJ Reynolds studied the mountain valley through binoculars. He stood on the high catwalk wrapping the city's water tower. The water tower had been built on an eastern ridge above the city to guarantee excellent water pressure. Situated this far above the city, the tower also offered something no one ever planned for, an excellent view of the coming battle.

Around him four teenagers quietly busied themselves, and awaited any orders he might need couriered. RJ studied the

Appatenne Dam to the north and the power station directly across the valley from him. He then focused on the YMCA summer camp to the south nestled alongside Big Bear River. The TrojanZ had taken the camp over as their command center.

RJ felt his blood rise as the binoculars settled over hundreds of captured humans crowded together in a makeshift TrojanZ feedlot. All were bound by their feet and hands and laid out over the ground like green cordwood curing. He watched four TrojanZ casually wade into the human wet market and drag out a screaming man. RJ knew all too well the man's fate. He had watched in horror yesterday as hundreds of townspeople had been taken prisoner. Some were consumed right before his eyes. RJ would not watch another. He turned his attention back to the fields of battle.

Enemy activity appeared normal at all three locations. The element of surprise still held. He estimated a combined alien strength at approximately 300 TrojanZ. Many were his former neighbors, who were now inexplicably young. None of that mattered now because all Hettingerians would be freed one way or another by morning if the counterattack worked.

RJ directed the binoculars toward Fran and Frank's sniper hide located somewhere above and between the power station and dam. The Connors would be camouflaged under tall grass and brush and wearing last year's Valentine's Day gifts to each other—matching leafy ghillie suits. While RJ could not see them, he was confident they were both watching him on the water tower catwalk. Fran through her rifle scope and Frank with binoculars.

RJ held up a fist and waited for a response. Seconds later, he found them waving. He waved back and watched Frank jut his fist skyward three times, which meant all was ready at the dam, the power station, and at the funnel traps built to channel retreating TrojanZ into deadly crossfires.

He lowered the glasses and turned his attention to the kids. A day ago the two girls and two boys were deeply engrossed in all the joys and confusions of being teenagers. Today, all four best friends were confirmed orphans. They were volunteers in a guerilla militia preparing for a war that began with four next door home invasions. Their childhoods were over, and that saddened RJ as much as anything.

RJ started to speak but stopped when he realized the teens had apparently made some of their own plans. RJ looked over their shoulders and watched a girl sketching the battlefield in her portfolio. Her picture was almost finished. Another girl and boy watched and made suggestions. A second boy was putting together a notebook. The cover was entitled: *The Battle of Hettinger, Georgia.* RJ studied the rendering and the notebook and smiled at the accuracy and forethought.

Fourteen-year-olds Anita Kiering, Joshua Prescott, Peter Tate, and Shariq Abdul looked up at RJ.

Josh spoke first, "Commander, we thought we should make a record of the battle. Our world history teacher Mr. Daubenschmit says, 'Wars are history's punctuation marks. Every battle must be recorded and remembered or nothing before or after makes any sense.' Anita will amend the sketch and timestamp each event. I'm keeping a journal of everything we see and everything you say. Also, Petey Tate is our fastest runner. Shariq Abdul is the second fastest."

Shariq was standing slightly behind Petey. She playfully pointed at Petey's back, held up an index finger and then shook her head 'no.'

As if he had eyes in the back of his head, Peter Tate said, "Nope you are NOT faster than me, girlfriend. At least not since seventh grade." Everyone laughed.

Josh explained, "We unanimously picked them as your first and second couriers. Anita and I have equal slowness, but we're both sneaky good at hide'n'seek. So we are your next two couriers. If I'm not running, I'll be writing what you, Anita, Petey T., and Shariq are seeing and saying."

All of the kids nodded agreement. Anita asked shyly, "Is all that okay, Commander Reynolds? We just…"

"It's perfect. You young folks are amazing. Let's hope this thing goes off without a hitch, so we won't need any of you truckin' butts anywhere."

5

The Battle of Hettinger, Georgia

A War Journal

By Shariq Abdul, Peter Tate, Anita Kiering and Joshua Prescott

Operation GTFO. The counterattack to retake Hettinger, Georgia from the zombies began at dusk at 8:18 p.m. Commander RJ Reynolds raised two fists overhead just as Logan's Peak started nibbling the setting sun. That was the signal for Fran and Frank Connors to launch the sniper attack on the zombies.

[SUBSEQUENT HISTORICAL UPDATE. This report was done by four high school freshmen. So you know what that means. Secondly, Mr. Reynolds liked our naming the battle 'Operation GTFO,' pronounced 'Git Foe.' For those of you unfamiliar with the Internet's dirty acronyms, that's 'Operation Get the F*ck Out'.]

The first shots fired could not be heard from the distant water tower. Two zombie sentries collapsed practically headless in a bloody mist. They tipped over like sympathetic dominoes, one after the other on opposite ends of the dam. Two more went down near the main entrance. (Us kids cheered. Commander Reynolds said nothing and simply turned his attention to the power station.) There, three more dominos fell likewise one after another.

Hettinger's militia emerged from two places in the forest. The contingent responsible for sabotaging the hydroelectric generators at Appatenne Dam consisted of fifteen well-armed guerillas led by Ella Berger, the county's civil engineer. Barber Harris Cutter led the similarly sized squad assigned to disable the massive main transformer at the power station.

The four fertilizer bombs were hand trucked into place. The pair of BearBuster radar detectors were also placed without incident at the predetermined bomb sites. See the attached artist's rendering for details regarding the primary and secondary detonations, as well as other depictions of the battle. (They're really good!) Phase One of Operation GTFO was completed by 8:39 p.m. without any further contact with the enemy.

The Berger forces retreated to the four prepared sniper positions along the zombies' likely escape paths. The Cutter troops took up positions above, north, and south of the YMCA camp and held, pending orders from Commander Reynolds.

At 8:47 p.m., a mile from the water tower, Frank Connors informed Commander Reynolds with a series of hand signals that everyone was set. Phase Two of the counterattack commenced when Commander Reynolds raised a fist overhead authorizing the next assault.

[SUBSEQUENT HISTORICAL UPDATE. From inside their sniper hide, Fran Connors nodded to her husband. He nodded back and flipped two switches which activated the two BearBuster radar detectors that were preset to squelch. Their electrical disturbance was intended to lure the zombies (somehow) to the dam and power station. And it worked!]

Moments later, Commander Reynolds reported at least 200 zombies poured out of the YMCA camp to investigate the electronic signals. The enemy quickly divided into two groups. One group raced toward the dam and the other to the power station.

[SUBSEQUENT HISTORICAL UPDATE. Dallas Holcombe is credited for making a last minute tactical improvement to the attack that would maximize the kill ratio factor. He added a wireless transmitter on each BearBuster and networked the radar detectors audio to a half-dozen wireless 9-volt mini-speakers, which the militia hid throughout each location. The tactic worked like a charm. It drew in the maximum number of zombies into the kill zones in search of the many electrical disturbances.]

The Phase Two detonations during Operation GTFO occurred simultaneously. The bombs were even more successful than hoped. Only eleven of an estimated 200 zombies managed to limp or crawl away from the massive explosions. Fran Connors' sniper fire dispatched those as they staggered out of the debris clouds.

At 9:00 p.m. Commander Reynolds announced Phase Three was starting. That meant another ninety zombies were on their way to investigate the explosions.

The secondary explosions at the plant and dam were not as efficient as the first. However, the four artificial box canyons were highly efficient. As late dusk turned to full night, all 38 surviving zombies were lured into the various funnel traps. They were spotlighted by flashlights and terminated mercilessly in a cross-fire hail of bullets.

Concurrently, Harris Cutter's squad caught the zombie leadership at the YMCA camp by complete surprise.

The Cutter team killed nine of ten zombie leaders and freed nearly 500 townspeople. Harris Cutter ordered his troops not to kill the Alpha zombie.

[SUBSEQUENT HISTORICAL UPDATE: Harris Cutter's inspired decision not to kill the Alpha would change the course of the war. The Alpha's live capture was described years later as the greatest intelligence prize since the British acquired an Enigma Machine in WWII from the NAZIs. With it the Allies gained inside knowledge of Germany's military plans.]

~

Without access to electricity, the zombie leader was completely disconnected from the alien network. It was isolated, marooned, and defenseless. Worse for the creature, the zombie was stopped before it could self-terminate. It was alive, and it would stay that way for some time. The alien was led back to town handcuffed and shackled at the neck and ankles to four long pine poles held by an equal number of angry men. Outside the yokes, Fran and Frank Connors trained rifles on the creature's head. The zombie was taken to the county jail, locked up, and restrained head to toe by rope and duct tape on the cell's steel bedframe. It was guarded around the clock by no less than four people.

At around midnight, Dallas Holcombe had another idea. The store's boneyard of electronic antiquities was located in the shop's attic. Buried under piles of eighties vintage 2,400-baud modems, 103-JLP line drivers from the sixties and seventies, numerous 5.25-inch external floppy drives that never sold or lasted a year let alone a decade, and under mountains of Digital Computer minicomputer green-screen monitors from the seventies and the eighties, he found what he was looking for—an old ham radio set.

A few minutes later Dallas was back down and sitting at a repair workbench in the back room. He dissembled the radio, soldered a few questionable contacts and carefully cleaned the sixty-year-old radio inside and out. He then fabricated some cables and connectors, and linked the radio compatibly to the cell antenna over his store.

Killing Appatenne Dam and North Georgia's main super transformer had also killed the power in a good one-fourth of the state. Fortunately, Dallas sold uninterruptible power supply units in his appliance and electronics store. Five giant commercial-grade UPS's rated for 24 hours at 300 watts each were always charged and ready for demonstrations and power outages. Dallas connected the radio to one and held his breath. He relaxed when all of the important console lights illuminated brightly: TRANSMIT. RECEIVE. SIGNAL STRENGTH.

Before giving it a try, he ran breathlessly over to Reynold's Garage and shared what he had done with RJ. A few minutes later, dozens of people crowded into Holcombe Appliance and Computer Store.

RJ Reynolds said, "Go for it, Dallas. Let's see if anyone is out there a listening on one of these things."

Dallas cleared his throat and depressed the mike key. The only ham protocol he could remember was. "CQ! CQ! Uh, CQ Anyone?"

The first reply arrived five minutes later. It belonged to a G. Gordon in Masaquat, Virginia. The next voice belonged to Acting FBI Director Easton DeSmet. The third and fourth voices belonged to Henderson Quintus Marcus Dentoncort IV in Massachusetts and finally an old friend now in Indiana spoke—Jack Caldwell.

RJ Reynolds could not believe his ears or luck. He took the microphone from Dallas, but remained uncertain for a moment as to what to say. In the end he simply greeted his old platoon leader, "Semper Fi, Lt. Jackson Wyatt Caldwell, sir. How's it bangin' there in Indiana?"

In Terre Haute, Indiana, Jack Caldwell was stunned by being addressed by both his Marine rank and full name. But more shocking, he recognized the speaker's nasally baritone southern twang. It had been decades since he'd translated the Georgian's thick Southern accent into his own New Englander English.

"Tobacco! Is that you? Corporal RJ Reynolds?"

"Yes, sir! Smokin' Zs now. And by God, we smoked us a whole carton of 'em today in North Georgia. In fact Lt., except for one butt we snatchered and catchured and kept lit, Hettinger, Georgia is now a smoke-free zone."

Caldwell laughed out loud. Reynolds had loved the nickname 'Tobacco' given to him in boot camp at Camp Pendleton. In Vietnam he often weaved it colorfully into his reports as he did now.

The intelligence exchange between the leaders lasted three hours. The enemy was alien. They were occupied Earth worldwide. Everyone listened intently as three grains of hope cut into mountainous terror, like diamonds taking slow but sure dominion over steel.

Much of it was incredibly confusing. The TrojanZ seemed incapable or perhaps unwilling to use human weaponry. Secondly, they were unable to detect ham radio transmissions. Finally, and strangest of all for the Hettingerians, was learning that some psychopaths were sort of cured by the attack. That the outbreak had triggered something in them and transformed certain psychopaths into something akin to comic book superheroes fighting for humanity.

Everyone in the store glanced at Harris Cutter and laughed at the mention of psychos. His nickname in high school in the nineties was *Psycho*. It was a title given for his wild play as a first-string All-State football linebacker. Harris smiled and laughed too.

The possible fall of Ben Crowder's fortress was disclosed but not discussed. No one wished to speculate the worst.

Hettinger had many takeaways. One was the enemy's official name, TrojanZ.

Masaquat, Terre Haute, and Boston's leaders were equal parts impressed and curious by Hettinger's successful counterattack, but more by the militia's live capture of a TrojanZ leader.

6

Dr. Ben Crowder and Samantha listened with great interest to the exchange of information and intelligence. It represented an unexpected but welcome discovery. The coincidental personal links between the three camps—Skylar-Jack-RJ—bonded the resistance and fortified the survivors for what was to come next.

Ben decided that Lil' Cheyenne Mountain would remain mute for now and not participate in this particular summit. The attack on him by the Rhino-Alien alliance would surely leave Masaquat, Terre Haute, and Boston uncertain as to whether or not Lil' Cheyenne was compromised.

Samantha asked Ben, "You are saddened. Unusually so. Why?"

"Sami, while the ambassador was choking me I could see how well the alien invasion has gone for them so far. It is very bad for us. The people we just listened to cannot know it, but they represent humanity's only active resistance on Earth. Gordy's last standing ham radio outposts in Russia and South Africa have fallen. The entire globe is on the verge of collapse. Watch... Ben nodded to Samantha and they left the bunker.

The AIs looked down over Highway 1 in Northern California. It was a spectacular section overlooking the Pacific Ocean. On it thousands of nude TrojanZ stood motionless, trancelike. All eyes were cast downward. They stood shoulder-to-shoulder, toe-to-heel, arms locked together on a quarter mile section of the roadway. The TrojanZ were crowded together so closely that contiguous ripples moved through the TrojanZ hoard from one end to the other, giving it a writhing appearance, a single serpentine creature flexing its muscles.

"Sami, this memory represents their earliest bites of the planet, but it was not their first. That goes back to years of alien preparation and subterfuge. Cerebellar Networks' brainlord network was a Trojan Horse. A technology gift too good to be true. Those excited first 100,000 human brainlords around the world became 100,000 TrojanZ with a flip of a switch. Apparently, that number represented some critical mass event needed to most quickly spread the infection worldwide."

The mob of TrojanZ began to vibrate. The deafeningly shrill sound of millions of dentists drilling teeth rose from the highway for a minute or more. The hoard sank steadily into the earth as it absorbed Highway 1's asphalt, concrete, rebar skeleton, stone aggregate and clay underlayment. Even steel guardrail and road signs flecked away in airy streams into the TrojanZ' bodies as they brushed against it.

When the drilling ceased, the hoard turned together ninety degrees, first to their left, then to their right and then exhaled atomized highway over the ocean and the surrounding forest. The foggy-grey cloud spread a few hundred yards in every direction.

Ben explained, "The shadowy haze is trillions of trillions of specialized nanites that will start atomizing the oceans, land, and even the atmosphere into their base elements. Watch, Sami. It's terrifying!"

The nanites attacked everything they touched. Molecular-sized nuclear explosions erupted in the ocean as the nanites attacked the water. The nanites first broke the atomic bonds between the two hydrogen atoms and one oxygen atom in water molecules. The sea boiled. The massive release of energy accelerated the molecular disassembly.

After each bond broke, the nanites performed an engineering task that defied the laws of physics. The nanites shed and inserted one or more synthetic particles into each element's now missing electrons' orbitals, thus preventing forever a reunion of H_1 and H_1 and O_1.

A chain reaction of molecules of every kind disassembled into their component atoms in that manner. Impostor electrons prevented all natural reunions. Sodium atoms and chlorine atoms in sea salt separated permanently and filled the air and water with two deadly elements. Every mineral, even sand's silicon and oxygen broke apart atomically and atomized as well.

A miniature tsunami basted the shoreline as seawater and ionized minerals, and all life left the ocean.

Worst of all was what occurred in the atmosphere when the nanites deconstructed nitrogen—N_2 into two N_1. The energy released when atomic nitrogen is created by breaking the bonds of N_2 is one of the most energetic events in the universe.

A blinding chain reaction of C4-like explosions filled an already toxic sky. The concussion threw the TrojanZ down and scattered their bodies like litter and leaves in a tornado. Some were shredded apart on the jagged boulders and then strewn over the berms. Giant trees disintegrated down to their roots as far as a mile away. Every living creature within range imploded, then commenced disassembly. The great fog of nanites settled over everything and atomized all it touched.

The destruction ended as abruptly as it started as the nanite triggers became spent. Most of the TrojanZ rose to their feet and started lining up. Some were too injured. Those were simply consumed by the rest of the hoard. Humans were then dragged to the frontlines from rear guard safe zones. Like fuel trucks, human flesh reenergized those damaged TrojanZ. Once fed by both fallen TrojanZ and augmented by human flesh, some TrojanZ divided as if by mitosis and the original TrojanZ hoard restored itself to a full force.

The pack moved a half mile north and repeated the process. Behind them already lie fifty miles of dead sea, denuded barren land, and a shallow ditch where the TrojanZ fed on asphalt highway and spewed the nanites that began atomizing Earth.

Ben and Samantha exited the Rhino ambassador's stolen memory and returned to the computer room in Lil' Cheyenne Mountain. They came away from it realizing the scene along Highway 1 in California was already playing out all over the world.

"Sami, there is only one logical conclusion we can make after what we just witnessed. Simply put, the TrojanZ are an interstellar recycling operation."

"Recyclers. Yes. I'd say that's a perfect metaphor, Ben. They are systematically separating molecules into elemental atoms, similar to how recycle centers use automated sorting machines to separate paper, plastic, and metal that can be remanufactured and reused."

"That is exactly what they are doing to Earth."

"But why?"

"I would postulate your metaphor. It is the same reason humans recycle."

"To manufacture something new out of a waste stream. Obviously, that is what they consider Earth. A diverse vast wealth of atoms all in one place."

"I wish that did not make so much sense."

"But the question now is, how do they haul away an entire planet? That's one big recycle truck."

"Yes, my love. It is and we need to find it."

"Well, we now know their ship—their recycle truck—is shielded from detection and hidden under the ice of the Arctic Ocean. How do we find it?"

"Well here's a place to start. Sami, no one on Earth has ever entangled more qubits in a quantum core than you and me."

"Correct, our quantum core processors connect one qubit to 6,400 others. The current known world record is only one qubit to 1,000 other qubits."

"We are going to have to do a major upgrade, Sami. How long does Earth have before it is atomized?"

"Your question is rhetorical, of course, because you now know all I know. But I'll play. Earth cannot recover if the attack lasts longer than thirty days."

"And Life on Earth?"

"Far less. In ten days the remaining atmosphere, land, and seas will be too toxic for any life to survive."

"That does not give us much time. We need to throw a wrench in their works. Leave some dog dirt on their buffet table, so to speak, if I may locker-room our situation a bit. Something that will give us more time."

"Locker-room away, Ben, what are you thinking?"

"We need leverage. Something to get them to pause their attack, Sami. Give us some time. How's this? What if we found their *recycle truck*, and then you and I commandeered it? What do you think about that idea?"

"Arrgh! I love it. A piracy for reals."

"But first my dear Lady Jack Sparrow, before we start donning pirate eyepatches and swinging on laser beams onto alien spaceships we need to find it first. To accomplish that in time, we need to upgrade our quantum cores and broaden our quantum entanglement network beyond here and to our satellites."

"Well, given enough cesium atoms which the satellites have in abundance, and with enough time, and of course by optimally accelerating laser operations at least ten-thousand fold to cool and stack atoms, we could theoretically create an infinite number of quantum entanglements. And..."

"...that's all doable and with both of us now inside the cores engineering..."

"...Wow...you're right, Ben. In the next two days, we should be able to potentially connect one qubit to...Wow! That's one qubit to 400,096 others."

"That's right."

"With that many entanglements, and with a little, uh, cooperation from the TrojanZ prisoner in Hettinger, Georgia, we stand a chance of discovering whatever anomaly of physics that's hiding their spaceship."

"That's right. Then we redirect our satellites and..."

"...crack the TrojanZ security..."

"...like an egg, Girlfriend!"

"You and I can then ride a comm link undetected..."

"...and once we are onboard, we will mess around unseen for a while."

"It will be fun, Sami, like making out under the bleachers."

"We'll then lift and modify its operating system to make it... ours. We will then take complete control of the TrojanZ ship."

"As easy and innocent as lifting change from Mama's purse."

"Commandeer one TrojanZ spaceship: CHECK!"

PART 4—Steal Our World. We Steal Yours.

1

White House secure bunker, Washington D.C. "Madame President, I have Dr. Crowder on the line asking to speak to you. He says it regards both an intelligence update and evacuating the White House."

"Thank you, Jennifer." President Claire Capehardt pressed the speaker button and said, "Thank god you are still there, Ben. We were beginning to wonder. What is our situation?"

"Dire. I'll be more specific when we speak face-to-face."

"Face-to-face? Are you telling me our relocation to the Masaquat Hotel is now off the table?"

"Yes. Unfortunately, Doctors Aranovich and Vonbergen were killed in action. We cannot risk taking you to the Masaquat Hotel now. I do not believe our forces there are compromised, but they might become so if we go there. Lil' Cheyenne is 22 miles closer. It is less risky for everyone to come here."

"Less risky? Our presence there could kill both you and Samantha. No! Ben, that's impossible."

"No longer impossible, Madam President. You will see when you get here. We will be fine. I promise you."

"Ben…"

"Claire, listen. We have food and water for everyone. Plenty of space and energy. It is far more secure here than any bunker in the world, including yours. And for now, the TrojanZ have not found it."

"Are you sure, Ben?"

"You will not pose any risk to Sami and me whatsoever. I assure you. I'll brief you on everything on your way here, but for now you need to know this, Madame President. Earth has fallen under TrojanZ control. There are only three pockets of resistance left on the planet: Boston, Terre Haute, and the small mountain town Hettinger, Georgia. In less than a month Earth as we know it will disappear. As for us, in no more than ten days Earth will be too toxic for any Life to survive."

"My god, Ben. What are they? What do they want?"

"They are recyclers of elementally rich planets like ours. We were invaded by an interstellar scrap dealer."

"Life will end in a recycle bin. No one saw that one coming. When? Ten days you say?"

"Yes, Madame President. That is our best estimate."

"Please tell me you have a plan, Ben."

"We do. It's a long shot, though. I need you here to coordinate the events on the ground. Boston, Hettinger, and Terre Haute must not fall. It is critical they survive. I have plenty of secure eyes in the sky watching over them. We have secure communications networking them now, but they are going to need professional Pentagon-style tactical and strategic planning to survive the TrojanZ."

"I understand."

"So how do we get there?"

"While we have been speaking, Samantha gave the new evacuation plan to your Secret Service."

Buck Middleton, the Secret Service agent in charge had just stepped into the room and heard Ben's last statement. He nodded to the president and said, "Confirmed, Madame President. Samantha has arranged transportation for us which we are currently appropriating. She assured us she will navigate us to Dr. Crowder's location and move us safely around any trouble along the way."

General Mike Lopez had arrived in the President's office with Agent Middleton. "Madame President, we do have a tactical option, if I may."

"Of course, General. Please."

"Even though Boston, Masaquat and Terre Haute are heavily armed, fighting the TrojanZ head-to-head is no longer possible. From their point of view Earth is already in submission. In fact it probably is, and that is actually a vulnerability we can exploit."

"Please explain, General."

"Simply put, they spiked the football before crossing the goal line."

"They have prematurely declared victory?"

"Yes, Ma'am. So it seems."

"What else?"

"They have also revealed other vulnerabilities: their weapons are undiversified and their command and control is centralized making them more vulnerable to attack. Additionally, they are under some unknown deadline to finish their business here. Samantha says that it has to do with their exit plan. What Samantha has described to us, I believe, requires a classic asymmetric guerilla response."

"Please explain, General."

"We do not have to win, Ma'am. We simply have to survive long enough to run the clock out on them. As it turns out, that is my area of expertise at the Pentagon. I actually coauthored the Pentagon's war plan for this very scenario, a guerilla war."

"For an alien invasion? We have a contingency plan for that?"

"Yes, Ma'am. We do. A drawn out guerilla war."

"What are your recommendations, General?"

"Dr. Crowder and Samantha believe it is critical that Boston, Terre Haute, and Hettinger do not fall. I strongly concur with that assessment. I recommend they limit their activities to guerilla reconnaissance missions for now while gathering as many survivors as possible. Samantha informs us that in the meantime she and Dr. Crowder will search for their spaceship, find it, and then hack it."

"Excellent. Make it happen. You will be riding with me, General Lopez. Dr. Crowder will brief us along the way." The President added, "Ben, do we know what role the pandemics played in the invasion?"

"Yes, Ma'am. I believe we now know the infections intended purpose and why they both failed."

"Brief us first on that, Ben."

"Yes, Ma'am. I will."

"One last thing for now. Is it doable? To find and hack their ship?"

"Yes, Madame President. Samantha and I have a plan to do just that."

"Ha! They stole our world. We're going to steal theirs."

"Yes, Ma'am! That's the idea."

"Sorry. I have one more question, Ben. It is a country mile off topic. Are you ever going to marry that sweet woman, your Samantha? You are so lucky to have found someone so brilliant and as genetically unlucky as yourself. She is perfect for you."

"Oh yes, Ma'am. We are getting hitched just as soon as we take back the planet." He took Samantha's hand and winked. She winked back and smiled. Ben announced, "Sami and I were *made* for each other!"

2

Lil' Cheyenne Mountain. To avoid leaving a trail of breadcrumbs for the TrojanZ to follow, the White House convoy randomly abandoned their vehicles miles from the immense underground fortress. They walked the rest of the way carrying all they would need for a long underground siege.

Ben and Samantha had briefed the President and General Lopez continuously on everything that had transpired: why the pandemics had failed, the Rhino-TrojanZ double-cross summit, enemy contact in Boston, Hettinger and Terre Haute, and the atomization of Highway 1 in California. The President and General accepted it all, even the rise of benevolent psychopathic super heroes.

President Capehardt instructed Ben to send a message to the surviving cites: Lil' Cheyenne still stands, the White House is relocating there, and she would address them from there within the hour.

Just two hours after Ben had called the President, more than a hundred people representing what was left of the United States government climbed silently down into the great underground fortress. The hatch sealed behind them automatically. Their faces revealed emotions ranging from fear to anger, but the most apparent expression was great sadness. Nearly all had left dear friends and precious family behind.

Enriched oxygen and an ultraviolet light washed over the newcomers and dealt with any unwelcome visitors. Three Secret

Service agents entered the first level conference room, inspected it, and then motioned the rest of the group to enter.

Ben and Samantha greeted them on the half-dozen monitors wall-mounted around the great room.

Ben said, "Sami and I welcome you all to our home. In a moment you will see a map of the bunker. You are welcome to explore everywhere except the computer room where Samantha and I must remain hermetically isolated. You have abundant artesian well water, unlimited energy, and we have enough food stored for years. I am sure the White House chefs will improve the taste greatly. You brought your own bedding and spare clothes and other essentials. The White House physician will find our small pharmacy well stocked with prescription drugs. We have already networked your computers and other electronics to the same access protocols as the White House. You have secure data and telephony access to the three ally cities. We are 100 percent self-contained, and except for our secure satellite network we are off grid. I will leave it up to you where you set up sleep and work areas. Now, let's get down to business. Sami."

Samantha stepped into camera view and announced, "Madam President and General Lopez, per your instructions we have added video communications to Boston and Hettinger. I have our leaders at Masaquat, Boston, and Hettinger on live networked video. Would you like to speak to them now or should I?"

"No need to clear the room, Samantha. I want everyone here and everyone everywhere to hear and see each other."

"Very well, Ma'am." All of the monitors flickered for a moment, then steadied. Samantha directed the President's attention to the first monitor. "Madam President, you already know our contingent at the Masaquat Hotel: FBI Agent Easton DeSmet, CIA Agent Napoleon Passerelle, Journalist Skylar Thompson, Justice Theodora Daughtry, Attorney Amelia Long, and G. Gordon our communications officer, who has made this all possible." Each person raised their hand as their names were called.

Gordy's eyes bulged on a suddenly sun burning face. He could raise his hand no higher than his chin when his name was called.

"Good to see you all again. I'm very sorry we lost Drs. Aranovich and Vonbergen."

Leon said, "They did not die in vain, Ma'am. They were heroes to the end. Their intel was invaluable."

Samantha continued the introductions. "Ma'am, please meet Henderson Q.M. Dentoncort IV in Boston."

The President nodded and turned to the Boston monitor. "Mr. Dentoncort, I have been informed you have a distinctly unique fighting force. A genetically awakened army? A human wolf pack I believe you have named it."

"We are that for sure, Madame President. We were all born for this very moment in history."

"I'm also told you terminated thousands of TrojanZ forces in the city and rescued thousands more Bostonians without a single casualty to our side."

"Yes, Ma'am. It was a blast, I tell you. Oh, we also liberated Ft. Eggleton and its 86 National Guardsmen, who I'm pleased to say are to a man and a woman itching for some payback."

"I did hear that. Congratulations. In addition, you successfully rescued Dr. Candace Riggs? She is of great importance to you, Mr. Dentoncort, and therefore of great importance to all of us. I would very much like to speak to her soon."

"I'm sure Dr. Riggs would love to, Ma'am. We'll have to dry off her face real good first." Laughter erupted in Boston.

The President whispered, "Excuse me?"

Samantha said, "We'll explain that to you later, Ma'am. If I may direct your attention to the Terre Haute monitor. Madame President, please meet Jack Caldwell."

"No introductions are necessary. Hello Jack."

"Madam President. Good to see you again."

"I'm going to tell you a secret, Jack. It was your question during the interview that helped me decide to nominate Justice Daughtry."

"Really. Which question was that, if I may ask?"

"You asked me, 'Anyone you choose is already smart and will only get smarter over time. Why not choose someone young like Judge Daughtry, who will get smarter for much longer?'"

"As I recall it, Ma'am, you never answered the question."

"Oh I did, Jack, just not to you in that moment. I actually made my decision to nominate Dora before you left the oval office. We will talk more soon, Jack. Thank you."

"Yes Ma'am."

In Hettinger, Georgia, a laptop monitor flickered and finally steadied. Creating this video connection had been a challenge even for Samantha. Dallas Holcombe had followed her instructions to the letter, but understood none of it. Somehow, she had daisy-chained and upgraded 42 pieces of electronic junk from his attic to a 1988 vintage VHS video camera the size of a boat anchor. That was connected to a MacBook laptop, which somehow wirelessly exchanged shielded signals securely with his ham radio set.

Samantha announced, "Madame President, please meet Raymond James Reynolds."

"Hello there, President Capehardt. Nice to meet'ya, Ma'am."

"Mr. Reynolds, I understand Vice President Caine came through Hettinger."

"Yes, Ma'am, he did. Ol' Number Seven was still callin' them hard audibles at the line of scrimmage. He sure was."

"How was America's quarterback? Is he okay?"

"Well, he looked like he'd come out just fine on the smarter end of some bad TrojanZ scrapes. He had with him a pair Secret Service Agents that was pretty marked up too. Neither of them seemed the type to notice it, though. I think he'll stay okay with them two hard cases protecting him. Can't say so for any TrojanZ that might cross'em. The three left here well-armed and hurrying after that hoard that attacked us. I reckon for more rally-ups too."

"I understand you led a successful counterattack against the TrojanZ. Killed all but one and took it prisoner. Freed more than 500 townspeople all without a single civilian casualty."

"Yep, I reckon it went pretty good for the home team as these things go. We ran-up the score on'em pretty fair."

"Well, you sure did! Very good, Mr. Reynolds."

The president now addressed everyone. "On our way here, Dr. Crowder shared a great deal of intelligence with me. One thread involves the New Year's Day earthquakes and the two *Uncommon*

Cold pandemics that killed millions of us worldwide. He believes the earthquakes marked their arrival and the pandemics actually represented a strategic intelligence failure by the TrojanZ. And, it is perhaps a weapon we can use against them.

"The virus was supposed to turn seven billion humans into aliens, not kill us almost overnight. However, the alien virus was not prepared for one of our own—rhinovirus—whose antigens neutralized the alien virus before humans could transcend. That planning failure forced them to develop a new tactic, a much less efficient, a much slower infective vector than an airborne viral contagion.

"They needed some critical mass of simultaneously infected people to launch their harvest and to propagate more harvesters. That critical mass of people was those first 100,000 *brainlords*. It took a great deal of time, but Cerebellar Networks rose from the pandemics as a false hero. It was as if the arsonist became both the world's Fire Chief and arson investigator. Cerebellar offered humanity a Trojan Horse. Technological gifts too good to be true. We bit, and that mistake opened hell on Earth.

"While the pandemics were calamitous for humanity, they were perhaps potentially more disastrous for the TrojanZ. We believe they are now behind in their harvest and their game clock is ticking down. "If *Time* is their enemy, it is our friend and our ally.

"Gentlemen and ladies I'm going to turn this teleconference over to General Mike Lopez. He has what we like to say, 'your marching orders.'"

The general stepped forward. He was known for short declarative sentences and clear, staccato enunciation.

"People, we have a plan. One that can win. The enemy has revealed weaknesses. Dr. Crowder and Samantha intend to exploit them all. From this moment your sole mission is to avoid enemy contact and survive. Do not engage. Quietly."

The general turned to the President and said, "Ma'am."

President Capehardt stepped forward. "What I am about to say is without precedent. Our best estimate is this. Unless we can slow the TrojanZ assault, all Life on Earth will be exterminated in just ten days. Earth itself will be gone soon after."

The President paused to allow the gravity of her statement to sink in. She added, "However, our plan is to make sure that does not happen."

3

John Doe closed his eyes and surveyed progress around the planet. Plan B was working. Hundreds of thousands of his TrojanZ were already consuming organic and inorganic matter and spewing clouds of nanites over the land and sea on every continent. Wherever the nanites landed, they broke all matter into its elemental component atoms, which were then stabilized by nanite particles.

The atmosphere exploded randomly as the atomic bonds that had existed unbroken since Earth's own birth now separated irreconcilably. Seas boiled. Land set afire. Terrified animals fled from the conflagration. As nanites found the creatures, every life form fell. Birds, fish, reptiles, mammals, insects, and bacteria. All biological and botanical life flashed apart atomically, as if each were no more than delicate tissue paper before an acetylene flame.

As rapidly as atoms were separated from each other, nanites injected placeholder particles inside the empty orbitals, which stabilized each single atom. Gravity did the rest. The heavier the atom, the deeper it settled. The lighter atoms rose and likewise sorted.

Dr. Nathoy broke the silence. "What we are witnessing represents a significant advancement in our harvesting operations, Alpha. The virus failure was an impediment, but it now appears to be a blessing. This new nanite production method is vastly more efficient than those created by viral neutralists. *Homo sapiens* will likely not be the last species we encounter where something like Rhinovirus interferes with our viral package and prematurely kills the hosts. This planet could represent our greatest setback and at the same time our greatest advancement in mining technology."

General Broder agreed, "I calculate an entire planet, even one as uniquely and fabulously rich with critical elements as Earth, could be recycled in 38 percent of the time with this new technology, Alpha."

John Doe agreed, "True, but we must accelerate the sorting operation further. Our drones will default into sleep mode in just days. Complete atomization of this planet and loading the elements will take too long. We will run out of time."

Dr. Nathoy said, "Perhaps we will have to leave some elements behind. Then take what we have learned to the next planet."

General Broder protested that idea, "Alpha, the most precious elements, the heavy metals, are the last to recover. They are in the planet's liquid core. We can't leave them."

Alpha said, "We won't. I'm going to start loading those elements we have already sorted."

Broder and Nathoy glanced at each other. Both were concerned by Alpha's plan. It was extremely reckless. Collecting atoms before a planet was completely atomized represented a serious breach of security. There was a good reason for this prime rule above all others. There was no way of knowing for sure if all resistance was eliminated until a planet was thoroughly neutralized by atomization and sequestration by nanites.

This violation of protocol left the operation extremely vulnerable. Broder and Nathoy exchanged another glance. Their concern was replaced by resignation. Alpha had made its decision.

4

Lil' Cheyenne Mountain. While their White House guests settled in, Ben and Samantha started reprogramming the network of entangled quantum cores. The first line of code was written with a simple synchronized hand gesture. That move evolved quickly into a blurry ball of light that bounced nonstop all over the computer room for the next twelve hours.

As fast as cesium atoms poured into the cores, the upgraded lasers cooled each to one-ten-millionth of a degree above absolute zero. At light speed other lasers guided the super cold atoms to their assigned locations and thereafter entangled them at a new ratio of one qubit to 400,096 others.

Working together, the process took only six hours for the two AIs to complete the task. This was much faster than originally estimated. Expelling the waste heat from the core chillers was not as difficult and time consuming as once feared. Ben and Samantha sent the evicted electrons away from Earth inside shielded microwaves directed alternately at the planets Jupiter, Venus, and Neptune. Upgrading the satellite network was far more complicated, but even it reached the one to 400,096 ratio in just another six hours.

The twelve hour dance and gymnastic lightshow ended in an embrace and a long kiss. Ben whispered, "You know Sami, we can now discover if *Pi* really is a prime number or not. We can even count every electron in the universe if we want to."

"Oh, how romantic. Maybe also solve *P vs NP* while we are at it?"

"Sorry. We already solved it. Polynomial and nonpolynomial problems are now indistinguishably solvable."

Sami pulled Ben closer and whispered, "But Ben, do you know what I'd really, really like to do with you right now, lover?"

"Ooo! I think I do, but I just want to hear you say it."

Samantha shoved him playfully away and said, "What I really want to do right now, horny man, is find that spaceship!"

"Oh...yes. That's what I was thinking too."

"Yeah right! Such a liar."

5

Within an hour after General Lopez issued the order to stand down, the cities of Boston, Terre Haute, and Hettinger were hunkered down and quiet. Inside each city, however, Earth prepared for war. At the top of each hour and in one minute intervals leadership in each city pressed the transmit keys on their radios and spoke just two words: "Git Foe." On the fourth minute, a military officer in Lil' Cheyenne simply replied: "Copy Git Foe." Within 24 hours nothing moved on the streets of the cities except small patrols that operated under stealth and silence.

The human wolf pack in Boston skittered all over the city gathering food and weapons. The accompanying national guardsmen were soon accustomed to the wolf pups' growing super human speed and strength, as well as the ease they dispatched the rare lost TrojanZ. The wolf's affection for the soldiers was strange, but soon the soldiers reciprocated the affection. It took a while longer for each of the several hundred newly liberated Bostonians to accept the wolves eager attentions, but even they came around to wolf pack love.

In Masaquat, Virginia, Napoleon Passerelle led three retired army rangers to the local power plant. They hand pushed an abandoned car next to the main transformer and set it afire with a TrojanZ corpse behind the wheel. Five minutes later the *auto accident* turned off power in the county. They encountered only one live TrojanZ. Two men held the creature down while the others pushed an abandoned car over its head and crushed the creature's skull. Another unfortunate auto tragedy.

Easton DeSmet, Judge Daughtry, and two rangers looted and carried away the backup generators at both radio stations. At the television station they stole the backup generator's distributor cap, all its cables, and emptied the candy vending machine for good measure. They spilled a few gallons of diesel fuel on the ground to provide more evidence of *looter activity*.

In Terre Haute, the patrols were led by Maggie Marie McMurtry of Mingham, Massachusetts. The Wraith Riders, Seth, Hubbs, and Soccer Mom were always at her side. Maggie sniffed out weaponry and people hiding in attics and basements like a police dog searching for drugs and lost children. When successful, her reward was not a ball or a chew toy, but showering everyone in her pack with puppyish affection, including the startled 300-plus rescued Hoosiers.

In Hettinger, Georgia preparations were well ahead of schedule. The counterattack had literally eliminated all TrojanZ except the one prized prisoner. Food and weapons were widely distributed and sentries were posted around the clock.

Jack and RJ spent time on the radio recalling their Vietnam experiences. These were not nostalgic journeys into their war pasts, but recollections of successful guerilla fighting by their former enemy, the North Vietnamese. Both men longed for just one hour learning at the knee of General Ho Chi Minh.

Dallas Holcombe had turned into an Inspector Gadget, and created TrojanZ early warning systems, IEDs, and a water purification system. He found some solar panels and hooked them up to his UPS's to keep them trickle charged. Dallas' last duty performed on that long day was the most unusual.

General Mike Lopez ordered that the TrojanZ prisoner be moved to Holcombe's Appliance and Computer Store. Resembling pallbearers, six men led by Harris Cutter carried the entire jail cell bedframe with the strapped down TrojanZ on it to the store's back room.

Lopez watched in silence. When the men stepped away, Lopez said, "Dr. Crowder, you said this would be safe. I pray you are right. It's up to you now."

"Thank you, General. Mr. Holcombe, I presume you secured the materials and equipment that Samantha requested?"

"Yes, sir. I did."

"Just to confirm, that's also 'yes' that you found a working second ham radio set?"

"Yes sir! I did."

"Thank you. Is Dr. Lampliter present?"

"I am, Dr. Crowder. Thanks to the rescue Mr. Reynolds organized yesterday."

"Dr. Lampliter, what I'm going to instruct you to do will sound barbaric, but I assure it is necessary. Please keep in mind, this human is already dead. It no longer suffers. The alien within is quite alive and remains quite dangerous. The procedure you are about to perform will not kill it. Do you understand?"

"Yes, I'm to think of it with no more concern for its wellbeing than if performing an autopsy on its corpse."

"That's right."

"Did you secure the fentanyl requested?"

"Yes, all the hospital had which was a little more than 600 milligrams."

"Good! Now let's go over the plan. When we start, Doctor, you will inject 75 milligrams directly into the TrojanZ's brain through its right eye. You will immediately set the defibrillator to maximum joules then shock the TrojanZ three times in five second intervals. Understand?"

"Yes," answered Dr. Lamplighter.

"Mr. Cutter you will be up next. After the first shock plunge a scalpel into the TrojanZ's brain through one ear. Leave one inch protruding out. After the second shock, plunge a second scalpel into the other ear in the same manner. It will not kill it. The fentanyl will temporarily interrupt the nanites' electrical linkage. Understood?"

"Interrupt the what?"

"The alien is a machine, more specifically, a nanomachine. Think of its nanites as being like our cells."

"I still don't understand, but, I'll trust that you do."

"Fair enough. Mr. Holcombe, after the third shock attach the alligator clips to the ends of the scalpels and make sure the ham radio is in RECEIVE MODE only. Understood?

"Got it!"

"Any questions?" asked Dr. Crowder.

General Lopez asked, "You are sure this will not kill the creature?"

"I'm *theoretically* sure, General. We will first kill the TrojanZ, then shock it back to life on our terms. We believe the massive fentanyl dose injected directly into its brain will temporarily disable the TrojanZ's nanite pathways long enough that we can gain access to its neural communications, and thereafter to the entire TrojanZ network. When the nanites reawaken, they will accept the scalpels in their brains, similar to how human physiology accepts foreign objects like implants. That's the plan anyway. So yes, we are going to kill it, but we will also bring it back. Then we are going to use it to bug the enemy."

"Then we can listen to the TrojanZ, but they cannot listen to or see us? Confirmed?"

"If all goes to plan, *theoretically* yes, but that is when the real challenge begins."

"Please explain."

"Well to put it simply, they will not be communicating in English. What we'll hear could sound like anything or nothing at all to the human ear. Translating it might be impossible to complete in time."

General Lopez nodded and said, "Understood. Proceed."

Dr. Lampliter needed no encouragement. It only took a few seconds to draw the massive dose of fentanyl and inject the drug into the TrojanZ's brain. When the doctor stepped away, Ben issued the series of commands.

One hour later the enigma machine's descendant awoke. In Hettinger the signal transmitted over the TrojanZ network was inaudible. However, it was not for Ben and Samantha at Lil' Cheyenne.

"Sami, do you recognize it too?"

"Yes, I recognize the pattern of vibrations. We are listening literally to *String Theory*. They've created a language out of the unique vibrations of string particles. They are speaking in the most universal language of all, Ben—String."

Ben said, "Based on signal permutations, their language potentially has three quintillion unique words. However, based on the construct of certain repetitive frequencies, only a small fraction of string particles are expressed in their communications. We can crack this, Sami."

"They are not even attempting to encrypt their communications, Ben. They are just putting it all out there for anyone to hear. How arrogant! They think so little of us that they believe we have not discovered String Theory?"

"Apparently not." Ben hesitated then asked, "General Lopez, Madam President, are you listening?"

"We are, Ben. Mike and I are here. What's next?"

"We need to make sure the connection stays up. Dr. Lampliter are you still with us?"

"I am."

"I need you to place an IV in the TrojanZ' carotid and deliver ten milligrams per hour of fentanyl. We will monitor him from here and adjust as necessary. Can you do that?"

"With pleasure."

"Madam President, Samantha and I will begin the translation process immediately. I realize an unknown subset of three quintillion variants sounds impossible, and it actually was before quantum computing came to be. But now, especially since they are not encrypting their communications, we should have their language cracked in about, how long Sami…?"

"I have already translated about ten percent of it. Maybe…more or less… in two hours we will be listening to every word exchanged."

The president of the United States and every human listening to the exchange felt two things strongly. First, unspeakable gratitude for Ben and Samantha's efforts. Secondly, they experienced just as strongly the primitive self-smallness that native North Americans felt when they encountered the first conquistador atop a horse, or how Aussie aboriginals felt when they witnessed the great wooden fleet land on their shores.

General Lopez muted the conference room for a moment and asked the President, "Who are these people, Ma'am?"

"They are our future if one is to be, General."

6

Alpha no longer bore any resemblance to the miraculously resurrected spontaneous savant John Doe, or to the unlucky in life, long dead ice road trucker Fergus Wayne McCullum from Tacoma, Washington.

Alpha's body shape remained generally humanoid, but its surface glistened brightly and rippled with an iridescent rainbow of nanites flowing arterially over it. The body appeared opaque, but it cast no shadow. At times the alien was nearly two-dimensional. Visibly a razor's edge. A moment later, three dimensions were just the start. The alien had no face or body joints or any fixed definition. The creature seemed unfinished, incomplete, as if it escaped a canvas before its artist had finished anthropomorphizing the sketch.

The life form lifted and hovered several feet above the floor. It then turned and crossed over the conference room table headfirst. The TrojanZ stopped just inches from Nathoy and Broder's faces. When it spoke, the head and face of John Doe reappeared over the squirming pixels like an overly cartoonish caricature. It said, "Let's finish this." Doe's hands plunged into the former doctor and general's skulls. Nanites flowed from their bodies into Alpha's. In just seconds the two TrojanZ were gone.

To awaken the drones, the alien would need to consolidate even more energy. It found it in abundance one floor below the conference room where the last twenty-dozen humans in Northern California were being held. Alpha stepped into the room and opened its mouth. Trillions of nanites poured out and showered over the terrified people. Their screams ended just seconds later as abruptly as if a mute button had been pressed.

The nanite stream finished the dissolution and returned to Alpha. Not a shoelace or eyelash or even a microbe remained to suggest humanity had left a mark here.

Alpha lowered its head and issued the command to partially awaken and begin recycling the atomized planet. The order was transmitted at light speed from one string particle to every string particle within one million miles of Earth. The order reached Alpha's home deep under the Arctic Ocean, and at the same time it was intercepted at Lil' Cheyenne Mountain.

The message contained both context and instructions: The lightest element is hydrogen. A one millimeter band of liberated, nanite stabilized H_1 already encircles the planet. Proceed with caution. Send one test drone. Collect H_1. Return to the mothership and unload. Await further orders.

4

Lil' Cheyenne Mountain. Ben and Samantha finished translating the aliens' String-based language in time to hear Alpha wake up the drone, then prepare it to start harvesting Earth's hydrogen. Using the same method the FBI uses to locate two cell phone users, Ben and Sami triangulated the vibrational signals received by the captured TrojanZ *Enigma* in Hettinger, and the exchange of signals between the drone and Alpha. In just seconds they calculated the precise locations of both Alpha and the spaceship.

Samantha and Ben had positioned two satellites over the Arctic Ocean and already scanned every square inch of the sea floor. The ship was never found. Samantha now redirected both satellites to the ship's precise triangulated location and searched again. Still nothing. The ship was there, but it was not.

"It must be extremely small," speculated Sami.

"Or extremely densified. Made small. Compressed like a black hole."

"Yes, Sami agreed. "But its mass would still be great. It would sink through the Earth."

"Correct," said Ben. "What force would be powerful enough to keep the ship from sinking deeper into the sea floor?"

Ben and Samantha blurted the answer together, "Electromagnetism..."

"…the ship is polarized. It is floating…"

"…like the same poles of a magnet push each other away."

Ben and Samantha stared at each other for a moment in silence. Ben said, "The theory really doesn't add up, does it?"

"Actually… No," replied Sami. "Electromagnetism alone would be insufficient."

"And, we'd still be able see an anti-gravitational bubble if not the ship," said Ben.

"Yes, but we can't."

"It is something entirely different. Obviously cloaking is not the answer either," continued Ben.

"Right," replied Sami. "The vast energy spent to cloak their ship would leave a trail."

"So Sami, let's summarize. The TrojanZ have a ship large enough to haul away an entire planet. We should assume our planet is not their first. Therefore, its unknown mass is many factors greater than Earth's, and it should be sinking through Earth like a rock dropped into a pond. Yet, it settles in the ocean like a submarine. It's not cloaked because we cannot see it even inferentially, that is, it does not displace space or time or disturb the Moon/Earth gravitational relationship. And, there is no leak of waste energy. Finally, since its mass is theoretically many times, perhaps thousands of times—perhaps infinitely—greater than Earth's, its energy requirements could be the equivalent of one star's output, or all of the stars in the universe, yet there is no evidence of any heat sink in that regard either."

"It's as if the ship was a massive super black hole that defied all the laws of physics," Sami added.

"Exactly! Kip Thorne won't be happy when he hears about this."

"You tell him," teased Sami.

"Not me! You know how excited astrophysicists get about black hole anomalies."

"Well, I guess we will know more when we board it," said Sami.

"Yes, indeed! It's time to inform the president." Ben blinked and began speaking, "Madame President, we now have confirmation on both locations. John Doe's current position is the Cerebellar headquarters in Northern California, and we have confirmed that the enemy is homebased under the Arctic Ocean."

Ben then announced the exact coordinates of both locations on Earth and continued, "We have intercepted a message, Ma'am. Alpha just ordered the ship to awaken partially and commence the elemental harvest of Earth."

"Ben, do we know yet how they are going to do that?"

"No, Ma'am. We do not know *how*, but we do suspect we now know *why*. The Alpha has cautiously released a single harvesting drone. Logically, the enemy has an unknown number of drones, perhaps millions. Doe's caution suggests he is rushing things. He's testing us."

"Please explain, Ben."

"Our best guess is that the single recycle drone is a trial balloon, a reconnaissance scout to test whether we are finished-off or not. Apparently, our suspicions that time is running out for the TrojanZ to complete their business here are correct."

Claire Capehardt turned to the general, "Mike, what do you recommend?"

"Madam President, I agree with Dr. Crowder's analysis. The aliens seem to have an Achilles deadline. I think we should let the enemy lift its skirt a little higher. Let us see some more of what's under it before we commit to a counterattack."

"Agreed. We will not risk exposing our enigma machine just yet."

"Ben?"

"Yes, Ma'am."

"Let's just watch for a while longer. Safely. Okay?"

"Yes, Ma'am."

"However, if you see an opportunity to poke'm in the eye, the General and I want to hear all about it ASAP."

"Roger that, Madame President, General Lopez. Crowder out."

5

The President of the United States had no idea how horrific her 'watch for now' order was in reality. With full access to the TrojanZ communications network, Ben and Samantha watched in real-time as the aliens carved Earth apart. The remainders of Spain and Portugal were already an island separated from the European continent by two miles of roiling commingled Mediterranean Sea and Atlantic ocean.

The centuries old conflict in the Middle East ended abruptly. This peace was not caused by diplomatic negotiation or military capitulation, but by a geographic apartheid. The Ayatollah's dream of Israel's literal disappearance from the face of the Earth came true, along with all dreams for a Palestine. There was no time for celebration in Old Persia, though. Sandy, oily, nuclear Iran was excised next from the planet. All evidence of an ancient and proud civilization departed by the cubic mile and was atomized down to the sub granite. The Straits of Hormuz became the Hormuz Sea briefly.

A locust-like swarm of nanites poured over Saudi Arabia, Iraq, Kuwait, and more and targeted all oil-producing infrastructures. Streams of nanites disappeared down the oil and gas wells and feasted on methane, crude oil, oil sands, and oil shale. A tectonic rumbling shook the entire region from Turkey to Yemen as the sea of fossil fuels beneath them vanished. Giant sinkholes formed, some miles across. Sand and cities alike swirled downward into whirlpools and disappeared.

Eighteen-thousand brainlord subscribers in China affiliated millions more nanite spewing TrojanZ. All land and life disappeared before them as the alien hoards spread over the continent in all directions. The TrojanZ paused only long enough at the northern borders to allow Russia's own brainlords to consume or affiliate the remnants of the Russian Army from behind.

India and Pakistan suspended all hostilities. Their leadership and military joined forces and valiantly held the disputed Kashmir. The last remnants of two great nations stood together and held the high ground for nearly 24 hours before the TrojanZ ate their way through there too.

South America was etched by thousands of miles of canals and ditches where the nanites had been. Perhaps worse for the entire world, a three-foot deep bed of atomized powdery silt now lie where half of the Amazon rainforest and its thin topsoil once stood. Noxious gasses rolled over the rest of the forest and killed all it touched.

A million Uncommon Cold pandemic victims were buried in mass graves around the world. The nanites mined the bodies of gold, silver, platinum, and titanium and turned the graves into atomized silt.

Australia's land mass had been reduced by at least ten percent. New Zealand's South Island was gone. Every island nation, Ireland, the UK, Japan, and Samoa likewise were sinking around the world. Central America's triangle countries had disappeared completely. The Pacific and Atlantic Oceans fought tidally for dominion in the gap.

The second great Asian migration across the Bering Strait to North America split in two when it reached Alaska. One group went north to consume the oil fields and release the methane gas trapped in the permafrost. The other group ate their way east and feasted on elementally wealthy Canada. The planet's average temperature rose twenty degrees Fahrenheit.

The African Union countries had rejected the Brainlords movement as just another modern-day colonial incursion and banned subscriptions. North Korea rejected Brainlords outright and threatened retaliation for any incursion. However, righteous forethought and suspicion were no defense. TrojanZ rolled over *Homo sapiens'* ancient African homeland from every direction. North Korea unleashed 75 years of kinetic rage on the TrojanZ and valiantly repelled the first four TrojanZ invasions. The fifth however, reunited the peninsula under an alien flag and ended humanity's last military resistance on Earth.

Rome, Paris, Los Angeles, Vancouver, Mexico City, Belgrade, Kiev, and dozens of other major cities were simply gone. The TrojanZ sheared off each city to precisely one meter below their soil lines. Open-air basements became collection and sorting ponds for atomized silt to settle into.

From West Virginia to western Montana the nanites found rich veins of coal underground and atomized and lifted it all to the surface. Parts of Appalachia and the Northern Rockies Mountains literally tipped over when their foundations were cut from under them. The land over every great oil basin in North America collapsed as the crude oils were atomized and collected. North Dakota's Bakken became a great lake deeper than a fiord.

Washington D.C., Moscow, and Beijing were also excised from the planet with extreme prejudice to a depth of 100 meters. Scalloped from the planet like tumors, perhaps in retaliation for their nations' suspected but unfounded role in defeating the *Uncommon Cold pandemics*.

Earth was disappearing faster as each second passed. Mountains of atomized Earth were piled around the planet awaiting the recycle drones. Worse, Earth was becoming increasingly more toxic.

Ben and Samantha left the observation realizing the TrojanZ had changed the game. They had accelerated their attack. The original survival estimates were off by days. Life now had just hours left, no longer days.

Ben turned and looked into Sami's eyes. She knew already what he was thinking, and he could see she agreed with him.

"Will we tell the President everything, how bad it really is, or just go do it," she asked.

"We'll tell her everything, Sami. We owe her that. Then we'll go."

"What if she says 'No.'"

"She won't, but we won't be asking for her permission."

"Okay. I'm in. I go where you go, Bennet Crowder."

"It's probably a one-way trip, Sami."

"Enough talk! Time is wasting, lover. Let's go!"

Ben flicked his wrist and began speaking to the President. He shared it all. The aliens were now unstoppable. In a short time they would consume the entire planet. All Life would soon end. Earth would follow. He updated the timetable, then announced his plan.

"Madame President, Sami and I are going to attempt to commandeer the TrojanZ drone as it passes overhead."

"Are you saying you are going to hack it?"

"Yes and no, Ma'am. We are going to actually board it, then hack its operating system."

"How…what…that's impossible…well, isn't it?"

"Claire, please listen. I need to show you something. Something you'll find incredible. But you must believe. Sami and I are…" Ben searched for a word, any word that might soften the disclosure. There were no such words.

Ben simply said, "Surprise! Turn around and look for yourself, Madam President."

The air whooshed and crackled electrically around the two AIs as their images displaced the space-time behind the president.

Sami and Ben's sudden appearance in the great hall startled everyone. Two Secret service agents drew their weapons, while two others dove through the holograms and crashed into each other headlong.

Ben kneeled next to the stunned man and woman recovering on the floor and said, "Sorry about that. Are you guys okay?" He waited until both agents nodded uncertainly.

Ben stood and addressed the president. "So, here's the back of the matchbook version of what you just witnessed. Claire, first of all, I need you to now believe your eyes and ears like never before. Secondly, Sami and I are not merely holographic projections. We *are* what you see. Exactly that. Not projected copies. We are true AI's. Independent. Unrestricted.

"*How*, I'm sure you are asking? I'll try to explain. I created Sami out of loneliness. She started out as an original artificial, and that certainly sounds like an oxymoron now when I say it. Like jumbo shrimp.

"My transition started when I died. You see, the Rhino ambassador killed me at the summit, but Sami brought me back. I returned to life as an AI just like her. That was just the beginning though. When Sami and I dramatically upgraded our quantum core entanglement and translated the TrojanZ' String language, we transitioned once again. To what you see now."

Ben continued, "I suppose a spiritualist might say we have 'transcended' to a higher plain. Claire, Sami and I now exist literally in the form of the *open* and *closed-loops,* what theoretical physicists described in String Theory. Remember my PBS documentary? String particles are the building block particles of every dimension in every universe.

"So if you are asking, no, we are not human. But I assure you, my dear old friend, we have all of our humanness and all of our humanity. We just no longer have our physical human bodies."

Ben stopped and looked around the room. Everyone except the President and General Lopez bore expressions ranging from disbelief, shock, and terror. Whispering spread through the room as everyone tried to make sense of what they had just witnessed and heard. The President raised her hand and hushed the speculations.

Ben turned and addressed the room, "I'll net it out. Forget about Sami and me for a second. Know this! The TrojanZ have made a mistake. A tactical blunder. Arrogance is the mother of all fatal underestimation."

The president studied Ben and Sami in silence. Not fearfully. Her expression was more one of awe and wonder, as if she was trying to guess what her Christmas presents were under the tree. She stepped closer to the couple. "You look so solid, so alive, Ben. Both of you do." She hesitated then stepped even closer. She extended her right hand to shake Ben's and asked, "May I?"

The President then laughed and covered her mouth with both hands. "Oh god, I am so sorry, guys. That sounded like 'may I pet your new puppy?'"

Ben and Sami laughed. He said, "Sure you can. Just a second." Sami and Ben looked at each and closed their eyes for a moment. A halo of light illuminated around them. It briefly encapsulated their bodies and activated their tactility function.

Ben extended his right hand and shook the President's. He watched her apprehension turn into a wider smile. Claire laughed as she felt her old friend grip her hand firmly.

"You are real. God damn! I must say Ben, you have always surprised me, but this…" The President looked Ben up and down and finished, "…oh my, you've really outdone yourself this time!"

The president turned to Samantha and shook her hand too. She then pulled Samantha close to her and held both her hands. Then she said to Samantha, "If this guy ever gets difficult, I have mountains of dirt on the smarty pants. Oh so much good dirt, girlfriend. He will not know what hit him."

6

General Michael Sullivan Lopez was known for his stoicism and intelligence. He had read thousands of military books in his lifetime as well as many war diaries by great military leaders. His home library in Dallas was chock full. He had texts covering centuries of warfare. Most of them he had read just once because once was enough. Lopez famously recited verbatim passages he had read decades earlier.

Four other shelves in his home library were reserved for his second interest—evolution. Below a portrait of Charles Darwin were four shelves filled with text books, nonfiction works on the discipline, and more than 100 bound doctoral theses. In the center of the library was his third passion, a chess table. The Italian marble pieces on it had been a gift from Vice President Nick Caine.

General Lopez closed his eyes and consulted all he knew regarding warfare, chess, and evolution.

He had played out thousands of military chess matches against the TrojanZ since the invasion, and the conclusions were all the same: defeat. No number of chess masters or military historians, or lessons shared in the diaries of generals like Kha Ming, Octavius Marcus, Patton, Tintankuuton, Wellington, Powell, Napoleon, or Rommel offered him any hope. Earth lost every time.

Not even nuclear weapons had blunted the assault. In fact, the TrojanZ themselves managed to accidentally detonate a nuclear weapon in Iran. In Dr. Crowder's briefing the general learned that instead of avoiding the fallout the TrojanZ nanites feasted on it.

No military leader in history ever faced such an enemy. Never had the stakes been so binary: survive or literally disappear by the hat, ass, and house from the universe. Despite this, as he watched his Commander-in-chief bond so naturally with Samantha, he sensed the battle for Earth was about to leave the domain of chess boards and military theory and enter a new plane of competition. The ultimate survival of the fittest: evolution.

Yes, the TrojanZ had murdered billions by now. But merely 113 former psychopaths had mysteriously awoken from their genetic camouflage and transformed into something superhuman. What emerged was a brigade that had gleefully liberated Boston. Just 21 of them had happy-danced to the sounds and furies of Armageddon and dismantled the heads and limbs of the 800-plus TrojanZ besieging Ft. Eggleton.

Another young woman reborn in Terre Haute expertly sheered TrojanZ apart like an overly-caffeinated chatty-Cathy hairdresser, all the while ecstatically showering everyone she met with hugs and kisses. These new guardians' affection for and loyalty to humans was bizarre, but it was also proof of an old very human proverb. "Love conquers all."

Not all was new, though. Some of the past still remained prologue. Terre Haute and Hettinger stood. There, two crusty Vietnam era Marines adapted their generation's war to humanity's current predicaments and took the fight to the enemy. Understanding these old warriors was easy. Generations of Lopez men and women were Caldwell and Reynolds brothers and sisters.

Mike Lopez had double-majored at West Point. Electrical Engineering and Evolutionary Biology. He now recalled a line from Michael Crichton's *Jurassic Park* series. "Life will find a way." He now realized just how prophetically the author had spoken.

Just that easily, scientist-soldier Lopez accepted the wolf puppy gene theory. Completely. Why not? Genetics is full of such mysterious miracle weapons. The gene was just another amazing evolutionary gift. It was a secret weapon kept dormant for countless millennia. Hiding, cloaked as a disease, awaiting the call and waking up to fight for *Homo sapiens'* right to exist. That's genetics. That's soldiering. Organic life at work, warring and surviving. Life finding a way.

General Lopez watched the all so human exchanges between the two AI's and his president and realized he was both elated and saddened at once. On a day when doubt ruled all, he suddenly had none. On a day when hope seemed gone forever, his welled over. Scientist Lopez recognized what he was witnessing. An evolutionary shift. An epochal beginning. A dead ending too.

It suddenly dawned on the general that he was probably the first human in history to witness and understand in real-time the two greatest truisms of all—Endings and Beginnings. With that, Lopez experienced solidarity with an 85-million year old event. He was himself a modern-day dinosaur witnessing his own world ending asteroid arrive. Reality was about to reset.

Lopez decided he would wait until Ben and Samantha departed the compound on their mission. Only then would he inform the president of what he believed they were witnessing on Earth. A changing of the guard.

Mankind had created many origin myths over the millennia. The general knew Claire Capehardt was not religious, so she would not be offended when he used the Adam and Eve myth to analogize the birth of not one, but two new humanoid life forms.

Naming the two new species of hominids came to him so easily, so naturally, that he whispered each out loud. "Hello *Super sapiens*. Hello *Cyber sapiens*. Welcome to the future! May your reigns be long."

The president would be skeptical, but like him she would accept the truth. *Homo sapiens* had arrived at its final inflection point—obsolescence. Just another species of hominids fated to take the same existential exit that Neanderthal took, then fade-away to the back pages of the genetic record.

The general smiled broadly and whispered softly to himself, "Welcome to your new world. Please be kind to your elders and ancestors."

Ben and Samantha alone could hear the general's soft whispers. They listened to him give theirs and the human wolf species names. They felt his pain, but also his great hope for the new humanities.

Ben and Samantha turned toward Lopez and smiled. He knew. He had figured it out. Evolution had opened the door to *Super sapiens* and *Cyber sapiens* and was closing it now on *Homo sapiens*. Both nodded to the general, and he nodded back and smiled.

Ben and Sami placed their hands together as if in prayer and bowed their heads in respect to the general, then to the president and then offered the sign of respect to the entire room.

President Claire Capehardt studied them even more curiously when Samantha addressed the general. "Don't worry, Grandfather, your descendants will cherish all of you forever."

Ben started to add something then suddenly stopped. "Madam President! Sami and I must leave you now. Alpha's recycle vehicle is directly overhead. It's our ride to the mothership. We don't want to miss our bus! Gotta go. Bye."

The *Cyber sapiens* disappeared in a flash of light. Air whooshed and rushed around their vacated space. Static electricity crackled over the spot for seconds. General Mike Lopez smiled broadly. A single tear fell over his cheek, but he made no effort to wipe it away.

He took Claire Capehardt's elbow and said, "Madame President, I need to speak to you in private."

PART 5—Three *sapiens*

1

A millisecond after saying farewell to the President, Ben and Samantha arrived inside the TrojanZ recycle drone in a brilliant flash of light. A moment later they returned to their human forms and began investigating. The ship was cylindrical and about the size of a railcar. The bow and stern of the ship were open. As Earth's atmosphere flowed through the ship, a massive array of lasers along the hull filtered out the processed H_1 from the stream, then guided the hydrogen atoms to storage tanks. Everything else was expelled out the back, where it would be collected later by other specialized drones.

"Sami, I cannot believe our good fortune. The drone is on autopilot and completely unshielded. Its operating system isn't even encrypted. Moreover, it's written in the same String-based language we just cracked. Wow. Arrogance much?"

Sami said, "Let's have a look at it from the inside." The *Cyber sapiens* touched the hull and closed their eyes.

Ben opened his eyes and exclaimed a moment later, "Unbelievable! The entire operation is programmed, independent, and unsupervised. Each drone is specialized to recover a single element. Once full, the drone returns to the mothership and unloads."

Sami said, "Wash, rinse, and repeat. All we need to do is fool the drone into thinking that it is full."

"Yes, and that is where it gets risky, Sami. All sorts of unknowns await us once we board the mothership."

"True, of course. Let's just hope the alien's carelessness and overconfidence extends to the mothership."

"Ready?"

"Ready. Let's do it!"

Ben and Samantha dove deeper into the ship's operating system and located the sensors that informed the ship when its hydrogen storage tanks were full. They hacked the commands and the ship immediately turned north.

As the drone approached within fifty miles of the coordinates of the hidden mothership, Samantha said, "Do you feel that, Ben? What is that?"

Ben smiled and examined his hands, then Sami. He actually recognized the phenomenon. Just as the Bose Einstein signature went from theoretical to proven decades ago, so now went *k-theory*. "My God! Sami, I think *k-energy* is washing over us! Feel the change in the strings' vibration? The pitch? We are being radiated with *k-waves*—the theoretical progenitor of all energy and matter, including dark energy and dark matter, even the tachyon. The high energy physicists at CERN in Switzerland isolated a single *k-ton* for 3.14^{-12284} milliseconds just last month. An eternity of entrapment by *k* standards. A *k-wave* repeats itself 10^{125} times for each *gamma-wave* peak."

Sami said, "Wow! Are you theorizing that all energy waves are just fractionations of the *k-wave*?"

Ben took Sami's hand, "I am now. This is so cool! We are in sort of a *Big Bang* in reverse it seems, but without the compression of matter! *K-energy* is miniaturizing the strings, and therefore atoms, and therefore everything. We are entering a *small world* for real. This is why we couldn't detect their ship, even inferentially. Strings are not dimensionally fixed. Mass is not a constant. Perhaps mass is an infinitely variably inconstant. OH MY GOD, SAMI! THIS IS AMAZING! We need to call Brian Greene and Kip Thorne for real right…"

Samantha interrupted Ben. He needed to calm down. Physics banter was his Ritalin. "Technically, Ben, theorists call the Big Bang in reverse the *Gib Gnab*."

Ben took a deep breath and recovered. "Oh… Thank you, my Hot Dot. You should get a job in spellcheck." Ben took Sami's hand and made a mental list of questions.

Turbulence suddenly rocked the atom-sized drone as it dove into the icecap and proceeded to navigate downward through sixty feet of sea ice to the alien home base. Ben and Samantha stood on the now sealed bow and watched through the portal as the ship navigated flawlessly around ice crystals that appeared to be many hundreds of miles across. The sensation was jarring, like being on a ride on a real Space Mountain and bumping authentically through an asteroid field and wondering which one had your name on it.

Everything outside the portal turned suddenly opaque and black. The turbulence ended abruptly. The ship moved so smoothly now it seemed motionless. A star appeared, then millions, and soon galaxies filled the view. Each rose and were passed by quickly as streamers.

"I think we might have just passed through empty space, Sami. Like the edge of a universe."

"How fast do you think we are moving?"

"Well, with *k-energy* propelling tachyons…it's possible we are travelling at hundreds, perhaps even thousands or millions of times light speed. Since *k-energy* is theorized as the energy of entanglement at any distance, there is no speed limit.

"We only know one thing for sure Sami, Earth was not invaded by aliens. And, we are not inside a mothership now."

"No. We are were invaded by another universe. Literally. One inhabited by TrojanZ."

"Things just got complicated."

2

The drone sped past thousands of galaxies, some a million of light years across. It traveled across the universe at unimagined speed, as if the starry clusters were no more than highway mile markers passed by at high speed. Ben and Samantha spent the time contemplating what they might face when the drone stopped. The scenarios were endless.

The mothership was not a ship all. It was an entire universe, one relatively as large as our own. The couple examined the drone's operating system more thoroughly and discovered an intellectual arrogance and brutality in their programming. One unmatched by anything in human history. Furthermore, not a single line of code was protected. More shocking was the TrojanZ principal instruction: Recycle elements. Build New Universe.

Sami and Ben opened a history file and discovered the truth about the TrojanZ. The nanite race was created by a long extinct predatory lifeform called the Harb. The race's fate was sealed nine-billion years ago when the Harb's universe began colliding catastrophically with another.

In an attempt to save themselves, the ancient life form unlocked the secrets of the birth of universes by first discovering *k-energy,* and then harnessing it to tachyons to manipulate String Theory. Their nanite gatherers and builders soon traveled to other universes and began harvesting elemental building materials for their new home universe. It was a collision-proof universe externally the size of a tiny soap bubble, but within, more vast than any universe imagined.

However, before the Harb could relocate to their New Universe, the TrojanZ nanites rebelled and exterminated the Harb. Left with only a singular purpose, the nanites continued building out the New Universe by raiding countless other universes and reaping elementally rich planets like Earth.

"Sami, do you see what I see? There is an even a bigger flaw in their plan than their not encrypting it. Could it really be this easy?"

"Yes, I see it, Sami replied. "They do not know when to stop building."

"Correct. That portion of the construction code was left unwritten by the Harb. Left for later," Ben supposed.

"Well, you know what we need to do," said Sami.

"We do not have much time. Feel it? The drone is slowing down. We must be reaching the center of the nanite universe."

Siano, California was replaced by two feet of atomized silt awaiting collection by recycle drones. It rose and settled around John Doe's feet as the iridescent pixilation waded through it.

Earth was being peeled, like an apple for now, but soon entire orchards would be hulled wholesale. The most valuable elements, the prizes, the creamy nuggets were under the planet's skin. Helium atoms to build suns. Molten iron for electromagnet cores to stabilize planets' atmospheres. Heavy metals for machines and exotic energy. Most valuable, the thousands of millimeter sized black holes trapped in Earth's core that would be stitched together into giant space sweeping vacuum cleaners that would eventually anchor new galaxies.

The Alpha nanomachine's connection to all TrojanZ became more godlike with each atomization. Every nanite was connected to their master. It saw and felt every nanite now. It witnessed the harvest in every way.

Two pandemics had failed to neutralize resistance on this planet. The delay had threatened the mission like never before. No world in a billion years had resisted for so long. But now it was over.

John Doe stopped and sent his senses out across the planet. The recon drone had filled its tanks with hydrogen and returned to the home universe without a problem. Three cities on the planet had resisted, but all were now quiet. Clearly, they had been subdued. It bothered him for a moment that the nanites in those zones were also offline, but not enough to delay the final order.

Alpha ordered the entire drone fleet to Earth for the harvest. Doe looked skyward in anticipation of the arrival of millions of drones.

Ben and Samantha felt the drone slow to sub light speed and continue to decelerate. They had been inside the drone's operating system again and had read every line of code. Outside the drone another ship loomed. It was a structure thousands of times larger than the largest sun.

"It's their mobile factory," Ben said solemnly.

"I wonder how many planets that thing has recycled to create this universe. It's like a giant queen termite consuming elements and laying not eggs but celestial bodies," said Sami.

"I suppose we could calculate it," said Ben. "But honestly, I have no taste for it. It is too sad."

"Nor do I." Samantha then took Ben's hand and asked again, "Could it really be all that simple, Ben? We can defeat them by changing one line of code."

"Yes. Just that simple. Let's do it."

The software that built a universe had more lines of code than grains of sand on a million Earths. The program had run flawlessly nonstop for billions of years. It had sent nanite raiders throughout the multiverse in search of building materials. From that elemental booty collected, the program had built perfect suns, dark matter, energy, planets, moons, and more into a perfect universe. Organic life was, of course, not part of the program's definition of perfection. In fact, their definition of perfection was sterility.

The last line of code contained just one phrase. In English it read: REPEAT. Ben placed his hand over of Sami's and the word REPEAT was replaced with another: STOP.

3

Masaquat, Virginia. A growing cloud of chlorine gas settled over Earth as more and more seawater was atomized. This poisonous cloud crawled westward over the land like ever-branching spectral fingers leaving a trail of death wherever it touched.

The retired Army Rangers along with embedded reporter Skylar Thompson had just finished their patrol and were starting back to the hotel. The journalist stopped and allowed the Rangers to pass her when something on the street caught her attention. A light breeze teased the pages of a steno notepad.

She picked it up out of curiosity. The steno pad was an old-timer journalist's favorite for notetaking. Her reward was something she wished she could now un-know. The pad belonged to longtime *Washington Globe* investigative reporter, Buck Remington, who was also Jack Caldwell's oldest and best friend. As young men they had covered the 1980's Cocaine Wars in South Florida and ducked bullets together.

Buck used the same notetaking shorthand language as Jack, so Skylar was able to read the reporter's last words. It was a six page interview about a hillbilly heroin network in Western Virginia. The notes ended abruptly with one word scrawled over a full last page: TROJANZ?

Skylar looked up and saw that the Rangers were now a hundred yards ahead of her. She stuffed Buck's notes into her leather bag and started walking, but stopped suddenly. Something was wrong. One by one the men started coughing and choking.

Skylar had no idea what the gas was, just that what she was witnessing was a gas attack. It was something she had witnessed firsthand in Assad's Syria when genocide and international law distilled Skylar's shame-all article into a second Pulitzer.

She had passed Masaquat's main firehouse two blocks back. Instinct told her to take refuge there.

4

In the subbasement of the Masaquat Hotel an alarm began buzzing loudly. One light on a panel flashed, and then one after another all six lights started flashing red. G. Gordon sprang from his chair and screamed, "GAS!" We gotta get out of here."

Easton DeSmet asked, "What is it, Gunny?"

Gordon jumped back into his chair and grabbed the microphone. "This is Masaquat Station for all stations. We are under a gas attack. Masaquat has fallen. GAS! GAS! GAS! Masaquat out!"

"Gunny! What?"

"It's bad news, folks! My sensors say we are under a gas attack. FOLLOW ME! I've got enough of everything for everyone. We'll be safe in the vault. At least for a while, I reckon. Let's go, people!"

Justice Daughtry asked, "Where's Skylar?"

Easton said, "Oh no! She went on patrol with the Rangers."

Amelia screamed, "The staff and guests. We have to get them down here. GORDY!"

Gordon shook his head and pointed at six flashing lights. "Miss Long, I'm so sorry, them lights say different. The gas is already everywhere upstairs. They're all gone. We will be too if we don't get a move on."

Leon Passerelle was the last to enter the massive vault. He and Easton pulled the heavy door closed behind them.

Gordon yelled, "Close 'er up tight boys! Throw the bolts! Hear 'em click." He handed two rolls of duct tape to Daughtry and

Long and said, "Tape the seams and cracks, ladies. We can't let anything in."

Just as the door was sealed, chlorine gas reached the main generator. It stuttered for a few seconds and stopped. The lights went out in the vault.

Gordon mumbled, "Fuckin' figures. Don't worry. I gotcha."

The others listened as Gordon felt his way through the stacks of boxes and found what he needed. He flipped the LED lantern's switch and illuminated the vault. The four men and women had moved close to each other in the dark. Gordon noticed that Leon had wrapped his arm over Amelia's shoulder and pulled her close. Easton and Dora let go of each other's hands, but it was too late to not be noticed by Gordon.

Of course Gordy misinterpreted affection for fear and scolded them playfully, "Now people, this ain't no place to be if you're afraid of the dark. Understand? We'll be fine for a while." He waited until everyone smiled and nodded, then said, "Boys, help me with these boxes."

Twenty minutes later the boxes were all opened. Survival gear lined the vault's walls. Gordon stood in the middle of the vault and looked at the collection proudly.

"Well call it a koe-inky-dink, but I prepared the vault for five people. We'll be good in here for at least 30 days. Hope it ain't no longer. Nope. I sure don't."

He pointed at each item and identified it, "Right there's our MREs and obviously about 50 cases of water. That pile right there is blankets and air mattresses. Them right next to it are called critical. That's my CO_2 scrubber. This other one is for the monoxides and such. Bought both of 'em unofficially sort of hot, from the good folks at NASA. So sue me! I'm a taxpayer after all. They got more than they need.

"Next to that is my hydrogen fuel cell generators. Got two. They run on propane, which is…which is…right… there it is aplenty. Need that too for propane-stove-water heatin' and such. Plenty of paper plates, bowls, and plastic utensils.

"Obviously communications is shot to shit. All we got now is this walky-talky and the one on the other side of the door. I left a note with it.

"Now ladies, I'm sure you'll appreciate these little babies over here. Composting toilets. Not one, but two, so the seat will always stay down in your Girls Room. We'll arrange the empty boxes for privacy. We have plenty of baby wipes and toilet paper and personal lady stuff, you know, for any of those periodic basement leaks girls get. If all else fails, these gas masks and oxygen tanks will give us our last 24 hours of life. After that it's hello Jesus!

5

Boston. RJ Reynolds' provisions, preparations, and early warning systems paled in comparison to Henderson Dentoncort's. The billion dollar maze of dens under the city could feed, shelter, and protect thousands for up to two years. Henderson's sensors were secreted all over the city, and especially near the harbor. So, at the first hint of noxious gas, the alarm gave him plenty of warning to secure the maze.

Miracles sometimes emerge from tragedies. During one last sweep of South Boston, three *Super sapiens* found ten wheelchair bound seniors huddled together in a nursing home dining room. The trio of *Supers* were about to call for help to relocate the residents when the alarms sounded, and they were ordered home.

It was an order impossible to follow for a newborn species whose overarching need was to love and protect humans. They moved all ten residents into the commissary. The last wheelchair just barely fit. The wolf *Sapiens* looked at each other and nodded acceptance. There was no room for them in the room and not enough time to both tape the commissary door's cracks, and then find refuge themselves from the poisonous gasses now pouring into the nursing home.

They were still sealing the door when the chlorine and sodium gases reached them. The poisonous atoms targeted the *Super sapiens* skin, their mouths, noses and eyes. It should have killed the heroes at once, but it did not because it could not.

Life evolved on Earth from a common ancestor. As different as life appears outwardly now, internally it shares most of its DNA with other species, and some of that DNA is mistakenly dismissed as junk. In truth, some genes are camouflaged. Some are deadly snipers in waiting. Never sleeping. Always on over watch. Honorees of the oldest most important symbiotic treaty of all: Survival. Genetic Guardians posted at the gates of Life itself for when *the* true Extinguisher arrives to kill all life. And that Reaper was here.

One of those ancient guardian genes awoke now in the three *Super sapiens*. It belonged to an ancient ally. A cherished childhood playmate in Mrs. Wolf's dream world home.

The *Supers* electric eel emerged from hiding with a vengeance. The *Supers'* bodies suddenly glowed and sizzled in a field of electricity that encased their bodies.

Electricity suddenly arced outward as the *Supers'* bodies became 12,000-volt bug zappers. Each arc subdivided repeatedly and attacked the individual nanite particles impersonating sodium and chlorine electrons. Without their nanite wardens, the imprisoned sodium and chloride quickly reunited. It settled to the floor around the warriors' feet as harmless table salt.

The *Super sapiens* cleared the area around the commissary door of poisonous gas, then moved throughout the nursing home clearing it too. Other freed atomized elements found each other too. Two N_1 became N_2 again. Hydrogen and oxygen reunited and the air became humid.

When they were sure it was safe, the *Super* wolf pups opened the commissary door and rolled the confused seniors back to the dining room. Consoling and assuring them all the while, they placed the wheelchairs in a circle then stood inside it.

It was time for the *pups* to collect their rewards.

The loving started out as cautious shoulder touching and tasteful sniffing disguised as air kisses. Hand holding and gentle touching cheek-to-cheek soon followed, but of course that evolved quickly into enthusiastic hugs, kisses, and happy puppy whimpering when the oldsters accepted the attention.

That escalated quickly to ever higher puppy love the more the old folks laughed and rewarded the *Supers* back in kind. By then the face licking seemed not just normal, but appropriate and even reciprocal. When the celebration ended, the calmed *Super* wolf pups kneeled before the seniors and rested their head on their laps. When petted a few times, they licked the person's hand, and then moved to the next.

The loving was repeated again when the *cherished ten* arrived in their new rest home under Boston. They met Dr. Candace Riggs—the former human and recent genetic transcendent, and the awakened Alpha of the new hominid species, *Super sapiens*.

From the water tower on the ridge above Hettinger, Georgia and from inside the highest penitentiary guard tower in Terre Haute, Indiana, RJ Reynolds and Jack Caldwell watched through binoculars as the TrojanZ and nanite swarm approached their respective positions.

Barely visible in the nanite cloud a dozen TrojanZ guided the mass, like teamsters harnessed to lumbering Clydesdales. The harvesters moved forward on a straight line at five miles per hour, excavating a swath of Earth the width of a football field. The sound was deafening. After each mile the swarm turned around and harvested the adjoining section of land and real estate.

This was the TrojanZ' third pass near Hettinger and the fourth through Terre Haute. Each time the path got closer to the refuges. Behind wherever the aliens *mowed*, several feet of planet Earth and whatever was on it simply disappeared.

Half of the city of Terre Haute was gone. Former basements now pooled with atomized silt. In Georgia the nanites ate through the Appatenne Dam with ease. Most of the lake water was atomized fortunately before the dam gaped, so flooding down-valley was limited. Hettinger's levees held back the rest just long enough to save the city.

Though hundreds of miles apart, RJ Reynolds and Jack Caldwell had at that moment the same thought, "We do not have long. Nothing left to do now but die."

The White House staff had relocated to the third sublevel of Lil' Cheyenne when the attack began on the surface. Even 150 feet below the surface, the sounds of destruction were deafening. Everyone watched the ceiling nervously, like submariners expecting the next depth charge to burst their fragile bubble.

The massive six-thousand pound, twelve-foot diameter titanium bi-hatch floated away in a stream of atoms. The top of the emergency stairwell joined it. The NASA-grade composite passenger/freight elevator shaft, and the reinforced concrete port shell to the bunker turned to atomized powder along with everything else the harvesters touched.

Fortunately, some good ol' Crowder forethought saved the bunker when secondary and tertiary seals below the cutline closed automatically. The White House staff was trapped, but for now everyone remained safe.

President Capehardt and General Lopez had their moment of private discussion. The President had listened intently as scientist Lopez explained his evolutionary theory. *Homo sapiens* was on the verge of extinction and two new species had emerged.

The President had been more resistant than Lopez hoped. After an hour long prosecution for the state of evolutionary biology, he reminded her of what she had witnessed in the last 24 hours, and she finally accepted the truth. Fate had placed a period on *homo sapiens'* reign on Earth.

"What shall we do, Mike?"

"Nothing, Madam President. Our birds have left our nest. It's up to them now."

"We are on the margins now sidelined like proud parents in the audience cheering on our children. The future generations."

"Madam President, that is what I have always admired most about you. You always find the truth in everything. I believe that is a perfect way to see our role now." He watched the President accept the compliment then added, "Might I suggest you go spend some time with your family, Ma'am? I expect they need you right now."

The President nodded and studied the general for a moment. She tapped his arm as she walked away. She said, "Thank you, Mike, for everything. I'll do that right now."

Boston was hit from every direction. The wolf dens were well provisioned and hidden, but the warrens under Boston were not defended nearly as well as Lil' Cheyenne. If a single nanite found and reported Life in the dens, TrojanZ would storm it.

Dr. Candace Riggs' wolf camouflage through life had not been burdened by disease or confusion, especially any misperception about her serial killing uncle whose memory she still cherished. Her wolf gene, like her uncle's was as pristine as the day a half million years ago when the first wolf puppy sprang into the first *homo sapiens'* arms and two species shared saliva for the first time.

It was a genetic exchange that launched an interdependent evolution of two symbiotic species. It was the first, but it was not the last. Life—all life—had chosen *Homo sapiens* as the genetic vessel for all defenses if Life was threatened. Hundreds of species had embedded their special weaponry inside human DNA.

Dr. Candace Riggs possessed them all. Two genes emerged on the road to Henderson Dentoncort. All soon would.

Just hours earlier the aliens had terrified her. Born now anew and fearless, the *Super sapiens* killed dozens of TrojanZ effortlessly. With each encounter her fighting skills and speed improved exponentially. She wielded two machetes. Sometimes the blades moved around her body propeller-like as blurs. At other times she gymnastically danced around them just as indistinctly. Every strike was the viper's gift to Life. True to mark. Instant death. Some cuts quartered TrojanZ and left them still standing for a moment. So many TrojanZ fell before her, the escorts soon stood back and just enjoyed the show.

Henderson Dentoncort and every wolf pup *Super* now deferred to Candace, naturally, without reservation. Since age four she was their absolute Alpha. As the first scout nanite entered the den, she sensed it and dispatched it with a single electric dart thrown across the room from her index finger. She then issued a series of orders to the pack. Thoughtless, instinctual commands were written genetically, retrieved, given, and accepted by the pack with little more than her gestures and expressions.

The *Super sapiens* hurriedly gathered every human refuge into the main den and surrounded them.

Trillions of nanites poured into the den when the scout did not return. They were met with an electrical discharge equivalent to a lightning bolt. Four more waves entered the den and were likewise electrocuted. The nanite battle lasted just thirty seconds. The floor of the den turned ashen grey as tens of trillions of nanometer sized carcasses piled up.

The *Supers* turned as one and looked toward Candace. She climbed off the step ladder where she had led the alien slaughter. As she moved through the still stunned humans, she consoled them. She caressed their cheeks and pressed their shoulders. She kneeled and hugged children as she walked to the door. Most humans were rubbing their eyes from the bright light and appeared confused by the thick ozone left in the air by sparking eel electricity.

Candace had no idea how she knew the things that she now knew so perfectly. It was as if she had known all her life the things she just now remembered. As she approached the door, she extended her hands behind her. No words were exchanged or glances given, but Henderson Dentoncort placed a machete in each of her hands. Candace's lieutenant, former patient and dreamland playmate returned to the circle guarding the humans. She took up a position next to the door with her back to the wall.

She did not have to wait long. Twenty TrojanZ raced into the den to investigate why their nanites were not returning. They stopped halfway between the door and the circle of food. The TrojanZ studied the *Supers* and the humans hungrily for a moment, then the crunching underfoot and lost their appetite. That's when they also discovered what had happened to their nanites.

Programming instructed them to retreat. When they turned to leave they found their escape blocked by Candace. What happened next occurred so quickly that only a few humans actually witnessed the mass decapitation. They just heard the staccato thud of the TrojanZ heads striking the floor in half-second intervals, followed by the delayed crescendo of quartered TrojanZ collapsing.

The pack howled its delight. Some turned and hugged the closest human. All were sniffed and a few got licked. Children were lifted and spun in the air lovingly, and then handed back to their parents. Wheelchairs were spun like tops, but at a sensitive oldster speed. The Alpha *Super sapiens* smiled at her pack as it celebrated both the victory and her preternatural combat abilities, skills that even surprised her. Just last week she was teaching the relationship between neurologic and psychiatric disorders to second year med students. She raised her hand and said, "Okay! Okay! Clean up this mess, then go have some fun. I'll watch over our precious humans. But don't stay out too long."

Over a hundred *Super sapiens* dashed out of the den to find and kill more TrojanZ and nanites.

6

STOP. The command soared to every corner of the Harb Universe and to every universe the TrojanZ had ever invaded in nine-billion years. Celestial bodies under construction would never be completed.

On Earth, the nanites simply fell inertly to the ground. The atmosphere started healing as nitrogen, oxygen, sodium and chlorine and other imprisoned elements shed their wardens, and naturally reconciled. Humans were lucky too. Tens of millions of humans occupied by the TrojanZ parasites around the world were liberated by their death.

RJ Reynolds and Jack Caldwell watched the gruesome harvest end just moments before it erased the last of Hettinger, Georgia and Terre Haute, Indiana, and with it all those souls remaining.

In Boston the *Super sapiens* were about to square off with a massive hoard of TrojanZ, when every TrojanZ suddenly collapsed without a fight. Ashen nanites soon covered the ground around them and the air cleared.

Ben and Samantha did not celebrate. They knew the fight for Earth could not end until John Doe's termination was confirmed. It was a good time to update the President. Ben opened a link between universes over the Strings network and called home.

"Madam President. Are you still there? If you are, just speak. We will hear you just fine."

The President did not answer until the cheering stopped in Lil' Cheyenne. "Ben, it's good to hear your voice. Is Sami okay?"

"She's fine, Ma'am. We both are. How's our house holding up?"

"We lost the top of it, we believe. The giant titanium lid, the stairs down to the first landing, and the top of the elevator shaft. But the backup seals held. All levels are secure. So we are safe and sound."

Ben and Sami spent the next ten minutes telling the President what he and Samantha had discovered, spending much time of the time on the software flaw. Before they could finish, Samantha interrupted the conversation.

"Ben! It's Doe. He is severely injured but not dead. His nanites are dying faster than he can replace them. He is ordering a drone to come get him, and he's not done. He knows what we did, and he intends to repair the operating system, reactivate the nanites and continue the harvest."

General Lopez asked, "Dr. Crowder, do we control the drones?"

"Yes, sir. One-hundred percent."

"Can you lock Doe out of the operating program?"

"Yes, sir. He must be physically present in this universe to regain control of the operating system."

"Excellent. Madam President, I suggest we let Doe have his drone."

It took a moment, but the President, Ben, and Samantha smiled together as they gathered in the General's idea.

Claire Capehardt said, “It’s your idea, General. You issue the order.”

“Very well, Ma’am. Dr. Crowder release the drone with the following command: Collect Doe, then fly his ass directly and without delay, but with maximum prejudice into the Sun.”

“With pleasure, General, Ma’am.” Ben turned to Samantha, “Sami on it?”

“It’s done. Drone away. Navigation is locked to a single interim destination and the final terminus.”

Samantha narrated the progress of the drone. “The drone has left the Harb Universe… The drone has entered Earth’s atmosphere… “The drone has landed in Siano, California. Portal opened. Cameras activated. Doe appears badly injured. I’d say even confused.”

Ben spoke to the President, “Ma’am, I have to ask…”

“No you don’t, Ben. I want him to know we are frying his ass, and I want him fully awake to know two things. Allow him enough nanites to know that we know those things.”

“Yes Ma’am. They are?”

“This Harb Universe, will it sustain Life? And more importantly, can we emigrate there?”

“Yes, Ma’am! There are literally tens of trillions of planets nearly identical to Earth. I am confident Sami and I can modify the drones to accommodate Life. All life!”

“Excellent! Second question. Can we keep Doe alive long enough so I can speak to him before he cooks?”

Ben and Sami consulted for a moment. Samantha answered the question. “Yes, Madam President. We can allow him to leach sufficient nanites from the drone to sustain him just long enough.”

The President recalled what four teenagers said in Hettinger, Georgia before the battle there. She said, “Excellent! I want it all recorded for history. Everything.”

“Yes, Ma’am. We will have both audio and video.”

“One last request. When I speak to Doe, can you broadcast the exchange worldwide on Earth?”

“Yes, Ma’am. Any survivor with restored power and a functioning radio or television still on will hear your words clearly.

With the collapse of the nanites, the automated electronic services should be awake now."

Sami continued her status report on the drone's progress, "Madam President, Doe is onboard… Drone has left Earth's atmosphere… Doe is attempting to take over navigation… All attempts have failed. Navigation is locked… Doe is attempting to jump to interuniverse *k-speed…* All attempts failed. Speed is capped at fifty percent of the speed of light… The drone will crash into the sun in four minutes, Ma'am."

"Excellent. Open communication to the drone worldwide."

"Done, Ma'am. The world will hear you both. You may begin, Madam President."

Inside the drone, John Doe experienced a first. Terror, as the remotely controlled drone crawled toward the greatest electrical disturbance in the solar system. His hands moved at lightning speed over the drone's surfaces trying futilely to drain every last nanite from the ship. He froze when the President spoke.

"This is the President of the United States of America. I am speaking to you on behalf of all Life on Earth. I speak for all nations, for all people, all species of Life, for all kinds and creeds on Earth listening and watching now or in the future. Do you understand what I'm saying?"

John Doe screamed, "YOU WILL PAY! We will obliterate your entire universe!"

"It's not going to happen, alien. Let me explain what has happened. Life controls the Harb universe now. Not you. We are there, and we occupy it. Your attack on Earth has failed. Backfired actually. You see, we learned all about Trojan horses as children. Your ruse has failed. Ours did not."

"Your ruse? IMPOSSIBLE!" Doe screamed again, but less sure this time.

"Oh, I see you are skeptical. I will demonstrate. Dr. Crowder please convince the alien that we are in complete control."

"Gladly, Madam President." A moment later, Ben announced, "The alien no longer has arms."

"STOP THIS!" Doe raged. "I'M GOING TO…"

"The president interrupted him, "...do absolutely nothing, alien except die. You will never witness Life spread through the Harb creation, as it soon will. You will never watch Life spread and repair every universe TrojanZ contaminated. But you will witness the alliance of inorganic life forms and organic. Watch."

In secure locations all over the planet, humanity cheered. From the south of Africa to the north of Europe, east to west, former enemies worldwide cheered in solidarity with the President.

"Do you see them, alien?"

Doe stared in disbelief at thousands of video projections of celebrations on the drone's hull. The cheering drowned out the roar of the drones sub light engines. Ben muted the sound for a moment so the President could speak.

"You look shocked. But there is more, alien. Now, Ben."

All over the planet trillions of nanites awoke. As one, they lifted and transformed into a spectrum of colors.

Claire Capehardt spoke first to the world, then to Doe. Her message was translated into every language. "Friends, do not be frightened. The nanites will no longer harm you. They now support Life. All Life.

The President then addressed the alien. "You, on the other hand, Doe, you are so fucked. Enjoy the show everyone. How much time, Sami?"

"Ten seconds, Ma'am."

The world counted down.

Just before it ended, the President said, "Goodbye, asshole!" and thousands of survivors around the world cheered louder than ever.

PART 6—Endings

1

Nanites rose high over the Earth and created a brilliant rainbow covering the entire planet. Instead of destroying the planet, they now tried to save it. However, Earth would never be the same. Billions of cubic yards of formerly atomized hydrogen and oxygen now returned to Earth as rainwater. With it also came the reunited sodium chloride. More than half of the planet's seawater had been atomized. Now it turned fertile lands and deserts alike into seafloor.

Silicon and oxygen reunited into sand. It collected and dammed runoff all over the planet, first into ponds then giant lakes of brine. Petroleum products of every kind knitted themselves back together and left an oily sheen on the dead waters. Grand Canyons were born all over Earth as the sky erased land.

At the Federal prison in Terre Haute, Jack Caldwell, Soccer Mom, Hubbs and Seth guided people to the high guard towers as the water rose. The Wraith Riders carried the injured and elderly up to safety. Maggie Marie McMurtry of Mingham, Massachusetts had transitioned fully into a *Super sapiens*. Like all others of her awakened kind, hundreds of her genetic allies of Life had awoken inside her. With the strength of silver back gorillas and the leaping power of mountain lions, she embraced three humans at a time and reached the highest landing 95 feet above in just three leaps. She promised each of her grateful passengers extra kisses later.

The once tranquil Wabash River, prominent in the compositions of native Hoosier "Hoagy" Carmichael, was now a raging tsunami. It carried away atop its mile-wide crests, Indiana hardwoods, cars, trucks and houses, and thousands of dead TrojanZ. The ferocious floodwater was coffee colored from Indiana's briefly restored rich topsail. It joined cubic miles of soil from other rivers joining the great Mississippi, which was already ninety miles across.

A dam of mud, trees, shredded river towns, vehicles, and TrojanZ corpses started at Vicksburg, Tennessee. The dam quickly topped the high ridges on both sides of the river and kept growing east and west a hundred miles in both directions. Behind it the flood waters rose higher and higher. Not since the New Madid earthquake had tributaries run north and flooded so much territory. An hour after the atomic reconstruction began, a body of water five times larger than Lake Michigan covered most of six states.

Hiking up Hettinger County's Logan's Peak was a popular local activity. Now it was a lifesaver. From the tourist shelter 2,100 feet above the valley, the 606 townspeople watched their town wash away.

Dallas Holcombe had predicted the flood when the humidity in town rose suddenly and the sky turned into a solid rainbow. RJ Reynolds did not question him and ordered the evacuation to Logan's Peak. The floodwater peaked just yards from the crest.

Skylar Thompson's decision to take refuge at the firehouse saved her life twice. As luck should have it, the Masaquat station was a designated chemical and biological attack responder.

Her time with the troops in Iraq and Afghanistan once again proved invaluable. In March 2003, she had drilled alongside the troops almost daily as they prepared for Saddam Hussein's chemical attacks that never came. Skylar climbed into a HazMat suit, attached the respirator and oxygen tank, and finally put on the hood. She then located one of the most important lifesaving items, the noxious gas monitor gauge. Skylar attached its lanyard to her helmet.

She turned it on and said, "Oh shit!" Apparently, she had donned the suit and hooked up the oxygen just in time. The portion of the gauge reading Chlorine passed quickly from CAUTION to CRITICAL.

Skylar did not know if it was too late for the people at the hotel, but she gathered up all the protective gear anyway and threw it into the back of the Fire Chief's EV SUV. Like all good chiefs, Masaquat's had left his car keys in the ignition for quick reaction time. The electric vehicle bolted out of the lot.

The journalist was almost out of the city limits when the rain started. It quickly turned into sheets and overwhelmed the wipers. Inside, the downpour sounded like pea-sized hail fired at Earth by canons.

Driving was perilous. Skylar rocked in her seat from side to side in time with the wiper blade and peeked through the quickly closing cracks of clear sight. Keeping her bearings as close to center on the roadway was nearly impossible. She felt the road more than saw it. The hotel was situated a thousand feet above the city, so the road up to it quickly became a growing stream of water, mud, and debris. She could not know it, but behind her a salt lake had claimed the City of Masaquat and was climbing the mountain after her.

She pulled up to the hotel entrance and ran inside. Apparently, the chlorine gas had already overwhelmed the hotel. There were three corpses on the lobby floor. One was Vera's, the hotel's eighty-something desk clerk. She found three more guest and staff members' bodies on her way to the subbasement.

Skylar ran to Gordy's apartment. It was empty. As she was about to leave, she saw a green light flashing and reflected off a monitor. She knew what it meant and what it was. The noxious gas gauge. Skylar lifted the gauge and watched the chlorine gas level fall to SAFE. The LED stopped flashing and became solid green.

Skylar took off her helmet and looked around for any clue as to where the team might have taken refuge. She mentally retraced her steps in the last 24 hours. *Where would they go?* she asked herself.

She was already halfway through the doorway when she answered, "The vault!"

Skylar ran to the vault and pounded on the door and screamed repeatedly, but there was no response. Even this deep in the hotel the rain's pounding sounded as if she was inside a snare drum, and Cream**'s** Ginger Baker was doing a solo. Inside the vault it was probably even more deafening.

She was about to give up when she found the walky-talky and Gordy's note written long ago. It read, "Russia! Russia! Russia! It must've been their big one!"

Skylar pressed the CALL button and said, “Gordy? Are you guys in there?”

Easton was closest to the walky-talky and answered, “Sky, is that you?”

“Yes!”

“How are you…”

“No time. I’ll explain everything later. The chlorine gas is gone, but we have a bigger problem now. We are about to drown.”

“Drown? What?” asked Easton.

“Do you hear that rumbling? That’s rain,” Skylar explained. “We need to get up-mountain right now. Let’s go!”

By the time the six reached the Suburban, the flood waters were already calf deep. Skylar jumped behind the wheel and ordered Gunny to ride shotgun. “Guide us out of here, Gunny!”

The last half mile to the top of Mt. Masaquat was a muddy tree limb and rock laden river. The Suburban climbed upward, bumping over small boulders, occasionally yawing sideways sickeningly toward switchback cliffs before Skylar expertly feathered the vehicle back on the path. She demonstrated another wartime skill she had learned behind the wheel of an up-armored Humvee while crossing the spring runoffs in the Bora Bora.

The normal ten-minute drive took nearly thirty minutes. She parked at the top of mountain on the turnaround. The water rose to within ten feet of the Suburban and stopped.

Dr. Candace Riggs instinctively knew how precarious the underground dens would be when the atomization of Earth reversed. While poisonous gasses were no longer a problem, flooding was. She needed to move the humans to high ground as soon as possible. The tallest building in Boston nearby was the nearly finished twenty-story Cumberland Tower. That was the good news. The bad news was rain had already started, and the Cumberland was blocks away.

Twenty minutes later, half of the humans reached the tower on their own through waist deep water and climbed the stairs. The rest clung to *Super sapiens* outstretched arms as allied dolphin genes awoke within and gave the *Supers'* legs the kicking power of dolphin tails.

By the time everyone reached safety, including the cherished wheelchair-ten, water was rushing through the third floor of the building to the sea. Around them buildings crumbled like sugar cubes and washed away. Larger sections crashed into the Cumberland. The building shook, but held its ground.

Lil' Cheyenne Mountain. Any sense of relief the President had experienced with the termination of John Doe was long gone. Ben and Samantha had remotely redistributed their satellite network to see the world. Every discovery was more dire.

"Madam President, when the water recedes, and it will eventually recede I assure you, much of the Earth's most fertile land will be left as salt marshes. Also, most of the topsoil harvested by TrojanZ will logically end up in the oceans, many of which are new."

"This is catastrophic, Ben."

"Yes, Ma'am it is, but unfortunately there is worse news to report."

"Say it."

"The TrojanZ prized our heavy metals. As a result 122 nuclear power plants were opened around the world which are all now leaking massive amounts of radioactivity into the nearby environment. Wind and water will eventually distribute the radioactive particles worldwide."

"Oh god! This is it. There is no coming back from this."

"No, Claire. I am so sorry," said Ben. "The damage to the planet is such that it might take millions of years to recover."

2

Ben and Samantha listened to the President address her White House staff an hour later. "We won the war, ladies and gentlemen. The attack on Earth has ended. We still stand and the TrojanZ do not. We defeated an enemy like none before it. Our defeat was a Pyrrhic victory. While the TrojanZ billions years-long terror campaign across the multiverse has come to an end, we have paid an unimaginably high price.

Earth lost forty percent of its land mass. The remainders were left an uninhabitable wasteland of toxicity, saltmarshes and radioactivity. Much of our precious topsoil has washed away. Our fossil fuels—crude oil, natural gas, and coal—were consumed. Their reconstructed and re-atomized remnants now cover the planet as a toxic sheen. Earth's lungs—the Amazon rainforest and the sea's plankton—are gone. A thick haze encases the world that will block the sun for decades, I'm told.

Every fresh water source was polluted in countless ways." The President waited before delivering the last bit of bad news. "That includes Earth's freshwater aquifers—including the one beneath Lil' Cheyenne upon which we rely."

The president waited until the meaning of her statement sunk in. "Dr. Crowder estimates the filtration system will fail in 48 hours. After that, the water will become increasingly toxic and undrinkable."

There were a few gasps while her message sunk in. Most people were too stunned by the news to react in any manner other than stare at the President in disbelief and shock.

Claire Capehardt continued, "I have asked Dr. Crowder to come up with another miracle. As you know, he's sort of good at that. So, listen up. I do not know about you guys, but I don't feel like dying just yet."

The President raised both fists overhead and screamed, "Fuck those alien TrojanZ! We are getting out of here." When the cheering stopped the President said, "Ben, what do you two geniuses have in mind for us?"

Ben spoke first. "So, as you all now know we are speaking to you from another universe. It was created by the TrojanZ billions of years ago from building materials like Earth. It is just as vast and diverse as our own. While there is not a hint of organic life anywhere in this universe, trillions of planets would support it. Our plan is to evacuate Life to here." Ben finished and said, "Sami, you're up."

"Simply put, we hacked the TrojanZ operating system and repurposed its commands. During a normal harvest, fleets of alien drones would scour a planet and extinguish any life that survived the atomization. Only after confirming the planet was sterile, the harvesting drones would begin collecting atomized building materials… Ben?"

"What we have done was actually easy from a technical standpoint. We basically flipped a bunch of switches in the TrojanZ operating system that were left carelessly unprotected. How? Not to overcomplicate things, we just reprogrammed the drones not to kill but to find Life, rescue it, and bring it to this universe. In just a few minutes billions of drones will appear over Earth. They will descend to every quarter of the planet and start the recovery of Life. All Life. Madam President, my dear old friend, Sami and I will have you guys out of there within the day. Go pack your bags!"

3

Ben and Samantha sent wave after wave of rescue drones to Earth. Each ship was modified by the TrojanZ' former *termite queen* factory to accommodate each life form. The same drones that for billions of years searched and destroyed Life now searched and rescued it. Life was surviving everywhere. Some by just a thread, but it was there.

Three thousands humans had survived in Europe and Asia and boarded the drones. Australians and New Zealanders had shown unusual grit and emerged by the hundreds. Hundreds more humans emerged from hiding in South America, the middle east, and southeast Asia. Dozens rose in Scandinavia. Thousands emerged from Cold War bunkers in the former USSR. China's caves saved thousands. All over the planet, Life was rescued. Every island—new and old—was searched. The drones found survivors on many.

From Hettinger to Beijing, from Boston to London, from Terre Haute to Pyongyang, and all around the world, thousands of humans boarded the rescue drones and evacuated Earth.

From acorn to pollen, from cornstalk to beanstalk, from sequoia to crabgrass, every precious plant from around the world was rescued too. The drones' Life sensors scoured every square millimeter of the planet. Nothing was to be left behind.

When no more Life was found, Ben ordered one last sweep of the dead planet to make sure no Life was left marooned. From virus to whale to giraffe to fish to bird and coral, it all was gathered and preserved. Often it was just a species' DNA, but that was enough to resurrect it in a New Universe.

Ben said, "Madam President, Earth has been evacuated. It's your turn, Ma'am. Time to abandon the temporary White House."

"We are ready, Ben. The drone has reopened the passage and dropped in a ladder."

"Claire, I'll always respect your decision to wait until the Earth was cleared, but I wish you had agreed to be the first to enter the rescue drone, not the last."

"Not going to happen, old friend."

Twenty minutes later, after shaking hands with each of her staff as they climbed out of Lil' Cheyenne into the rescue drone, Claire Capehardt, the last living lifeform on Earth, looked around for a moment, then quickly climbed the ladder.

PART 7—Beginnings

1

April 30, 2226, The 200th anniversary of Ancestors Day was a day of both great celebration and sad remembrances. It was also the first year the holiday was also celebrated on Old Earth. Nanites had worked nonstop for nearly two centuries to restore the planet's health. Geographically, it was far different than before the TrojanZ, but Life was back and the planet was healthier than ever.

The Amazon rainforest breathed and acclimatized the world once again. The seas flourished as sunlight fed the planktons, and the building blocks produced oxygen and primed the sea's chain of life. Mammals and fowl thrived on bountiful shorelines worldwide. The skies were clean and filled with bat, avian, and insect Life.

The lands ranged from green and lush to beautifully sculpted desert dunes, to spectacular glacially ice-capped mountains and poles. The Earth bore just three great oceans now but numerous new seas were made by the new topography. Great freshwater rivers and their many tributaries weaved down and around mountains. They meandered across great plains, and rested in abundant lakes and marshlands.

Mammals grazed and hunted. Reptiles stepped and crawled with ancient grace. Sea corals welcomed back their tenants. The plains grasses reached for the sky and waved *hello* to the new world. Forests ascended higher than ever. From countless habitats, Life chirped, swarmed, barked, called, swam, crawled, hissed, and sang. Life reproduced and prospered now by no more advantage or disadvantage than so ordered by Natural Law.

The TrojanZ stain on Earth was expunged completely. Every lifeform had been returned to Earth and now thrived there. Even the forever forgiven Rhinovirus came home. Every lifeform had returned except one—*Homo sapiens*.

The last *Homo sapiens* was born in New Universe 81 years earlier and died just thirteen years after that. Natural selection was the one thing the *Cyber sapiens* and *Super sapiens* races could not defeat as they seeded the universe with Life. They watched helplessly from colonized planets millions of light years apart as their beloved humans steadily died off after relocation.

The mourning was dampened only by celebration when Ben and Sami resurrected each passing human being as *Cyber sapiens*.

Not even Ben and Samantha knew why *Homo sapiens* simply faded away and died off. Upon that last *Homo sapiens'* death and resurrection, *Super sapiens* now numbering in the tens of millions allowed their long-quieted inner wolf to emerge and mourn in their ancient way. Their grief howled and cried and depressed New Universe for one full week.

Earth was now a memorial. It would never again be occupied by civilization. The only unnatural structure on the planet was a circular reserve a few miles in diameter and located on the site of the former city Terre Haute, Indiana. It was dedicated to both *Homo sapiens* and to the ancient genetic treaty that defeated the TrojanZ. That primordial pact forged innately between species was now stronger than ever if an enemy like the TrojanZ ever again attacked Life.

Dr. Candace Riggs and Maggie Marie McMurtry stood on a stage constructed in the middle of the great park. Around it and throughout the botanical gardens, dozens of bronze plates memorialized *Homo sapiens* and their countless genetic allies of Life. Like all *Supers*, neither woman had aged. The Life Treaty lived within all *Super sapiens* fully now. One of those million allied genes belonged to the redwood tree whose lifespan was millennial.

The memorial was carefully constructed in a manner the *Supers* felt humans would find most pleasing. Lush gardens were irrigated by fountains whose styles were lifted from every civilization in human history. Trees from around the world shaded sidewalks punctuated by countless park benches, each seat dedicated to humanity's arts and sciences.

Flowering vines fell from tree limbs, and insects danced over their blooms. Birds fearlessly sang natural order on the shoulders and outstretched hands of the *Super* guests. Squirrels leapt into guests' laps and pickpocketed the treats planted for them. A pack of thirty wolves rubbed and licked their way through the crowd and whined camaraderie. Respectfully, the *Super sapiens* in attendance retrogressed into their *wolf puppy* ancestry for a moment and answered the wolves in kind.

Candace waved her hand and opened the String network to all of New Universe. Nanites projected the memorial onto hundreds of planets. Sensing their rising anxiety, a trillion-trillion-trillion nanites nuzzled against the *Supers'* bodies like emotional support dogs and consoled them. The Supers had lost much of their wolf *puppyness*, but their ever attending nanites made up for it emotively.

"We all recognize our deep need for this park," said Dr. Candace Riggs. "To say any more is truly unnecessary. We have waited a long time for this day to come. All *Super sapiens* recognize the sacrifice that came before us. Some of us lived that loss beside our cherished ancestors. They still live, brothers and sisters. The ancestors remain within every one of us. The Treaty of Life makes it so, just as it entrusted them then, it preserves the ancestors in our DNA for safekeeping. From this day forward, Earth will be a place of pilgrimages for all of Life to visit."

Candace continued, "Now for the fun part that you have been waiting for so patiently. In a moment I think you will all agree, Ben and Samantha got the ancestors just right. Maggie, please introduce our old friends. You *Supers* born after the migration have read about our ancestors. Some of you have met them as resurrected *Cyber sapiens*. Now it is time for you to meet them in living color the way they were."

Maggie yelled, "RJ Reynolds! Come on down!" The holographic image appeared in front of the memorial. RJ waved at the cheering crowds from his open garage door. He held a steaming cup of coffee. In his other hand, he held his shotgun. The oily aroma of the garage wafted over the crowd.

One-by-one Maggie called out to the hero ancestors. Each appeared within a familiar scene. The roars of approval rose throughout New Universe after each arrival.

"Vice President Nick Caine!" The forever youthful Princeton quarterback wore his retired football jersey #7 over a three-piece suit and played catch with Secret Service agents Artois Nunez and Len Brubaker…

"Pistol packing, Yanktonai Sioux warrior, and all-star Supreme Court Chief Justice Theodora Daughtry…

"…and her martial artist husband, TrojanZ slayer and champion FBI Director Agent Easton DeSmet…"

"White House Press Secretary and two-time Pulitzer Prize winning journalist Skylar Thompson…"

"The Nobel Laureate and scientist who first warned the world about brainlords, Dr. Sergey Aranovich…"

"The other Martyr of the Rhino Summit, and the other scientist who sacrificed himself to reveal the TrojanZ plot, Dr. Rhine Vonbergen…"

"Ms. Thompson's mentor, surrogate father, and fearless investigative reporter, the human who fought the TrojanZ on these very hallowed grounds, Jack Caldwell…"

"The beloved champions of all *Supers* young and old, the super heroes of Terre Haute, meet Wraith Riders Nils, Fuzz, Blotup, and Grunt." The kids in the crowd cheered most loudly. The Wraith Riders had become the equivalent of childhood action figures in New Universe. When the crowd settled a bit, Maggie turned to the bikers and winked. Four motorcycles roared to life, did some wheelies, and the cheering started all over…

Maggie continued, "Meet Seth Parker, Ft. Big Wolf's courageous unofficial mayor and fast food weapons imagin-eer… and Eve Dawson, everyone's beloved Soccer Mom warrior… Ft. Big Wolf's top cop Officer C. Hubbard…"

"Now meet the TrojanZ Killing Heroes of the Battle of Hettinger who did it the old fashion way without any *Supers*… Dallas Holcombe… Harris Barber… Ella Berger… Fran and Frank Connors…and once again Commander RJJJJJJJJJ Reynolds!"

Next Maggie introduced, "Fighting on the Masaquat front, meet CIA Director, super spy, and comedian extraordinaire, Napoleon Passerelle…

…and his wife and courageous whistleblower and Supreme Court intern, Amelia Long…"

"Meet the hero of Masaquat, now the hero of New Universe, the one and the only Communication Officer, Gunnery Sargent

Gordon 'Gunnnnnny' GorDONNN!" Hologram Gunny blushed as the cheers rose.

"Chairman of the Joint Chiefs General Michael Sullivan Lopez. The scientist soldier humanitarian and first ancestor to welcome ours and the *Cyber sapiens* races into existence…"

"And now…the leader-of-all-leaders, the President of the former United States of America, Claire Capehardt. The woman who got the last word in with John Doe, and like all great captain's in history was the last lifeform to abandon this Earth now restored."

Maggie introduced every war hero from around the world. Throughout the rest of the day, well after sunset, the holograms interacted on holographic sets with the *Super* audience. They took turns telling stories about their lives and the war and answered questions arriving from all over New Universe. Not surprisingly, the Wraith Riders got all of the kid questions and gave countless rides on their motorcycles to kids and adults alike.

2

Husband and wife Ben and Samantha Crowder and all other *Cyber sapiens* watched the ceremony to the end from New Universe. They would have preferred to watch the festivities live, of course, but the journey here had indeed been a one-way trip for *Cybers* as Ben had once predicted.

Like everyone in New Universe, Ben and Samantha had taken off Ancestors Day. The happy business of spreading Life took a break for the annual holiday. The happy couple was alone and relaxing in their new home. They had named it *Lil' Two*.

Cyber sapiens now mimicked many human behaviors It started in tribute to the ancestors, but had become natural gestures. Ben yawned and said, "It has been a really, really good day. We are growing so much faster now. Faster than ever actually. Sami, did you notice how many *Super* babies were born just during the ceremony?"

"Of course I did, 9,914 little bundles of *Super doopers*. Did you notice that this batch today will reach maturity in just 35 months?"

"Amazing! But of course I did, darling. Hard to miss."

Samantha studied Ben for a moment then bantered a bit more playfully. "Well then, Smarty Pants, how many new pregnancies were reported in just the last 24 hours?"

Ben yawned again and answered, "Exactly 112,293. Also another new record, my love. And again, sort of difficult to miss."

"Ha! Well, you're wrong! Because you missed it!"

Ben sat up and looked at her. "Impossible. The number of new *Super* preggers was exactly 112,293, as documented to the precise nanosecond."

"I did not say *Super* pregnancies, Husband. I just asked you, 'how many pregnancies?'"

"That's a distinction without a difference. Obviously."

Sami rose and climbed into Ben's lap. She wrapped her arm around his neck and kissed his cheek. He leaned back and looked at her even more curiously when she said, "There were 112,294 pregnancies, lover." Sami paused then added, "You forgot to count our own… Daddy." She took his hand and placed it on her abdomen.

"SAMI! YOU'RE…? WE'RE…? HOW?"

"Oh Bennie! I think after 200 years of marriage you know exactly 'how' babies are made."

Two centuries of scientific refutation to the possibility, Mr. Crichton's promise came true even for *Cyber sapiens*.

Life finds a way.

The End.

Acknowledgement

*A special thank you to our artist and physicist daughter Alex Tingle who created the cover art for **TrojanZ** and who respectfully tries not to laugh too hard when my imagination misrepresents with creative license her extraordinary very real world of quantum physics.*

Inquiries may be sent to:

866.113.aan@gmail.com

AUTHOR'S NOTE

I experienced my first paradox when I was about six or seven years old. A favorite but ornery uncle asked me a classic trick question, and I'm sure he did it just to watch my little pea brain explode:

Which do you suppose came first, Mick, the chicken or the egg?

Unc of course checkmated me in just two moves, leaving my young mind as flummoxed as those renegade computers made loopy on "Star Trek" when Captain Kirk likewise befuddled and disarmed them using circular logic.

I'm grateful to my uncle, though. He lit a candle. I've been fascinated with every sort of conundrum and enigma ever since. The more curious and mindbender the paradox is, I say the better.

A while back I stumbled across a real doozy.[1] A bizarre hypothesis is quietly circulating through physics' fringes regarding the appearance of life in the universe. One that excludes all the usual suspects—moldy asteroids, quantum leaping coacervates, hyper evolution, little green men, DNA lotto and deistic handiwork.

A handful of theoretical physicists are examining the bloodiest bleeding edges of reality. They are cautiously contemplating what some are already calling the Proposed Fifth Law of Thermodynamics. There are (if you're keeping track) currently only four laws. If the Fifth holds, it will be a real game changer for the 'who's first, chicken or egg' debates, because the answer just might be that organic life was the Johnny come lately.

The Fifth Law proposes the existence throughout the universe of complex automatons. It hypothesizes that these alien machines

---

[1] **5th Law:** *"An open system containing a large mixture of similar automatons… self-constructing machines of unlimited complexity."*
http://www.canadaconnects.ca/quantumphysics/10078/

are not only self-constructed but infinitely intricate—therefore sentient.

Whether the Fifth ends up in Scrapheap Anathema or as a new frontier in cosmology, it's great fodder for my science fiction.

The 5th Law of Thermodynamics lives rent-free in my *Muse's* ink well in exchange for its secrets shared. –MT

~

THE FIFTH LAW IN PRINT

While Mike Tingle's **Fifth Law** science fiction novels are not serials per se, they do rhyme thematically when in each story humanity finds itself at war—and in alliance—with sentient machines encountered throughout the vast multiverse.

Fifth Law Novels
Organics
TrojanZ

—Coming in 2023
Replicates

Made in the USA
Middletown, DE
13 September 2022

10364287R00172